INSPECTOR FRENCH AND
THE MYSTERY ON SOUTHAMPTON WATER

Freeman Wills Crofts (1879–1957), the son of an army doctor who died before he was born, was raised in Northern Ireland and became a civil engineer on the railways. His first book, *The Cask*, written in 1919 during a long illness, was published in the summer of 1920, immediately establishing him as a new master of detective fiction. Regularly outselling Agatha Christie, it was with his fifth book that Crofts introduced his iconic Scotland Yard detective, Inspector Joseph French, who would feature in no less than thirty books over the next three decades. He was a founder member of the Detection Club and was elected a Fellow of the Royal Society of Arts in 1939. Continually praised for his ingenious plotting and meticulous attention to detail—including the intricacies of railway timetables—Crofts was once dubbed 'The King of Detective Story Writers' and described by Raymond Chandler as 'the soundest builder of them all'.

Also in this series

By the same author

*with other Detection Club authors

FREEMAN WILLS CROFTS

Inspector French and the Mystery on Southampton Water

COLLINS
CRIME
CLUB

COLLINS CRIME CLUB

An imprint of HarperCollins*Publishers*
1 London Bridge Street
London SE1 9GF
www.harpercollins.co.uk

This paperback edition 2020
1

First published in Great Britain
by Hodder and Stoughton Ltd 1934

A catalogue record for this book is
available from the British Library

ISBN 978-0-00-839327-4

Set in Sabon Lt Std by Palimpsest Book Production Ltd, Falkirk, Stirlingshire

Printed and bound in Great Britain
by CPI Group (UK) Ltd, Croydon CR0 4YY

MIX
Paper from
responsible sources
FSC™ C007454

This book is produced from independently certified FSC™ paper
to ensure responsible forest management.

Find out more about HarperCollins and the environment at
www.harpercollins.co.uk/green

CONTENTS

PART I: TRANSGRESSION

PART II: DETECTION

PART III: MYSTIFICATION

PART IV: ELUCIDATION

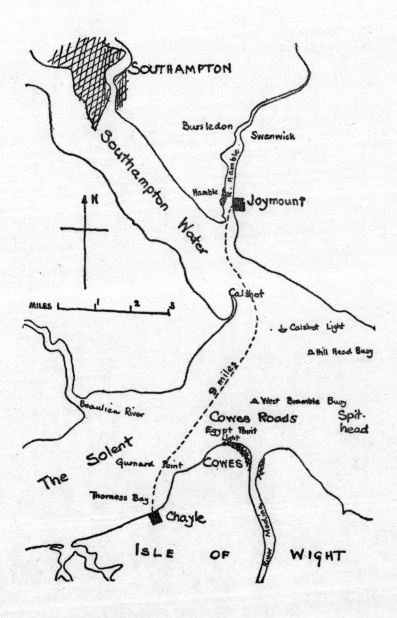

PART I

Transgression

Joymount is Perturbed

'And now, gentlemen, I shall call upon our managing director for his report.'

Sir Francis Askwith, chairman of the Joymoun Rapid Hardening Cement Manufacturing Company, Limited, put down his agenda paper, glanced at his colleagues, leant back in his chair, and waited.

The faces of the seven men seated round the boardroom table were grave. This was no ordinary meeting of routine business to which they had been summoned. A crisis had arisen in the history of their company, and they were there to take decisive action.

They were representative enough of the directors of a small firm. Four of them were 'passengers.' Sir Francis, though still a distinguished looking man, was bent from the weight of his seventy odd years. He was a retired County Court judge, personally charming, but as a chairman simply a figurehead. The two men seated on his left were also past their prime, too old indeed to take a useful part in the business. A fourth man, though only in the thirties, was obviously a son of sport, and seemed out of his element in this temple of diplomacy and finance.

The other three, however, were of a different calibre. One was the very type and essence of the prosperous business man—middle-aged, quiet, efficient, and with that unmistakable air which comes from personality. A man whose opinion one would unhesitatingly take and whom one would be glad to have as a partner in a crisis. Unfortunately the Joymount Rapid Hardening Cement Manufacturing Company was small fry to him and he did not give its affairs sufficient attention greatly to influence their conduct.

Next him sat the youngest of the party, a man still on the right side of thirty. This was Walter Brand, who as well as being a director, overlooked the financial affairs of the firm. Appearance and manner indicated that he was something of a live wire.

The remaining member of the board sat at the foot of the table, opposite the chairman. His name was James Tasker and he was the managing director upon whom Sir Francis had called for a report. He was a clean shaven, slightly undersized man of about fifty, with a long nose, rather foxy eyes and a thin-lipped mouth like a trap. In him the critical observer would have recognised the real head of the concern, and the critical observer would have been right. James Tasker was an able man. There was nothing about the technique of his business that he didn't know. He was an adept at encompassing sales and a genius in the handling of men.

Slowly he now rose to his feet, still turning over the papers which lay on the table before him. The others watched him anxiously. They had come there to hear bad news and now they were going to hear it.

'Mr Chairman and gentlemen,' began Tasker in a dry but cultivated voice, 'as we haven't had a full meeting of the board since this matter arose, and as it was not convenient to give details on the notice summoning the meeting, I may perhaps recount the circumstances from the beginning, for the benefit of those who are not fully familiar with them.'

He paused and looked at the chairman.

'I think we should all like you to do so,' Sir Francis returned, and Tasker with a little nod resumed.

'I need scarcely go back to the start of our enterprise seven years ago. Then our prospects looked as promising as anyone could wish, and like many another firm, we set out to make our fortune. Like them, we found we had made a mistake. The memory of the depression is too recent and too painful to need recalling. As you know, we all but closed down last year. Almost, but happily, not altogether. For, again as you know, during the summer of 1933 our business began slowly but quite steadily to mend. I shall ask you to look at the graph I have prepared, a copy of which is before each of you. This covers the life of our enterprise, showing its early success, then its gradual decline, its sinking into the trough of the wave and its apparent recovery.'

There was a slight movement as his hearers bent to study the sheets before them. The history of those later years had indeed been something of a tragedy, a tragedy of which they had not yet reached the end. As they looked at the sinister record, the mind of more than one went back to the circumstances under which the company had been formed.

For many decades the use of Portland cement had been growing, till in the early years of the present century it

5

had become the world's chief building material. But it had one serious drawback: it took something like a month to set really hard. Then there came the French invention of *ciment fondu*, a product which grew hard in as many hours as the older material had taken days. Other similar inventions followed and soon various firms in England were making one form or another.

The Joymount Company were producing a material of the *ciment fondu* type. The company had come into being through the observation and enterprise of the young man Brand, who as a reward was afterwards given his directorship. Bathing one day near the mouth of the Hamble, a small stream with a large estuary which flows into Southampton Water not far below Netley Hospital, he noticed how like the slob left uncovered by the tide was to that used near his home for the manufacture of cement. Cement, he knew, was already made in the Isle of Wight, where they had the two prime necessaries, this kind of slob and chalk. Here on the Hamble the chalk was not so much in evidence, but he made enquiries and found that it was to be had within reasonable distance. Brand reported his discovery to his then chief, a chartered accountant in the City. This man had had investigations made, and Brand's opinion was found to be justified. The young man had had the manufacture of ordinary Portland cement in his mind, but it turned out that he had done better than he knew. An unexpected deposit of bauxite supplied the further ingredient required for making the *ciment fondu* variety. A small company was formed, the necessary ground and rights were purchased, and in 1927 the new works were a going concern. From the first it had done well—until the slump, when as Tasker had just mentioned, it had all but closed down.

'You will see from this,' went on Tasker, demonstrating on his graph as he spoke, 'that with the coming of the slump our profits began to fall. Up till September 1932 we kept on working at a profit, but then we unhappily crossed the line of solvency and for a year we worked at a loss. This loss increased until May 1933, when it amounted to something like £100 a week. That meant about £5,000 a year, and generous as you, gentlemen, and our shareholders have been, we could not stand such a drain for long. As you know, the question of closing down was considered again and again. We did not, however, take this desperate remedy because we believed that if and when recovery came, we had here a valuable property which in the long run would recoup our losses.'

Tasker had the ear of his audience. All were listening with concentration. The bright July sunshine pouring in through the open windows contrasted with their gloomy faces. The silence of the room was broken only by the faint cries of seabirds, circling round the firm's little wharf in the hope of getting their dinners with the minimum of toil. Brand, who was something of a philosopher, could not help thinking how similar were the aims of birds and men.

'In June 1933,' Tasker continued, 'there came a welcome change. In July our average losses dropped to a little over £80 a week. In August it was down to £50 and in September to £10. In October, for the first time for over a year, we showed a profit—only £25 a week, but still £25 on the right side. In November the figures were better still: our profit had gone up to £60 a week. That is to say that from June to November we had a steadily increasing and highly gratifying improvement every month. In short in November last we had all the signs of a speedy return to real prosperity. So far I think all you gentlemen are aware of the facts.'

Tasker glanced round and one or two of his hearers nodded.

'But now,' he went on, 'we come to a disconcerting and unwelcome change. The direction of the curve, as you can see on the graph, changes suddenly. From November to the present moment it is going down as steadily as before that date it was going up. In December our profit of £60 a week dropped to £50. In January it had gone down to £35, and each succeeding month it has gone down still lower, until in April we were once again faced with an actual loss on our turnover. It was only the trifling figure of £15, but in May this deficit had risen to £45, and last month, June, it was £80. You will see from this that our losses are rapidly increasing. In fact it is not too much to say that if things continue in the same direction, we shall be faced in a short time with bankruptcy.'

There was a slight movement among the other men as Tasker reached this conclusion. Then Bramwell, the type of the successful business man, spoke.

'I was in South America when this matter was discussed and I didn't hear the full details. What exactly has gone wrong? Is it increase of costs or shortness of sales or what?'

'Sales,' returned Tasker. 'Our sales have gone down steadily.'

'Costs all right?'

'Our costs are perfectly satisfactory. Our plant, as you all know, is as modern as any, I think I may say, in the world. And we have adopted full scientific management, motion study, costing, office planning and labour saving devices of every description. I'm ready to stand over it that our costs will compare favourably with those of any works anywhere. I may add that we've a thorough good lot of men.'

'I thought so,' Bramwell returned. 'From what I have seen of the works, everything seemed to me quite excellent. Thank you, Tasker.'

'At our last meeting in June,' went on Tasker, 'when I reported how serious this matter was becoming—when you were in South America, Bramwell—it was decided that I was to make a special investigation into the affair, so as to be able, if possible, to put before you today, not only a full explanation of what was happening, but also a recommendation as to the best means of meeting the situation.'

Tasker seemed to find a difficulty in proceeding. He was obviously a good deal perturbed. This question of a possible shutting down meant more to him than to any of the others. Tasker was not a rich man, and if his salary as managing director disappeared on the top of the money he had put into the concern, it would leave him really hard up. Brand, it was true, was also dependent on what he could earn, but Brand was a young man and unmarried, whereas Tasker would soon be past his prime, and he had a wife and son and daughter to support. It would not be an easy thing at his age to get another job.

To the others the affair was not so serious. All were comfortably off, and though no one contemplates the loss of money with equanimity, the failure of the Joymount Works would be to them a comparatively small matter.

After a momentary hesitation Tasker continued speaking.

'The first thing, as Bramwell's question just now has suggested, was to find out what had gone wrong. As far as we ourselves were concerned, there was no mystery about it. Our sales were simply dropping. The number of new buyers had fallen off and our regular customers were taking a smaller quantity. I got in touch with a number of these regular customers, but none of them would give me any satisfaction.

'Then I approached certain of our rivals. Here also there was not much information to be had, but from one or two men whom I knew pretty well I learned something at last. And I will say that it was pretty surprising. In each case their sales had gone down too.

'There seemed to be only one explanation for it: engineers and architects had for some reason become suspicious of rapid hardening cement and had gone back to the use of the older Portland. My friends and I studied the technical journals for an explanation of this—entirely without result. So far as we could see no failures had taken place, nor were there any articles or correspondence on the subject.

'I then went to the Board of Trade and asked for the latest returns of the use of rapid hardening cement in this country. You will understand my astonishment on finding that so far from there having been a diminution in the amount used this had actually increased.'

Tasker fumbled among his papers. 'I don't know if you would like the figures,' he said. 'If anyone would, they're all there. Roughly speaking, they show that our output had dropped by some twenty per cent while the total used in the country had gone up by five per cent.

'Where, then, had the extra stuff come from? It seemed to me at first that in spite of the tariff, cement must be being imported in large quantities. But I was wrong in this too. Careful enquiries through a friend in the Customs department showed that there had been no increase to speak of in the amount shipped into the country.'

'Extraordinary,' interjected Sir Francis, looking round on his colleagues.

There was a little murmur of agreement, but no one seemed disposed for further comment and Tasker went on.

'There seemed, therefore, to be only one solution left—that some British firm or firms were putting out a greatly increased amount of the stuff. I went to Robertson's manager and put it to him straight—I may say that he and I have been personal friends for many years, quite apart from business. I said, "Look here, Tony, your firm has been one of our best customers since we went into this business. Now you've cut down our orders by twenty per cent. What's it all about?"

'Well, he wouldn't say for a while, but at last under a promise of secrecy he told me. We were being undersold. Not in the actual price charged, but rebates were being given for even lorry- or wagon- or ship-loads. They were not large rebates, but where things are so tight that every penny has to be counted, they were large enough to make the difference.'

The chairman moved suddenly. 'But,' he said, 'if we are being undersold, as you tell us, how is it that we are still able to sell our product at all? I understood you to say that our output is only down about twenty per cent.'

'I'm afraid that's not difficult to answer,' Tasker returned with a grimace. 'The amount available with these rebates is limited, and my friend's firm can't get all they'd like. Production, however, is increasing rapidly, and as it does so, Robertson's will take more and our share will go down still further.'

'It doesn't look very rosy,' Sir Francis remarked hesitatingly, with which opinion there were murmurs of agreement.

'Did you find out who was underselling us?' asked Bramwell.

'I did,' said Tasker slowly, 'and I think it will surprise you more than anything else. It's Chayle.'

'Chayle?' Bramwell retorted. 'You don't say so?' while there were expressions of surprise from several other members.

'Yes, Chayle. I shouldn't have believed it, but it's the fact.'

Chayle, or to give it its correct name, Messrs Haviland & Mairs, Ltd, of Chayle, Isle of Wight, was the only other works in the district which were making the same rapid hardening cement as the Joymount Company. The works, which had been started two years before Joymount, were situated at Thorness Bay, on the Solent, some four miles along the coast to the west of Cowes. So far as was known, they were considerably larger than Joymount and equally efficiently organised, but none of the members of the Joymount staff had been over them. Tasker knew both Haviland and Mairs slightly, but neither seemed anxious to pursue the acquaintanceship, and they remained on distant terms.

'I don't understand that,' Bramwell went on. 'Chayle's not such a lot bigger than we are ourselves. How could they turn out enough stuff to affect the market?'

'That's my difficulty too,' Tasker agreed. 'I don't see how they could.'

'Is that the only firm that's putting out the stuff cheap?' asked the sporting director unexpectedly.

'It's the only one I could hear of.'

'Must be costs,' Bramwell declared. 'We've just agreed that our methods and machinery are as good as can be had, but it looks as if we'd have to revise our ideas. They must be turning out the stuff cheaper than we are.'

Tasker shook his head. 'It's not that,' he declared. 'I'm absolutely positive that no firm could do what we're doing any cheaper than we do it. Let me go on.'

'Sorry,' said Bramwell; 'I thought you had finished.'

'I did what seemed to me the obvious thing,' Tasker continued. 'If Chayle were putting out cement cheaper than we could, it followed, I thought, that they must be putting out an inferior cement. I bought some of the Chayle stuff and I told our chemist to test it.'

'King?' Sir Francis asked.

'Yes, King. King's a very good man at his job, as I think you all know; a really first rate chemical engineer. I had every confidence in his opinion. I told him I wanted his report for today, and I got it last night.'

'And did he come up to scratch?'

'I think so, Bramwell.' Tasker spoke with more emphasis. 'If he's correct, the affair turns out even more serious than appeared at first sight. I was right and I was wrong. I was right that the cement was different from ours. I was wrong that it was inferior. It's not inferior.' He paused, then added slowly: 'It's better.'

There were murmurs of concern and incredulity.

'It's not quite the same in chemical composition,' Tasker went on. 'I needn't go into the exact formulæ, I don't suppose any of us would be much the wiser if I did. But it's all here if anyone wants it. It's nearly the same, you understand, but not quite. And the interesting thing about it is that the difference does not merely consist of a slight variation in the proportions of the ingredients—that's to be expected and makes little matter—the difference consists in the presence of certain entirely new elements. It's quite evident that the Chayle people have made some discovery that's going to make us a back number.'

'You mean they've got a new cement?'

'Virtually a new cement.'

Once again there were murmurs of concern. This was certainly a bad look out for their enterprise. If the Chayle people were turning out a better article at a cheaper price than they were, nothing could save them from going out of business. Presently Sir Francis broke the silence.

'You suggest,' he said to Tasker, 'that our Chayle friends have made some discovery or invention in connection with the manufacture of cement. But surely if they had done so they would patent it and allow the rest of us to use it under licence? That would surely pay them better than trying to run a secret process, as I presume you mean they are doing?'

Tasker shrugged. 'I don't know,' he replied slowly. 'I thought of that, and I'm not sure that you're right. In the first place, the covering of a process by patent is not easy. There is always the chance that by introducing some small modifications the protection may be evaded—in which case you have spent your money and lost your process. Besides there's a lot of money in patenting. If they've got hold of something good, they would want to patent it all over the world: covering it in this country only wouldn't be much good. I don't know: I think they might find it better to run it as a secret process.'

The sporting gentleman moved uneasily. 'If Tasker's right in all he's told us, there must surely be other firms than Chayle in it. It's surely physically impossible that they should put out enough to make all this difference?'

'I agree,' Bramwell declared. 'What do you say to that, Tasker?'

'I've said that I don't know. There may be others, working probably in agreement with Chayle.'

Again there was an uneasy silence, broken once more by Bramwell.

'How long can we go on, Tasker?'

'Well, that's just it. Unless we see light somewhere, we can't go on at all. As you know, we're in debt to the bank as it is. We were beginning to work some of it off, but for the last four months we've had to give that up. We're increasing the debt at present, and the bank is not going to stand for much more of it.'

'Been kicking up trouble?'

'Not exactly, but the manager asked me to see him and he gave me to understand our credit was about at its limit.'

'I don't like to think of shutting down without a struggle,' declared Sir Francis.

There were murmurs of approval, but no concrete suggestions, and Sir Francis went on.

'It seems trying to take an unfair advantage of you, Tasker,' he said with a twisted smile, 'but you told us in your statement—and of course we knew—that you were asked, not only to tell us what exactly was happening, but also to recommend the best way of meeting the difficulty. The first part of that commission you have carried out in your usual entirely competent way, but what about the second? Have you been able to think of any way out of our difficulty.'

Tasker shrugged, while the others exchanged perfunctory smiles. 'I'm afraid that's not so easy,' he admitted. 'I can't see any very satisfactory steps that we might take.' He hesitated, then went on more slowly. 'There is just one possibility. I don't myself think there's much in it, but I give it for what it's worth.' Again he paused and the others watched him more eagerly. 'It's King's idea. He'd like to be allowed to try to evolve a similar process. He points out that we know something that we believe none of our competitors knows. We know that the Chayle stuff is different to the rest of the cement on the market because of the extra ingredients it contains. King thinks that, knowing this, he might discover a way of making it.'

The suggestion led to a good deal of discussion. The possibility of King's success, the time that he might require, the estimated loss during this period, even the morality of the proceeding was called in question. Finally Bramwell brought the talk to a close. 'With your permission, Mr Chairman, I think we should have King in and see what he says himself.'

Some such demand had been foreseen, and King was in readiness. Brand was sent for him.

The chemical engineer was a good-looking young fellow of some eight-and-twenty, with dark keen eyes and an alert manner. Obviously moreover he had personality and character—for good or evil. His appearance suggested that what he undertook, he would perform; that in emergencies he would keep his head, and that if a way out of a difficulty were possible, he would find it.

'Mr Tasker has been telling us about your researches into this new cement,' Sir Francis began, when a seat had been found for the young man at the table. 'He says that with the knowledge you already have, it might be possible for you to find some way of making the stuff. We want to know what your feeling about that is, and what you think of your chances of success.'

'I should like very much to try, sir,' the young fellow answered. 'I think there's a reasonable chance of pulling it off. Of course you will understand that I couldn't pledge myself to do so.'

'We understand that and we're not asking impossibilities. What we have to decide is, firstly, whether your chance of success justifies our running at a loss while you are carrying out your experiments, and secondly—I'm being quite straight with you—whether we would be better advised to call in some further, and perhaps more experienced, technical help.'

That this idea should be most distasteful to King was as obvious as it was natural. 'I should ask you to give me a chance, sir; first, at all events.'

'Well, we'll settle that later. Tell me now how long you should want.'

Some other members of the board put questions, then King was thanked and asked to retire. A short further discussion brought the business to an end. King was to be given one month to see what he could do. At the end of that time the whole matter would be reconsidered. If his progress had been substantial, the time might be extended. If not, they would either get additional technical assistance or close down.

This settled, Sir Francis left the chair and the meeting came to an end.

2

The Fight Begins

Brand remained behind when the other men left the room. He was acting for the secretary to the board, who was on leave, and he wished to draft the minutes while the proceedings remained clear in his memory. For a moment he stood at the window, lost in thought.

He was glad on every count that King had been given his opportunity. During the seven years in which they had been associated at the Joymount Works, he and King had become pretty good friends. Their intimacy, however, was due rather to the accident of their being thrown together by their work, than to any special personal attraction. In ordinary circumstances they would probably have remained no more than pleasant acquaintances, but at Joymount there were two reasons which drew them together. The first was that they were the only two men in the concern of similar age and social position, and their outlook on life was therefore more or less alike. The second was that contact was maintained outside their work. Both lived at the same boarding house, or, as the proprietor called it, private hotel. Both moreover were keen on things mechanical, and both delighted in motor boating and racing, a hobby which their position on Southampton Water enabled them to indulge fully. The only discordant note (literally) in their friendship was that for some unknown reason King believed he could sing, and at all sorts of inopportune moments his upraised voice could be heard dealing despotically with fragments from the classics, the more popular melodies of Schubert being special favourites. This habit considerably annoyed Brand, who was himself musical.

For a time Brand considered the outlook as it concerned himself, and then his thoughts reverted to King. There was no doubt that King would put his whole energy into his task. Serious as this Chayle affair was for Brand, for King it might well prove even more vital. King had a very comfortable billet at Joymount and he would not want to lose it. To a large extent he was his own master, and his relations with Tasker and the other members of the staff were pleasant. His salary admittedly was not lavish, but it was adequate, and he had reasonable leisure and in a mild way as much society as he wanted. So far, his case was similar to Brand's.

But King had an even stronger reason for desiring success than merely to keep his job: a reason which Brand did not share. If he got hold of a good process, it might mean a very big thing to him. It might at a stroke render him independent, even wealthy. It would certainly make him professionally a very big man. He might even better the Chayle process and become the world's first authority on rapid-hardening cement. No, there was no fear that King would not do his best.

And King's best was supremely good. At the works he was jack of all trades and master of all. As well as overseeing all the tests, he took charge of the quarry from which the limestone was obtained, of the dredging of the slob, of the machinery, the crushers, the rotary kiln, the ball mills, the screens, elevators and other appliances; of the decauville tramways laid throughout the works, of the wharf at which the 'puffers' and small craft were loaded.

And his management was quite first class. As a result of his effort the organism functioned like clockwork. He saw chalk and slob leaving their respective deposits and arriving to the second at the crushers and mixers. The moment the kilns were ready for more slurry, that was the moment at which just the required amount of slurry was delivered to them. When enough clinker was produced to move, that was the instant the conveyor was ready to carry it to the ball mills. No machine was delivering less than full output because of supplies of material running short: none was choked through getting too much. The plant in fact was continuously putting out the maximum of which it was capable. To have to scrap all that excellence would be to King as bitter as gall.

Brand glanced out of the window before turning back to the table to write his minutes. It was a gorgeous July day, with rich warm sunshine and a cloudless sky. The outlook was delightful. Before him stretched the estuary of the Hamble, its drab sloblands hidden by a full tide, blue as the Mediterranean. At the other side, quarter of a mile or more away, was the little village of Hamble, and the low grass-covered shores of Hamble Common, stretching down towards Southampton Water. By standing at the right of the window and looking sideways across it, Brand could get a glimpse of Southampton Water itself, and the opposite coast near Calshot. Occasionally from this window he had seen the forms of great liners creeping up to Southampton. Seaplanes were constantly in view, indeed the heavy drone of aircraft from the Calshot depot was seldom out of his ears. Brand liked the country. Apart from everything else, he would be sorry if he had to leave it.

By the time he had written up his minutes, the steam whistle had blown for the dinner hour. There was a small canteen in connection with the works and from this lunch for the three chief officers was sent up to the boardroom. Brand cleared his books away as Tasker and King came in.

Though it was an unwritten law that during lunch shop must not be talked, for once the rule was relaxed. The minds of all were too full of the morning's events to think about other matters. But it was not until the coffee was finished and cigarettes were lit up that the discussion became purposeful.

'I've been thinking over one point,' declared King after a short silence, 'and though it's outside my province, I perhaps might mention it. I wondered if there wasn't another line of investigation that you, Tasker, might follow? Not to tell you your business, you know, old man.'

Tasker looked at him gravely. 'If any of us try to stand on our dignity now,' he declared, 'we'll deserve all that may be coming to us. Anyone who can think of *anything* that might help us is a public benefactor and deserves a medal. Go ahead.'

'I thought you'd feel like that,' King returned. 'There's probably nothing in this idea, but I think it's worth discussion. Why not carry the war into the enemy's camp?'

Tasker lit another cigarette. 'Meaning just what?' he demanded.

King lowered his voice. 'Why not see Haviland or Mairs or somebody from Chayle and put it to them that they're underselling us, and how are they doing it? You could speak in a sort of joking way. I don't suppose they'd give you a straight answer, but you might get something out of them.'

Tasker did not reply and Brand interposed: 'You've never spoken to either of them on the subject?'

'No,' said Tasker at length, 'I never have. I've thought of it, I admit, but it seemed to me I might do more harm than good—that we'd be better if they didn't know what we were after.'

'You needn't mention the new cement,' Brand pointed out: 'only that they're underselling us.'

'Merely to ask how they're underselling us would scarcely be productive, I'm afraid. Had you any idea of what I might say, King?'

'What I had in mind was that you might insinuate that we'd be willing to pay something to come in with them.'

Tasker nodded approvingly. 'Ah,' he said, 'that's talking. I could put it that we'd like an idea of what it would cost us to come in as you suggest. What do you say, Brand?'

Brand thought it was a darned good notion.

'All the same, I'm not sure that we should move at once,' Tasker went on. 'I think, King, it depends on your success or failure. If you succeed it would be better that they shouldn't know that we were alive to the question at all. If you fail, it would be a second string to our bow.'

This seemed reasonable to both the others, and it was decided that action on the matter should be postponed. Then King turned to a subsidiary point. 'By the way, Tasker, how would you propose actually to get in touch with those two? Would you call on them?'

'No: making too much of it. I'd accidentally meet Haviland in the train. He goes to Town to the meeting every Friday, and returns by the 4.50 from Waterloo to Portsmouth. I've only to get into the tea car and be surprised and pleased when he turns up, and I think we could drift naturally enough into conversation.'

'Good idea,' King approved. 'Now, Tasker, there's another thing I want to speak to you about. These experiments that I've undertaken; there's a lot of work in them.'

'I shouldn't have thought you'd mind that.'

'I don't mind it, as you know perfectly well. I'd be quite willing to spend the rest of my life at them. But I've only been given a month. That means that a lot of experiments will have to run simultaneously. I can't do a number simultaneously. What I want, Tasker, is some technical help.'

Tasker made a grimace. 'What would that cost us?' he asked.

King shrugged. 'Not very much. A couple of young men at four or five pounds a week each. I shouldn't want anybody very skilled, because I would supervise everything myself. They would just have to be operating chemists—not theoretical men.'

'For one month,' said Tasker. 'All right: I agree. You'll get them yourself?'

'Yes, I'll ring up Town now and have 'em down tonight.'

'I wonder,' Brand suggested, 'if I could lend a hand also? I'm not so busy now, and Harper, that clerk of mine, is a good fellow and could do some of my work. I'm not a chemist, but I know something about it and I believe I could work under King's instructions.'

'Fine!' King exclaimed delightedly. 'That'll be four of us. We should be able to make things hum. You agree, Tasker?'

Tasker nodded. 'Everything depends on this stunt of yours

23

coming off,' he pointed out. 'It would be a fool's game not to go all out for it. Yes, I agree. Anything else you want?'

King grinned. 'Never knew you in such an accommodating mood before,' he said. 'I hope it continues. No, if I can't do it with three helpers I can't do it at all.'

These arrangements were carried out. In reply to King's telephone, two energetic young chemists, Radcliff and Endicott, arrived late that night and next day began work with fervour. Brand spent the mornings in his own department, but from lunch time till late at night he was with the chemists, endlessly carrying out experiment after experiment under King's direction. King developed a habit of disappearing on mysterious errands—usually in the evening or at night—from which he returned, tired and dirty, and with samples of clays and slobs and chalks discreetly hidden in suitcases. These samples then became the subjects of renewed experiments. It was all very intense and efficient.

Unfortunately however the reward of such concentration showed no signs of materialising. Brand broached the subject one night about a fortnight later, as he and King were returning to their rooms.

'What about it?' he asked. 'Do you think you've got any forrader?'

'Too soon to say,' King answered, but Brand could see that he looked anxious and more than a trifle despondent. 'As you know, I've been working on four separate lines of approach. I've proved two are no go. I feel sure, therefore, it must be one of the others. We'll know in about a week.'

'Has Tasker been saying anything?'

'Yes; he wants to try and pump Haviland on Friday.'

'Oh, he does, does he? And what do you think?'

'Well, I can only agree. Didn't I suggest it in the first

instance? All the same, it shows what he thinks of my chances.'

Brand nodded. Though he sympathised with King, he fully approved the proposal, which was adopted at a later conference.

It was with considerable interest that the two younger men went round to Tasker's house on the Friday night to learn the result of his efforts. They found him puzzled.

'Well,' he said, 'I met the old boy on the train as we arranged. He was very civil, much more so than ever before. Very civil and very open.'

'Open? He wasn't giving much away, I bet,' put in King.

'He was. He was giving so much away that I felt overwhelmed. I'll tell you. You'll have a spot?'

Tasker busied himself for a moment with whisky and tumblers. Then, having pushed the cigarettes over to his visitors, he went on.

'Our scheme worked perfectly. I got into the tea car on the 4.50 from Waterloo, sitting at the other side of the aisle from where I had seen Haviland on previous occasions. Fortunately for me, things worked out splendidly. People came in, but my appearance must have put them off, for they all avoided my division. The result was that when Haviland appeared, he dropped naturally into mine. I was surprised to see him and said so. I was also pleased, and when he made a remark I could not hear it owing to the noise of the train, so moved across the passage to his table. It was all done, I flatter myself, quite naturally, and he could not have suspected an intention. At least, I think not; Haviland's about as cute as they're made. Well, we chatted, very amicably, as you can imagine. Then when we'd had tea I thought the time had come, and I said in a joking way, was it he that was causing all this flutter in the dovecot, giving rebates that made his neighbours green with envy? He grew pretty wary at that, and I could see him hesitating while he thought how he should take me. He decided on frankness: artless candour; unreserved ingenuousness; I could almost see his mind work.'

'Then he did make a statement?'

'Oh, he made a statement all right, and a good statement too. He began by saying that he naturally hadn't meant to discuss the affair with a brother manufacturer, because when looked at from one point of view their action mightn't seem over friendly. But of course I was not the man to take such a narrow view. They were taking a present loss in the hope of future gain, and he knew I would agree that they had every right to do it. I would agree that every honest method of gaining trade in these bad days was legitimate?

'Naturally I agreed: all was fair in love and business. He had felt sure that I would.'

'Sort of mutual admiration society?'

'Quite. Then he went on to make his statement. He said that Mairs had come into money. A rich uncle of his had died leaving a quite substantial pile. Their trade and connection had dropped badly during the slump, and Mairs had agreed to put part of this money into the business with the object of giving their customers more attractive terms. Temporarily, of course. They hoped in this way to re-establish their market. They believed they would only have to continue selling at a loss for a short time. Once their connections were re-established, they would revert to their former terms. So what do you think of that?'

King made a gesture of unwilling admiration. 'There's

the same brain that found the process,' he declared. 'It's a good tale, a jolly good tale—and a damned lie.'

'You think so?'

'Sure of it. And what's more, Tasker, I think you owe him one for imagining you'd swallow it.'

'As a matter of fact,' Tasker returned, 'I don't suppose he did think so.'

'Then why did he tell you?'

'Because it might be true. He'd believe I couldn't disprove it.'

Brand shrugged. 'He'd be right there. No outsider could disprove it.'

'No,' said Tasker surprisingly, 'he wouldn't be right. I have disproved it.'

Both his hearers stared. 'Go on,' said King at last.

'As a matter of fact,' answered Tasker, 'the different cement disproves it; and demonstrates the existence of the process as well. But some other information I got disproves it finally and beyond question. For this I can claim no credit: I got it by chance in the club.'

King grinned. 'Well, you're a downy bird, you are! Keeping a lot of perfectly good information up your sleeve. What's the story this time?'

'Pretty convincing,' Tasker declared. 'I was having coffee in the club after lunch when Macfarlane came over. I don't think you've met him, but he's my stockbroker. He's a big chap with a breezy manner, and he began singing out that he was glad to congratulate me on the boom in rapid hardening cement. I asked what boom, and he began to joke and called me a fly dog and wanted to know had I gone to some other broker to invest my ill-gotten gains. You can imagine the style.'

'But what was it all about?' Brand asked.

'That's what I asked him, and I had the devil's own job to get an answer. He evidently saw he'd put his foot in it, and he wanted to draw back. But I wasn't having any, and at last under pledge of secrecy he told me that it was rumoured in the City that rapid-hardening cement was booming. He'd had it from another broker that the Chayle people were making a fortune—both Haviland and Mairs were investing hand over fist. It was supposed the other firms in the business were doing the same. So there you are.'

The others looked at him in blank amazement. Then King swore. 'So it's bigger than we thought,' he declared. 'They must be producing the stuff even cheaper than we imagined.'

'On the other hand,' Brand pointed out, 'if the rich uncle was not a myth and the sum was very large, it would account for the investment as well.'

'No,' said Tasker emphatically, 'that's just the point. Don't you see? If the uncle story were true, only Mairs could invest. But Haviland's doing it too. King's right. This is a bigger thing than we thought.'

'Gosh!' moaned King. 'If I could only get on to it!'

'If you don't,' Tasker returned grimly, 'we're just about down and out.'

For another hour the trio sat discussing the outlook, and it was with an added sense of the precariousness of their position that they finally separated.

3

A Foolish Pact

As the days passed and the end of the allotted month grew nearer, King's temper became steadily shorter and his face more anxious. Not only had he not found the secret, but he was obviously beginning to doubt that he ever would. In vain he and his staff had worked—enlivened by snatches from the 'Marche Militaire' or the 'Unfinished Symphony'—sometimes till two and three in the morning, sometimes indeed till they dropped asleep over their experiments; the elusive process remained elusive still. He had pushed his four methods of attack as far as he knew how, but they had proved unproductive. Indeed in a moment of discouragement he admitted to Brand that he did not see his way further and that failure was staring him in the face.

'If I don't get it, it's the end of me,' he said bitterly. 'I'll not get a chance like this again: not ever. Here's fame and a fortune on the one hand; and on the other—just ruin. I must have been all but on the secret again and again, and for the sake of missing some little point, I'm going to lose. It's so sickening it makes me ill to think of it.'

It was getting on to three in the morning and the two young men, tired almost to tears and oppressed with the numbing sense of failure, were walking slowly to their rooms. The night was wonderful even for late July, clear and calm and balmy. The moon, which was nearly full, was sinking in the west, but was still high enough to make their immediate surroundings bright as day, and to show up as a faint smudge the coast beyond the Hamble.

King railed openly upon fate. It was the first time Brand had heard him relinquish his cocksure pose, and he was the more impressed. For a time Brand commiserated with him, but so sorry for himself did King presently become, that Brand's feeling of sympathy began to evaporate.

'My dear chap,' he said at length, irritated by the other's entirely selfish diatribe, 'you're not the only one that's going to suffer. If you fail, we'll all be out of a job. Tasker may be able to pull along, but even he'll be badly hit. I have nothing but what I make. I'll never get a job like this again. It's not only you.'

King turned and looked at him sombrely. 'I know that perfectly well, Brand,' he said. 'You seem to take it pretty coolly. I wonder if you realise what failure is going to mean to you? I doubt it. Just think before it's too late.'

'What good'll that do?' Brand retorted. 'Thinking about it won't alter it. I'll not starve. I'll get something, if it's only a clerkship.'

'Will you?' returned King aggressively. 'How do you know you will? I suppose you realise that thousands of clerks are walking the streets today because they can't get jobs? Don't think that because you've been a director that an employer'll want you. I tell you, he'll avoid you. He'll say, "Here's a man that's been boss of his department.

30

He'll be too big for his boots as a clerk. I want someone less high and mighty." That's what he'll say. And he'll have plenty of others to choose from. I tell you, Brand, if this place goes down, you go down with it. Don't you make any mistake about that.'

In his more weary and dispirited moments, these had been the very thoughts which had been forcing their way into Brand's mind. They represented a dark shadow, a sort of evil nightmare, which in spite of all his efforts had been weighing more and more heavily upon his spirits. What King said was true. He was by no means sure of employment. Hundreds of men as good as he were without it: why should he prove an exception? King might even be correct in suggesting that his very qualifications would be against him.

And if he couldn't get a job what was to happen to him? All his little capital was in Joymount. If the company went down that would be gone. He would be penniless in a terribly short time.

Brand felt a little sick as he considered the picture. He tried to banish it. He told himself that his feeling of horror was due merely to physical weariness and that a few hours in bed would remove it. But all the time he knew he was wrong; he realised that now for the first time he was facing the facts. He saw that if he lost his job there was no telling to what depths he might not fall.

'Confound you, King,' he grumbled, 'you're not a very cheery companion. We're tired and we want a sleep. That's what's wrong with us. Let's get to bed and things'll look better in the morning.'

King slipped his arm through Brand's as if to hold him back. 'No,' he said, 'don't be in a hurry. I want to get this

31

thing straightened out. I want to know what it's going to mean to both of us if we fail. It's not merely idle. I may tell you I have something in my mind. But we must know where we stand before we begin to discuss it.'

'Let it wait till the morning.'

'No, we've got our chance now. Goodness only knows what may happen in the morning. Hang it all, man, don't be such a fool. Do realise that the whole of the rest of our lives may be at stake.'

Brand smothered a curse. 'Well,' he said testily, 'what's the great idea?'

'I'll come to that in a moment. I want first to know what the result will be to you if we fail to find this process.'

For the first time Brand grew interested. King's manner had changed. He seemed now neither tired nor despondent. Rather he appeared to be choking down an almost uncontrollable excitement. He radiated energy. In spite of himself Brand felt himself being carried away by it. And suddenly it was borne in on him that King had never been despondent at all. He had never really railed against his fate. All that had been put on—for some reason.

'Come along out with it, old man,' he said goodhumouredly. 'If you've got a notion, let's have it.'

'I want to know,' King repeated in serious tones, 'what the result of failure's going to be to you. Let's get that down into words first. Then I'll tell you what I've been thinking.'

Brand was still more impressed. He could no longer doubt that the chemist had some proposal of importance to put up. He did not reply and King went on.

'We've agreed that if the works go down we'll lose our jobs. Have you private means, Brand? I don't want to pry into your affairs, but this matters. I may say I have none.'

'I have none either,' Brand returned slowly. 'I had a little capital—technically, I have it still, but every penny of it is in the concern. It took it all to get me my directorship.'

'Then if the company goes, that money goes too.'

'I'll have nothing,' Brand admitted.

'Same with me. And what about relatives, Brand? I should be absolutely alone and penniless if the works go down. Would you?'

As King spoke, an even fuller realisation of his position swept over Brand. Alone and penniless! What a ghastly thought! If the works went down that would be his fate. Alone and penniless. For the first time Brand felt himself in the hideous grip of panic.

King did not push his question. He had evidently got the effect he was seeking. For a few moments he did not speak, then very softly he said:

'What would you give for security?'

The phrase struck into Brand's consciousness. What would he give for security? Why, *anything!* Security was the thing he wanted—more than anything else. Security didn't matter so much when one had it. Faced with its loss, it became about the most important thing there was.

'Security!' King went on. 'And not security only. What would you give for a fortune? Well, Brand. What would you give for security and a fortune—as against ruin?'

Security! A fortune! The words conjured up a vision so gorgeous, so utterly to be desired, that Brand felt carried away. Yet he answered soberly.

'What's the good of talking like that? You know as well as I do that I'd give anything I had—which is just nothing at all.'

King made a gesture of dissent. 'That's just where you're

wrong, Brand,' he said earnestly. 'You could give something that would do the trick. I don't say absolutely—there is a chance of failure. But I'd put the chances of success at ninety-nine to one.'

Brand stared. 'For heaven's sake get on with it,' he urged.

Though they were alone on the moonlit road King bent forward and lowered his voice. 'The process would save us,' he declared. 'And there's a way by which we might learn it.'

Brand continued to stare. 'How?' he asked laconically.

'By going to the Chayle Works and seeing how it's done.'

Brand laughed scornfully. 'Bless my soul, King, is that all? That's like the groans of the mountain leading to the appearance of the mouse. And do you imagine they'd be accommodating and show us?'

'Don't be more of an ass than you can help, old man. My scheme's watertight. They wouldn't show us, no. But then we wouldn't ask them.'

'I don't know what you're driving at, King.'

'As a matter of fact we wouldn't trouble them at all,' King went on in that ridiculous low voice. 'We'd pay our call—er—privately.'

'Do you mean that we should break in?' said Brand bluntly.

King shrugged. 'Technically, I'm afraid so,' he admitted coolly; 'actually, no. What I mean is this; we should go to the place at night, climb over the wall, have a walk round and see what's going on. We should almost certainly get the clue.'

Brand whistled. 'But that—' He hesitated. 'That, King, would be burglary. Breaking and entering. Not to put too fine a point on it, man, you're suggesting stealing the blessed thing!'

'And what are we doing now?' King answered tensely. 'What have we been doing for the last three weeks, with the approval of everyone concerned? Trying to steal their idea! Buy their stuff: analyse it: find out what it contains: try to get their process. Are we trying to improve the manufacture of cement? Not we. We're trying to get hold of their profits for ourselves. What do you call that but stealing it? And you've been as busy as anybody.'

Brand shook his head. 'But that's different. What we've been doing is legitimate enough. We're surely entitled to the work of our own hands and brains.'

'Brand, I'm surprised at you! That's just hypocrisy and you know it! You know as well as I do that what I propose and what we've been doing are identical—except for the place in which we shall do it. We've been trying to pick their brains here, now we shall try to do it there. That's all the difference.'

Brand was beginning a protest, but King broke in fiercely. 'And what about their stealing our jobs?' he queried. 'They were doing quite well out of their concern. We were all making our living comfortably and satisfactorily. Then they see how they can make some more. Do they think about us? No, we may starve, so that they can double their share. What about that? Do you think it's not legitimate to protect ourselves against that sort of thing?'

Again Brand tried to speak and again King broke in. 'Well, there it is,' he declared with a gesture as if he was holding out some imaginary offering. 'It's up to you now. I can't do this thing by myself. I must have help and there's no one but you. Will you come in and save not only your-self and me, but everyone in the Joymount Works? Or will you stay out because of a scruple—a false scruple, mind you—and let us all be ruined? Come now, Brand. If it doesn't matter to you personally, remember all those to whom it's life and death, and don't put yourself and your scruples, if you have any, before them.'

Brand was silent. This proposal of King's was utterly unexpected, and he scarcely knew what to say. He did not set up to be in any way straighter or more moral than the next man, but he did draw the line at burglary. Besides for burglary you could get the devil of a sentence. Years!

But was this burglary? If they stole nothing tangible would it be burglary? King said not. Was King right? On thinking it over, Brand wasn't sure. Would they really be guilty of more than trespass?

The more he thought of it, the more he hated the idea. But, he asked himself, did his own mere likes and dislikes matter in such a case? Did the greatest good of the greatest number not demand from him the sacrifice of his own preference?

Brand saw that it was not a choice of good or evil that faced him. It was a choice between two evils. A somewhat tarnished conscience and the chance of prison on the one hand: on the other, ruin for all his friends at the works.

Ruin also for himself! Why should be throw away the rest of his life for a scruple, and a doubtful scruple at that?

King's voice once again broke into his thoughts. 'I forgot to say, though it is a bit important—I forgot to say that if we carry out the scheme I propose, there is not the slightest chance of it ever becoming known. I've given it a lot of thought and I've got a watertight plan. So you needn't be afraid of that.'

It was this last argument that really tipped the scale with Brand. He did not give way all at once. For an hour and more they paced backwards and forwards, he objecting, King protesting. But at last he agreed. After all, if it wasn't quite straight, it wasn't so very crooked. And it wouldn't hurt the Chayle people: there was ample room for both firms.

'Good man,' said King, when he announced his decision. 'I knew you wouldn't let us all down. Now do you realise that it's after four o'clock? Let's get to bed and we'll talk about this further in the morning. And I needn't say, not a word to a soul.'

It was not till after lunch next day that the matter was again referred to. King, having seen that his two assistants, Radcliff and Endicott, were fully occupied, beckoned Brand into his office.

It was a tiny match-boarded place with a large window looking south towards Southampton Water. It was not very clean and not at all tidy. Books and catalogues had over-flowed the shelves on to the desk and floor. There were papers everywhere. King cleared a chair for his guest by the simple expedient of tipping it sideways.

'Now,' he began, 'let me tell you what I've done and then we'll hold a council of war.'

He lit a cigarette, then tilting back his chair, he stretched a long arm into a corner and picked up a rolled plan.

'This,' he went on, spreading it on the desk, 'is a section of the twenty-five-inch Ordnance map. You see where we are. This land is the north-western coast of the Isle of Wight, and this water above it is, of course, the Solent. This is Thorness Bay, between three and four miles west of Cowes along the coast. These buildings on the shore of Thorness Bay are the Chayle Works. You see their position, on the flat ground of a little valley between low hills, and opposite the estuary of the Beaulieu River. Incidentally, as you know, they are about nine miles from here.'

'Well, I ought to know that.'

'Of course. I simply want to begin at the beginning. You also know the works. You've seen them a thousand times from the Solent, but have you ever been close to them?'

'Now you mention it, I don't think I have. Not within a mile, I should say. With the launch you cross the mouths of bays. Different to tacking about with sails.'

'I thought you mightn't have. Well, I've gone in close and had a good look. And the first interesting thing I saw was that there's a high wall all round the place. Incidentally I noticed that they've made a tiny harbour and there are usually two or three small steamers or motor boats in it.'

'I've seen that myself.'

'Quite. Well, one evening I went over to Cowes and walked out after dusk. I went right down to the works and found that the place is like a medieval fort. There are only two gates, one opening on to the end of the pier, and the other to the approach road.'

'Secret process all right,' Brand suggested.

'Yes, and I got something more interesting still. In conversation in a nearby pub I found out that the wall was new. It was built three years ago.'

'So dating the putting down of the plant for the new cement?'

'Of course. Naturally I wanted to see inside, but I couldn't manage it. So I did the next best thing. The ground rises on the Cowes side—clay cliffs, you know, and there are hedges and shrubs which provide cover. I went back the next evening with some food and a rug, slept in the launch in Cowes Harbour and before it was light went ashore and walked to Chayle. By the time dawn was breaking I was on this higher ground. From there I could see the buildings. I checked them up with those shown on the Ordnance map, and found that two new ones had been erected since the map was made. I had a pretty good glass, and the walls of these two buildings looked new. I assumed they were built at the same time as the surrounding wall, and contained the secret we wanted.'

'You didn't stay there all day, surely?'

'As a matter of fact, I didn't. I watched till lunch time and I saw some interesting enough things. First I saw the staff arriving, the labourers first and then later the office lot. They were very like our own crowd, and I could almost guess their various jobs from their appearance. A very small night squad left, together with a tall lame man with a basket; obviously the night watchman. I noticed also that though there was a fairly continual stream of motor lorries in and out of the works, the entrance gates were kept closed. They were specially opened for each vehicle, and closed again after it had passed. And at the pier, where they were loading bags by a decauville tramway, they had a man at the gate all the time.'

'They're taking no chances.'

'Are they? Well, after that I became a Scots visitor, come to the Island for my health. I discoursed to all and sundry in the bars of any pubs I could find, until later in the afternoon, I had a bit of luck. Who should come into a pub but the night watchman.'

'How did you know him?'

'I thought it was he. I had taken a pretty good squint at him with my glasses. I got talking to him and stood him a pint. He was a taciturn devil, but a second pint loosened his tongue. He was the watchman, and he told me a good deal about the works. I needn't trouble you with just how I pumped him. He told me that about three years ago the firm had put in some new kilns. It was then they built the wall and the two new buildings. The buildings were for the kilns, but he obviously didn't understand the details, and in any case I couldn't be too curious. They were doing well and putting out a lot of stuff, and the wages of everyone had been raised. I thought that was enough about the works and I turned the conversation on to himself. He told me his name—Clay—and about his parentage and early life, all complete. Incidentally, he is now entirely alone in the world. He had driven a lorry for the firm; he said said there was nothing on wheels that he couldn't drive. Some three years ago he had had an accident. It wasn't his fault, so he said: some blinking fool had come charging out of a drive just before him. He had been hurt internally by the wheel and couldn't work. They had made him night watchman and he had a not too bad screw and was comfortable enough.'

'Interesting, if not exactly relevant,' Brand declared. ''Pon my soul, King, you've not done so badly. You've got about everything—except what we want.'

'Quite,' King admitted drily, 'and I suppose you now'll agree that to get that we must have a look inside those new buildings? And that's what I want to do—tonight.'

'Suppose they're locked?'

King shrugged. 'Our first snag is the wall,' he pointed out. 'We'll get over the wall tonight. If after that we come to a locked door, well, I've thought about that. We may be able to deal with it. And if not, there may be a window. Now, Brand, in this thing you're taking instructions from me. Go home now and get a sleep and after dinner we'll set off.'

'I don't want a sleep. I'm quite fresh.'

'You won't be in the middle of the night. You want a sleep and you're going to have it. Go along, don't make trouble, there's a good chap.'

Brand, knowing in his heart that King was right, went. He lay down on his bed, and in what seemed about ten seconds, but was really over four hours, King woke him to say dinner was ready.

4

The First Attempt

About ten that night King and Brand left the boarding-house, having put up the usual story that they were going to work late at the office and didn't know when they'd get back. The weather was fairly suitable for their purpose. It was fine and calm, though a little too bright. The moon was full, but happily this was to some extent neutralised by a heavily clouded sky and a haze over the water. There would be ample light for anything they might require, but they would have to be careful about being seen.

King led the way across the boarding-house yard to a small shed which he used as a workshop. He was a handy fellow and a good carpenter and metal worker. This shed was to him a holy of holies, even more sacred than his laboratory at the works.

'We've got to take one or two things,' he explained. 'What do you think of that? I've been making it for the last week.'

'That' was a ladder, partly wooden and partly rope, very strong and very light, and in its design bearing traces of King's ingenious mind. When erected it took the shape of an A without the crossbar. One side of the A was of wood, folding into two, and stretching to about fourteen feet when extended. To the top was fixed the rope ladder, of about the same length and forming the other side of the A.

'You see,' King pointed out, 'when it's folded there's plenty of room for it on the launch. When we get to the wall we extend it and it reaches to the top. We go up, throw the rope ladder over, and that gets us down the other side. See?'

Brand paid his due meed of admiration. He had got over his scruples and was looking forward like a boy to the adventure.

'Well, you take it, will you? I'll bring the rest of the kit.'

Brand shouldered the ladder, which was surprisingly light, and King having picked up a package which lay ready, they left the shed.

'I suggest we don't take the ordinary path to the works,' King said in a low voice. 'If we met anyone our baggage might require explanation. Let's go by the shore.'

To Brand this seemed obvious wisdom. They went down to the beach and pushed along the rough grass just above high-water mark. Here they were unlikely to be seen, and the grass of course would not retain footprints.

'What have you got in the package?' Brand asked as they trudged along.

'Pad of old sacks to lay over possible glass on the wall,' King returned. 'Four torches, two for use, two spare. Masks in case someone should see us. Bunch of skeleton keys for various kinds of locks. Gloves so as not to leave finger-prints. That's the lot. Have I forgotten anything?'

Brand thought not. He was, indeed, rather impressed by the completeness of the preparations. One thing at least was evident—that King had had the expedition in his mind for a much longer time than he had led Brand to believe. He said so.

'Why, yes,' King admitted coolly. 'From the very first I had to consider a possible failure of the mere chemical investigation. But I couldn't consider complete failure. Some scheme of this kind seemed to be indicated.'

How typical of King! thought Brand. If success in anything he undertook was humanly possible, King would succeed!

They were now in the neighbourhood of the wharf. Owing to the works' sheltered position on the Hamble Estuary, the building of a harbour had not been considered necessary. A small wharf of open-work ferroconcrete piles had simply been erected parallel with the shore, and a little dredging in front of it had provided depth for the small craft which used it. At the end of the wharf was the boat-house belonging to the works, in which Brand and King kept their respective launches. The dredging had been carried round the end of the wharf so that there was access to the boathouse at all states of the tide.

'We'll take your launch,' said King. 'It's the smaller and more silent of the two.'

Now they trod softly lest they should be heard by the crew of the little coaster moored alongside. Gently unlocking the boathouse door, they bestowed their stuff on Brand's launch, a squat craft with a broad square stern, like a fifteen-foot length cut from the bows of some larger boat. King added a light pair of sculls, but when Brand was about to cast off, he stopped him.

'Not yet, old son,' he whispered. 'We've got to have an alibi. All the best criminals do it. Come up to the works.'

They walked round to the road entrance of the works, which like Chayle, were also surrounded by a wall, though in this case only four feet high. There they let themselves in. The watchman saw them and came forward.

'Good night, Taylor,' said King. 'We're going to work late—perhaps all night. You needn't trouble about us. We'll let ourselves out when we're done.'

The old man touched his cap. 'Good night, gentlemen,' he answered. 'You're busy these times?'

'A special job,' King called back. 'Thank goodness, it'll soon be finished.'

Reaching the laboratory, King locked the door behind them, switched on the light and lowered the blinds. Then they passed into his private office, also locking its two doors, from the laboratory and passage respectively. King here switched off the light and got out his torch.

'We'll leave the light on in the lab,' he said, 'and if it's seen, it'll be supposed we're there. Here's our way out. I fixed it up this afternoon.'

As he spoke he took a rope from a cupboard. One end was already made fast to a cleat which had been screwed inside the cupboard, and every couple of feet it had a knot. He threw the other end out of the window.

'Down you go,' he said. 'You needn't be afraid: it's amply long enough.'

'I say, King, you've thought this out all right,' Brand admitted, as he climbed on the window sill and gingerly lowered himself down.

The laboratory was on the first floor of the office block, and a climb of some twenty feet brought him to the ground.

He let go the rope. For a few seconds it shook violently, and then King stood beside him.

'If we go back in the morning the same way, pull up the rope, and leave by the door, Taylor'll swear we've been in the building all night. Radcliff and Endicott will swear to it too, for I've done some work that they don't know about, and if I produce it tomorrow, they'll say we must have worked all night to get it finished.'

Again Brand complimented him and they turned towards the shore. The ground on which they had alighted was hard and would not leave footprints, and as there was nothing to bring Taylor or any other person to that part of the yard, the chances of the rope being seen were negligible. They reached the wall, slipped over it, and tiptoed silently down to the boathouse.

'We'll give her a good push out,' King whispered, 'and she'll float clear of the wharf. Then we'll use the sculls. Steady a moment till I fit these mufflings. No lights, of course.'

Having shipped the rowlocks and bushed them with soft rags, they pushed off. Without a sound they floated under the counter of the steamer and out on to the dark water beyond. Then Brand dropped in the sculls and pulled silently away.

Not till they had gone a mile and were well into Southampton Water did they turn on their lights and start their engine. They kept inshore out of the channel through which the great liners nosed their way up to Southampton, passing to starboard of the Calshot Lightship and the Hill Head Buoy, and only coming as it were into the open when they crossed Cowes Roads from the West Bramble Buoy to Egypt Point. Then they again hugged the shore till they came off Gurnard Point. There King, between free snatches of the 'Marche Militaire', stopped the motor and turned out the lights.

'We've only another mile to go,' he explained. 'We may as well do it with the sculls. Let's put on our masks and gloves first in case we forget them.'

It was thicker here, which in a way was all to the good. So far they had had no trouble, being able to pick up the lights through the haze. Brand did not like the look of the weather. It might easily thicken up enough to make getting back difficult. However, there was no use in meeting trouble half way. With the muffled sculls Brand was able to pull in almost complete silence. The boat floated easily along. There was no wind and scarcely any swell. The only sound was the faint jabbling of the tiny wavelets on the bows. Presently King spoke.

'We can't risk going to their harbour,' he said. 'We'll land on the shore here. It won't kill us if we get our feet wet.'

'No trouble about getting ashore,' Brand returned, 'but what about getting aboard again? It's about high water now and if we're too long we'll find the launch high and dry on the shingle.'

'We'll anchor a bit out and wade in. It'll be all right.'

Brand raised no further question but pulled straight in. King moved up into the bow and seized a boat-hook.

'Steady,' he said presently, and then, 'Back water a stroke.'

Brand obeyed and King dropped the anchor overboard.

''Bout two feet of water,' the latter said. 'Now let's see we have everything. Got your torches? Right. You take the ladder and I'll manage the rest.'

'Right,' Brand said in his turn. 'Go ahead.'

They were glad it was summer when, having taken off their shoes and rolled up their trousers, they stepped into the water. They had not, however, far to wade. The beach shelved quickly and they were soon on dry land. There was still a narrow, shingle-covered band between the water and the foot of the low clay cliffs, and along this they walked. Presently the cliffs fell away, and then the wall of the works loomed up before them. King selected a spot and placed his ladder and mat—there was glass on the coping—and in a few moments both men were inside. King had evidently memorised the map, for he led the way without hesitation.

The space on which they had descended was waste ground, being littered with old planks and barrels and the debris inseparable from such a plant. To their left was the gable of a large building, and they moved along it away from the boundary.

'This is an old building,' King whispered, 'but the next one, a few feet further on, is one of the new ones.'

They passed on till they came to the new shed. It was brick built and of considerable length, but neither very wide nor very high. A row of windows with sills about eight feet from the ground, were faintly illuminated, but through muffled glass. Above was an elaborate system of ventilators. From within came the heavy rumble of moving machinery.

'The new kilns,' King whispered.

As he spoke they kept on moving cautiously along the shed wall. Now they realised the advantage of the moonlight. They could see about them without using their torches.

There was no door in the long side by which they were

walking, nor in the gable which they presently reached, though a conveyor passed through the latter to feed an adjoining bin. The second long side was also unbroken save for windows, but at the opposite gable they came on the door.

It was a large oaken gate, strongly built and containing a wicket fitted with a Yale lock. King clicked his tongue with annoyance when he saw that the wicket was locked and that his skeleton keys were useless.

'We can't get in,' he whispered. 'Come and let's look at the second shed.'

With great care they crept forward to the second new building. Here they found that similar conditions obtained. The shed, apparently identical in size with that they had just left, was also locked. From it also came the same sound of moving machinery.

Brand whispered his disappointment, but King shook his head. 'Never mind,' he breathed; 'I half expected this. We'll get in next time.' He paused for a moment irresolutely, then went on. 'I want to have a general look round. There's no use in both of us risking being seen. Go back to the ladder, like a good chap, and wait for me.'

Brand nodded and when King had vanished like a shadow, he crept silently back to their point of entry. Then at the bottom of the rope ladder, he settled down to wait.

It did not seem to him that they had made much by their expedition. They had already known that there were new kilns in the sheds. But if they couldn't get into the sheds to examine them, he couldn't see that they were any further on.

King, however, had seemed quite satisfied. Apparently he had not expected to be able to get into the sheds. Why, then, their expedition? It was all very puzzling to Brand, but he had immense faith in King and he supposed that some purpose had been gained.

One thing at least he was pleased about. Though they had 'broken and entered' in the technical sense, they had done nothing of which he need be very much ashamed. And his motives were really not bad. He did not think he could be seriously blamed for his action.

Time soon began to drag. Brand wondered what was keeping King. He grew more and more restless, until an approaching shadow resolved itself into the chemist.

'That's all for tonight,' the young man breathed. 'Just let's see we've left no traces and we may go.'

Brand was bursting with curiosity, but felt his questions must keep. They crossed the wall, retrieved their mat and ladder, and set off towards the boat. Then he began.

'We haven't got much and that's a fact,' King returned, 'but then I didn't expect to get much this trip. It was simply a preliminary reconnaissance. We'll have to do it once again and then I hope we'll get all we want. I had a bit of luck since. I've been all over the offices.'

'Great Scot! How did you manage that?'

'By a fluke, pure and simple. When I left you I crept over towards where I thought the offices must be. I was nearly nabbed by a couple of fellows who were evidently going round having a look at the machines. However, I took cover in time and they passed without seeing me. It looks as if they just had a skeleton shift on at night to keep the automatic part of the plant running.'

'Yes, I wondered we didn't see more signs of life.'

'That's the reason. You remember, I saw only a tiny shift leave the works in the morning. Well, I really wanted to see where the watchman hung out, and whether he was a live wire or spent the time asleep. Then I had my bit of luck. Just as I got near the door of a likely building it opened and my friend of the pub came out. He's a good man that, doing his trick when no one's looking after him. I hid behind a convenient barrel and he passed without seeing me. When he'd gone I hesitated for about half a second, then I thought the opportunity too good to miss and I slipped in through the door he'd come out of, he'd left it open. I peeped into a comfy little room with a fire and light and his supper set out on a shelf, then hurried on down a passage which I guessed led to the offices. It did, and I went all over them: main clerical offices, some private rooms, technical office and lab. I was in them all. Great piece of luck!'

'But did you get anything?'

'I didn't get the secret, if that's what you mean. But in a case like this no knowledge is to be despised. Don't worry, Brand. With luck we'll be all right yet.'

'The watchman didn't see you coming away?'

'No, I got out before he came back.'

Brand continued his questions, but his companion was irritatingly close and refused absolutely to reveal his plans. From the way he spoke however Brand was sure that he had plans, though what they might be he couldn't imagine.

On the return journey they simply reversed their previous proceedings. The tide had fallen round the launch and they got aboard without trouble. They rowed to Gurnard Point before starting up the engine, and reverted to the sculls at the entrance to the Hamble. Without lights they approached their own wharf, and in silence and unseen got the launch back into the boathouse. As before they left their stuff in the launch while they went back to their rope and climbed to King's office. Then talking noisily, they set out the work which they had presumably done, turned out the light in the laboratory and went down to the entrance. They made a point of seeing the watchman and bidding him good night, King calling his attention to the time by saying that they had got on well and that it was not so late as they had expected. Then picking up the stuff from the launch, they walked back to their boarding-house, stored their impedimenta in King's workshop, let themselves into the house and went to bed. Whatever advantage they had or had not gained, Brand was at least certain that they had not given themselves away.

This opinion was confirmed next morning. Both Radcliff and Endicott were obviously impressed by the amount of work that had been done during the night, and Brand felt that their testimony, coupled with that of the night watchman, would make their alibi unbreakable. Nor could any trace of their presence remain at Chayle. If all King's plans worked out as well as that of the previous night, the Joymount Works would be saved!

The time, however, was getting short. Unless King could get an extension from the board, only six days were now left. This was Thursday, and the board met on the following Wednesday. And the board would not grant an extension, Brand felt sure, unless they were satisfied that King had made substantial progress in his investigations and seemed likely to achieve success.

He was filled with a desire to discuss the affair once more with King. But on that Thursday and the following day, Friday, King vanished from the works. No one, not even Tasker, knew where he had gone. This, however, was in order, King had been given complete freedom of action during the period of the investigation.

Again on Saturday he did not turn up, but that evening Brand saw a light in his workshop and went over. The door was locked, and after a short delay King opened it.

'I say,' Brand greeted him, 'you're a nice one. Where on earth have you been all this time?'

'Different places,' King rejoined grinning. 'Exeter and London mostly, if you want to know. Why?'

'Why?' returned Brand, 'What do you mean by "why"? Don't you think I want to know what's going on?'

King chuckled. Are you on for the decisive expedition tomorrow night?' he asked.

'Back to Chayle?'

'Yes. Just the same as before, except that—this time we'll get what we want.'

'I'm on, of course. But why do you hope for better results?'

'I don't hope; I know.' King swung round and pulled out a drawer beneath his bench. 'Look there.'

In the drawer were a number of Yale keys, evidently in process of being filed up. King bent over, glancing at the door as he did so.

'The Chayle keys,' he whispered triumphantly.

Brand could only stare at him in utter amazement.

The Bowl of Sugar

'But, my dear chap, you must tell me.'

It was half an hour later and the two men were walking along the winding road in the direction of Swanwick.

'There's no mystery about it,' King answered. 'From the very first, as I told you, I foresaw that if I was to succeed, I might have to have a look round the Chayle Works. In this case keys might be wanted, so from the very first I began to work out plans for getting them.'

'Tell me,' Brand said again.

'I'm doing it as quick as I can,' King returned. 'From our expedition on Wednesday night I learned not only that we wanted keys, but that the keys were Yale and that they were small in size. Now it's not usual to have large outer doors opened with a small sized key, and a possible reason for this occurred to me. In all probability the principals carried the keys about with them, and therefore wanted them to be as small as possible. I assumed that if I could have a look through the pockets of Haviland or Mairs, I should find a bunch of about eight small Yale keys.

It seemed worthwhile taking a chance on this assumption, and I took it.'

'But, good heavens, King, you don't mean that you were prepared to search their pockets?'

'Scruples again? Don't be such an ass, Brand. You're in this thing up to the hilt and you needn't pretend to have scruples about one part of it and not another. However, in this instance, you weren't responsible. I'd better not tell you any more.'

Brand was sorely troubled. If King had done anything like this, he most certainly did not want to be mixed up in it. Why, it was pocket-picking! Then he thought of the benefit he and others were going to get from King's work. King no doubt disliked it as much as he did himself, but King had gone through with it. He, Brand, could not in decency take the benefits of King's action if he refused to pay the price.

'I'm sorry, King,' he said. 'Only a passing distaste. I'm with you, as you know.'

King nodded. 'I know you are, old man. I agree with your scruples, mind you. I'm all for conscience myself, so long as it's not overdone. But don't ever let's forget: we're not out to hurt anybody, only to prevent other people hurting us.'

'I know, you ass. Get along, will you, and tell me what you did.'

King had looked hurt, but now he smiled again, as if delighted with himself and his achievement.

'My problem, then, was in some way to get my hands into either Haviland's or Mairs' pockets and see if such a bunch existed. How was I to do it?

'It was Tasker who gave me the hint. He said that Haviland came down to Portsmouth every Friday by the 4.50 from Waterloo. I also could travel by that train. It provided a suitable meeting place. Trains, moreover, were conveyances in which people frequently went to sleep. Could I do anything on those lines? I was personally unknown to Haviland, and I thought I could.

'I worked out the details and on the Friday after Tasker saw Haviland—yesterday week, in fact—I went up to Town and travelled down in the tea car with Haviland. There was plenty of room and I chose a seat from which I could watch him unobtrusively. He didn't look up from his paper when I got in, and I let him get out before me, so I don't think he noticed me at all. But I saw what I wanted to see—that he took two cups of tea and that into each cup he put two pieces of sugar: that is, four lumps in all. From various enquiries I had made I knew Haviland was a man of habit, and I assumed that he took four lumps in his tea each time he travelled by that train. As it turned out I was justified.

'That of course was all preparation, but on last Thursday I began to carry out my plan.

'First I wanted to travel by some Southern Company's tea car train in an area in which I was a complete stranger. I chose the 2.28 from Exeter to Waterloo. I went to Exeter on the Thursday and travelled up by that train. I chose an ordinary compartment and went along to the restaurant car for tea some ten minutes after the other passengers. I dallied over my tea and was one of the last to be finished. By the time I had paid my bill my own and the next compartments were empty. Then choosing a moment when the attendants were out of the car, I took a cigarette out of my case and got up to go. I was not observed, but all the same I acted carefully. I dropped my cigarette in what I claim was a realistic way on one of the tables of the next division. Naturally, I had to stoop to get it, and when I straightened up again a sugar bowl, complete with its contents, was in my pocket. I got back to my carriage, packed the bowl in my suitcase and congratulated myself that my first fence was successfully taken. I suppose they missed the bowl, but it had not vanished from my table and there was nothing to connect me with its loss.'

This was not at all the kind of story that Brand wished to hear. King grinned at his expression. 'What's the saga about the tangled web we weave?' he demanded. 'Is that the way you feel?'

'I don't pretend I like it,' Brand admitted. 'However, I suppose we can't get what we want without paying for it.'

'True, oh philosopher,' King returned genially, 'and invariably it's best to have somebody else to do the paying. Why,' he grinned, 'you should be all over me with gratitude, you self-righteous divil!'

'So I am, really. I told you I was with you.'

'You are, old son; trust me to see to that.'

The words were spoken with good-humoured raillery, and yet for a moment Brand wondered if they did not contain the suspicion of a threat. He glanced at his companion, but King's expression was entirely disarming. 'Go ahead,' Brand urged. 'I want to hear the rest of the tale.'

'As I said,' King resumed, 'there I was with my first fence taken. I had a little white china bowl with a green rim and the words "Southern Railway" on its side in the correctly shaped loop, and in the bowl were a couple of dozen pieces of sugar, each rolled in its paper cover, bearing the maker's name and the directions for opening it in blue letters and in red. The genuine article, all complete and no deception.'

'I've seen them,' said Brand.

King shook his head. 'Ah, but you've never possessed any for your very own. Well, I turned then to another point. Haviland, I felt sure, would like a nice sleep next day in that 4.50, and that seemed to suggest a sleeping draught. I estimated that about half an ordinary draught would meet the case. It would be pretty certain to send him off, but the sleep would not be too heavy: he could be wakened at Portsmouth. Here I confess I was working in the dark, and I would have been glad of a bit of medical knowledge. However, I had to take some risks.

'I had already learned that he took four lumps of sugar at tea. Four lumps must therefore contain half a draught. That is to say, there should be one complete draught in every eight lumps. Very cautiously I opened my suitcase and counted the lumps in my bowl. There were twenty: little paper packages, I mean; for each package contained two tiny half lumps. If I threw away four packages it would leave sixteen in the bowl, and I should therefore require two draughts. Fortunately I had them: in fact, it was having them that suggested the whole idea to me. Some time ago I had suffered from insomnia and had been ordered one of those barbituric compounds. I had some five-grain tablets over. You're beginning to see the idea?'

'I think so: dimly.'

'I'll make it clear. My next step was simple. I went to an hotel, locked my bedroom door, and set to work. First I carefully took the paper wrapping off my sixteen lumps. Then with a little twist drill which I had brought I drilled holes in the resulting thirty-two half lumps. I divided each of two of my sleeping tablets into sixteen portions, and I put one portion in each half lump. I crumbled my extra lumps up, and with the loose sugar I coated over the holes, moistening it just enough to make it cake and stick. When I had finished I was satisfied that nothing would be noticed. Then I replaced the paper wrappings, put the lumps back in the sugar bowl, and I was ready for the great experiment.

'Next day was Friday, and at intervals during the morning I took first single tickets to Portsmouth, Fratton, Petersfield and Haslemere, so that I could leave the train as soon as I had done my job. Then at four-fifty I repeated my manœuvres of the previous week, except that when Haviland took his place in the tea car I sat down in the same division, only still at the opposite side of the corridor. I was at the single table, you understand, and he at the double.

'My success now depended on my having luck on two points. The first was that no one else should come and sit in that division, the second that Haviland's sugar bowl should not be markedly fuller than my doped one. On this second point I saw at once that I was all right, and to my great satisfaction no other passengers entered.

'The first thing I did on sitting down was to put the sugar bowl on my table back against the window and to prop the menu card up in front of it. I was carrying the doped sugar bowl in a despatch case, and this I put on the table, and behind the raised lid I managed to exchange the bowls. My doped bowl, that is, was now on the table hidden from Haviland by the card, and the "good" bowl was in my despatch case on the seat beside me. You follow me?'

'Absolutely.'

'You must understand that while Haviland could not see the bowl and would think, if he noticed and thought about it at all, that my table had been left without sugar, this would not apply to the attendant. It would spoil the whole scheme if the attendant brought another bowl of sugar, but he would not do so, because he would see my bowl over the edge of the card.'

Brand nodded without speaking.

'I then went to the attendant and said that I had a nasty headache, and would he please let me have my tea as soon as possible. He was most sympathetic and brought it at once. As soon as he had gone, I leaned across and asked Haviland if I might borrow his sugar as mine had been forgotten. He was reading and he pushed it over without a word. I found I had no difficulty in changing the bowls, so that in ten seconds, when I handed back the bowl, it was the doped one that was on Haviland's table.'

'Bless my soul, King, but that was good,' Brand commented with unwilling admiration.

'Thanks to my bits of luck, things were going all right,' King admitted, 'but I was by no means out of the wood. You can imagine I was fairly excited, but I choked this down. I didn't want Haviland to remember me more clearly than was necessary, so like himself I buried myself in my newspaper, and we had no conversation. In due course his tea came, and over my paper I watched him take his two cups and put in four doped lumps.

'When he had taken his second cup I poured out my own second, and again I asked him for the sugar, apologising in a word as one would. Again he pushed it over without looking at me. This time, as you can imagine, I repeated my manœuvre and once more changed the bowls, so that I handed him back his own original bowl of "good" sugar, while keeping behind my menu card my own bowl of doped. I then had occasion to take a book out of my despatch case, and this gave me the opportunity to make the further necessary change of the bowls. When the doped bowl was back in my despatch case, I can tell you I felt a lot happier.'

'I don't know how you ever thought of it,' Brand repeated.

'This was my next fence safely taken, but still I didn't feel safe. If the old boy should become suspicious and accuse me of anything, a search would give me away. I therefore took my despatch case to the lavatory. There I filled the basin and dropped in all the sugar from my bowl. While it was melting I burnt the paper wrappings, destroyed the ashes. Then I broke the bowl, and threw the pieces out of the window one at a time. When the sugary water had been run off and the basin washed round, the last trace of the affair was gone, and at least for what was past, I felt absolutely safe.'

'I should say so!' Brand agreed.

'I had got over all my fences so far, but there was one still to be taken, infinitely the worst of the lot. I went back to my seat and waited, and soon I had the satisfaction of seeing Haviland lie back in his corner and shut his eyes. In five minutes I could have sworn he was asleep.

'Just then we stopped at Haslemere, and I was able to make sure. He was sound asleep. And here I had another amazing piece of luck. The people in the next division of the car got out, leaving the end in which Haviland and I were sitting otherwise quite unoccupied. The attendants had finished clearing up and had also vanished. I decided that when we left Haslemere I must get on with the business.

'I crossed the corridor and sat down beside Haviland. As I have said, he was at the double seat side of the corridor. I slipped my hand into his pocket. He never moved.'

'Ghastly risk,' Brand commented.

'It wasn't really,' King replied. 'I could see the door through which the attendant would enter, and I could have got my hand out of Haviland's pocket before he reached me. But if I was caught I had an answer ready. I would say I had been sitting across the corridor and had thought Haviland was ill and had crossed over to see. He *would* be ill—doped—and I would have been justified.'

'You foresaw everything.'

'I tried to. But as a matter of fact I wasn't disturbed. No one came in. Then I had a terrible job. I soon spotted the keys. I saw a chain going into his right trousers pocket, and I guessed the keys were attached to it, and so they were. But from the way he was sitting, it was the very devil to get them out. However, my luck stood. He never waked and I managed it at last. They were just what I expected—a bunch of seven small sized keys, mostly Yale.

'I had prepared a dozen wax moulds in tin cases. I couldn't get the keys off the chain, so I had to sit there beside Haviland while I was taking my impressions. It's some job, as I expect you know, to take impressions of Yale keys—much more difficult than with ordinary keys. I didn't hurry therefore, but worked as carefully as I could. By the time I had finished, we were coming into Petersfield. I got the keys pushed back into Haviland's pocket and moved across the corridor just as we ran into the station.

'It seemed to me that if Haviland didn't wake at Portsmouth, I should be better out of it. I therefore got out at Petersfield. No one saw me leave the car.'

'My word!'

'I had luck all through,' King declared. 'Half a dozen things might have happened to prevent my success, but they just didn't. I really had amazing luck. But I'd like to know what did happen to old Haviland. Did he wake up at Portsmouth, or did they send him to the police station or to hospital, or what?'

'What happened to you?' asked Brand.

'After leaving the train? I got a bus from Petersfield to Winchester, and from there made my way here in the ordinary way. The affair had a perfectly tame ending. *But*'—King absolutely beamed with delight—'in my drawer are the Chayle keys, and nobody knows it or will know it but you and me.'

'It's just about the brainiest bit of work I've ever heard of,' Brand admitted. 'And what do you propose to do next?'

'Nothing, tonight. I'll not be ready with the keys. It's a perfectly hellish job filing them up. An error of a hair's breadth will put you wrong and make the whole job useless.'

'Tomorrow night, then?'

'Yes, tomorrow night. We'll repeat last Wednesday's performance, except that this time we'll get into the sheds. And then, Brand, then, old man, we shall know what we shall know!' King chuckled in triumph, and though Brand hated the means, he chuckled too when he thought of the almost certain end.

As the two young men rounded a bend on the road they met Tasker. He stopped and they began to chat.

'You were away the last couple of days?' he presently said to King.

'I spent the night in Town,' King returned, 'and I dare say you can imagine how. I was trying to get information about this wretched problem.'

'So I supposed,' Tasker agreed. 'I'll be glad when this period's over, King.' He smiled crookedly. 'Of course, I know that a definite arrangement was made that you would do as you liked this month and I'm not grumbling, but I do think the head of a business should know what the other members are doing.' He became more serious. 'I wish you could give me some information. I'm getting upset about what we're going to do. Here's Saturday, and on next Wednesday the board meets, and if you haven't got your process by then, we'll be in the soup. Can you not tell me how you're getting on?'

King nodded. 'Your criticism's justified, I admit. Obviously you're entitled to know everything that's going on, and that before anyone else. But I ask you to believe me, Tasker, that the reason why I haven't told you whether or not I'm going to succeed, is that I don't know. It's like this, you understand. There are several lines of enquiry into this thing, any one of which might get us what we want. Well, I've worked four of these to the very bone, and they've led nowhere. Now I'm on to the fifth. It seems promising— more promising, I think, than any of the others—but I can't say whether it'll turn out trumps, because I don't know. But I'll say this: there's a reasonable hope of success. Certainly I'll know by Wednesday whether there's any use in going on, or whether I'm beaten.'

'Well, an agreement is an agreement and I don't want to force your confidence. But your success or failure is going to make a hell of a difference to all of us.'

'Don't I know it! And you know that if I can do it, it'll be done.'

Tasker supposed that that was so, and with a nod passed on.

6

Disaster

All the next day, Sunday, the two young men anxiously watched the weather. Fog had come down, a regular pea-soup fog. Fog in moderation would be their greatest ally, enabling them to go on their dubious occasions with despatch and secrecy. But fog in excess, as it was now, was an enemy which might easily upset their whole plan of campaign. Brand was one of the best amateur navigators on Southampton Water, but even he shook his head over the possibilities of reaching Chayle, as he gazed into the blank wall of mist which surrounded them.

'We can do it by dead reckoning,' King urged. 'We'll have to in fact. I must give myself some time to experiment with what I find. I daren't wait for another night.'

'That's all very well,' Brand returned. 'But it won't help us if we find ourselves ashore in the Medina or athwart the bows of some liner.'

'We must just take the risk. If we've luck, the fog will be all to the good. We don't want to be seen by coastguards or lightkeepers. And if it's as thick as this your liners'll be at anchor.'

Fortunately in the afternoon it cleared slightly. It was still very thick, but it was not utterly hopeless. They could see twenty yards instead of five.

They took the same precautions as on the previous occasion. The whole technical staff had worked on that Sunday, but when four o'clock came King said he was fed up, that that was enough for the day, and that they'd go home. He was the last to leave the room, and when he did so the rope was hanging out of his office window. Having made sure that the watchman had seen them leave the building, he and Brand returned by this emergency means. In this the fog was their ally, preventing any chance of their being seen by passers-by. Getting down to it at once, they managed by dinner time to produce what looked like a fair night's work. This would be required for the building up of their alibi, and if they were asked where they had been between four o'clock and eight, they would say, gone for a long tramp to clear the cobwebs of the laboratory out of their brains. If they couldn't prove this, the fog would prevent anyone else from disproving it.

After dinner they once more told the boarding-house people their story of late work. As before they picked up the ladder and kit, carried them along the beach to the boathouse, and put them on Brand's launch. Going round to the entrance to the works, they made the same point of greeting the night watchman, turned on the light in the laboratory, locked the door of the private office and reached the ground by the rope. With the same caution they got out the launch, rowing away from the wharf with muffled oars.

So far everything had been easy; the fog had not seriously inconvenienced them. But now as they rowed out into the Hamble Estuary it began to grow more important. It was not dark, for above the fog the moon was still nearly full. But all contact with their fellows was cut off. They were floating on an illimitable extent of black water, surrounded with a faintly luminous haze, and apparently alone in the universe. Tonight King was rowing and Brand, bent over watch and compass and chart, was steering.

'We'd want a patent log for this job,' Brand grumbled. 'Hang it all, dead reckoning by time alone is not much good, particularly when you're dealing with tides.'

'We'll do our best,' King answered shortly.

When they had reached what Brand judged was the same point as on the previous occasion, King started the motor and lit the lights. Brand headed as straight as he knew for the Calshot lightship. If they went anywhere within a couple of hundred yards of it they should see the light, and if they saw the light the greater part of their difficulties would be over. All around them were horns and bells and fog sounds of various kinds. But in most cases it was impossible to tell the direction from which these sounds were coming, particularly as their own motor was making a quite respectable noise. King added to the raucous sounds by a free rendering of themes from the 'Unfinished Symphony'; at least Brand believed that to be their source.

'Keep a good look out, King,' Brand said after a few more minutes; 'we should be on to the Calshot Light any moment.'

He had scarcely spoken when King cried out. Right ahead a little ball of light was slowly growing.

Brand turned sharply to port and the luminosity swung

round to their starboard bow, drew abeam, remained abeam for some seconds as they traversed the arc of a circle into a sou'-sou'-west direction. Then it slowly faded out on their quarter.

'Jolly good,' King said warmly.

'Lucky so far,' Brand agreed. 'Now for the Egypt Point light. We'd have no trouble if it wasn't for these confounded tides.'

The tides in this waterway are indeed confusing, not only for the amateur, but for the professional also. Two separate waves or pulses of tide come into Southampton Water and the area connecting it to Cowes Roads: one via the Solent and a later one through Spithead. The result is that there are really the equivalent of four tides in the twenty-four hours instead of two. A good deal of experience had given Brand a fair idea of how the currents ran, but even so, a mistake would be the easiest thing in the world. Fortunately their problem was not complicated by wind, or they might indeed have given it up as hopeless. Fortunately also the distance was not great, only some three miles. With luck they would do it in quarter of an hour.

Both agreed that they must keep the launch to its normal full speed, as the danger of losing their way was so much greater than that of collision. As a matter of fact they saw no ships, though once the deep-throated roar of a big foghorn sounded unpleasantly close.

At the end of fifteen minutes King reduced the speed to dead slow. If they missed the Egypt Point Light nothing would be easier than to run ashore, and though such a contingency on soft slob mightn't harm the launch, if they struck a stone it might hole her.

For three or four minutes they nosed slowly along, and then for a moment the fog thinned and they caught on their starboard bow a light. It waxed and waned.

'Got him!' Brand breathed triumphantly. 'Bit of luck the fog lifted! We were heading straight for the shore.'

'We're pretty well all right now,' King returned. 'We've done the worst at all events.'

They swung round west till the light came on their port bow. For a mile or more they ran west, then turned south-west for another two or three.

'We should be nearly there,' said Brand. 'Shut off that motor and get out the sculls.'

As he spoke Brand steered due south. The fog had come down thicker again and they could see a very short distance over the water. But it felt damper to the skin.

'It's going to turn to rain,' Brand remarked. 'Lucky for us if it does. Steady!' he went on in a more urgent voice. 'I hear the wash of ripples on the shore.'

King held water and a moment later they grounded gently. King silently unshipped his oars and lowered the anchor overboard. Then loading themselves as before, the men got out over the bow. This time they stepped into less than six inches of water. There was no fear of the launch going aground, as the tide was still flowing.

They were sure from the distance they had come that they must be on the west side of the works. Accordingly they turned east. The fog once again had thinned and they could see they were opposite low irregular clay cliffs. Soon these tailed out and they knew they had reached the low ground on which the works stood. A few more moments and the wall loomed faintly up, and with a sigh of relief they realised that their first difficulty had been overcome.

Without a word they repeated their previous actions. King extended the ladder and set it against the same point on the wall, and then climbing up, laid the mat across the glass and went down inside by the rope ladder. Brand followed and after halting a moment to listen, they crossed to the new shed and passed round it to its door.

Now came the critical point of their adventure.

Had King got hold of the right keys, and if so, had he been able to make sufficiently correct duplicates? Both men held their breath as King produced his bunch. And then a great feeling of relief swept over them, as one of the keys went into the lock, turned, and the door opened!

'Look out, Brand,' King whispered, 'some of those machine fellows may be in here. You'd better stay near the door, and if I'm nabbed, get home as quick as you can.'

The shed was dimly illuminated and a glance showed that it contained, not one, but two, rotary kilns. They were revolving noisily, but as they automatically fed themselves with slurry and fuel and discharged the clinker, it did not follow that anyone was looking after them. However, Brand slipped behind a tank which stood near the door, while King crossed over to the kilns and disappeared between them.

He was away only a few moments. 'There's no one in the shed,' he said as he came up. 'Let's get out while we can.'

Cautiously they reopened the door, and after glancing round, they slipped out, closed the door behind them and made their way to the second of the new sheds. Here, again, their luck held. Another of King's keys opened the door and once again they found the shed untenanted. It also contained two kilns in motion.

'This fairly beats me,' King declared when he had finished his tour of inspection. 'The process must be connected with these four secret kilns, but I'm hanged if I can see how. They appear to be perfectly ordinary kilns, except that they're only about a third the normal length. And then to make the thing worse, they've got a full length one outside.' He hesitated for a moment. 'Come,' he went on, 'let's get out of this. Some of these chaps may come in to do a bit of greasing at any time.'

Still unobserved they left the shed and retreated round its corner into hiding. King swore in exasperation. 'It beats me,' he repeated. 'I was sure that if we could get into those sheds we would find all we wanted, and I'm blessed if I'm a bit wiser now we've done it.'

Brand was nearly as much upset. 'That's a blow, King, I will admit,' he said. 'After all our labour and what we've risked!'

'I'm not going to leave till I've found the darned thing out,' King went on. 'Hang it all, if they can invent the process, I can surely follow it when I see it working before my eyes!' He paused, then went on uneasily: 'I wonder could I have another peep into the offices? It's a pity when we're here not to get all the information possible. One more effort might give us what we want.'

Brand was not enthusiastic, but King quickly talked him over. 'I expect one of these keys will open the private door, so that we needn't go near the watchman's hut. Come on, Brand. It's worth an effort.'

Brand reluctantly agreed, and they moved off along the shed wall. The fog by this time had slightly cleared. It was still thick, but they could now see for fifty or sixty feet. As the vapour thinned, the moonlight had grown stronger, and nearby details were clearly visible.

Since they started their investigation they had had a streak of wonderful luck, but now they reached its end. Suddenly a dreadful thing happened, so quickly that Brand scarcely realised what was taking place until it was over. As they slipped round the corner of the shed, they all but ran into a man.

'Oh,' he cried in a high-pitched voice, 'there you are! I've just seen your ladder. The boss will have something to say to you! Put them up, will you!'

Brand was slightly in advance as they turned the corner and now to his horror he saw that he was looking into the barrel of an automatic pistol. It was the first time he had ever had that view of a pistol, and even in his excitement he found himself thinking how much more sinister that little circle of steel looked than any other single object he had ever seen. Instinctively he raised his hands above his head, feeling as if the end of the world had come.

But neither Brand nor his adversary had reckoned on the alert mind of King. As the unknown raised his hand King dropped to a crouching position, and before either of the others realised, he had sprung swiftly forward and upward, while his right fist, shooting out, caught the man with the pistol a sharp crack on the point of the chin.

Brand had never seen anyone so completely knocked out. The man collapsed without a struggle. He fell backwards with a horrid thud on to the ground and lay still.

'Lucky we had our masks on,' said King, as he dropped on his knees beside him. 'He'll be none the worse, but he'll scarcely come round till we've gone.'

'I wonder if he's alone?' Brand observed, also kneeling down.

'Sure to be,' King returned. 'It's the night watchman,

Clay: the man I talked to in the pub. He's been on his rounds—'

King's voice trailed away into silence. But Brand did not notice. He was not listening. A dreadful misgiving had shot into his mind, and it seemed from King's sudden stiffening that he was experiencing it too. This man, Clay, was looking very odd. Very still, very ghastly . . . Brand shone his torch on the ground.

'King,' he said in a queer, hoarse tone, and pointing with a shaking finger, 'that stone! He hit his head on it!'

King for a moment did not answer, then his voice came also strange and toneless. 'My God, Brand! Get water. There's some in that barrel.' He pointed vaguely in the direction in which they had come.

With his heart thumping painfully Brand hurried away. He found the barrel, filled his cap, and ran back. King moistened his handkerchief and bathed the man's face.

'More water,' King muttered.

Brand, trembling now in every limb, hurried back to the barrel and refilled his cap. When he got back he found that King had opened the man's clothes and was feeling his heart.

'Well?' breathed Brand.

King, his face grown nearly as white as that of the watchman, shook his head. 'Give me that water.' He took the cap. 'Can you feel anything?'

Brand knelt and put his hand over the watchman's heart. There was no movement there. Not the faintest trace of a pulse remained. Brand looked up in speechless horror. For some moments there was silence, and then King spoke. 'We must face it, Brand,' he said in that same queer, toneless voice: 'he's dead!'

Brand felt almost sick.

'Oh, King, he's not?' he whispered, but as he said it, he knew. There was no doubt. Clay was dead.

Slowly the two men rose from their knees and stood looking down at the inanimate body.

'The poor fellow!' Brand said desperately. 'Can we do nothing?'

King seemed stunned. For once his energy and efficiency had deserted him. He shook his head helplessly.

'The poor chap!' Brand repeated. 'And he was only doing his duty. But you couldn't help it, King. It was the merest accident.'

King slowly pulled himself together.

'A lot of good that'll do us,' he returned, and in his voice there was that same dreadful horror. 'Who's going to believe that?'

Brand started. This was a new point. He had been so taken up with the actual tragedy that the possible consequences to himself and King had not occurred to him.

'What do you mean?' he gasped.

'What do I mean?' King retorted, now once more himself. 'What do you think I mean? If we're caught here there's a charge of murder against us. That's what I mean.'

Brand was appalled. For the moment he had not seen that this consequence was inevitable, but now it burned itself into his consciousness.

'But it was an accident,' he stammered, loath to face the hideous truth.

'Don't I know it was an accident? What's the good of harping on that? Do you think any jury on this earth would believe it?'

Instinctively they stepped back a few paces from the recumbent figure and King went on. 'No; we may make up our minds to it: if we're caught, we're as good as hanged! Nothing in this world could save us.'

Brand shivered. 'But they wouldn't believe it was deliberate, King. Our characters.'

King swore bitterly. 'Our characters, yes, that would help us a lot! We're here to steal another man's property: we're caught in the act by his servant: we resort to physical force to escape: we kill the servant. Characters, indeed! I tell you, Brand, it doesn't matter what we meant to do. Don't be more of a damned fool than you can help. I tell you if we're caught we haven't a dog's chance.'

Brand took a deep breath. 'Then let's get away quick before we are caught,' he urged.

King shook his head. 'For heaven's sake, Brand, pull yourself together,' he growled savagely. 'We've got to do a whole lot more than that. Don't you see that if we go straight away, we're certain to be traced? Do use your brains! We've got to fix up something better than that. Let's carry the poor chap to the ladder where no one's likely to come, and then we'll think out our plans.'

With shrinking they moved the remains, then drawing back a short distance, sat down on some old boxes. Action had calmed Brand, but now an overwhelming feeling of horror surged up in his mind. He knew that he must fight it down. He must keep cool and so help King. How thankful he was to have King! King was a tower of strength in an emergency. King would find a way out.

'Now let's see,' began King, still in that hoarse, toneless voice, 'just how we stand. First, we'll take what's against us, then what's for us, and then what we should do. It's now'—he glanced at his wristwatch—'just getting on to twelve and if we're home by four in the morning it will do. Say we take an hour to go home. That means we've three hours here to consider things and make a plan and carry it out. So don't let's spoil everything by being in too great a hurry. Remember, it's our lives that are at stake.'

Brand, feeling that the last thing he could settle to was calm consideration, crushed down his feelings and told King to go ahead.

'The first thing they'll think of,' King resumed, 'will be our motive. They've got this secret process and they've evidently expected that people might be after it, as they've armed their watchman. Therefore they'll begin by wondering whether whoever killed the watchman was after the process. You see that?'

'Only too well.'

'Next, they'll ask themselves, Who wants the process? Some other manufacturer of rapid-hardening cement, naturally. What other such is there? Joymount is the only other in the neighbourhood. What about Joymount? You see? I've thought about all this because I foresaw—not what has happened—but that we might somehow give ourselves away and have to consider where we stood.'

Brand moved uneasily. 'I agree so far. But they couldn't prove anything. Besides, there's our alibi.'

King shook his head. 'I wonder if you have any idea what a police enquiry is like? The least slip and we're done for. The ground here is not too hard and it's a bit damp. If in any one place we've left a footprint, it would finish us. If it was someone from Joymount it could only be someone scientific and fairly high up in the concern. They'd probably fix on you and me right away. They would get us to walk across some soft ground by some trick—and there we'd be. You see: it's practically impossible to do anything without leaving a trace. I mention a footprint only as an example. There are dozens of other ways in which we might give ourselves away.'

This was about as much as Brand could stand. 'For goodness' sake, King, that's enough. Let's have what's for us for a change.'

'There's much more for us than there is against us,' King went on. 'I've only mentioned this so that you may agree that all possible precautions are necessary. For us we have the facts that no one else has seen us here: that no one saw us coming: that no one knew we were coming: that so far as we know we have left no traces anywhere. Then besides our own statement, we should have the evidence of our own watchman that we were in the Joymount lab all night, and the evidence of Radcliff and Endicott that we must have been, owing to the work done. We have a good alibi, and it's particularly good because it's normal and ordinary and without coincidence. All that's in our favour.'

'It seems to me complete.'

'It's not complete by any means. A clever detective could break it down. However, in its way, it's good. That's what's for us.'

This calm dispassionate discussing of the issues was having its effect on Brand. His first rush of horror and panic was subsiding, and this catalogue of what was 'for them' he found definitely reassuring.

'You said you would discuss what was against us, then what was for us, and then what we must do. Have you thought of the last point?'

King made a grimace. 'I haven't, and that's a fact.

I foresaw a good many things that might have happened, but never anything like this. No, you'll have to keep quiet and let me think. Thank goodness it's a warm night.'

For over an hour they sat there in the semi-darkness, till Brand began to feel that unless something happened soon he would get up and scream. Then suddenly, just as he was about to make a move, King stood up.

'Have you thought of a plan?' he asked sharply.

Brand admitted that his only plan would be to get away from the works and back to Joymount as soon as possible.

'That's no good,' King returned shortly. 'That means that we're caught within two days! Now I've got a plan. Not a good one, I admit, but better than yours. As you can't propose an alternative, you'll have to adopt it. That agreed?'

'Of course, King. What is it?'

'Nothing very pleasant or very easy, I'm afraid. Still, it's our only hope. In a word, we'll have to fix things so that it will look as if Clay had disappeared voluntarily. No suggestion that he died here must ever arise. You see?'

'That would be splendid, but how can we do it?'

'I think we can do it. Now first you wait here while I slip into that office for a moment. And while you're waiting you may think out these two problems. First, how can we most easily get the body to the launch? And second, where can we hide it until tomorrow night? It'll be my job—with your help—to dispose of it finally: it will be yours to keep it till then. And you needn't get excited if I don't turn up for an hour or more. I'll be back in plenty of time for all we have to do.'

It was not what Brand wanted, to remain there with

that terrible piece of evidence, but King was making himself responsible for their joint safety, and he must do what King asked.

King vanished silently into the fog and Brand was left alone with the body and his thoughts.

7

A Watertight Scheme

That long hour during which King was working out his scheme had been very trying to Brand. And yet now that King had gone, he realised how much the man's presence had meant to him. It had been a sort of sheet anchor to keep him from drifting into panic. Now that its restraint was removed, it was all he could do to prevent his nerves from slipping from control. To keep himself in hand he set to work with resolution on the problems King had left him.

Of the two questions he had to consider, the first seemed to present no difficulty at all. Clay, though a tallish man, was slight. It should be easy to carry the remains to the launch. True there was the getting of them over the wall, but with King and himself, one at each side of the wall, it should be simple enough.

The second question was more difficult. Assuming they had reached Joymount, what was to be done with the body? It could not be left in the launch: others beside themselves had keys to the boathouse. And the launch could not be left in any place other than the boathouse: no question that it had been out must ever arise. The body would have to be removed from the boathouse, that was clear.

Brand wished King had been a little more explicit as to his plans. If he had explained how he proposed to get rid of the body, it might have suggested a hiding-place. Was it for instance to be taken by water or overland? By the launch or by car?

By car? Did not that suggest something?

He, Brand, had a car, a small Triumph saloon, which he kept in a separate garage, the former harness-room of the boarding-house. He wondered if the garage might be the solution of his problem? No one but himself had a key for it, and once the body was there, he thought it would be safe.

And there would be no difficulty in getting it there. The ladder and mat had to be carried to King's workshop in the same yard; the body could be carried also.

Brand was pleased with his solutions. If King's whole scheme was as good as his part of it, they should be all right.

How he wished King would hurry! He had been gone now for half an hour and it was terribly trying sitting there alone in the fog. Brand wondered what he was doing. Surely not still trying to discover the secret? So far as he, Brand, was concerned, the secret could remain a secret for ever. He hated the very thought of it. Not the secret, but how to get out of their terrible predicament; that was what they must concentrate on.

Then it occurred to him that they didn't now want the secret. They couldn't use it if they had it. If they were to show that they knew it, suspicion would at once be aroused. No doubt its theft would be assumed, and all firms which might profit by it would be watched. No, the secret instead of being an asset to them, would now be a deadly danger.

What, then, could King be doing? Terribly Brand felt tempted to go in search of him. But he did not know where King was, and he feared he might miss him.

Suddenly a horrible idea occurred to Brand, only to be banished immediately from his mind. Was King entirely trustworthy? Had he gone off himself, leaving Brand to be caught and to bear the consequences of their joint action? King was a very able fellow and in many ways a good fellow, but Brand had to admit to himself that he had never felt absolute confidence in him. He sometimes wondered what would happen if King's self-interest were to clash with his duty . . .

Then he felt ashamed of himself. He had worked with King for seven years, and King had never once let him down. No, King was doing something for their common good. Of that he was satisfied.

As if to reward him for his loyalty, the figure of King at that moment materialised through the fog.

'How have you got on?' Brand asked eagerly.

'Better than I had hoped. Tell you later. We've got to get this poor fellow away now and see that we've left no traces.'

'Right. I've thought it out. There'll be no difficulty.'

'Good. Then let's get at it.'

They did not, however, cross the wall as Brand had imagined they would. King utterly refused to allow the weight of one of themselves and the body on the ladder at the same time.

'You ass,' he said petulantly, 'the thing'll break. I designed it to carry one person only. You don't want to be found here in the morning with the body and a broken leg?'

In the end they tied the body to the rope ladder, and when both of them were on the top of the wall, pulled it up, lowering it outside in the same way.

King was extraordinarily thorough. He would not leave until they had examined with their torches the scene of the tragedy and every other place they had been, lest some trace of their presence should remain. But nowhere could they find any.

The walk along the shore took it out of them, for while one carried the body, the other had to bear the whole of the remaining impedimenta. Fortunately the fog, while still persisting, was much thinner and they were able to find the launch without difficulty. King waded out and brought it in, the body was lifted aboard, and with muffled sculls they rowed due north. Then the engine was started and Brand once again took charge of the navigation.

The clearing of the fog enabled them to see the navigation lights from a reasonable distance. They had no trouble therefore in reaching the Hamble, and by nosing gently along the coast they were able to make out the wharf and so find their way unnoticed into the boathouse.

They left the body in the launch while completing their alibi at the works. As before they climbed up to King's office, pulled up the rope, came out through the laboratory, said good morning to the watchman, incidentally calling his attention to the time, and then returned to the boathouse. From there with much labour they carried the body and their apparatus to the boarding-house yard, placing the former in the garage and the latter in King's workshop.

While King agreed that the garage was an excellent hiding place, he had further ideas which puzzled and annoyed Brand. First he insisted on the outer clothes being stripped off the body, a revolting job which nearly made Brand sick. Then he would not allow the body to be laid on the back seat of the car, as Brand had intended. Instead he placed it on the driving seat with its feet on the pedals and its hands on the steering wheel. It had to be propped up in this position, a job which Brand loathed almost as much as the other. But King was not satisfied till an elaborate system of supports had been devised to give it as nearly as possible the position of a man driving the car.

He would not explain what was in his mind, however, merely saying that they had to remember that the remains would stiffen, and that they must therefore be left to stiffen in the proper position for the scheme. 'Now,' said King, when at last the horrible business was done, 'I'll be away all day. Some things have to be seen to. You keep those two fellows working on at the same experiments. And if you're talking to Tasker you may give him a hint that things are going all right: no more than that. Then tonight I'll want you to lend a hand with getting rid of the body.'

'How are you going to do it?' Brand asked uneasily.

'We haven't time to discuss that now,' King returned. 'We must get to bed in case someone in the house notices the time we come in and it is checked up with the watchman's statement. Now, Brand, listen carefully to what you have to do. Carry on today as if nothing had happened. Then tonight go to bed at the usual time. Ruffle up your bed as if you had slept in it and at once slip into my room. Of course put out your light first and lock the door, taking the key. I'll either be in my room or I'll come in shortly.

You better hide under the bed in case someone else should go in. You'll want your rubber gloves and your torch. I should bring two torches if I were you. That all clear?'

'All clear.'

'We'll leave about two. The job should take a couple of hours. Then all our troubles will be over. You're sure that garage of yours is properly locked?'

'Positive.'

'Then see you don't let the key out of your possession. Oh, and by the way, you should know I'm going to Town early this morning.'

With this Brand had to be content. Letting themselves softly into the boarding-house, they crept on tiptoe to their respective bedrooms.

In spite of his excitement, Brand's head no sooner touched the pillow than he fell into a dreamless sleep. Nothing is physically more wearisome than mental anxiety, and in addition to that Brand had recently had a lot of night work in the laboratory. He woke refreshed and in a more normal frame of mind, though the horror of his and King's position still weighed heavily upon him.

He took an early opportunity of seeing Radcliff and Endicott.

'King won't be in this morning,' he told them. 'He's gone to Town. He and I came back last night and you see we got the acid reaction finished. He wants you to go on with the second stage of that aluminium salt.'

'He's a most desperate swotter, and so are you,' Endicott returned. 'How many nights have you been working at that blessed salt?'

'The whole thing's nearly done,' Brand answered. 'He says he expects to get all he wants in a day or two.'

'But what does he want?' Radcliff asked. 'I never could
see that he was getting anywhere with all these experiments.
Is it a very profound secret?'

'No secret at all in a sense,' declared Brand. 'I don't
understand it myself, but it's some idea that he's got. He
thinks he can find a way of cheapening the cement-making
process. He put it up to the directors and convinced
them to the extent of allowing him to carry on these
experiments.'

'That's the yarn he told us when we came. I don't think
much of it myself.'

'What do you mean? You don't suppose, Radcliff, he'd
let you know enough to put two and two together, do
you?'

'Well,' Endicott shrugged, 'it's no business of ours. So
long as we're paid for what we do, that's all we want. I
suppose if he's nearly finished, that means the end for us?'

'It was to be a temporary job, wasn't it?'

'Oh yes, we're not grumbling. It's been interesting enough
and the money's been all right.'

All through the day time dragged terribly for Brand, and
as it slowly passed, his nerves grew more and more on
edge. He did his utmost to control himself and to act as
if nothing abnormal had occurred, but he found it a
dreadful strain. However his work kept his mind to some
extent occupied and at last he turned homewards from the
works.

At dinner he had a shock.

'Did you hear of the theft at Chayle?' his neighbour
asked, a bank official on sick leave.

'Theft?' Brand returned. 'No. What was that?'

'It's in the evening paper. It seems they've had a theft in

the cement works. About four hundred pounds was stolen from their safe last night.'

A hand seemed to grip Brand's heart. 'Good Lord!' he said, he hoped not tremulously. 'From their safe? You mean burglars with safe breaking appliances?'

'No,' the bank official returned, 'nothing so exciting as that. The safe was unlocked, not broken open. It seems the night watchman has disappeared too. He must have somehow got hold of a key and taken the money.'

In spite of the need for caution, Brand could not repress a shiver. So this was what King was doing when he left to inspect the offices! No doubt the key of the safe was one of those of which he had obtained mouldings. Evidently that had been his scheme, to remove something valuable, so as to account for the absence of Clay and make it appear it was voluntary. A clever idea, yes: but, *stealing money*! Oh, how Brand hated the whole thing! It was utterly and absolutely loathsome!

And King should have told him. He should not have allowed such a piece of news to be sprung on him. King was much too—

Brand hastily pulled himself up. He must not fall into a reverie in this way. Already he thought his companion was looking at him strangely.

'I say,' he went on, 'that's a mysterious business! How on earth could a night watchman get hold of the key of a safe?'

'So you might say. However, they'll find him quickly. It seems he's lame. A lame man could never get away with a job like that.'

'A fool to try,' Brand considered.

'No doubt. Still, you never know what these fellows will

do for a bit of money. And four hundred would be a pretty big sum to a man like that.'

'That's true.'

Brand thought he did not acquit himself too badly in the ensuing conversation. Talk about the theft became general, belief that the culprit would have a short run for his money being universal. Then to Brand's overwhelming relief, someone said something about cricket, and the subject dropped.

Later in the evening King came in. In a loudish voice he declined the landlady's suggestion to serve up dinner, saying he had dined in the train coming down. At this someone said: 'Been in Town today, King?' which was evidently what he wanted. He answered that he had been up on some chemical business for the firm, and dilated on the heat in the city.

'Did you see your neighbours at Chayle have been having excitements?' said someone else.

'I saw that,' King returned in interested tones. 'Nothing very big though: four hundred, it said.'

Brand marvelled at the natural way in which he spoke. He had had no idea that King was so good an actor. Without the slightest trace of self-consciousness and with just the correct amount of detached interest, King added his remarks to the conversation until presently the subject was changed.

Time crawled slowly on, and at last bedtime came. In his usual way Brand said good night and went up to his room. There he did as King had told him. He ruffled up the bed, turned out the light, locked the door and silently made his way into King's room. King was not there, but he entered shortly. He saw Brand, nodded, and when Brand would have spoken, put his finger to his lips.

'Wait till we go out,' he whispered softly.

Brand watched his preparations with interest. King took from his clothes cupboard the rope ladder which they had used at Chayle. It was now fastened to a crossbar of wood. King opened the window, fixed the bar across it, and let down the ladder. This window overlooked the cobbled yard in which was the garage, which, no doubt, explained King's choice of his own room rather than Brand's. Brand's room was round the corner of the house, looking out in front towards the Hamble, and beneath it was a flower bed of soft earth which would have taken excellent footprints. Having set out the gloves, torches and one or two other appliances, King lay down on his bed. Brand took the only armchair the room contained.

King left the light on for a time which he fixed by his watch, probably, Brand imagined, for the time that he usually read. Then he turned it off, the bed creaked as if he was settling down to sleep, and silence followed. It was not till a torch shone out that he saw King seating himself on a chair in the window.

Once again time dragged in the most dreadful way. Again and again Brand thought his watch had stopped. But always he found the hands had moved infinitesimally since the last time he had looked at them. He was still horribly upset at the idea of the theft. This was quite deliberate evil-doing which nothing could excuse. It was quite different from the theft of the process, if they had been able to accomplish that. That somehow was, or could be conceived of as being, all in the way of business. But to steal four hundred pounds of actual money was an entirely different proposition. The very idea was hateful.

And there was also its hideous consequence. This poor

Clay had been an honest man. Now by their action he was branded a thief. It was utterly abominable. Of course in a way no one would be hurt. As King had said, the man himself was dead and he had no relatives. Still Brand felt that to have blackened the character of a dead man was a thing which would always weigh on his mind.

And yet from his own point of view, nothing better could have been done. This plan of King's would certainly do what it was intended to—it had done it already. The man was gone—and no suspicion of murder had been raised. Granted that the rest of the horrible affair could be carried out as efficiently, no suspicion of murder should ever be raised. And if so, no suspicion would ever fall on them . . .

After incredible ages King made a move. Quarter to two showed on Brand's watch when a torch shone out. Then taking the gloves and torches, first Brand and then King swung themselves out of the window and carefully climbed down to the yard.

Once again the weather suited them. Tonight also the sky was heavily overcast, and while in the diffused moonlight they could see their way about, their figures were not too obvious should anyone chance to look out. They landed on the cobbles and silently crossed the yard.

'We've got to get out that car without it being known,' said King. 'If we push it a hundred yards along the road, no one'll hear it starting up.'

Noiselessly they let themselves into the garage. As King had foretold, *rigor mortis* had set in, and they had some difficulty in moving the stiffened body from before the wheel to the adjoining front seat. A more difficult and much more horrible job was re-clothing it in its own garments, which King had brought, tied up into a bundle.

However, the revolting work was done at last and they pushed the car down the road, out of earshot of the house. King produced a large scale map of the district.

'Do you see this road leading from Southampton through Swaythling to Fair Oak? Now just there,' he pointed, 'a little farm road comes in. I want you to drive there now. You can go through Bursledon and by Thornhill Park in the direction of Swaythling, turning left before you come to the Itchen. I'll go with you as far as Bursledon, where I'll pick up a car I hid there during the afternoon and follow you to the farm road.'

'Then you weren't in Town?' Brand asked in surprise.

'Of course not: I was fixing up for tonight. But never mind that now. If you're sure of the way, go ahead.'

'I know the road,' Brand returned. 'I've driven over it several times.'

'Right.'

King got into the back and Brand, with his awful passenger beside him, started the engine. In a moment he was able to slip in the clutch and they moved off. He drove in silence for a time, then he could bear his thoughts no longer.

'I say, King,' he said over his shoulder, 'what about that four hundred pounds?'

King leaned foward. 'I know, Brand. I see it's distressing you. Well, I may tell you I absolutely hated it, but what could I do? It was the only way out. It didn't hurt Clay himself, and he has no living relatives. All the same I loathed it. But you see it has worked.'

'It was a hideous thing to have to do.'

'I know. But it was that or us. Nothing but a theft of money would have accounted for the man going. But don't let's talk of it now. Time enough when we're out of the wood.'

Brand felt slightly comforted by King's expressions of regret, though he realised that his feeling was irrational, as these did not in any way alter the facts. He wished King would be less secretive as to his plans. Brand shrewdly suspected that his silence was due to distrust of himself: that King wished him to be so completely committed to the undertaking before he knew its details, that he would be unable to withdraw if later he wished to do so.

Presently they passed Bursledon, and on a deserted stretch of road King got out.

'I'll follow you at once,' he said. 'I hid the car in an old sandpit. When you get to the farm road just pull up and wait for me.' With a nod he vanished and Brand once again let in his clutch.

That drive was the most terrible Brand had ever taken. Though he could scarcely see it, he was all the time profoundly conscious of the silent form at his elbow. Owing to the stiffening, the figure sat up on the seat as if it were alive, but occasionally when the car lurched it swung over against Brand. When he had pushed it back three or four times he was in such a condition of nerves that he could have screamed. His mind also was full of dread lest for some reason he should be stopped. If for instance some smash-and-grab raid had taken place in Southampton or elsewhere, the police would stop and examine all cars. How he wished he had insisted on the figure being placed on the back seat and covered with a rug, as he had suggested. But King had not agreed to this, saying that if by some unlikely chance he should be stopped, such a rug-covered object would inevitably be examined, while the body on the front seat might in the dark be taken for a living passenger. Brand had given way, but now he bitterly regretted it.

However the drive was accomplished without incident. In due course he reached the rendezvous. Brand pulled in to the side, switched off his headlights, and settled down to wait. It occurred to him that he must account for his stop, and he had just decided to get out and open the bonnet, when King arrived.

He was driving an old and battered Austin Seven, which he manœuvred close to the edge of the road, just ahead of Brand. Immediately he jumped out.

'Turn the car, Brand, and park behind me,' he said in a low voice, 'and switch out your lights. This is a very deserted road and we'll take the risk of no one passing.'

Brand turned the car to head south and backed towards the Austin, King motioning him on till the two cars were almost touching.

'Now we've got to get the body into the Austin and sitting at the wheel. It'll be a bit of a squeeze, but it should be possible. Come on, Brand: we're nearly through.'

This proved another dreadful and horribly difficult job. However at last it was accomplished. Brand's forehead was running sweat when they had done.

'Now the notes and the key of the safe into the pockets and I think we're ready.'

King took a roll from his breast pocket and thrust it into that worn by the body, then he put a key into the trousers' pocket.

'That's all, I think.' He stood for a moment buried in thought. 'No, by Jove! I was just going to make a mistake.'

As he spoke he lifted a tin of petrol from the back of

the Austin and put it into the Triumph. 'That's all at last. Now for our great effort.'

Once again King stood thinking, then he seemed to come to a decision.

'You get in, Brand, to the seat alongside the driver. Leave the door open behind you. Look sharp like a good chap. That's right. Now start her up. Good. Now listen to what you have to do. Get her going at a walking pace, then get her into second—still at a walking pace. The ground's sloping a little down and she won't stall. You follow? Then get out—sharp, and shut the door. I'll accelerate with the hand throttle and steer her into that railing. She'll go through it and down into the stream below. A drop of petrol will do the rest.'

So that was King's scheme! A faked accident! Well, it was a good one, if not very original.

Fearful of the appearance of a police patrol, Brand did not stop to think. He climbed into the car and started the engine. Then leaning over on that ghastly figure, he pushed over the gear lever, slipped her into first, and let in the clutch. She moved off at a crawl, King walking beside her on the other side and steering through the window.

'Now second speed,' King called, and Brand made the change. The speed increased, but King was able to run alongside. 'Out!' King shouted, and Brand leaped out, slamming the door.

Immediately he heard the engine roar and the car bounded forward. It left them as an arrow leaves a bow, and still accelerating strongly, rushed ahead. The two men ran after it as fast as they could.

Events now happened quickly. Immediately ahead of the car was a sharp right-hand bend on an embankment approaching a bridge, the edge of the slope being protected by the railing to which King had pointed.

The car, now travelling at thirty miles an hour, did not round the bend, but carried straight on against the railing. There was a crash and the sound of ripping wood, and the car vanished downwards. Further crashes came from below, then all was still.

'That may have been heard,' King breathed. 'The petrol, quick!'

Brand raced back to the Triumph, and picking up the tin of petrol, rushed forward again to where the 'accident' had taken place. King was bending over the wreck.

'Just as well it didn't go on fire at once,' he said quickly. 'I've set the controls as they would have been if this had been a genuine smash. I was bothered about that point, but I couldn't see how to meet it.'

As he spoke he was hammering with a stone at the connections to the carburettor. 'This'll account for the fire,' he went on. 'Pour that petrol of yours over everything. Anything that could give us away must be burnt.'

By the time the body and cushions were soaked in petrol, the carburettor was broken off. Petrol was running out there also, the tank being above the dash. King, who seemed to have foreseen everything, pulled a short length of fuse from his pocket and laid it with one end in the spirit. There was the scrape of a striking match, and a moment later the two men were running silently to the Triumph. Brand started it up instantly and they began to glide slowly south.

Suddenly there came a burst of light from behind, and looking back, they could see the tops of flames rising above the bend in the road.

'That's done it!' King cried. 'Now back as fast as you like!'

They returned the way Brand had come, through Thornhill Park and Bursledon, stopped at the point at which they had started up the engine, and pushed the car back to Brand's garage. Then creeping across the yard, they climbed the rope ladder to King's room. King drew in the ladder, hiding it in his wardrobe.

Next morning, King having seen that the coast was clear, Brand left King's room for the bathroom, returning from there to his own room. When they met at breakfast both were satisfied that not the slightest suspicion of their nocturnal activities had leaked out.

One or two small matters still required attention, and before going to the works King carried them out. He cut up his wooden and rope ladders and burnt them in the fireplace in his workshop. He also burnt their rubber gloves and the pad of sacks they had used to cross the wall at Chayle, melted away the wax key impressions and broke up their mould cases, buried the remainder of the keys he had made, and in fact destroyed every trace that remained of their adventure.

'I'm thankful to hear that everything's gone,' said Brand when King explained afterwards what he had done. 'Please goodness that's the last of the whole ghastly business. If I was only sure of that I would take the closing down of the works without a grouse.'

'The works won't close down,' the amazing King replied. 'I got the process as well as the money that night.'

PART II

Detection

8

French Gets an Outside Job

Chief-Inspector Joseph French threw down wearily the file of papers with which he had been occupied, and rising from his desk, moved over to the window of his room for a moment's relaxation. This room to which he had moved on his promotion—Chief-Inspector Mitchell's old room—was one of the most pleasantly situated in the whole building of New Scotland Yard. Instead of his former view of the brick walls of a courtyard, he now looked out upon open space; the Embankment beneath, then the Thames with its constant stream of traffic, the London County Council buildings across the river, and to the right Westminster Bridge, seen partly in plan and partly in elevation. It was a larger room moreover than his old one and more comfortably furnished; in fact it was altogether more in keeping with its occupant's new status.

Over a year had passed in French's life since that tremendous event which had entitled him to write the word Chief before his former designation of Inspector. It had been an event long hoped and waited for. However, now that it had come and passed, it seemed to him less important than formerly. His life indeed had not changed so much as he had imagined it would. He was a little nearer the upper ranks of his superiors and a little further from the uniformed men, whose salutes, when given, were more punctilious and respectful. But alas he was also a little further from his former colleagues, Inspectors Tanner, Willis and the rest. He had tried in every way he could to prevent that slight feeling of restraint from creeping in between himself and these old friends, but without success. He found, as scores of thousands have before him, that a rise in position means a corresponding increase in loneliness.

His work also, though different from what he was accustomed to, was not greatly different. There was less investigation, but more consideration of the investigations of others. There was the reviewing of several cases simultaneously, rather than the concentrating on one. There was more allocating of work, with the puzzle of keeping several men busy, while still available for instant use in emergency. There was the constant solving of the problems of his subordinates and the straightening out of the tangles in which they not infrequently became involved. There was more money and a better position, with correspondingly more responsibility and less chance of leaving his troubles behind him when he went home. Though French remained entirely delighted with his promotion, he had found that the extra money and standing exacted their full cost.

One thing however he did miss, and that was his country jobs. Since his promotion, except for the blissful time of his holidays, he had not been away from the Yard for even one day. As he stood now by the window watching a tug pulling a flotilla of barges up against the ebbing tide, he wished he could once again get out on some special job. Indeed the gorgeousness of this brilliant July morning made the allure of the countryside and sea seem almost irresistible.

Was it a coincidence, he afterwards wondered, that just as this thought should be passing through his mind, the Assistant Commissioner's bell should ring? French liked and admired Sir Mortimer Ellison, particularly since he had come so closely in touch with him in that business of the murders on the launch in the Channel. Sir Mortimer indeed had been a good friend to French, and his kindly manner and the full recognition he always gave his subordinates, made it a pleasure to work under him.

French hurriedly left the window, and stepping along the passage, knocked at the Assistant Commissioner's door.

Sir Mortimer made a gesture with his rather elegant hand which French knew meant, 'Come in, close the door, sit down on that chair, and listen to me.' French did all these things.

'Joint application from the Chief Constables of Hants, the Isle of Wight and Southampton, for a man,' began Sir Mortimer. 'Some rather involved case which I'm afraid I haven't read with the care it doubtless merits, but it sounds like a burglary plus the Rouse car case over again. Four hundred pounds were stolen from a safe in a cement works on the Isle of Wight and a man was found burnt in an Austin Seven near Eastleigh. Apparently there's some connection, not obvious on the face of things. The local police however think there's more in the affair than meets the eye: they don't say what.'

'I saw about the burning of the car in the paper, sir.'

'I did too. Well, the information we've got is not very illuminating, but there's one point which makes me think it must be important, and that is that I happen to know

Colonel Tressider intimately—that's the Chief Constable of Hants. He's what's referred to in certain circles as a downy bird, French. If he thinks something wants looking into, you may take it from me that it does.'

'Yes, sir,' French returned, not knowing a better comment.

'In fact,' Sir Mortimer went on in his somewhat dreamy voice, 'I think so much of his opinion that I should like to do him proud.' He smiled sardonically. 'What about going down yourself?'

Instantly the interview took on a new significance to French. 'If you think so, sir, certainly,' he said promptly, but not too promptly. Was this already the answer to his wish?

'What do *you* think?' Sir Mortimer returned bluntly.

French hesitated with discretion. 'The only thing that I'm handling that's urgent is that Cromer affair, but I'm nearly through with that and if it would be time enough to go to Hampshire in the evening, I could finish it. All the other cases are allocated and the men concerned can push ahead by themselves.'

Sir Mortimer nodded. 'A few hours can't make much difference. Yes, go down in the evening. You're to report to Superintendent Goodwilly, of Southampton, who will give you all the particulars. If you could see him tonight it would be an advantage, as you could get to work in the morning before every clue is lost. Right then, I'll reply to Colonel Tressider and Company and you can ring up Goodwilly.'

French was filled with delight as he returned to his office. This job would just give him the change of work and that breath of the country—and possibly even the sea—for which he so greatly longed. With considerable eagerness he finished his Cromer work, put his papers about other cases in order, and handed them over to a colleague. That evening he set off with Detective-Sergeant Carter by the 6.30 from Waterloo.

It was a good train and they reached Southampton on the tick of eight o'clock. A few minutes later they were being shown into Superintendent Goodwilly's room at police headquarters.

Goodwilly was a comparatively young man only recently promoted to his present job. French took to him at once. He had a determined face with a pleasant and kindly expression and a pair of extremely intelligent eyes. His manner was direct and unassuming, but at the same time competent. French felt that he would get from him loyal support and that small minded jealousies would not hamper the conduct of the case.

'The three Chief Constables concerned had a conference and fixed up this application, Chief-Inspector,' said Goodwilly after the usual greeting and preliminaries had been gone through. 'You'll see them later. In the meantime I am to tell you all I can about the case.'

'I shall be glad to meet them,' French returned politely. 'But as to the facts of the case, I'd much rather have them from you, Super.'

Goodwilly was pleased, as French had intended him to be. He settled himself more comfortably in his chair and went on.

'The case is really not a Southampton case at all. It's divided into two parts, and part of it is being handled by the Cowes men and part by the Eastleigh staff. It just happened that both asked me to have some enquiries made, and the result of those enquiries proved that the two cases were connected. I can therefore give you a general outline of what has taken place, but you will have to go for your details to Cowes and Eastleigh.'

'We gathered from the Chief Constables' letter that the two different events were connected, but we could not understand how.'

'I'll tell you that now. Will you smoke, Chief-Inspector?' Goodwilly held out a pouch and a box of cigarettes. French filled his pipe and Carter took a cigarette.

Goodwilly had produced a file of papers, but he evidently knew the facts by heart, for during the whole course of his story he only looked at them once. He spoke easily, putting the events into more of a narrative form than officialdom usually achieves.

'The first thing was a telephone message from the Super at Cowes, asking me to have enquiries made for a tall thin man with a pale clean-shaven face and a limp, dressed in certain clothes and so on. Here,' Goodwilly handed over a paper, 'is the description. It is, as you can see, pretty complete, except that no photograph was available.'

French glanced over the paper and nodded. 'Quite good that,' he admitted.

'The message came in at eleven-five on last Monday morning and gave a skeleton of the events which had occurred. It was supplemented later by further details. Briefly the facts were as follows—'

The Super interrupted himself to get a map of the district, which he spread on the table.

'Here, on the Isle of Wight just opposite the mouth of the Beaulieu River, is situated the Chayle Rapid-Hardening Cement Works, owned by Messrs Haviland & Mairs. It's a medium-sized works, with a small harbour on the Solent,' and Goodwilly gave a short description of the place. 'Mairs is the partner who looks after the finance. On Monday morning he went as usual to his accountant's room and in due course opened his safe. At once he saw that some money was missing. He checked up his figures and found it amounted to £415. He locked the room, told Haviland of his discovery, and phoned for the Cowes police. Superintendent Hanbury went out himself and conducted an enquiry.

'The first thing he learned, after the immediate circumstances of the theft, was that the night watchman had disappeared. No one had seen him that morning and his supper, uneaten, was laid out in his hut. Hanbury sent at once to the man's rooms—he lodged close by—but he had not returned that morning. It was believed that he usually had his supper between one and two in the morning, so whatever had happened to him had probably happened before that hour.

'All concerned naturally assumed that these two events were connected and that the watchman, Clay, had robbed the safe and disappeared with the swag. Hanbury's first step was, therefore, to obtain this description of Clay which you have seen, and to send it round the Island, as well as here and to Portsmouth, and other points along the mainland.'

'Do I understand you to say that the accountant opened the safe with his keys?' French asked. 'I mean, was the safe opened with a key to abstract the money, or broken open.'

'The safe was not damaged in the least, so it must have been opened with a key.'

'I suppose there is no doubt that it was really locked when Mairs left it on the previous working day?'

'I understand that Mairs is positive that it was, and also that he unlocked it on the Monday morning before making the discovery of the theft. Besides we think we've found the key that was used, as I'll tell you later. But in all this I have only hearsay evidence. You'll have to get those sort of details direct from the persons concerned.'

'Naturally,' French agreed, 'but the more information I can get now, the better for me.'

Goodwilly nodded. 'I understand that all right, Chief-Inspector,' he agreed. 'Well, that's really about all I learned from Cowes. Oh, I'm wrong. There was one other point.

'Mairs was able to say that he had got the money from the London and Southern Bank in Cowes at various times within the last couple of weeks, and that it consisted principally of single notes, though there were a number of fives and a few tens also. The Super went to the bank and was able to get the numbers of the fives and tens. There were four tens and fifteen fives, the remaining £300 being in singles. These are the numbers of the fives and tens,' and the Super passed over another paper.

'Those should be useful,' French commented.

'As a matter of fact,' Goodwilly returned, 'I don't think they will be, as you'll probably agree when you've heard the rest of the tale. Well, that all took place on Monday and referred to the Chayle works.

'On Tuesday morning another case was reported, this time from Eastleigh. At first it seemed totally separate from the other, and it was only later that we found the two were connected. Superintendent Crawford stated that a man had been found burnt to death in an Austin Seven. The man could not be identified and all that was known was the car number, OU 0091. As OU was the registration combination for Southampton, Crawford asked me to have the number traced.

'I sent a man to the County Council Registration office

106

in Civic Square and he learned that the car belonged to a Mr James Norman, of an address in the suburbs. My man went to the address and saw Norman. He said that the car had been his, but that a month previously he had sold it to Messrs Fisher, garage proprietors, who do a big motor trade in the town. The man went on to Fisher's and they told him something that brought him back at the double to report.

'They said that about nine o'clock on the previous morning, Monday, a man had come in and asked if they had a small second-hand car for sale. He was a middling tall man, thin, clean-shaven and with a very pale face and a limp, and spoke in a high-pitched voice. He was dressed in rather poor clothes—well, I needn't go on. He answered the description of Clay in every respect. He had been shown two or three cars, and had finally bought Norman's old Austin Seven at thirty pounds.

'When I heard this I went down to Fisher's myself. They confirmed the description, and they remembered how Clay had paid. It was in notes, two tens and two fives. These notes had been paid into the bank on the previous day. I wasn't long till I was with the bank manager, and he got the records looked up. All four notes were among those which had been stolen from Chayle.'

'Pretty good,' said French. 'The man clearly didn't know that the numbers of fives and tens were noted.'

'So it would appear,' Goodwilly agreed. 'Well, there was the identification of the dead man. I got on the phone to Crawford and he came in and saw me. It happened that Colonel Tressider was with him at the time, and he came along also.

'Crawford told us that the car had failed to take a sharp bend in the road from Swaythling to Fair Oak and had gone down a bank and stopped at the edge of a river. It had caught fire and been burnt out. The front of the car was a bit damaged, though as the ground was fairly soft, this damage was not as great as might have been expected. The carburettor however was broken off and that had allowed the petrol to escape, no doubt accounting for the fire. In this old model the tank was over the dash and the petrol had run out by gravity.

'The remains had been examined by a doctor, but there was not a great deal that he could tell. The man was fairly tall and thin and lame in the left leg, as was Clay. Thirdly, the back of his skull was fractured, which the doctor said would have caused death. It was probable therefore that he was killed directly when the car went down. Lastly, he had had a tooth stopped, the doctor thought, fairly recently. How recently he couldn't say, but he was certain of the stopping. We 'phoned across to Hanbury at Cowes to try if he could find the dentist, but so far he has not replied. If the dentist is found it should put the identification beyond question, though personally I don't think there's any doubt about it as it is.'

'No,' French said thoughtfully, 'all that seems pretty conclusive. It's not easy to see, all the same, just how the accident happened.'

'The doctor mentioned a possibility, though only very tentatively, because there's no evidence either for or against it. It seems this Clay, who was a youngish man, was formerly a lorry driver in the employ of the Chayle firm, and some three years ago he was injured in a smash he had with another vehicle. You'll see that Hanbury gives us a short history of the man after his description. That's how he got his lameness. But in addition to the lameness he was hurt internally. Now the doctor thinks that because of that weakness, on top of the excitement of his break, the man may have had a fainting fit. Of course without having seen Clay's doctor, ours couldn't give a considered opinion. But it's a point to be gone into.'

'It sounds reasonable.'

'It does. One other find that Crawford made was a key. It was lying below the body as if it had been in the trousers' pocket. It had obviously been made by an amateur and the wards, but not the handle, corresponded exactly with the description of the Chayle safe key. We've sent the key over to Hanbury to try it in the safe, but we've not heard yet if it fits.'

'It'll fit all right,' French considered.

'I think it will, Chief-Inspector. However, we ought to know very soon. Well, as the three of us were there, the Colonel insisted on our having a sort of conference on the case. It didn't seem quite right, because our own Chief Constable was away and after all it had nothing to do with me. But there we were and we had it. As we talked about it one or two points came out that seemed a bit difficult to explain. I've noted them down.'

For the first time Goodwilly seemed a little at a loss. He paused, looked up his notes, hesitated again, and then at last went on.

'Looking over the affair as a whole, what I might call a strange irregularity in the design seemed to reveal itself. I'll try and explain what I mean. If this Clay had managed to get a key for the safe, it followed that he must have been a man of brains and resource. You understand that no key was missing. The key which was used must have been specially made for the purpose, and this of course works in with what Crawford found. Now it's not an easy thing to cut a key which will open so complicated a lock as a safe's. And further, it wouldn't have been easy to get hold of the original key to copy. It seemed to all three of us that Clay must have been extraordinarily able.

'Well, the Colonel then and there got me to ring up Hanbury and put these points to him. Hanbury said he had considered them, but had been utterly puzzled by them. He had not had time to complete his enquiries, but such information as he had gained made what had been done seem almost impossible. Only two keys for the safe existed, and one was kept continuously by Haviland and the other by Mairs. Neither had lent his keys to anyone, and both were positive that no one could have got at them to copy them. That's one side of it.

'On the other hand, a man of this almost superhuman cleverness was so idiotic as to buy with the stolen notes a car which could be identified without difficulty by any police officer in the country. He didn't even trouble to change the number-plate. How he could have expected not to have been dropped on beats me. And it beat both the Chief Constable and Crawford.'

'It's a strong point,' French agreed, while Carter nodded appreciatively.

'A man with the education and knowledge and ability to get hold of that safe key, would have known that the numbers of five and ten pound notes are recorded when they leave and enter banks. And he would also have known that the registration number of a car gives its entire history. There seemed to all three of us something here which required looking into.'

'I agree,' said French.

'We talked of it for a while, and then the chief said that while we mustn't make too much of a thing of which we hadn't the full particulars, it seemed to him that this apparent dual intelligence was really fundamental. By that he meant that there were two intelligences at work, in other words, two people. Well, I needn't repeat our conversation, but at last the Colonel put up a theory which so far as it went seemed reasonable to both Crawford and me.'

'I begin to see why Sir Mortimer thinks so much of Colonel Tressider,' French interjected.

'If he does, he's quite right. The Colonel's one of the best—from every point of view. Well, he suggested that there were two of them in it, this watchman and someone else, probably a clerk. While the safe was open this clerk might have directed his principal's attention to some other matter, and then managed to slip the key out of the lock, take a wax impression, and slip it back without discovery. He might moreover be an amateur metal-worker, and so have been able to cut the key. He would see however that he couldn't just steal the notes: if he did that, suspicion would be bound to fall on him by elimination. So he would look round for a scapegoat and find it in Clay. He would give Clay part of the spoils to make a getaway, and so draw aside the hue and cry. Of course he wouldn't put it like that to Clay, but it might be put so that a stupid man would think he was getting a very good thing out of it.'

'He might have given him all the fives and tens,' Carter suggested.

'You're right, Sergeant: I hadn't thought of that,' Goodwilly admitted handsomely. 'That would leave three hundred pounds' worth of untraceable notes for himself. How does that strike you, Chief-Inspector?'

French moved uneasily. 'I agree there were probably two people in the thing,' he answered slowly. 'As to whether it is otherwise correct, I don't know. I'd rather think over it a bit before saying.'

'Well, that wasn't so immediately important,' Goodwilly went on, 'but Colonel Tressider proceeded to add another twist that neither Crawford nor I had thought of. He asked was there any trace of the notes on the body? Crawford said he had found what looked like paper ash, but he couldn't tell if it was from notes. The fire had been fierce enough to destroy everything inflammable.

'The Colonel then said, "Suppose it was some other paper and there were no notes."

'Well, we looked at him, and I for one didn't twig at the moment what he meant. Then he explained. Was there any reason, he asked, why this burnt car business shouldn't have been a fake? He reminded us of the Rouse case and of a case in Germany, and of one or two others of a similar kind. Suppose, he asked, the clerk or second guilty person, whoever he might be, had done Clay in for the notes and engineered the accident to cover things up?

'Neither Crawford nor I were enthusiastic about this, but the more we thought of it, the less absurd it began to seem. So far as we could see, there was nothing actually impossible in the idea, and as the Colonel said, it certainly would work in with the ingenious mind of the man who had got the key.'

'Was there any detail in the accident itself which would support such a theory?' French asked. He was not greatly impressed by all this. The Colonel seemed to have been looking out for complications, instead of taking the simplest explanation of the facts. His own experience was that the simplest explanation of any mystery usually proved to be the truth.

'Well, there were a couple—three if you include the general one that we had known all along: that it was difficult to see why the accident should have taken place at all. Because there wasn't a particle of evidence to support the fainting theory. But a more interesting point was why the accident should have occurred just where it did. Crawford said that that particular spot was the *most* suitable place for an accident that he knew. A case could undoubtedly be made for the selection of the site.'

'That's true,' French admitted dubiously.

'Then there was another point which Crawford brought out,' Goodwilly continued: 'the finding of the safe key beside the body. If this had been a genuine accident, the key would scarcely have been there. If Clay had been on the run, the first thing he would have done would have been to get rid of it. He would have known that if it had been found on him, he was done for. That looked to all three of us a bit like a fake.'

French nodded. 'You're right there, Super,' he declared. 'That's the strongest argument you've brought forward, by a long chalk. What did the Chief Constable say to that?'

'He was impressed. He said that it proved nothing and that we must not jump to conclusions, but it did indicate a case for investigation. And seeing that the case might be the concern of three police forces, he thought an outsider to co-ordinate the work might be useful. He rang up the other Chief Constables and suggested getting a man from the Yard.'

French grinned. 'And what did you and Crawford say to that?'

'It didn't worry me; it really wasn't my show. Crawford

didn't like it, I could see, but when the Colonel pointed out to him that if he took it on, he would be dependent on whatever information Superintendent Hanbury chose to give him about the Cowes end of it, he thought a man from the Yard would be a good idea.' Goodwilly grinned in his turn. 'I didn't know it at the time, but I learned later that Hanbury and Crawford have their knives in each other about some private quarrel. So there you are, Chief-Inspector. That's the history of the affair to date, so far as I know it.'

'Well,' said French. 'I think you've proved your case for investigation. What occurs now? Am I given a free hand to do what I like?'

'Of course. What's been arranged is this. Crawford and Hanbury have been told of your arrival and been instructed to lend you any men you want and help in every way they can. But I may say, Chief-Inspector, they didn't need those instructions. You'll find them a decent pair ready on their own to do everything. And here's a general letter to any other police force in the county on whom you may want to call, with the same instructions. And if you want a private room as a headquarters, you can have one here.'

French got up. 'Splendid,' he said. 'You couldn't have done better. Thanks, Super, very much. Now, perhaps, you'd phone Crawford that I'll go out to see him in the morning, and I'll trouble you no more tonight.'

The interview soon came to a close, and within half an hour French and Carter had found an hotel and turned in.

9

French Sees the Burnt Car

Had French been a believer in omens, he would have given thanks to his gods when he looked out next morning. It was the first of August, and there was the look of August in the cloudless sky and the rich warm sunshine which would later become a grilling heat. French loved heat. Splendid! This was better than his room at the Yard.

He and Carter caught an early bus and by nine o'clock were seated in Superintendent Crawford's room in the Eastleigh Police Station. Crawford was a big dark man with a heavy manner. He looked a man who would be slow to move, but who when once he got going, would have something of the momentum of a steam roller. He was civil, but not effusive, and French imagined that some feeling of grievance that an outsider had been called in still lurked in the deeper recesses of his mind.

French, however, had no complaint to make of his treatment. Crawford gave him all the details of the case with clarity, showed him a number of photographs of the smash, and then said that within reason he and his staff were at

115

French's disposal. What, he asked, would French like him to do?

French thought that a visit to the scene of the tragedy was indicated, and Crawford immediately rang for his car to be brought round.

'Does any technical question arise about the car, Super?' French went on. 'If so, wouldn't it be well to take an engineer? I don't know if you're an expert, but I'm not.'

'If I had been handling the case, I should have taken one. I know something about cars, but I'm not an expert. In any case, I suppose you'd want one for court, if the affair ever goes there.'

'You're right. I had overlooked that. Let's have one.'

French, as a matter of fact, had not overlooked the point, but he had found that a little mild flattery was useful in dealing with those whose cases he had taken over. He was not dishonest in supplying it. He found that it gained him help and made things easier, and why should he not therefore adopt it?

Crawford drove to a large garage which bore notices that here was the true and only Austin agency, and saying he wouldn't be long, disappeared inside. Presently he returned with a sharp-featured young man in a check overcoat.

'Mr Dexter,' said Crawford. 'He's a director of this business and an engineer, and if anyone knows more about cars than he does, I should like to meet him.'

Dexter was obviously delighted to be let in on the case which had thrilled the whole neighbourhood. He did not say so, however, merely explaining that he was glad to do anything to help his good friend, the Super. It was all very amiable and pleasant. He got in behind with Carter and in a few minutes they reached their objective.

It was just as French had been led to expect from the description. The road, curving sharply to the right in the direction in which the wrecked car had been travelling, was on an embankment some fifteen feet high, approaching a river bridge. It was bounded by a grass border about eight feet wide. From the further edge of this border the ground sloped rapidly down to a sort of berm or level shelf beside the river. The only protection along the edge was a wooden railing, consisting of uprights some six feet apart, bearing on their tops a longitudinal member about three inches square in section and set diagonally. This railing was painted white, and served to draw attention to the curve. At night it would certainly have shown up clearly in the beams of a headlamp.

At the bottom of the slope, on the rough, irregular ground beside the water's edge, lay the car. It had smashed the horizontal rail and one upright of the paling, and this glancing blow had deflected it slightly towards the right. Running diagonally down the bank, it had turned partially over on to its left side and ploughed into a tiny hillock. The earth was heaped up in front of it, as snow heaps up before a railway plough.

The fire had obviously been fierce, particularly about the fore part of the car body. Here most of what could burn was gone. Floorboards, cushions, upholstery, paint—all were badly damaged. The key and human remains had been removed, but nothing else had been touched.

French stood looking round him, as he mentally registered these details. Then he turned to Crawford.

'Did you make any search for footprints, Super?' he asked.

Crawford shrugged. 'We searched,' he admitted, 'but it

was impossible to come to any conclusions. The whole place was tramped over by sightseers. As a matter of fact,' he admitted in a burst of confidence, 'the importance of possible footprints was not realised at first.'

'Naturally,' French returned smoothly. 'In any case on this grass I don't suppose impressions would have been left.'

A detailed inspection of the car added but little to their knowledge. The radiator had been pushed bodily backwards by the mound of earth, and the bonnet covers were crushed and shapeless. One had been forced up, revealing the broken carburettor. The rest of the car was but slightly damaged structurally. Both front wings were crushed, but the chassis seemed uninjured.

'Now, Mr Dexter,' said French, 'let's begin with the speed. Do you think you could estimate what that was?'

Dexter shook his head. 'Quite impossible to say. Very approximately I think it might have been from twenty-five to thirty miles an hour. The car must have been moving to plough into that earth, but a really high speed would have smashed things up a lot more.'

'Good enough. Now perhaps you'd have a look over the car and tell us what damage is done. Take all this down, Carter.'

Carter nodded. He had already produced his notebook.

'There's not so much wrong, so far as I can see,' answered the engineer. 'Radiator, fan, carburettor, wings and so on, you can see for yourselves. What may be important, such as the steering gear, I can't tell you about because it's buried. The front axle is probably bent, but you'll have to get the car lifted before we can be sure.'

'We'll ask you to lift it for us presently, won't we, Super?

In the meantime, do you think I'm right in assuming that the striking of that railing and this heap of clay would account for all the damage?'

'Yes, I think so,' Dexter said slowly. 'It would set back the radiator and that would damage the fan and so on. It would crush up the wings, too, of course.'

'The carburettor?'

Dexter hesitated. 'I suppose it would have done that too,' he said slowly. 'I don't see exactly how, but it's not easy to account exactly for everything.'

French grinned. 'I'm afraid, Mr Dexter, you'll have to bear with us. In the police we have an absolute obsession for detail. If we don't find out how that carburettor has got broken, we'll feel our day has been lost.' He bent down and examined the damaged brasswork. 'Speaking subject to your correction,' he went on, 'it seems to me that the carburettor has been hit by something pretty heavy. Are those scratches on it the nature of the beast, or have they come since birth?'

'You're quite right, Chief-Inspector,' Dexter agreed. 'Those marks are not natural. Clearly the carburettor has been broken by a heavy knock, and those marks show where it was hit.'

'Then what hit it?'

Dexter shook his head. 'That's what I can't tell you,' he declared. 'But there's no doubt that something has.'

'Well,' French said lightly, 'if we can't get it, we can't. It was an unfortunate part of the accident, at all events, because I presume that's where the petrol came from that caused the fire?'

'It looks like it.'

'But is there any doubt of it?' French persisted.

119

'No, I don't think there is,' Dexter returned, but his manner seemed dissatisfied.

'What is it?' French asked. 'I can see you're not quite happy about that.'

Dexter shook his head. 'No, that's not right,' he declared. 'I'm happy enough, as you call it. Simply it seemed rather a big fire for all the petrol that would have come out.'

'Oh?'

'You see, that's the old form of tank, above the dash. With that pipe broken the petrol would run out all right, but it's a small pipe and it wouldn't run out very quickly. I should have thought myself that the fire would have been confined to the front of the car. But I see I'm wrong.'

'Impossible to be right in everything. By the way, how do you think the petrol got alight?'

'That I'm not very clear of either. When you get a fire it's generally due to a short circuit somewhere, or else, if the engine is badly smashed up, to the petrol getting on to too hot metal. Here I don't think it could have got on to anything too hot, and I don't for the moment see what could have sparked. But there again some connection may have been broken which is now covered with clay.'

'That you'll be able to tell us later. Now, Mr Dexter, you mustn't jump to conclusions by my asking you this question. It's a routine question which we put in all cases of this kind. Can you see anything which might suggest that the accident was a fake? You remember the somewhat similar Rouse case? It was there held that the fire was not an accident, but was caused deliberately. Can you see evidence for or against that idea here?'

Dexter seemed a good deal interested by the suggestion. 'Some of these questions that you've been putting showed

120

me that something of the sort was in your mind, and I agree that the smashing of the carburettor and the lighting of the petrol might at first sight look like it. But my experience is that you simply can't account for everything that will happen in a smash. Because we can't explain these two things, it doesn't follow they were done deliberately. You follow what I mean?'

'Of course. But you can't see direct evidence, one way or another.'

'I think I can,' Dexter returned, somewhat to French's surprise. 'You see those controls? The car's in top gear. Now suppose there was some hanky-panky about it, I don't believe it could have been got into top gear. You suggest, I suppose, that the driver was dead before the accident, and that the accident was no accident at all, but was deliberately brought about?'

'I suggest nothing,' French returned; 'all I ask is whether you see any evidence for or against some theory of the kind.'

'Well, I see evidence against it. If the driver was dead, the smash could only have been caused by starting the car from outside, and running along beside it while it was gaining speed, and trusting it to run straight for the last few yards without a hand on the wheel. Now it wouldn't be possible, in my opinion, to get the lever into top gear under such circumstances. The speed would be too high.'

French nodded.

'That may not be quite convincing,' Dexter went on, 'but I think this is: In such a fake the only way you could get your acceleration—necessary acceleration, mind you— would be from the hand lever. Obviously you couldn't get it from the foot pedal; you'd have to be inside the car to do so. *But*, if you used the hand lever, it would stay put. The hand lever doesn't snap back to normal when freed, as does the pedal. Now this lever is in the normal position, giving minimum acceleration. Therefore the pedal must have been down at the time of the crash. Therefore a living person must have been in the car, and therefore it looks to me like a genuine accident.'

'That's very valuable, Mr Dexter, and just what I wanted. You understand that all we've discussed is confidential, don't you?' He turned to Crawford. 'Well, Super, if you agree I think we'll ask Mr Dexter if he'll get his breakdown plant and have the car taken to his garage, where it can be better examined. Will you do that for us, Mr Dexter?'

'Yes, if I may borrow your car, Superintendent?'

'Of course,' said Crawford. 'Take it with pleasure.'

When the engineer had disappeared French turned to the Super.

'What do you think of our friend's argument, Super?' he asked. 'It seems to me he's overlooked something pretty obvious.'

'You mean?' Crawford returned.

'Well, he's looking at only one possibility of fake. He's considering only how the car could have been driven down to where it is. He's forgotten that the fake might have come after that.'

'You mean that he's assuming it went on fire as a result of the fall?'

'Just that. If it didn't and if the fire was produced deliberately after the crash, his argument simply washes out.'

Crawford seemed a good deal impressed. 'It's a fact,

Chief-Inspector,' he admitted. 'If that were so the controls could have been altered between the crash and the fire.'

'Exactly, Super. You're a thought reader.'

'Then you're still doubtful that it was an accident?'

French looked grave. 'Tell me, Super,' he asked, 'did your people lift that bonnet cover?'

'Certainly not,' Crawford answered decisively. 'We touched nothing except to remove the body.'

'And do you think that the crash would have opened it just enough to enable the carburettor to be got at? You see, it's prised up just high enough for that and no more.'

'I see what you mean. You think the crash wouldn't have broken the carburettor?'

'Well, do you? Seems to me it was protected by the radiator. Admittedly, the radiator was pushed back, but it was just as good a protection as in its normal position.'

Crawford made a sudden gesture. 'Absolutely correct, I should say! And if so, the smashing was done deliberately and we're on to something very like murder.'

'It's beginning to look that way to me. I don't believe that carburettor was broken by the crash, and I don't believe that petrol was set on fire by the crash, and I don't believe the dribble of petrol that could come out of that pipe could make a fire of the size there's been here. But can we prove it?'

'Ah, that's the rub.'

'It usually is. However, let's try. If that carburettor wasn't broken by the crash, it was deliberately struck by something. Can we guess what that might have been. We have the marks on it to guide us.'

Both men bent down once more and examined the scratches and dints on the brasswork.

'You see,' said French, 'they're quite irregular. If it had been hit with a hammer there would be little plane surfaces, bounded by tiny arcs of circles. But these blows are so irregular that they might be called jagged.'

'A stone?' the Super suggested.

'That is what I had in mind,' French admitted. 'If so, that should give us a clue. There are plenty of stones about here, though none of them are loose.'

Crawford nodded. All over the ground were stones of various sizes, bedded in the grass-covered soil.

'Let's look around,' Crawford suggested with something almost of eagerness in his heavy manner.

They began searching, but it was Carter who had the luck. He had been poking about while the others were talking, and now he gave a cry. French and Crawford hurried over.

Beneath a low growing shrub was the bed of a large irregularly shaped stone. It was fresh, showing the stone had recently been lifted.

'That about settles it,' French said slowly as he stood looking down. 'If we could find that stone, and if by any impossible chance a fingerprint should show on the clay, it might fix the thing for us.'

Again they searched, and this time it was French who gave the cry.

In a clump of bushes lay a rough stone some eight or nine inches long, which had obviously come from the bed Carter had found. French lifted it carefully. The grass beneath it was fresh. He turned it round and at once gave a little grunt of satisfaction. On the sharpest of the points were tiny flakes and scrapings of brass.

'That about settles our hash,' he said grimly. 'Your Chief Constable was right and we're on to a murder.'

124

Crawford, greatly impressed, agreed. 'They nearly got off with it, too. If we had paid attention to the expert, they would have. And he's a good man, is Dexter.'

'He was right, as far as he went. He just didn't go far enough.'

As French spoke he was examining the stone more minutely. 'You see,' he went on, 'it's covered with dulled fingerprints. The man has worn gloves. We'll get nothing more from the stone. Bring it along, Carter, all the same.'

For a moment there was silence, then French went on: 'Let's see now how we stand. We're assuming that the victim was murdered and put in the car and the car run down the bank. Owing to the difficulty of getting up a high enough speed, the smash was not complete and fire did not result. But fire was necessary to remove traces of the murder, so petrol had to be spilled. Breaking off the carburettor seemed the obvious way, and it was broken off. But advantage was taken of the chance to set the controls in a more natural position. Personally, I imagine that more petrol was used, but I don't see that we can prove it. That right so far?'

'It's my reading of the facts.'

'Now will the state of the body throw any light on this theory? What about that fracture at the back of the skull?'

Crawford made a sudden gesture. 'By Jove, Chief-Inspector, you're right there! I noted the difficulty of accounting for a heavy wound at the back of the head when the man must have been pitched forward, but I supposed it just must have happened. I bet now it never happened. I bet that wound on the back of the head was inflicted before the car ever ran down the bank. What do you think?'

'Yes, I'm inclined to think so too. Let's go, Super, and have a look at the remains and a word with the doctor.'

'We'll have to wait till Dexter comes back with my car.'

'He'll not be long.'

As if to justify French's opinion, the Super's car at that moment swung round the corner and rapidly approached. It drew up beside them and Dexter alighted.

'The breakdown truck will be here in a few minutes,' he explained. 'It won't take long to lift so light a car, and we'll have it into the shop within the hour. Give me another hour for an examination, and I'll let you have my report.'

'Splendid!' French approved. 'Then I think we'll leave you to it. What about getting along, Super?'

An examination of the remains gave French nothing more than he had already known, and they drove on to the doctor's house. Luckily the doctor was at home.

He had not, however, much to tell. The fracture of the skull postulated a very heavy blow. It certainly could have been due to accident, as for instance, if the deceased had fallen heavily on his back and had struck his head against some solid object. Or it could have been due to murder: someone coming up behind his victim and striking him with a heavy blunt instrument. No, it could not possibly have been self inflicted. As to whether it could have been caused by the car accident, French and the Super could form just as good an opinion as he could. If the deceased had been thrown violently against the car, so that the back of his head struck some hard and rigid object, then the injury might have resulted. Whether the deceased was or was not thrown in such a way, it was not his province to say. That, it seemed to him, was a matter for the police.

French with a smile acknowledged the justice of these observations, and they bid the doctor good morning.

'He believes it was murder,' said French when they were back in the car.

'You think so?'

'I'm sure of it. He wasn't going to say so, but he doesn't think the injury was caused by the accident. I should say that from his manner.'

Crawford nodded. 'Probably you're right. I believe myself it's a true bill, and I congratulate you, Chief-Inspector, on your morning's work. It's a big step to have taken in so short a time.'

'My dear man,' French returned, 'it was a joint achievement by all three of us. But we're by no means out of the wood. It'll only worry us to know it was murder, unless we get the murderer.'

'And what's the next step?'

'Chayle, I suppose. I don't think there's much more to be learned at this end.'

But it turned out that there was one thing more. As they reached the police station a constable came forward. The Superintendent at Cowes had found the dentist who had attended to Clay's teeth, and he had just arrived. Should he be taken to see the remains?

Crawford took the man across himself, and Carter accompanied them. French did not, sitting down instead at the Super's desk to consider what he had learnt.

If this car accident were really faked—and by this time French had little doubt that it had been—it showed evidences of that highly developed intelligence which the Chief Constable had postulated. The 'accident' was of the same order as the obtaining of a key to open the safe: something which could only be done by an exceptionally gifted man. Here indeed was proof of the Chief Constable's very shrewd deduction.

If, however, the unhappy watchman had been in his death the victim of a more able intelligence, had he not also been this other person's dupe from the first? French thought so. There was nothing to suggest that Clay could have been a partner in the theft.

But if he were a dupe from the beginning, how had the real actor bent him to his purpose? What inducements had he used to force Clay to disappear from the works and to buy the car and do whatever else was necessary for the scheme?

Here was a difficult problem. Handicapped as he was by his lameness, which would at once have made him a marked man, Clay would never have put himself in such a position, unless some extraordinarily powerful pressure had been brought to bear on him. Probably it would be necessary to go into Clay's life. That indeed was a promising line of research. It should give contacts suggesting the nature of the pressure used, which in its turn might point directly to the guilty party.

French had not time to proceed further with his analysis. He had just jotted down these general ideas when Crawford and Carter returned with the dentist.

'It's Clay, all right,' Crawford said as they entered. 'You're quite sure, sir?'

'I'm perfectly sure,' the dentist returned. 'As you gentlemen probably know, mouths vary enormously, and to persons like myself who have studied the subject, each mouth is distinctive. With my card index'—he tapped a box he was carrying—'I can at once recall any mouth upon which I have ever worked, without possibility of error. It's as certain as a fingerprint.'

No doubt that the dead man was really Clay had arisen

in French's mind. At the same time it was certainty that he wanted and not opinion. Well, here was certainty, and so far as it went it was all to the good. French was pleased with his progress.

His morning's work however was not yet over. It was now nearly two hours since they had parted from Dexter, and the three police officers returned to the Austin depot to see if his report was ready.

It was. Dexter reported that he had made a detailed examination of the car and had found nothing to account for the disaster. The steering gear was in perfect order, except for a bend to the cross-rod which had obviously been caused by striking the earth. In fact all the damage— very slight under the circumstances—had almost certainly been the result, and not the cause, of the crash.

'That's about proof of the murder theory,' said Crawford when they had left the garage. 'I suppose it means an adjourned inquest?'

'I should think so,' French returned. 'And I think we'd better keep what we've learned to ourselves.' He looked at his watch. 'I say, Super, it's getting on to one o'clock. What about a spot of lunch with us? About this time my thoughts usually turn towards eating and drinking. And as for Carter's, his never seem to leave the subject.'

Crawford agreed with alacrity and they went to the nearest hotel. A period of intensive action of another kind ensued, and then French and Carter left for Southampton with the object of catching the 2.20 p.m. boat for Cowes.

10

French Learns of the Process

The two men enjoyed every minute of their hour's sail to the Island. The early promise of the day had been more than fulfilled. It was hot in the brilliant sun, but the *Medina's* forceful stride made a pleasantly cool breeze. The colouring was intensely vivid. The blue sky produced an azure sea, and both were relieved by the green of the trees on the shores to right and left, and lower down, the reddish brown of the clay cliffs near Hill Head.

It was all new ground, or rather new water, to French, and he found it fascinating. He was interested in shipping, and the presence of four of the world's greatest liners grouped in one small area thrilled him. Then his attention passed to the huge floating dock, empty at the moment, and standing up out of the water like a couple of long and high, but narrow, blocks of buildings. On each was a crane whose jib pointed straight up to the sky: twin spires of this cathedral of commerce. After these mammoths ordinary steamers, yachts and lighters seemed small beer, and French watched the giants till they were out of the immediate neighbourhood of the harbour and well down into Southampton Water.

He was struck by the contrast between the populous area adjoining the city and the lonely shores of the estuary. Except for clusters of houses at places like Hythe and Lee, the country seemed thinly inhabited. Depressing looking shores too, particularly on the west side, which was low and swampy. To the east the ground rose higher and was better wooded. An important feature in the landscape, the great squat circular tanks of fuel oil shone greyly in the sunshine. Then came Calshot, with its group of low sheds surrounding the Martello-tower-like castle. They went close in to the shore here, as they opened out Cowes Roads and the stretch of water where the Solent and Spithead join.

French looked with a thrill on these historic sheets of water, whose names he had known since he was a boy. Far away to the south-east he could see on the horizon two of the three old forts that he knew were there, looking like the tops of round postal pillar boxes projecting from the sea. It brought back tales he had read as a child of ships of the line, frigates and corvettes, lying in Spithead, waiting for the wind that would take them out to meet the French or the Spanish or the Dutch. Then they were crossing Cowes Roads, with Egypt Point on their right and the tree covered slopes of Osborne on their left, till presently they entered the estuary of the Medina and came to rest at the pier in Cowes.

French had rung up Superintendent Hanbury, and as the two men stepped from the gangway a sergeant of police introduced himself. The Super, he said, was engaged and could not meet them, but he would be free by the time they reached police headquarters. It was a short distance, and if they wouldn't mind walking, he would show them the way.

The sergeant was respectful and sufficiently talkative, but not communicative about the Chayle affair. French therefore dropped the subject till they were shown into Hanbury's room.

Superintendent Hanbury was a contrast in appearance to Crawford. Also a big man, he was fair instead of dark: with blue eyes, a pale skin and a little turned-up fair moustache. He had a pleasanter expression than Crawford and greeted French in a more friendly way.

'Sorry I couldn't meet you, gentlemen,' he apologised, 'but our magistates are sitting today and I have to be within reach of the court. You want, I suppose, to go out to Chayle? Or is there anything else you'd like first?'

French said he'd like to begin with a little chat about the affair, to which Hanbury agreed with readiness. He described in detail all he had done, but without adding materially to French's knowledge, except on the single point that he had tried the key found in the burnt car, and that it did open the safe. He quite saw the difficulties in the theory of Clay's having robbed the safe, but could suggest no alternative. He was immensely impressed with French's idea that the car disaster was a fake, but the suggestion that Clay had been murdered did not seem to him to throw any real light on the matter. Finally French, seeing he wasn't going to get any further information, said he would like to go out to the works.

'I can run you out, but I can't stop with you,' Hanbury offered. 'I have to be back in court shortly. When you're ready to come back, ring up, and I'll send the car out again.'

This was very satisfactory to French. He much preferred to

make his own enquiries in his own way. He therefore thanked Hanbury, and said that as he couldn't have the advantage of his presence, the arrangement would suit him very well.

Hanbury had wished to introduce French to the two partners, Haviland and Mairs, but it happened that both were attending some meeting in Southampton, and would not be back till later. 'You'd better see Samson,' the Super thereupon decided. 'He's their engineer and a live wire. I expect he can tell you as much as the others.'

French was accordingly introduced to Mr Noel Samson, a tall thin young man with a big nose, a deep bass voice and a discontented manner. After a few moments' conversation, he asked what he could do for his visitors.

'First,' French answered, 'I want you to please show us round the works so that we may get a general idea of our bearings. Then I want to see the watchman's room and the safe from which the money was stolen, and anything else that you think might bear on the affair. Then I should like a statement of what you know. Then—'

Samson had begun to smile as he listened to this recital. Now he laughed outright. 'Steady on, Chief-Inspector: I'm only finite. You want to be shown round the works? Very good: come along. When that's done we can think of the next step.'

Samson proved himself a good guide. He took his visitors everywhere and explained the various processes in rotation. Then they examined the watchman's room, where he had sat between his five periodic inspections: at nine, eleven, one, three and five. As they walked Samson told them what he knew of the matter and answered a number of questions on various points of detail.

On the whole French did not learn a great deal more

than had been told him by Superintendent Goodwilly. It seemed that Clay was normally on duty from eight to six—ten hours. He was employed to keep a general watch on the premises, in spite of the fact that a small shift worked at night to tend certain machinery, such as the rotary kilns, which ran continuously. He brought two meals with him for the night, and it was known that he had the first between twelve and one and the second about four. On the night of his disappearance neither had been eaten, which seemed to indicate that he had left the works early.

Though in direct discussion French did not learn a great deal from the engineer, he was puzzled by the man's manner. There was in his every word and action a strong sense of grievance. For some reason Samson was a disappointed man. French noted the fact for future consideration.

'Well, Mr Samson, that's fine so far as it goes,' he said at last. 'What about having a look at that safe?'

They were sitting in Samson's office, and without replying the engineer put a call through his telephone.

'I was asking,' he said to French, 'if Mr Mairs had come back, and I find he's just arrived. As he is our financial expert, and the safe that was burgled was his, I think I'd better hand you both over to him. If you want me again I'll be here.'

French expressed his satisfaction at this arrangement, and they walked to Mairs's office. Grosvenor Mairs was a small round-faced man with a headlong way of walking, swinging his head forwards and sideways at each step as if he were a diver about to take a plunge. He had a boisterous offhand manner, but there was something coldly calculating about his eye which suggested that he was very well able to take care of himself. Samson effected the necessary introductions and left them.

'I'm glad this matter has been put into the hands of the Yard,' Mairs said. 'Nothing against our local force, you know, and all that. But it stands to sense that the Yard must be better equipped to deal with serious crime, and both Mr Haviland and I think that this is a very serious crime.'

French was interested. 'Why do you say that, Mr Mairs?' he asked.

Mairs hesitated. 'I think Mr Haviland would like to talk to you about that when he comes in,' he said. 'He'll be here shortly. In the meantime, if there is any other information that I can give you, please ask me.'

This seemed a propitious moment to investigate the matter of the safe. Mairs was obviously anxious to help. He showed French the safe and unhesitatingly answered all his questions.

But here again French found that Goodwilly had told him practically all there was to know. The safe was in Mairs's own office, was large, and of an old pattern, and contained the books of the firm in addition to any cash that might be in hand.

'Who knew that the money was in the safe, Mr Mairs?' French asked.

'Well,' the junior partner returned, 'it was probably known by all the staff that we kept money in the works and that the safe in my office was the most likely place to keep it. But that we had four hundred in it on that particular night was only known to myself and the two clerks in our cashier's department.'

'They didn't talk?'

'They say not, and I believe them, for both are reliable fellows who have been with us for years. But, of course—' Mairs shrugged.

'Of course,' French agreed politely.

'But there's one thing which you should know,' Mairs went on. 'Our wages come to between two and three hundred a week, and are paid each Friday. The money is obtained from the bank on Thursday, so as to allow time to divide it into the pay envelopes. If the thief had come on a Thursday night he would have found nearly seven hundred pounds instead of four.'

'And that would be known to all your staff?'

'All the staff wouldn't know how much the wages came to, but all would know that we had more money before pay day.'

'Quite. That's certainly interesting.'

From Mairs French picked up what further information he could. He got the names and addresses and histories of the clerks and others who knew that money was kept in the safe. He learned the details of Clay's history, none of which seemed to help, and also that Samson was an exceedingly able man with high qualifications as an engineer and chemist, who had been with them since the start of their works, nine years previously.

As Mairs gave this information a call came through on his telephone. 'Right,' he answered, 'we'll go now.'

'That was Mr Haviland, Chief-Inspector. He would like to see you in his office if you will come across.'

He led the way, Carter as usual bringing up the rear like some great dog.

Haviland presented an extraordinary contrast to Mairs in manner and appearance. He was a heavily built man, with a walrus moustache and a deliberate air. He shook hands with French, nodded to Carter, and asked everyone to sit down.

'I'm glad to see you here, Chief-Inspector,' he said ponderously. 'I may tell you that I took the liberty of asking the Chief Constable whether Scotland Yard could be called in. He told me it had already been done. I was much pleased.'

'It was considered desirable to co-ordinate the different police forces which were dealing with the case,' French replied.

'You are discreet, Chief-Inspector,' Haviland returned. 'However that's your business. But I should like to tell you that both Mr Mairs and myself take a very serious view of this affair. I should also like to ask you a question or two if you have no objection?'

French smiled. 'No objection, sir, but I don't guarantee to answer.'

'You can answer these. First, I am informed that the man found in the burnt car really was Clay. Is that so?'

'Yes, sir, that's so.'

'Next, it was hinted that the accident to the car was really not an accident at all, but that it was caused deliberately. Can you tell me anything about that?'

French hesitated. Was anything to be gained by keeping this secret? It would come out at the inquest in any case.

'There's reason to believe it was not an accident,' he said quietly.

'Ah,' Haviland glanced quickly at Mairs, 'we feared it might be so. That rather confirms a very unpleasant idea which occurred to each of us independently. I'll tell him, Mairs?'

'I think you should.'

'Well, Chief-Inspector, I am one of those who feel that there's no use in calling in your doctor or lawyer and not telling him the whole facts of your case, and I imagine the same obtains in circumstances such as we find ourselves in now. We both feel that there is more in this matter than is apparent on the surface. In short, we feel that this theft would not have been carried out—and murder committed, because I suppose that car business was murder?'

'We think so.'

'So should I. Well, we feel that all that would not have been done for four hundred pounds, or rather for the chance of what money might have been in the safe—for we doubt that the thief knew what was there.'

'You may be right, sir. At the same time there are thousands of people in this world who would commit murder for the chance of such a sum.'

'Not in these circumstances, I think.'

'That postulates some other motive,' French pointed out.

'It does,' Haviland returned, 'and that's what I'm coming to. There was something more valuable than four hundred pounds in these works. Not in the safe of which we are speaking. But in that one which you see there'—he pointed to a large green Milner safe in the corner of the room—'there was something worth perhaps hundreds of thousands, perhaps millions. That's what we're afraid of, Chief-Inspector.'

French whistled softly, and even Carter sat up and looked thrilled.

'Tell me, sir.'

Haviland did so. He told of their setting up the works and engaging Samson, a man with a brilliant record, as their engineer and chemist. That was nine years previously. For five years things had gone on without incident, then Samson had come to himself and Mairs to say that he thought he was on to a discovery, which if it worked out as he hoped, would revolutionise the manufacture of rapid-hardening cement. He put his facts before the partners and they authorised him to engage in experiments. These were long drawn and costly, but at length Samson had made his process a commercial possibility. It was an exceedingly simple discovery. Did the Chief-Inspector know anything of the manufacture of cement?

French's ideas were of the haziest.

Very well, roughly what happened was that chalk and earths of various kinds were mixed and ground with water into a slurry. This was then burnt into clinker in large rotary or other kilns. The clinker was then ground fine, and—there it was: cement. In this process the burning of the dried slurry to clinker was an expensive item, and that was where Samson's discovery came in. As the Chief-Inspector doubtless knew, there were certain substances called fluxes in existence. These were mixed with, say, metals, to promote fusion when heated. Now Samson had discovered that certain chemicals in certain proportions enormously assisted the fusion of the dried slurry into the viscous semi-liquid which afterwards became clinker. So much so that the slurry could be fused with a very much smaller application of heat than formerly. The Chief-Inspector could see the result of that. With the new process there was a great saving of coal and of the time during which the slurry had to be kept in the kiln. He need not go into figures, but the Chief-Inspector might take it from him that the process meant an enormous thing, running, as he had said, possibly into millions sterling. Now the formula for producing the flux, and the method of using it when produced, being complicated, had necessarily been reduced to paper, and the papers were kept in the safe in that office. What he and Mr Mairs had feared was not the loss of a paltry four hundred, but the loss of their secret.

The Chief-Inspector would now understand their anxiety upon the whole question.

French, considerably impressed, agreed that this was an important contribution to the problem. He pondered in silence for a few moments, then began in his slow deliberate way to ask questions.

'From what you say, the secret formula has not, I take it, been stolen.'

'No. If it had been, you would have heard something more about it before this.'

'Were there any signs of the safe having been interfered with?'

'None. None that any of us could trace at all events.'

'That doesn't prevent its having been removed and photographed and replaced.'

'We realise that only too well.'

'Who knew that this document existed and that it was in the safe?'

'So far as we know, no one but Mr Samson and Mr Mairs and myself.'

For the first time Mairs spoke. 'Don't you think we should get Samson in while we're talking this over?' he suggested.

'I think so,' Haviland returned. 'What do you say, Chief-Inspector?'

French thought it would be advisable, and Haviland put through a call. Presently Samson looked in.

'Come in, Samson, and find a chair,' Haviland said. 'We were just telling the Chief-Inspector about the process. He wants to ask some questions.'

'I was asking, Mr Samson, who knew that your notes were in the safe?'

'No one—except the three of us here. So far as I'm aware, no one even knew that we had a secret. I did the experiments myself and no one knew what I was working on, and when we altered our system we simply said we were adopting a slightly different process. I don't think anyone realised it was either secret or valuable.'

'Surely your big wall and your closed gates would have suggested something of the kind?'

'Oh well, we had to take some precautions. While casual visitors were safe enough, a qualified chemist might have smelt a rat.'

French paused. 'Tell me,' he went on presently, 'are such processes not patentable? Why run it as a secret process?'

The partners exchanged glances. 'That's a very pertinent question, Chief-Inspector,' Haviland answered. 'It's one which we considered seriously ourselves. The reason we decided against it was this: We're producing cement at about eighty per cent of what it costs our rivals. Now if we say nothing about our process, we can sell our product at our ordinary price and take our profit. As a matter of fact we do sell at our ordinary price, but we give a slight rebate for full wagon- or ship-loads. That ensures the sale of every ton we can put out, and it's not a large enough cut to look suspicious.'

'I follow.'

'Now suppose we patent the process. At once the engineers of the world are at work to modify it so as to evade our monopoly. Quite likely someone discovers a better process. Then we're down and out. Even if we fight and hold our rights—a ruinously expensive business—we should be forced to allow other firms to use the process on licence, prices would come down generally, and our

141

profits would be correspondingly reduced. I don't know whether I have made myself clear?'

'Quite clear, sir.' Again French paused. 'Now you say that only you three gentlemen knew of the existence of the secret process. But if you're right that this affair represents an attempt to steal it, you must be wrong in that?'

Again the partners exchanged glances. 'I think we all see that difficulty,' Haviland admitted. 'It certainly does look as if someone knew, but how anyone could have found out we can't imagine.'

'Then, with regard to the stealing of the money, you think it was only a blind?'

'We imagine so. We suggest that the thief was in search of the process and that he left, or thought he had left, some trace of his presence, and decided to take anything he could lay his hands on to make it look like an ordinary burglary.'

'And do you think Clay was party to the affair?'

Haviland shrugged. 'Clay was a man of good character. I should have said he was quite honest. Of course you never know . . .'

'If you're right in all this,' French said after another pause, 'there seem to me two lines which will have to be gone into carefully. The first is, Who would have benefited by stealing the process? And the second, Who could have got hold of the keys of your safes?'

Haviland made a gesture of agreement. 'That's it, Chief-Inspector; that's exactly what we thought ourselves. But there you've got us. It mightn't be difficult to say who would have benefited by stealing the secret, but your second question is unanswerable.'

'Well, let us take the first question first. Who in point of fact would have benefited?'

'We think,' Haviland returned slowly, 'only a technical man—someone with a technical knowledge of cement manufacture. Mr Samson tells us that no outsider could have understood the formula.'

'Have you any such in your works?'

Haviland looked at Samson.

'Not to my knowledge,' the engineer answered.

'Then as to possible suspects outside your works?'

Haviland shook his head. 'That's a hopelessly big question, I'm afraid. There must be hundreds. Given the unlikely fact that the existence of our process was known, there are literally hundreds who could make a fortune out of it.'

'You mean that anyone finding the formula would sell it as his own?'

'Yes, I think so.'

Once again French sat silent, lost in thought.

'Those rebates you give for full loads,' he said presently. 'Are you sure they haven't give you away?'

Haviland shook his head. 'That we're giving the small rebates is of course known, but we don't believe the discovery could suggest that we had a process. We think the rebates would be explained in one of two ways: either that we're selling at a loss to keep our plant running, or that we've got better scientific management than other works.'

Haviland paused, then went on: 'As a matter of fact I put up a story to meet the difficulty. I gave out that Mr Mairs had come in for a fortune and was spending a little to make up the loss on our sales, so as to keep our works going through the bad times.'

French nodded. 'Very ingenious, sir. How did you give that story publicity?'

'I told Mr Tasker. It was he who spoke of our rebates. He's the managing director of the Joymount Works, over at Hamble.'

'What is their business?'

'Cement of the *ciment fondu* type, same as ours.'

'Oh,' said French. 'Are there many similar works round here?'

'No, only the two, Joymount and ourselves. The big works on the Medina make an improved Portland cement, and wouldn't be interested.'

'And was Mr Tasker,' French asked slowly, 'the only person to whom you told the story?'

'Yes, he was the only one who mentioned the rebates.'

French hesitated. 'His question, I suppose, didn't seem to you suggestive?' he said at last.

All three men stared. 'Suggestive?' Haviland repeated. 'You mean?'

'I mean,' French answered, 'that here is a firm which would be vitally interested in your discovery; a firm located on your threshold, so to speak—much nearer than any of your other rivals. They have discovered you are underselling them—because that's what you're really doing—and their managing director tries to pump you on the matter. I asked whether you found it in any way suggestive?'

Once again the three men stared, this time in silence.

11

French Gets Down to It

It was Haviland who presently broke the silence.

'I wonder if I quite understand you, Chief-Inspector? Are you suggesting, to put it bluntly, that Tasker or some of his people stole the process?'

'I'm asking if you thought so,' French returned with a smile.

Haviland shook his head decidedly. 'I certainly did not,' he answered. 'And I don't think—?' He looked at Mairs and Samson.

'Such a thing never entered my head,' Mairs declared.

'Nor mine,' Samson added.

'I don't think there's any evidence for such a view,' went on Haviland. 'In fact I think Tasker's speaking of the rebate cuts the other way. If he were contemplating the theft, he wouldn't have drawn attention to himself like that.'

French nodded. 'I simply asked for your views, because you gentlemen seem to have given the affair such close thought.'

'I don't see,' Haviland went on, 'how Joymount could

have discovered that we had a process. Nor do I see how they could have got the keys of the safe.'

'Someone got them,' French pointed out. 'Why not Joymount?'

'Well, how could they have?' Haviland persisted.

'What about an accomplice among your own staff?'

Haviland shook his head. 'I don't know who it could have been.'

French was not convinced of Joymount's innocence, and he noted the matter as one to be gone into thoroughly. There was however no need to say so.

'You're probably right, sir,' he went on smoothly. 'I see difficulties in the theory myself. Now about the keys. I understand there are only two in existence?'

'Yes,' Haviland answered, 'and that applies to each safe, the one the money was stolen from and that one in the corner. Mr Mairs, who acts as our accountant and cashier, has one pair of keys, and I have the other.'

'How do you keep them?'

'I keep mine on a ring, fastened to my trousers with a chain. I only undo the chain at night, and then I put the keys under my pillow.'

'You're satisfied that no one could have got at them?'

'Perfectly.'

'And you, Mr Mairs?'

'I keep mine in the same way. When the question of the process arose we discussed this matter of the keys and agreed as to what we should do. I'm also satisfied that no one could have got hold of mine.'

'What keys altogether were on the bunches?'

'So far as the works were concerned, the same on both,' said Haviland. 'Besides the two safe keys there was a key of the wicket in the outside gate, of the two new sheds where we have our new small kilns, and of the office block, and each of us had one for his private room. In addition I had one or two private keys connected with my house.'

'That is true in my case also,' Mairs added. I had three private keys on my bunch as well as those belonging to the works.'

'Well,' said French, 'from that it seems obvious that the keys couldn't have been taken away for long enough to open the safe. Therefore they must have been got hold of momentarily and an impression taken. Now when could that have been done?'

Haviland shook his head. 'That's just it,' he remarked.

'Let's get down to it,' French returned. 'Suppose one of you gentlemen opened the safe and had occasion to turn back to your desk for a moment. Suppose a clerk or other person was present. Could not he have snatched out the key, taken a wax impression of it, and replaced it without your notice?'

Again Haviland shook his head. 'Impossible,' he declared. 'You've overlooked the chains. If either of us had unlocked the safe and wished to return to our desks, we should have had to lock it first and remove the key. We *never* took the chains off, except at night.'

At this Mairs nodded emphatically and French had another try.

'You're both absolutely positive you didn't lend the keys to *anybody*. Your private keys, for instance, which were on the same bunch?'

Neither man had done so. Neither would have done so on any account whatever.

'Then it looks as if they must have been taken at night,'

French went on. 'A mild sleeping draught, not strong enough to arouse suspicion, but enough to keep the patient quiet while the operation was in progress? What about that, gentlemen?'

Once again the partners shook their heads. They were positive that nothing of the kind had occurred.

French was silent. This certainly was a bit of a teaser. If these men were correct, it was beginning to justify Hanbury's expression that the impossible had happened. Well, French had been up against that difficulty before. If statements proved that the impossible had happened, the answer was: so much the worse for the statements. For the first time French began to wonder if these Chayle people knew more than they had admitted. How, he wondered again, could he find that out?

Haviland moved suddenly as if an idea had occurred to him. For a moment he seemed to be considering it, then hesitatingly he spoke.

'Your talking of a sleeping draught has just suggested something to me. I can't believe there's anything in it, but perhaps I ought to tell you.'

'Please do, sir,' French invited, while Mairs and Samson stared with surprised interest.

'It was last Friday,' went on Haviland. 'I had been in Town for the day and I came down by the 4.50 to Portsmouth; via Ryde, you know. Well, the whole story is simply that I fell asleep in the train. There was nothing in that: it has happened, I'm afraid, many times. But on this occasion I slept very soundly—I didn't wake when we stopped at Portsmouth. In fact the car attendant seems to have had trouble waking me. But when he did so I was at once all right.'

148

'One can generally tell if one has been drugged,' French pointed out. 'Did you imagine that on this occasion?'

'No,' Haviland said with decision. 'I thought it natural enough. I had had a heavy day in Town, and if you remember, last Friday was very hot, and the car was hot and stuffy.'

'You didn't then think you had been drugged,' French went on, 'but now in the light of our discussion are you equally sure?'

Haviland hesitated again. 'No,' he said at last, 'that's why I've mentioned it. It has occurred to me that the tea had a slight taste. I remember thinking it wasn't as good as usual.'

French nodded. 'Were there many other passengers in the car with you?'

'I don't think so; I really didn't observe. As I said, I was tired, and while I was awake I was reading.'

'No one sitting at your table?'

'No one.'

'Nor across the alley way?'

Haviland hesitated again. 'I think there was a man, but I didn't look particularly at him.'

'You can't give me any description of him?'

'I'm afraid I can't. I had no reason to look at him.'

French tried hard to get a line on the passenger, but without success. Then he reverted to the case generally. In spite however of all his efforts he failed to learn anything further.

There was just one other thing to be done at Chayle. Having taken Haviland's and Mairs's fingerprints, French carefully tested the insides of both safes and satisfied himself that no prints other than those of the partners were to be found. He had not indeed expected to find any, owing to the fact that the man who had broken the carburettor of the Austin Seven had worn gloves. However the search had to be made. Having completed it, Carter rang up Hanbury for the car, and when it arrived the two men took their departure.

French was well satisfied with his progress as he and Carter travelled back to Southampton. He had triumphantly solved his first problem—whether there was or was not a case for investigation. He had shown that murder had been done, and he had initiated enquiries which he hoped would soon lead him to the murderer. Certainly a good day's work!

But it was not French's way to linger over the past. Now, as at all times, it was the future that mattered. What was to be his next step?

He wondered if he had enough data to form a tentative theory of the crime. He was afraid not, and yet in the course of his interview with the Chayle partners, two possibilities had emerged.

The first was that the Joymount people had learnt of the process and were trying to steal it—or had stolen it. This would involve their having bribed Clay to help them, and when they had got all they could out of him, having murdered him to preserve their secret. This idea met the inherent possibilities of the situation, and was to some slight extent supported by Tasker's question.

The second possibility was that the Chayle partners had themselves murdered Clay. No motive had been indicated, but one could easily be imagined. Suppose, for instance, they had found that Clay had discovered the process and was about to sell it. This suggestion also met the facts, and was supported by the fact that the Chayle statements involved an impossibility, and must therefore at some point be incorrect.

French saw that he was skating on extraordinarily thin ice, and yet thin ice was better than no support at all. Suppose one of his possibilities were the truth. Was there any test as to which it might be?

He thought so. The sleep in the train! That train journey had been, so far as he could find out, the *only* occasion on which moulds of the Chayle keys could have been obtained. Had Haviland been drugged on that occasion? If so, it would remove the contradiction in his evidence—that the keys could not have been copied—and also prove the existence of an outside criminal. French saw that an early investigation into that tea-car episode was indicated.

But though these ideas seemed reasonable enough as starting-off points, French was far from satisfied with either. As the little steamer pushed its way along past Calshot and the Hamble he went back again over the facts. Then something more likely flashed into his mind and he gave a little sigh of satisfaction.

Suppose some outsider had penetrated into the works with the object of stealing the process—a representative of Joymount or some other person. Leave out for the moment how he came to suspect its existence, and also how he got the keys. Suppose he did suspect and had the keys, and had entered the enclosure to make a search. Very well.

Suppose now that while he was making his search he had been challenged by Clay. Suppose he hit Clay over the head and killed him.

This seemed very promising to French. He pursued the idea.

If he were right so far, what would now happen? Well, there would be the intruder with a body on his hands. His immediate and overwhelming need would be to get rid of that body. How would he do it?

He could scarcely leave it where it was. This would call attention to the murder too quickly. Nor could he bury it nor throw it in the Solent. In each of these cases discovery would be too likely. What would he do? Obviously stage an accidental death—if he could. And how better could this be done than by a car accident and fire?

This was a startling theory, but it looked as if it might be the truth. What would it involve? First it would involve the murderer buying the car. He would have to impersonate Clay. And here at once a clue was suggested. A man's face could be whitened and he could walk with a limp and speak in a high-pitched voice. But he couldn't to any considerable extent change his height or build. Therefore the murderer would have to be a thinnish man of slightly over middle height. That would be something to go on.

This theory would explain that really almost insoluble problem: how Clay came to be mixed up in the affair at all. It would explain the reason for the car accident. It would explain the buying of the car with stolen notes of five and ten pound denominations, for an essential of the scheme would be that it must be believed that Clay himself had bought the vehicle. In fact, it presented the first really intelligible theory of the crime.

Of course the murder of Clay at Chayle would work in with either of French's tentative possibilities—the guilt of Joymount or of the Chayle partners. As a touchstone of these two he had already thought of the sleeping in the train. Was there any corresponding enquiry which might indicate whether Clay had or had not been killed in the works? For some time he considered this point, then he thought that there was.

Could he find out how Clay reached the mainland?

If it could be shown that the watchman was alive when he made the crossing, that of course would be an end to his idea. If on the other hand the man's crossing could not be traced, it would tend to support it.

Here then was plenty to be getting on with: the getting of details of Haviland's sleep in the train, of how Clay crossed to the mainland, and of who could have impersonated Clay when buying the car. Incidentally French noted that the latter could not have been either Haviland or Mairs—Haviland was too stout and Mairs too small, but so far as size and build were concerned, it might easily have been Samson.

On reaching their hotel, French got Carter to ring up Hanbury. French was sorry, but he wanted two things. First, could the Super find out how Clay had crossed to the mainland? and second, could he get him a photograph of Samson, if possible without this being known?

Hanbury much regretted that he had done nothing with regard to the first point. However he would get on to it at once. But with regard to the second, he fortunately could oblige the Chief-Inspector. He happened to have such a photograph in his possession. It was a group of certain of the staff of the works taken on the occasion of Chayle winning a football challenge cup. The portrait of Samson was good and would bear enlargement. Hanbury would send the group at once.

This was a piece of extraordinary luck. The photograph arrived while French and Carter were at breakfast next morning and presently they set off for Fisher's garage. They found Fisher civil enough, but inclined to be annoyed by the number of police representatives who desired his story.

'I told Superintendent Goodwilly all this,' he said in a slightly aggrieved voice. 'I think he might have passed on the information to you.'

'He did so, Mr Fisher,' French returned pleasantly, 'but we've gone a little further since then. What I am now working on is the identity of the man to whom you sold the car. Now I have here a photograph of some of the Chayle staff and I want to know if you can pick out Clay. If you can, it settles the question once and for all.'

As long as Fisher was not being asked merely to repeat himself he was anxious enough to be helpful. But neither he nor any of his assistants could find the purchaser in the group.

'You're quite sure it wasn't this man?' said French at last, pointing to Samson.

'Is that Clay?' Fisher returned. 'No, it certainly wasn't. That's very interesting now. If the man wasn't Clay, who was it?'

'That's the rub, Mr Fisher,' French agreed. 'Now I'll tell you a secret. That's not Clay, but a man I thought might have been impersonating him—Clay in fact is not in the group. Thank you, Mr Fisher, you've helped me considerably.'

There, so far as French could see, went one of his two theories. From the height and build point of view, Samson was the only one of the Chayle hierarchy who could have impersonated Clay. He had not done so. Therefore it looked as if Chayle was out of it.

This theory, of course, had always been the unlikely one of the two. It was much more probable that some outsider

154

was guilty. French felt that his next step must be to get a similar photograph of the Joymount staff and see if Fisher could do better with it.

Where, he wondered, might such be obtained? It was unlikely that his amazing luck in connection with Samson would be repeated.

It was, however, very nearly repeated. French, having made sure that there were no Joymount photographs at the police station, drew a bow at a venture. He went to the office of the principal local paper, and showing his credentials, put his query. He had seen a very good photograph of a football team that the Chayle cement works had put into the field. Was there a similar photograph of members of the Joymount staff? Or were there any photographs of any kind which included them?

His shot scored a bull's-eye. Though not superstitious, he was a little frightened at this run of luck, for he had found that rapid early progress in a case usually meant a block later on. However as long as the luck lasted he could only be thankful for it.

It chanced that the Southampton *Argus* had a photograph of the Joymount staff. It had been taken some three years earlier on the occasion of the visit of a Canadian commission which was studying the manufacture of rapid-hardening cement. On the mount below were the names of the members.

It was just what French wanted. Removing the reference, he went back to the garage and showed it to Mr Fisher.

But here he was disappointed. The man who bought the car might conceivably have been one of four of the group, but neither Fisher nor any of his staff could say that it was so.

French noted the names of the possible four. They were: Mr Walter Brand, director; Mr Frederick King, chemical engineer; Mr James Campbell, fitter, and Mr Robert Armour, fireman.

Of these there could be no doubt as to which were the most likely. French determined that he must go into the recent movements of the chemist, King, and probably also of the young director, Brand.

But though this would be an early item on his programme, French decided it should not be his next step. Joymount was a matter of guesswork, whereas in another direction he had what might prove to be a direct clue. If an outsider were guilty, that outsider had obtained a mould of the keys. Had this been done by drugging Haviland in the train? This question was more urgent than Joymount. He would take it first.

From the hotel timetable he found that the 4.50 from Waterloo reached Portsmouth Harbour at 6.56. When the train came in that night he and Carter were waiting on the platform.

Once again he had a piece of unexpected luck. It happened that the tea-car staff on the train was the same as had been on duty on the evening in question, and the head attendant remembered the incident clearly.

'I know the gentleman well,' the attendant said. 'I don't know his name, but he comes down every Friday afternoon and always has tea and toast. He comes to this station.'

'Goes over to the Island,' explained French, anxious to do more than merely ask questions.

'I dare say,' the attendant returned.

'Yes, he lives near Cowes. He went unexpectedly to sleep, you say?'

'Yes, I never saw him asleep before. That night, it was last Friday, six days ago, he came down and had tea and toast as usual. There were no late teas, and we got the tables cleared and all shipshape before we passed Haslemere. I happened to be speaking to a friend at Haslemere and I could see along the platform that no one got into the car. I didn't go through it therefore after leaving Haslemere. Besides, you understand, if anyone had wanted anything they could have rung. Petersfield was the next stop, and I wasn't out on the platform there; so when we left the station I walked through the car, just to make sure no one had got in and that nothing was wanted. We do that, you know.'

'I know,' said French. 'It's an attention that's appreciated.' Again French tried his gentle flattery.

The man seemed pleased. 'We do our best, sir. Well, when I went through the car after Petersfield, I noticed this gentleman was asleep. We stopped at Fratton and Southsea and then here at the Harbour. I went through the car to see that nothing had been left behind, and there I saw the gentleman still asleep. I spoke to him, but as he didn't wake, I shook him by the shoulder. Well, sir, you'll hardly believe it, but I couldn't wake him. I called another of the attendants to help me carry him to the station-master's office, where a doctor could see him if necessary. But when we tried to lift him he woke. He seemed a bit upset, but I will say he did the decent. He gave us five bob between us, and thanked us. I asked him would he like someone to get him a taxi, but he said no, that he was all right. So we left him, and that's all I can tell you about it.'

'That's very clear,' French complimented. Then he became very confidential. 'Now I'll tell you something. Can you keep a secret?'

The man, interested by this unusual attitude on the part of a chief-inspector of the Yard, made the obvious reply.

'Very well,' French went on, 'not a word of this to anyone. We believe that while in the tea car a certain small object of value was stolen from the gentleman. That's what we're investigating. Now it looks to me as if he was drugged. What would you say to that?'

The attendant wouldn't be surprised. The passenger was more heavily asleep than was, in his opinion, natural.

'Suppose he was drugged,' said French, 'how could the drugging have been done?'

The attendant didn't see that it could have been done at all. No one could possibly have got at the trays before they were served, of that he was certain. After they were served the Chief-Inspector could form as good an opinion on the matter as he could. No, he couldn't say how the other passengers in the car were distributed, but he did remember that the gentleman was alone in one of the wider compartments.

French was very persistent in his questioning, but without further result. The attendant obviously did his best, but he had noticed nothing suspicious. Nor could French himself think of any scheme which could have been adopted.

French then produced his groups. The man quickly recognised Haviland and Mairs, but no one else. When at last French indicated King and Brand, he said he thought King's face was familiar, though he couldn't say whether he had travelled in the car.

Though French had not learnt all he would have liked, he realised the importance of the attendant's statement. It seemed almost certain that Haviland had been drugged, and if so, it would explain how copies of the keys were made. It would prove that the murderer of Clay was an outsider, and it would practically prove that he was looking for the process. To know all this was a great step forward. Well pleased, French returned with Carter to Southampton.

An interesting note from Superintendent Hanbury was awaiting him. The Superintendent and his staff had gone into the question of how Clay had gone from the Island to the mainland, and he enclosed his preliminary report.

Clay had called at the garage in Southampton—Hanbury was not aware of French's theory that Clay had done nothing of the sort—at about 9 a.m. There was only one service from the Island which would have enabled him to do this, the 7.30 a.m. boat from Cowes. Hanbury had therefore made enquiries from everyone aboard this boat or concerned with the run. No one had seen Clay. Moreover two separate witnesses were prepared to swear that no lame man had crossed at all.

Hanbury was evidently staggered by this discovery. It followed, he pointed out, that the watchman must have crossed in some private boat or launch, and he was now trying to find out if this was the case.

Here was another satisfactory piece of news. It did not prove the truth of French's theory that Clay had been murdered in the works, but it strongly supported it. Things were getting on nicely.

But when French looked ahead he found the prospect less pleasing. In the first place the question of the drugging of Haviland must be cleared up. The whole business of the tea car must therefore be gone into more thoroughly.

Then as to *who* might have drugged Haviland and murdered Clay, he was still at a complete loss. Tasker's questions about the rebates, and the general circumstances of the case had suggested that the Joymount staff should be considered, and of these King was the most likely man. But there was no real suspicion against either King or anyone else.

Feeling that he had a lot of work before him, French went up to bed.

PART III

Mystification

12

Joymount Makes a Fresh Start

Every time Brand allowed his thoughts to dwell on the tragedy during those first few days after it had happened—and they were seldom turned to anything else—he felt sick with horror and distress. It was not so much fear of the results to himself, though this weighed on him heavily enough in all conscience. But even if every trace that they had made had been wiped out and discovery was absolutely impossible, he would still have been horror-stricken. What he found so terrible was the realisation that with his connivance an innocent man had lost his life and had been branded as a thief without any opportunity of clearing his name.

King also seemed upset, though to nothing like the same extent. Indeed King warned Brand very seriously about the danger of allowing his feelings to become known. 'We're safe enough as it is,' he pointed out on more than one occasion, 'and we'll continue to be safe as long as no one suspects us. If we're suspected and the police begin to investigate, goodness only knows what they won't worm out.' Brand saw the sense of this, and did his utmost to keep his manner normal.

But it wasn't easy. Particularly difficult was it when the papers came in. Brand opened these with a dreadful eagerness. On Monday night and Tuesday morning there were accounts of the robbery and the disappearance of Clay, bald uninspired accounts which, without actually putting it in words, took the watchman's guilt for granted. On Tuesday the evening papers had the story of the car. The details given were the obvious ones which would strike the casual observer, and it was evident that the writer had envisaged no possibility other than accident. So far, so good.

But when he opened his paper on Wednesday morning, Brand got a dreadful shock. To the headlines which he expected was added the caption: 'ASTOUNDING DEVELOPMENT.' With a rapidly beating heart he read the paragraph.

The identity of the dead man had been discovered. Clay, the watchman who had disappeared from the Chayle Works, had bought the burnt car from a Southampton dealer, and his was the body which had been burnt.

With horror-stricken features Brand sought King. But King only smiled. 'That's all right, you thickheaded ass,' he said. 'That's according to plan. They were intended to find that out. So long as they're satisfied it was Clay who bought the bus, isn't that what we want?' And Brand, though still dreadfully worried, felt a certain relief.

That same Wednesday, August 1st, was a red-letter day in the history of the Joymount Works. For that Wednesday was the day of the board meeting, the last day which had been given King to bring his researches to a successful conclusion. Brand was present with Tasker when King came in to discuss the statement to be put before the directors.

King had prepared a long and involved report, the gist of which however was simple. He had discovered a process—he was careful not to use the definite article. That was really all that mattered. He went on to say that they were not yet in a position to work the process, because certain machinery would have to be made which was not yet even designed. But he had the essentials, and the directors might look forward with absolute confidence to a reduction of about twenty per cent in manufacturing costs.

'That sounds,' Tasker declared on reading the document, 'almost too good to be true. You're sure there's no snag? Are you quite positive you can do what you say?'

'Absolutely,' King returned. 'The doubtful part is done. There remains only some straightforward research and design. There's no question of the result.'

'If you let us down we shut the shop.'

'I'll not let you down, Tasker. Give me the order to go ahead and I'll have the process working in a month.'

Tasker sounded almost overcome. 'If you do that,' he said slowly, 'you'll not only save the works and all our jobs, but you'll make your own fortune. I'll see you get a proper return.'

'Just like you, Tasker; I knew you would. Well, Brand will confirm that neither of us have wasted much time since this day four weeks. We couldn't have done more than we did.'

At the board meeting a restrained optimism reigned. It was obvious that while the directors were impressed, they were not completely convinced. But under the circumstances their attitude was only to be expected, and King was entirely satisfied with some rather hesitating congratulations and an order to go ahead with the purchase of the new plant.

Another period of intensive work followed. First Radcliff and Endicott were got rid of on the grounds that the directors weren't standing for any further pursuit of King's elusive process. Then King threw himself into the complexities of mechanical design. New short kilns had to be made, and also the mixers for putting in the special compound which was the essence of the process, in other words, the flux. In this work Brand could not help, and King completed it single-handed in ten days. Orders for the stuff were then placed in such a way that none of the manufacturing firms could find out what they were really making. Only one article, one casting, one bolt almost, was ordered from each. At last one hundred and twenty-eight firms were engaged in making special parts to a very accurate standard. When the parts came in King would assemble them with his own fitters. With the same object of secrecy two other precautions were to be taken. First, no new buildings were to be put up. The kilns—there were only to be two—were to be erected in an existing store, temporary alternative storage accommodation being taken in Southampton. Secondly, they were going to copy the evident blind used by Chayle. The existing kiln was to be retained, and though only one-third of it would be used, it would look from outside much the same as ever.

When the machines had been designed and the last order for their parts had been despatched, Brand was surprised to find that the preliminary work was not complete. Once again King required his help for a further series of chemical experiments.

'What's it all about now?' Brand asked. 'I thought you'd got everything. Why more investigation?'

'Well,' King retorted, 'I think you might have guessed that for yourself. Suppose we make the confounded stuff, and suppose Chayle finds it out? They must do so as soon as we put it on the market, if they use the same methods we used in the first instance. What's their next step? They tumble to what has happened, and they're so sure they're right that they accuse us of stealing the blessed formula. Where would we be then?'

'They couldn't prove it.'

'Perhaps not. But if we couldn't prove where we got the thing, it would amount to a fairly close approximation. We must be guarded against that.'

'But how can you guard against it?'

'The way I intended from the very start. I must put through a complete series of experiments, showing to any expert exactly how I gradually came nearer and nearer the solution till at last I hit on it. By my own experiments, mind you. If I can prove that we'll be all right, no matter what suspicion arises.'

'And can you devise such experiments?'

'Yes, of course. I have notes for the complete series, with a couple of dead ends where I made natural mistakes and went back to the main channel—all clear as day. I have only to work through the series and post my results, so that any small oversight may be found and rectified.'

Once again Brand was filled with admiration for the efficiency of his companion. With this work completed they really would be safe, even if by some unlikely chance it became known that they had the formula.

In the meantime the Clay affair had proved a great deal

less than a nine days' wonder. Each morning newspaper comment had shrunk, till on the fifth day it had vanished altogether. There had been notices to the effect that the inquest had been opened and adjourned and that Scotland Yard had been called in. It was therefore evident that the police were still working on the case, but of what direction their activities were taking, there was no hint.

To Brand it seemed like living on the edge of a volcano. He was swayed backwards and forwards between positive terror when he considered the police activities, and relief when he thought of King's precautions. But all the time the fact of the death of Clay hung like a physical weight on his conscience.

The days, continuing slowly to pass, brought at length that of the adjourned inquest. Brand had waited for it with a horrible sinking anxiety, and even King had shown signs of the strain he was undergoing.

Both men would have given a great deal to be present. But both saw that to identify themselves in any way with the affair would be sheer madness. Each endeavoured to hide his internal qualms beneath as nonchalant an exterior as he could achieve. Each flattered himself he succeeded fairly well.

There was an account of the affair in the local evening paper. Each got a copy and locked himself away in his room to learn the worst.

And very bad both found it.

The inquest had apparently aroused enormous interest and the proceedings were very fully reported. After a well-padded opening on the unusual and dramatic nature of the events and the popular interest shown by the crowding of the hall where the enquiry was held, details of the evidence were given.

The first witness was a labourer, who when cycling to an early farm job, noticed that the white railing on the top of the road embankment approaching the bridge near Fair Oak, had been partially broken down. As the railing had been intact on the previous evening when he was returning to his home, the labourer stopped to investigate. He saw the ruins of a burnt out car lying on the bank of the river. He went down and examined it. He found that it contained human remains, also burnt. There being no possibility of life remaining, he touched nothing, but cycled to Eastleigh and reported the affair to the police.

Superintendent Crawford followed. He stated that on receiving the report of the previous witness, he had called up the police doctor, and proceeded with him to the place. He described in detail the ground, the state and position of the car and body, and the marks he had found where the car had passed off the road and through the railing. After the doctor had provisionally examined the remains, he had had them removed to Eastleigh. He had been about to proceed with an investigation into the affair, but his Chief Constable having pointed out that the case would probably be concerned with other police districts besides his own, he had agreed it would be better to get a man from Scotland Yard to co-ordinate all the enquiries. He had therefore left everything till the officer arrived, which he had done on the following morning.

The doctor corroborated the Superintendent's evidence. He described the remains with a fullness of detail which made Brand shudder. Questioned as to the blow on the back of the head, he said this might have occurred through the accident, provided the back of the head had been driven with sufficient force against some part of the car. He did not himself see how such an occurrence could have happened, but he considered this point out of his province. The injury could certainly have been due to foul play, but in his opinion it could not have been self-inflicted. The post-mortem showed that it would have been sufficient to cause death.

Herbert Dexter, the motor engineer, was then called. He gave technical details as to the damage done to the car, and said he considered it must have been going about twenty-five miles an hour when it went down the bank. The coroner questioned him on the smashing of the carburettor and the setting fire to the petrol, and the witness said that in his opinion the crash down the embankment would not have accounted for either.

Wilfred Boothby, dentist, Cowes, stated that he had examined the mouth of the deceased, and that he had identified dental work which he had done. The man was John Clay, an employee of Messrs Haviland & Mairs, of Chayle.

Haviland was the next witness. He described Clay's appearance and gave his history while with the firm. In particular he told of the motor accident in which the deceased had been involved, and the injuries he had received therefrom, and his subsequent appointment as night watchman. He gave Clay a good character, saying he had believed him thoroughly honest and reliable, and declaring that he would be greatly surprised to know that he had been guilty of stealing the firm's money.

Mairs gave details of the disappearance of the money. He said he had obtained it from the Cowes branch of the London and Southern Bank, told of the keys of the safe and how they were kept, and detailed the steps he had taken in acquainting the police of the loss.

Arnold Fisher, garage proprietor, recounted the purchase of the car which was afterwards found burnt, and described the purchaser. He explained that while the purchaser resembled the description of Clay, he had been unable definitely to identify him. He had paid the notes he had received for the purchase into the Southampton Branch of Lloyds Bank.

Two bank officials were called, one from the bank in Cowes to give the numbers of the notes paid to the Chayle works, and the other from Lloyds Bank in Southampton, to say that he had received certain of these notes from Mr Fisher.

The last witness was Chief-Inspector French of New Scotland Yard. Asked by the coroner to tell them in his own words what he could of the affair, he said he had been sent to make an investigation into the case because for various reasons the local authorities had suspected foul play. He had begun with the burnt car, and from inspection he had doubted that the injury to the carburettor had been cause by the crash. He then told of his finding of the stone, and said that in his opinion this proved that the 'accident' was a plant which had been staged for some purpose which might be suspected, but which he regretted could not so far be proved. He had then considered the injuries received by the deceased, and it had seemed to him that as the man Clay had been thrown forward when the wreck took place and had been found lying forward, the injury to the back of his head could not have been caused by the crash. As the doctor was of opinion that this injury on the back of the head would have killed Clay, he, French, had come to the conclusion that the deceased had been murdered before being put in the car, and that the 'accident' was intended simply to cover up the murder. He was not, however, in a position to charge anyone with the murder.

This statement had caused a considerable sensation, though rumours of the truth had not been wanting. French was questioned on a number of other points, but he was unable to give any further material information. When French had finished, the coroner had addressed the jury, his remarks being given verbatim. When he had summarised the evidence, he went on to deliver himself of a theory to account for the facts. 'We do not know,' he said, 'just what took place. Whether the deceased man, Clay, made the key and robbed the safe at Chayle has not been proved. Still less, however, has it been shown that anyone else could have done so. If Clay were murdered, it follows that some other person or persons are involved, and it might well be that this other person or persons were guilty of the theft also. Or it might be that the other person or persons discovered what Clay had done, stole the money from him, and committed the murder to hide their crime. These matters, however, do not concern you,' and he went on to tell the jury that their business was simply to state in their opinion the identity of the dead man and the cause of his death, adding, if they thought they could do so conscientiously, a clause saying whether they considered anyone to blame for the death, and if so, whom. The jury, after a short deliberation, returned the expected verdict of wilful murder against some person or persons unknown.

With terrible distinctness Brand saw that this verdict removed once and for all any chance of his and King's action being considered an accident, if knowledge of it should reach the police. The very fact that they had not come forward with a statement would damn them utterly.

If it became known that they had gone to the works and stolen the secret, nothing could save them from the gallows.

On the other hand, the whole proceedings were rather a relief inasmuch as they appeared to indicate that the knowledge of the authorities was still very limited. They seemed to imagine that Clay had bought the car from Fisher, and if this really were so, he and King were surely pretty safe. Of course, Brand had heard that the police didn't always tell everything they knew. But the acid test was that no enquiries had been made at Joymount, and until such began, he believed he need not worry overmuch.

Then a fresh fear attacked Brand, a fear which for some time had been lurking in the background of his mind, but which up till now had been overshadowed by the greater dread of the inquest.

It was due to a comparatively insignificant cause—merely that King was looking increasingly worried. Each day recently he had seemed to grow more and more anxious. He would say nothing, but Brand found it impossible to avoid the conclusion that some hitch had occurred in the programme.

A few days after the inquest he once again tackled King on the subject. King looked at him queerly, then said: 'Come for a walk afterwards. I'll tell you then.'

All that afternoon Brand worked in a state of nerves which made him anything but a desirable chief for his clerks. That something had gone wrong was now obvious.

But when they went for their walk Brand was less impressed by the difficulty than King seemed to think he should be. 'What is it?' Brand had asked urgently. 'What has gone wrong?'

'Nothing has *gone* wrong,' King answered. 'It's to prevent something going wrong that I've been anxious.'

'Tell me.'

'Well, let's try and reconstruct what must have happened. When the detectives went to Chayle, we may take it Haviland and Mairs told them of the process. Would they not then have tumbled to the real motive at the back of things? To me it seems unquestionable.'

'But what if they did?' Brand queried. Wasn't this the very contingency against which King had provided by this recent series of experiments? 'Aren't we safely out of it?'

'Don't go too quickly. If their attention were directed to the process and they assumed it was stolen, their first question would be, Who would profit by the theft? They would think of Joymount as the only firm in the neighbourhood which would do so. Remember it would be no use to our friends on the Medina, because the process only works with cements of the *ciment fondu* type, which they don't make.'

Brand nodded and King continued.

'Well, if they thought of Joymount, they'd think of me: the technical member of the firm. And if they thought I had wanted help, they'd think of you. So that, you see, Brand, we mustn't risk real suspicion.'

'But how can we avoid it?'

'Well, there's one way and only one. If we don't sell our stuff at a cut price or grant rebates we're all right. Only those who benefit from the theft will be suspected.'

'But we'd benefit from decreased costs in any case.'

'No doubt, but that would be our secret. Scotland Yard wouldn't know it. If we granted rebates they would.'

Brand hesitated. 'But,' he said slowly, 'would the

directors stand for that? Remember they're expecting to cut prices and quadruple our turnover.'

'Ah,' said King, 'now you're talking. At last we've got to what I really wanted to discuss with you. Tasker could fix the board. We've got to tell Tasker what's happened.'

This was an exceedingly unpleasant idea. Brand at once demurred to it. They couldn't tell either Tasker or anyone else: it would be too dangerous. Not that he doubted Tasker. But there it was: a secret shared by three persons was no longer a secret. Besides, were they sure that even Tasker would believe that the death of Clay had been an accident? And if he didn't, would he consent to become an accessory after the fact?

'I know that's a point,' King admitted, 'but it seems to me we've got to risk it. Either we undercut Chayle, in which case we bring Scotland Yard down on us; or we don't, in which case we put ourselves in Tasker's hands. There, it seems to me, is the choice. Which would you prefer? Of course there's another: that we throw up the sponge and go out of business.'

For an hour they argued. Finally Brand had to admit that his companion was right. If Tasker were not told, he and the board would insist on a cut price. If he were, he could wangle the board. Of the two evils, the telling of Tasker was the lesser.

'Good!' said King when this conclusion was reached. 'Will you fix up with Tasker for a pow-wow?'

Brand agreed, and with heavy heart and a foreboding of ill, he left King and returned to the boarding-house.

13

Joymount is Again Perturbed

Next morning, when the correspondence had been dealt with, Brand approached Tasker.

'King wants a discussion about this new process,' he said. 'We've got something rather dreadful to tell you. You'll have to prepare yourself for a shock, Tasker.'

'What is it?' Tasker grunted, as he continued running his eye over a letter.

'I can't tell you without King. But it's horribly serious. You'll be upset.'

Tasker laid down his paper and looked fixedly at the younger man. 'I can see you're upset,' he said quietly. 'If it's important there's no time like the present. Get him in now.'

After ensuring that they could not be overheard, King told the whole story. He began by reminding Tasker how he, Tasker, had selected him to investigate the falling sales of the Joymount Company, and how he had discovered the cause. He painted a moving picture of the fate of the concern and of each one of themselves if something were not done to avert the threatening disaster. He showed that the discovery of the Chayle process would not only be the only hope for Joymount, but, and on this he laid great stress, the discovery need not injure Chayle. 'As you know as well, and perhaps better than we do,' he declared, 'we were not out to injure Chayle, but only to prevent Chayle injuring us.'

Tasker, who had by this time become somewhat grim, replied by a nod, and King went on to describe his decision to search the Chayle works, his enlistment of Brand's aid, their first scouting visit, the discovery that the keys would be necessary, his trick to get the impressions, and the second visit to Chayle with its ghastly result. Then he told of the efforts he had made to escape from the appalling situation in which they were placed, how he decided that only the disappearance of the watchman would meet the case, and how a motive for that disappearance must be provided. He described his search of the offices, his finding of the money and his conclusion that here was the very thing for his purpose. He made it clear that he knew that the dead man was alone in the world, and that any stain that might be put on his name would not affect any living person.

Then he went on to recount his despair at having, after the immense price which they were going to have to pay, to admit failure—to admit that the price would be paid for nothing. He told of the struggle he had to prevent himself hurrying away from that dreadful building, then his reminding himself that now he had an opportunity which would never recur, and that if he didn't take advantage of it, Joymount and himself and his friends, were down and out. In the end he had conquered his panic and had opened the two safes. In Haviland's he saw what he was in search of. With a supreme effort he had forced himself to sit down and copy the precious document word for word.

Finally he told of the getting of the body away; of the hiding it in Brand's garage for the night; of his dressing up in Clay's clothes, powdering his face, putting on a limp and speaking in a high pitched voice when he purchased the car; of his driving it about through that livelong day from place to place, till in the late afternoon he thought it safe to hide it in an old sand pit; of the staging of the accident, and lastly of the series of experiments he had carried out to explain how he had reached the process, should such explanation ever become necessary.

As the story gradually unfolded, strong emotion began to show beneath Tasker's iron control. He seemed utterly appalled. For a while he could scarcely speak coherently. Then he conquered his feelings and grimly and with terrible clarity he pointed out that if the case went to trial, no jury on earth would doubt that murder had been done. The others unhappily agreed, and Tasker went on to add that he was now himself definitely an accessory after the fact, but that he would have to carry this risk, for he could not give King and Brand away. He accepted their story, and quite apart from his own fate and that of Joymount, he could not deliberately expose his two friends to the risk of being hanged for a murder which he honestly believed they had not committed.

The younger men were a little overwhelmed by the way in which their chief accepted responsibility for their actions, but Tasker swept their appreciation aside without ceremony. Shrewd man of business that he was, he quickly saw King's point about the cutting of prices.

'We'll carry on at our present figure,' he said with instant decision. 'We'll not sell so much cement, but we'll get a fine profit on what we do sell.'

'That's what I had hoped you'd do, Tasker,' King returned. 'But can you get that through the board without giving away the whole story?'

'Oh lord, yes,' said Tasker contemptuously. 'Anyone could get anything through the board. Bramwell won't be there, and nobody else knows anything about cement, or, one would think, anything else. When will you be ready to get going?'

'In about a fortnight.'

'Well, there's nothing more that we can do about it, except to sit tight and say nothing.'

With these sentiments the others were in the fullest agreement and the discussion presently terminated.

In due course the board meeting took place, and the directors did as Tasker had foretold and agreed that the selling price of their product should remain unaltered. They extended to King their warmest congratulations, and at Tasker's suggestion they decided he was to get five per cent of the profits of the process, in addition to a substantial increase of salary.

Tasker made a very big point of the necessity for absolute secrecy if their process was not to be copied by other firms. This, he pointed out, would see the end of their profits. He was so emphatic that the directors seemed really impressed.

In due course the parts of the new machines were supplied and were assembled by King. Within about six weeks of receiving the authority to proceed, he had the process in operation.

The results delighted all concerned. When the costs were made up secretly by Brand he found that the change was going to save even more than King had estimated. A veiled delight reigned at Joymount. The works were saved!

Everybody's job was saved, and soon there would be more money for all! The start of the process seemed indeed to usher in a happier period, particularly to the three principal officers of the works. No manifestations were made by the police. Brand's doubts and fears began slowly to subside, and thoughts of arrest and what might follow arrest faded gradually from his mind. It looked as if the authorities were either satisfied that the law had been broken only by the dead man, or that their wider enquiries had drawn blank. Brand began to feel some assurance that he would hear no more of this appalling episode in his life.

Then a new development arose which gave both him and his two fellow conspirators very furiously to think.

One morning early in November Brand was summoned to Tasker's office. With him he found Haviland and Mairs.

Brand knew the Chayle partners slightly, having met them at business conventions, though neither had been before at Joymount, nor had he or Tasker been—officially—at Chayle. They greeted him courteously.

'Our friends have come to discuss a matter of business with us,' Tasker explained, 'and as it appears that we won't be able to keep long away from figures, I thought I'd better ask you to come in at once.'

Brand murmured that he was glad to meet the visitors. Conversation was general for a few moments, and then Haviland got down to it.

'In these days of cut-throat competition,' he began, 'we have to watch very carefully what our rivals are doing. I suppose that applies to you too?'

Tasker told him it most certainly did.

'We have developed a systematic watch on the market,' went on Haviland in his slow ponderous way. 'We have to, and I expect you do it too.' Again he paused, but Tasker merely nodding, he continued. 'Now part of our routine is to analyse at frequent intervals the cement our friends—and rivals—put out. We've been doing it for three or four years.'

'It's a practice I much admire,' Tasker said smoothly, 'though I'm afraid we don't go into it so closely ourselves. Price changes, and—er—rebates is what interests us most.'

Haviland agreed. 'We don't overlook that side of it either, but we find the chemical analysis also valuable. Now we analyse samples of *all* cement that comes on the market, and we therefore analysed yours among the rest. No objection, I hope?'

Tasker smiled. 'Of course not,' he declared. 'How could there be?'

'We didn't of course intend anything unfriendly: it was only in the way of business. But in the case of your stuff, Samson, that's our expert, made an interesting report. He found that the cement contained a higher proportion of certain minerals than usual, and that it reacted in certain definite ways to other tests. I may say he found that your cement was a cement well known to us, and which in point of fact we have been making for a considerable time.'

'That's very remarkable,' Tasker returned in an interested voice. 'There's no secret about this cement that we're putting out. We've adopted a slightly different process, invented by our chemist, King. You tell me you've something of the same kind?'

'We have been turning out that identical stuff for nearly three years.'

'Very remarkable indeed. Of course it's a common thing in a way. History tells us that again and again inventions have been brought out by several people simultaneously.

There seems to come a period in the world's history when things get ripe for a new product, and then it appears—in different places.'

Haviland hesitated for an appreciable interval. 'That,' he said drily, 'is indeed very true. But that,' he added with what Brand thought was a horribly sinister emphasis, 'is not the only way in which such a phenomenon can be explained.' He paused, then before Tasker could speak, went on. 'But we didn't come here to occupy your time in discussing causes. We should be satisfied to leave causes alone. What we wanted to discuss was something more pleasant. We wondered whether this move of yours mightn't lead to—well, to something in the nature of an agreement between us?'

During all this preamble Brand's heart had been sinking lower and lower. So far as he could see, there was only one thing that it could mean. In some utterly unforeseen and incredible way their actions at Chayle had become known. And now here were the partners come to exact their vengeance.

This last remark of Haviland's however gave the conversation an entirely unexpected twist. Brand could have sworn that their visitor was leading up to something very different. It puzzled him, and therefore made him the more uneasy. Could it be, he wondered, that the Chayle partners only suspected what had happened, and that this suggestion of an agreement was simply some ingenious kind of trap to give them their proof?

These ideas shot through Brand's mind, but he could not consider them in detail. Tasker was speaking.

'That's a very interesting proposal,' he was saying, 'and one we should be glad to follow up. At the same time I don't know that I exactly follow. What, roughly speaking, was the nature of the agreement you had in mind?'

'Well,' Haviland returned, 'here we are, both of us, manufacturing this new product at a good profit. Now this is a situation in which we could easily cut each other's throat. It would seem,' he smiled heavily, 'a pity to do so. It appeared to us a case where union would be strength.'

'You mean that we shouldn't attempt to undersell one another?'

'That among other things.'

Tasker got up and went to a cupboard. He took out a box of cigars and handed them round. 'As this promises to be a longer session than I had anticipated, we may as well be comfortable,' he explained, and returning he brought out whisky and soda and four glasses.

'This is very nice of you,' Haviland remarked, and Mairs also murmured appreciatively.

For a few moments the conversation strayed from the point at issue, then Tasker brought it back.

'Speaking entirely offhand,' he said, 'I imagine we should be very pleased to agree with you that neither of us should undersell the other. As a matter of fact, as you know, we are not underselling you at present.' He smiled disarmingly as he added, 'But you are underselling us.'

'We are,' Haviland admitted readily, 'but that would be a matter of arrangement. If we could see eye to eye about the main business, details of that kind would settle themselves.'

'I think,' said Tasker cautiously, 'that I may say that we should be prepared to consider very carefully any proposals that you might make us.' He looked at Brand, who nodded his agreement.

'Of course,' Haviland went on, 'as long as our joint works are producing only a small proportion of the total rapid-hardening cement made in this country, the matter is not so serious. But if either of us increased the output by issuing licences to other firms to manufacture on our process, that might make a considerable difference to the other one.'

'I follow,' said Tasker, nodding. 'You think that we should agree not to issue licences or buy up works or extend our own works other than by mutual agreement?'

'That might be part of it, yes,' Haviland agreed. 'But there's an even more important aspect of the subject, and that is the present profits we are both making. Now we know our profits, and seeing that we are both working the same process, we can estimate yours.'

'But I don't think we know that we are both working the same process,' Tasker countered. 'You say that our new product is the same as yours. Well, you have made tests, and if you say so, I am willing to grant it—I don't known personally. But I don't know how you can say our processes are the same. There are many roads to Rome.'

'It would seem from what our engineer, Samson, tells us that the processes must be the same. However let that pass for the moment. If you don't think I know what your profits are, let me say, you are making certain profits.'

Tasker smiled. 'I'm glad to say that at least is correct.'

'Quite. And you said, I think, that your chemist, Mr King, had got your process going quite recently?'

Tasker hesitated momentarily. 'I don't think I said so, but it's quite true. He's been working at it for a long time, but it's only comparatively recently that we've been manufacturing on any scale.'

'Quite. That was my information. Now we've been talking

a good deal about this affair, but it's only now we are coming to the real issue. We have, as it were, been chipping at the cocoanut, but have only now penetrated to the milk. You have been working it for a short time, whereas we have been putting out the stuff for over three years.'

Tasker simulated a mild mystification. 'Yes?' he said. 'So I gathered from you. But I don't know that I see just where that leads us.'

'I probably haven't made myself clear,' Haviland said politely. 'On account of this matter of dates, we consider that we were the originators of the process. That we have in fact a priority claim on it.'

'But, of course,' Tasker agreed. 'We don't dispute it for a moment. As a matter of fact I don't mind admitting that it was the fact that you were underselling us that started King to work.'

'Quite. And we have therefore a claim on the process.'

'A theoretical claim for priority, yes. But only theoretical. We did not understand that you had patented your process?'

'Nor have we. But we think that scarcely relevant. In fact, Mr Tasker, we don't mean a mere admission of our priority. We think it carries a royalty.'

'I'm afraid,' Tasker was more polite than ever, 'that this time it's I who have not made myself clear. Our engineer reached the process—our process, I mean—by means of a series of independent experiments. I think that can be demonstrated.'

'My dear sir!' Haviland was overwhelmed. 'Please don't imagine that I doubted it. I'm satisfied he could show us every step in the evolution of the affair from nebulosity to the completed process. What I doubt is that it affects the question. I base our claim on mere priority.'

'But you surely don't take up the position that where two persons independently make an unpatented invention, the second in point of time is liable to pay the first a royalty?'

'I'm afraid I haven't really considered any abstract cases at all—simply this concrete one—that's rather neat, I think,' Haviland laughed heavily—'this *concrete* one of our own cement. In this case we really do think we're entitled to a royalty on your profits from the process.'

Tasker went through the form of considering the statement. 'I'll admit,' he said with a smile, 'that this is a totally unexpected point of view. I don't know that I've ever heard of such a claim being advanced. But perhaps we are talking about different things. I was taking "royalty" to mean something substantial. You doubtless mean a nominal sum as an admission that you were first in the field?'

'Not entirely nominal, I'm afraid. Not to waste your time by beating about the bush, I may say at once that we think the circumstances entitle us to seventy-five per cent of the extra profits made by the process.'

Tasker smiled again, but Brand saw that behind the smile his eyes were hard and cold. 'You're not serious, Mr Haviland,' he said easily. 'As I said, a trifling admission that you were first in the field, yes. But what you suggest is equivalent to our working the process on licence from you; and pretty stiff terms at that.'

'Well, that is exactly the suggestion. You don't think it reasonable?'

'Oh now, you don't really expect me to treat it seriously. An agreement on the matters you mentioned earlier—yes, we'd be delighted. But a royalty of seventy-five per cent!' Tasker laughed with evident amusement.

'Well,' said Haviland, 'I'm sorry you don't see eye to eye with us there. In fact we thought the terms were moderate. Let us however leave the question over and you perhaps will think of terms that you would suggest for an agreement. I'm glad at least that you think an agreement is desirable.'

'I agree to that,' Tasker answered. 'Of course you realise that our positions are a bit different. You are your own master and can do what you like: I have a board of directors behind me. However I can assure you that we on this side will give the matter very careful consideration. I don't know,' he added pleasantly, 'that I'm including in that a seventy-five per cent royalty, you know.'

'We'll exclude nothing,' Haviland rejoined smiling. 'We'll enter our conference with untied hands, free to consider anything. Isn't that the best international practice? Come, Mairs, we mustn't keep these good people for the whole day.'

He turned it off with a joke, but his eyes also were unsmiling.

Courteous to the last, Tasker and Brand saw them to their launch, and waved their arms as is the manner of friends. But Tasker's face was grim and set as they returned towards the offices.

'We're for it, Brand,' he said shortly. 'They know!'

14

An Alliance with the Enemy

As Brand watched the receding launch, he seemed to see disappearing with it his own happiness, his security, and his hopes for the future. For of course Tasker was right. Instead of the whole hideous affair of the Chayle Works being over, it looked as if it was just really beginning.

And there was no knowing to what this new development might lead. They were going to be blackmailed, but was that all they faced? Did it only mean that their profits would be reduced? Or could Haviland supply evidence which would lead to a conviction for murder?

Brand's heart sank lower than it had done at any time since the ghastly affair began. Oh how he wished he had never gone into it with King! What would he not give if he could wake up and find it was only a nightmare! How joyfully he would accept the loss of his job and capital, if only he could be cleared of this dreadful shadow which was hanging over him!

He was steadied by Tasker's matter-of-fact voice. 'We've got to do a bit of thinking over this, Brand,' the managing director declared. 'If we're not careful those chaps will give us trouble.'

Brand pulled himself together. 'Let's go back to your room and get King,' he suggested.

'No,' Tasker returned, 'that's just what we mustn't do. If we have a conference the moment they go, it'll show there's something up. No, Brand; you go back to your office as if nothing had happened, and don't see King. But bring him along to my house after dinner.'

This was obvious wisdom and Brand acted on it. But when he reached his room he found he couldn't work. He had been doing a job with one of the clerks and he simply couldn't concentrate on it. He had to make an excuse and get rid of the man.

He saw King at the lunch hour, but merely said that something serious had happened and that they were to go up to Tasker's in the evening to discuss it. It was not till they were on the way that he told the full story.

King was a good deal upset. He had looked upon his scheme as a complete success, and this suggestion of failure at its very root was a blow not only to his peace of mind but to his self-esteem.

The managing director was waiting for them in his library. Brand at once felt comforted by his manner, which seemed unimpressed and normal.

'Cold night,' Tasker began. 'You're just in time for coffee.'

They settled themselves round the fire, Brand and King with cigarettes and Tasker with his pipe. Tasker began to talk about football, and it was not till the maid had brought the coffee and withdrawn, that he turned to business.

'Very awkward this affair,' he said to King. 'I suppose Brand has told you about it?'

'He has,' King returned drily. 'It seems to me worse than very awkward.'

'We don't know how bad it is,' Tasker declared. 'We don't know how much these people have guessed and how much they can prove.'

'You mean,' King asked, 'that they may be bluffing?'

Tasker nodded. 'That's our first question at all events.'

'Rather risky, a bluff of that kind,' Brand said doubtfully.

'You think so?' Tasker shook his head. 'What could we do?'

'Nothing, of course, as things are. But suppose we hadn't been to Chayle, we could take them to court for defamation of character.'

'No,' said Tasker; 'we couldn't. During that interview they didn't say a single word that was actionable.'

King nodded. 'That's true. There appears to have been a suggestion that if we thought the cap fitted us we ought to put it on, but from what Brand tells me, they never said it fitted.'

'What they're doing is blackmail,' Brand pointed out. 'Would they risk that if they weren't sure of their ground?'

'I think so,' Tasker answered, 'if they believed they were right.'

'Even if they couldn't prove it?'

'Yes, I think so.'

'I'm inclined to agree,' King observed. 'Scotland Yard has been into this thing. Now I can scarcely believe that Haviland and Mairs should have found out something Scotland Yard missed. But if the Yard had got anything, they would have been here to see Brand and myself. They haven't come. Therefore it looks to me as if nothing was really known.'

190

Tasker made a gesture of negation. 'I doubt if you can reason that way. It seems to me that Chayle might very well know the truth, and yet wish to keep it from the police.'

'I don't follow,' interposed Brand.

'Look at it this way.' Tasker sat forward and demonstrated with his hands. 'They have a secret process of which the existence is not generally known, and from which they're making huge profits. Very well, we get hold of it. Now the thing of all others that Chayle will want will be to prevent the knowledge of it from spreading.'

'You mean,' King returned, 'that if its existence were known, everyone would be out to get hold of it.'

'Yes. Every chemist would be working on it and sooner or later someone would get it.'

'That's right. But if Scotland Yard discovers this affair, the existence of the secret becomes known over the whole world.'

'Quite. Therefore they won't want Scotland Yard to discover it.'

Brand moved uneasily. 'But do you really mean to suggest that they would keep back evidence from the police? If the thing came out afterwards they would then be accessories after the fact.'

'Ah,' said Tasker, 'now you're talking, Brand. That's what we must consider. Would they take a risk like that?'

'There mightn't be any risk,' King pointed out. 'They might, for example, admit they'd had the clue for some time, but say that its significance had only just then occurred to them.'

'I suppose that would be possible with certain clues.'

'It mightn't be believed, but it couldn't be disproved.'

191

There was a short silence, then King made a sudden movement. 'The more I think of it,' he said, 'the more convinced I feel that they have no proof. They're bluffing to get us to make the first move. I suggest we sit tight and see what happens.'

Tasker turned to Brand. 'What do you say to that?' he asked.

'I suppose it's right enough,' Brand admitted doubtfully. 'What do you think yourself, Tasker?'

'I'd rather have your opinions,' Tasker returned, 'as you're principally concerned. If there's trouble it will be you two that are for it, not me.'

'How do you make that out, Tasker?' Brand queried. 'It seems to me we're all in it together.'

Tasker shrugged slightly. 'I'm with you, heart and soul,' he declared, 'in what we do now, and no action of mine will let either of you down, so far as I can help it. But you must realise that if the thing were to come out, there'd be no use in my suffering as well as you.'

'But you couldn't help it.'

Tasker smiled. 'Of course I could help it. Hasn't King given me a written statement that the discovery of the process is his own work, resulting from his own experiments and from nothing else. No. I know nothing of any visit to Chayle. But,' he made a gesture as King would have spoken, 'don't let's consider a remote contingency like that. You both think that we should call their bluff?'

'Yes,' said King, ignoring his chief's somewhat sinister suggestion. 'It seems to me that if we don't fall for what they've said, they'll be bound to show their hand.'

'Right. You agree, Brand?'

Brand agreed, though again doubtfully.

'Well, I agree too. I'm glad to have that settled. Have a nightcap before you go.'

Four days later Tasker wrote a non-committal note to Haviland, saying that he had now had an opportunity of considering the points raised at their recent interview, and he, Tasker, felt sure they could complete a pact of non-aggression and co-operation on the lines suggested, as he considered this would be just as much in the interests of Joymount as of Chayle. Nor did he think his directors would have any objection to granting a purely formal recognition of Chayle's priority in the discovery. He concluded by declaring Joymount was ready to discuss the matter further at Chayle's convenience.

'That should do the trick,' said King when Tasker had called him and Brand into his office to approve the letter. 'They're bound now either to drop it or to show their hand.'

Brand agreed, though he could not visualise any prospect of the Chayle people dropping the affair.

This opinion was shortly justified. Haviland, after also waiting four days, replied that he was glad to have Tasker's note and to find that the Chayle proposals met with his general approval. Doubtless, he added, the financial suggestions would eventually also commend themselves to the Joymount authorities. He thought that a little further discussion might be useful, and as it was hard to find time in a busy day for matters outside the ordinary routine, he suggested that Tasker and his friends should come to Chayle at nine o'clock on the following Tuesday evening.

The three Joymount men thought this letter looked badly. There was a restraint about it which seemed to indicate a disturbing confidence on Haviland's part. Moreover the obvious desire for secrecy was ominous. When the trio got into Brand's launch for their trip to the Island on the Tuesday evening, each was feeling less easy in his mind than he would have admitted.

Whether by accident or design the Chayle harbour was free from shipping when they arrived. Mairs was waiting for them on the wharf, and opening the wicket gate with his key, he led them to the conference room. Haviland and Samson were there. None of the Joymount party had met Samson, and mutual introductions took place.

Haviland was a good host. He quietly saw that his guests were disposed in comfortable chairs and supplied with drinks and cigars. For a few moments the conversation remained on general topics, then Haviland turned to business.

'I didn't say it in my letter in so many words,' he began, 'but we all thought that our discussions should be kept as private as possible. Even our watchman doesn't know you're here.'

Tasker briefly approved this policy and Haviland went on. 'I suppose we may take up our discussion where we stopped at our last meeting. You were to consider generally the question of an agreement between us. From your letter I understand you have done so?'

'The three of us present have considered it together,' Tasker agreed, 'but I have not mentioned it to my board. I should prefer only to put before them cut and dried proposals.'

'Quite so,' Haviland said. 'And your opinion on the proposals?'

'Generally speaking,' Tasker answered, 'we are in favour of an agreement, but the proposals are scarcely detailed enough for us to reply fully.'

Haviland nodded. 'It was to arrive at detailed proposals that I thought we should meet. May I ask if you have thought of anything concrete that you would like to incorporate?'

'I think,' said Tasker, 'that seeing that this matter is your suggestion, your proposals have probably been more carefully thought out than ours. I suggest that we take yours first. Personally I imagine they will cover the ground.'

Haviland shrugged. 'As you like. I've got here some tentative clauses which we put forward as a basis of discussion.' He took some sheets from a drawer and handed them round.

It was not without trepidation that the Joymount trio glanced over the sheets. There were seven short clauses, not legally phrased, but mere abbreviated notes of what the future document might contain. As the visitors read them they saw that the crisis was upon them.

The first five were innocuous, indeed valuable. They laid down, roughly speaking, that the existence and the nature of the process being used by both firms was a secret, and must be kept so; that the prices charged by both were to be similar and agreed between them, as also were to be any rebates or allowances made; that the work generally was to be carried on in a spirit of agreement and conciliation; that neither firm was to obtain advantage at the expense of the other; and that each was to keep the other advised of its various contracts. If necessary, the stock of either was to be used to assist the other to fulfil rush orders. These five clauses indeed represented a working agreement of a valuable nature.

None of the Joymount men, however, dwelt on these clauses. Their troubled gaze leaped to Nos. 6 and 7.

These were the shortest, the most direct, and the most devastating. They read:

6. Joymount to agree that the new process is the absolute property of Chayle.
7. Joymount to work the process under licence from Chayle, and to pay Chayle 75 per cent of all profits received therefrom.

Brand was horrified. This was as bad as anything he had foreseen. Chayle would scarcely have made such claims unless they knew exactly what had happened. He glanced at Tasker with an anxiety which he tried hard to hide.

Tasker, he thought, was playing his part well. He glanced down the items, and when he reached Nos. 6 and 7, he raised his eyebrows, whistled faintly, and gave a little smile. It was an admirable suggestion of the good-humoured toleration of an obsession.

'This is like certain living creatures,' he said pleasantly; 'it's sting is in its tail. Well,' he looked at Brand and King, 'I think we can say at once that the first five clauses are excellent and certainly form a basis of discussion. In fact, I don't at first glance see that they could be improved. But the last two clauses'—he broke off and laughed easily—'I don't suppose, Haviland, that you put those forward seriously?'

'I assure you, Tasker, that we are most serious about them.' He in his turn glanced at his associates. 'You agree, Mairs? And you, Samson?'

Mairs and Samson agreed fully. Mairs, indeed, thought that Clauses 6 and 7 represented the real kernel of the agreement. Samson nodded his approval.

'But,' Tasker went on in the same slightly contemptuous way, 'you can't ask us to agree that the admitted fact that you found the thing out first nullifies all our work on similar lines.'

'My dear Tasker,' Haviland replied with a certain earnestness, 'I suggest that we all understand each other perfectly. There is no need to put unpleasant facts into words. But I do ask you to believe that we know just where we stand in this matter.'

Tasker shrugged. 'Very well. You know where you stand. But we don't. I suggest that if you are really serious you must say exactly upon what grounds you make—well, what seems to us such a ridiculous demand.'

Haviland still spoke earnestly. 'We would rather not,' he said. 'Very decidedly, we would rather not. Such a statement would be unpleasant, and we don't wish to have an unpleasant interview.' For a moment he paused, then went on again. 'I may perhaps say two things. First I ask you to believe that we're not jumping to conclusions. We *know*. Second, we do think, and I'm sure in your heart of hearts you agree with us, we do think that our request for seventy-five per cent of your extra profits is moderate.'

Tasker shrugged. 'I entirely sympathise with your desire for a pleasant interview,' he declared. 'At the same time,' he smiled, 'seventy-five per cent of our profits would be worth one unpleasant interview. I'm afraid before we can consider your suggestion, we must know quite directly your reasons for making it.'

This, Brand thought, was the stuff at last. He expressed his approval, as did also King.

Haviland on his part, seemed undecided as to what he should do, and looked to his two henchmen for counsel.

197

Mairs also hesitated, but Samson said: 'Go on. You better tell them.'

'Well,' Haviland said with a shrug, 'as you will. I'm sorry, and I say again that I don't wish to be unpleasant or to make our association irksome. We know, in a word, what happened to Clay, and we know where your discovery of the process came from. As to *how* we know it, you can't expect us to tell that. If you think for a moment, you'll see that would be unreasonable.'

'I can't profess immense surprise,' Tasker said in unmoved tones. 'We three guessed that you might possibly suspect something of the kind, because of course what you mean to suggest is that we murdered Clay and stole your secret? That's it, I suppose?'

'That's it,' Haviland answered with all the directness for which Tasker had asked.

'I wondered if it was that coming across tonight,' Tasker went on smoothly. 'Our answer is that if you suspect such a thing, as good citizens you must go to the police with your suspicions. We're not asking you to shield us. We're quite ready to answer to the authorities for our conduct.' He smiled. 'It seems to me, Haviland, that it's you people that are in the difficulty, not us.'

Haviland made a little gesture of depreciation. 'That, as you know very well, is perfectly true. We don't want to go to the police, and you know why. If we go to the police, the existence of the process comes out. You see, I'm being perfectly open with you. Now, if its existence is known, chemists everywhere would be on to it. If we all sit tight and work amicably on the basis we suggest, we all remain happy and comfortable and we all make a good profit. We make more than you, I admit, but then we're entitled to more.'

Tasker evidently decided the time had come to play his trump card. 'That's all very well, Haviland,' he said, 'but there's surely one thing you've overlooked. Suppose, for argument's sake, we were guilty of this affair—which, incidentally, I categorically deny—and suppose you suppress the evidence you say you have against us, you then become accessories after the fact. How do you get over that?'

'Very simply. The evidence against you we held for a considerable time before we saw its significance. If in the future we found it convenient to go to the police, we would say that this significance had only just then struck us. But don't'—he made a gesture of dismissal—'let us continue this unprofitable discussion. I suggest that we leave the thing alone for a day or two. In the meantime, both of us will think it over, and then we can have another meeting. Perhaps by that time you would be in a position to make some alternative proposal? I assure you we are entirely ready to agree to any reasonable terms.'

King moved suddenly. 'There's just one question I should like to ask, Tasker. Suppose that we went mad and agreed to these gentlemen's terms, what guarantee have we that the matter would really be dropped? There are six of us present here. Well, we're all right. None of us is going to say anything. But is this alleged proof known to any other persons, and if so, how do we know that they would be equally accommodating?'

Haviland waved his hand. 'There would be no fear of anything of that kind,' he assured them. 'No one knows what has happened except the six of us here present. You can understand that such knowledge would be—nearly—as dangerous to us as to you.'

They had a little further talk, then Tasker said it was getting late. He agreed they couldn't finish their business that night, and he proposed another meeting in a week. They readily agreed. At the Joymount Works? In the evening? They agreed also. With a cold cordiality, the Chaylites saw their victims to their launch.

15

Chayle Puts on the Screw

It was a silent party which embarked on Brand's launch and chugged across Cowes Roads and up Southampton Water to Hamble. Though none would admit it, the disappointment each felt was tinged with real fear. Even if it didn't seem likely that the Chayle men would lodge information against them, they felt their security was gone. No one could tell what might eventuate from such a situation.

'Haviland managed that well,' said King at last. 'We don't yet know for sure whether they're not bluffing. Of course, Haviland's position about that is unassailable. They couldn't tell us how they knew lest we should find some way to get round their proof.'

'I think,' Tasker answered, 'we must assume they do know something. At all events there was one part of Haviland's advice which we must admit was good; that we think over the affair. Let's do so and meet again at my house on Friday evening.'

'Yes, that's right,' said King. 'Same time?'

'Same time.'

On Friday night it would have interested a student of human nature to observe how the characters of the three men had come out in the conclusions to which each had come. The timidity of Brand, the tenacity of King and the caution of Tasker were reflected as by a mirror from their various statements. When they had settled down once again in Tasker's study, each gave his views.

Brand was the first. 'I've thought about this thing since Tuesday,' he began, 'in fact, I don't believe I've thought of anything else; and I've come to the conclusion that Tasker was right in what he said in the launch coming home. I believe they do know something. Whether they know enough to get us arrested I can't say, but I think we must assume they do and act accordingly.'

'I agree with Brand,' interposed Tasker. 'Let's deal with this before we go any further. What about you, King?'

'I agree,' King admitted. 'Even if it's only bluff, it's too dangerous to disregard it altogether.'

'Then let us take that as settled. Well, Brand?'

'If we take that as settled,' Brand went on, 'it seems to me we are pretty well in their hands. It's not so bad in a way, what they propose. Without the process we're faced with ruin. What they propose would keep us going, and even give us a small profit. If we were kept from bankruptcy and had an easy mind about the Clay affair, I think we wouldn't do so badly. Personally I'd be satisfied.'

'It would be mere existence instead of the riches we've been expecting,' King burst out.

'Let's finish with Brand,' said Tasker. 'Then, Brand, you'd be in favour of accepting their proposal?'

Brand nodded decisively. 'Yes, I would. But I'd want it tied up so that they were committed to the thing and couldn't afterwards go behind us to the police. As to the money,' Brand twisted unhappily on his chair, 'we can't deny they're entitled to the whole profits. We did steal their blessed process, and we've no real right to anything out of it.'

Tasker nodded. 'Well, that's a perfectly reasonable position. First vote, for agreement. Now, King, let's hear what you have to say.'

'I agree with Brand that we must treat the Chayle threats seriously, whether they're bluffing or not,' said King. 'But I don't agree with him in anything else. I think we should refuse the financial demands.'

'*In toto?*'

'*In toto.* I look at it like this. We know they're making enormous profits. If they go to the police these profits will probably be lost. Well, they're not going to risk that. If we hold on as we're doing, they continue to make their profits. We don't take any away from them because the market's big enough for us both. I propose we refuse, for I'm certain they'll do nothing.'

'And Brand's morality argument?'

'If there ever was anything in that argument, which I doubt, it's too late in the day to bring it up now. Besides we've discussed it before. How often has it been pointed out that we went into this, not to injure them, but to prevent them destroying us? And that's all I now propose.'

Tasker smiled a little grimly. 'Well, that's not so bad. We've now got two absolutely opposite opinions. Brand for acceptance, King for refusal. Does that mean that I've got to settle it?'

'Looks like it,' said King.

'If I were tactful,' Tasker went on, 'I'd say I sympathised with both your points of view. As I'm not, I'll say I don't agree with either of you. I don't think, Brand, that we should just throw up our hand and sit down under this. On the other hand, King, I think a mere blank refusal would be unwise. I'm therefore all for compromise. I suggest we meet them, but bargain for better terms.'

'I would agree to that,' Brand said at once.

'There's another point,' Tasker went on. 'I for one don't hold with the people who think that money counts for everything. For instance, of all the strikes I have known, not one has really been about money. Superficially, money of course. But really in every case it was not money but a sense of injustice which took the men out. It's human nature. Here I question if the same thing mightn't obtain. These people have worked out their process at possibly a lot of trouble and expense. Now they see us sailing in and getting the benefit of their work. I can imagine them saying, "We're damned if they're going to get away with it."'

Brand was impressed with this argument, but King scorned it. 'I don't believe that,' he declared. 'I'll counter it at all events. We *can't* agree to their terms, because agreement would be an admission of guilt.'

Tasker nodded. 'I've considered that point, but I don't think you're right, King. We say to them: We're innocent, but we admit the circumstances look suspicious, and though we're satisfied we could prove our innocence, we don't want the annoyance of having to do so. We're therefore willing to pay a certain amount—not a great deal, but a certain amount—to avoid this unpleasantness. That strikes me as a reasonable attitude and not in the least compromising'

Opinion still remained divided. Brand agreed that Tasker's idea was better than his own, but King wanted a fighting policy. 'The strongest defence is attack,' he declared, whereupon Tasker told him not to be an ass and made disparaging remarks about *clichés*.

In the end Tasker put the question to the vote. With some unwillingness King came round and Tasker's proposal was carried unanimously.

Brand felt a good deal happier for the discussion. He now saw, as he had not seen when considering the affair himself, that however strong the Chayle people's position might be, they hadn't it all their own way. It now again began to look as if the Joymount lives and liberty, their capital and their jobs, were after all reasonably secure. Chayle would have no motive to give them away and a strong one to refrain from doing so.

In due course Tuesday arrived and with it the next conference. The Chayle party again came over in their motor launch, engineered and navigated by Samson. Tasker had not taken the same precautions for secrecy as had Haviland: in fact it looked almost like bravado that a steamer should actually be loading an emergency cargo during the visit. Not however to be outdone in courtesy, King waited on the wharf for the visitors and conducted them to the office.

Tasker made no attempt to outshine Haviland as host. His attentions to his visitors were entirely adequate, but he made no pretence at undue friendliness. In this Brand thought he was wise. It gave him a stronger position than if he had seemed to be currying favour.

The preliminaries over, Tasker got to business. He made a short informal speech, taking up the position which had been decided on at the Friday conference. Firstly, he said, the Joymount people admitted nothing whatever. The death of Clay was the real kernel of the affair, and they absolutely and categorically denied having murdered him. Further, they believed they could prove their innocence, if challenged. Their consciences were entirely clear. However they saw very well that certain circumstances looked suspicious, and they realised that police suspicion would be irksome. They wished to avoid this.

The avoidance of such annoyance would undoubtedly be of some financial value to them, though not of a great deal. They were willing however to pay for it, and if they could get the necessary assurances from the Chayle representatives that no question of police interference would arise, they would pay a royalty on all cement produced under the new process. Of course they could not believe that Haviland had been serious when he suggested seventy-five per cent as the amount of the royalty. He, Tasker, thought twenty-five per cent would be an excessive figure, though they might be willing to go to this extent.

Haviland, suave and urbane, replied to this effort by saying that he and his companions were glad to learn that their Joymount friends were in agreement with them on the principle involved. Once the principle was admitted and agreed on, details could be settled amicably.

Tasker then said that as they were now actually in agreement on principles he thought that they might as well begin at the beginning of their proposed schedule and check over the items in turn. If they found that six articles out of seven were settled, it would encourage them to deal with the unhappily contentious seventh. With a view to facilitating their discussion, he had taken the liberty of drafting out a set of seven clauses, as the basis of their convention. These were simply Haviland's clauses, slightly extended and modified to meet the Joymount point of view. The only question that really had to be dealt with was whether Chayle could accept these unimportant modifications. If they could, their work was done. If not, they must try to find a compromise. With this Tasker produced his draft.

'I'm sorry,' he apologised, 'that I've only one copy. As a matter of fact I typed it myself, and as I'm not a typist I funked the mysteries of carbon copies. However I think we can manage.'

The document was to all intents and purposes a legally phrased draft of Haviland's seven items. The alterations were comparatively trifling, with the single exception that for the words 'seventy-five per cent' in Clause 7, 'twenty-five per cent' had been substituted.

As in Haviland's draft, the first five clauses were in effect an agreement that the two firms would work together on equal terms and for their mutual benefit. As it happened, these non-contentious clauses spaced out so as to finish on Sheet 1. On Sheet 2 were typed Clauses 6 and 7, Clause 6, which agreed that the new process was the absolute property of Chayle, and Clause 7, which laid down that Joymount would work the process under licence from Chayle, paying a royalty thereon.

The principal alterations introduced by Tasker were that Chayle thereby gave to Joymount a licence to use the process, which could not under any circumstances be revoked; that it mentioned the salient features of the process, to distinguish it from any other that might subsequently be evolved; that the royalty was to be calculated, not on the profits, but on the excess profits of the new process over those of the old; and of course that the royalty was to be twenty-five per cent and not seventy-five per cent of such profits.

Following the example of Tasker a week before, Haviland expressed a lively satisfaction with the draft, which, he said, seemed at first sight to be exactly what they wanted. 'Except of course Clause 7,' he went on. 'We cannot think that you're serious about the change in it.'

Tasker repeated his suggestion that each clause should be taken in turn, and this was done. The first six clauses were debated, and after some further slight modifications had been introduced into the draft, were agreed to. Then they came to Clause 7.

The framework of the clause gave little difficulty. Tasker accepted a modification that the royalty should be calculated from a figure to be certified by an agreed firm of auditors, and everything was settled except the question of the amount of the percentage.

'Well,' Tasker began, when at last they were face to face with the real issue, 'I think I've already made our position clear. The process is ours, but because of the peculiar circumstances we're willing to pay twenty-five per cent to be saved the annoyance of a police investigation. It's not worth our paying more for this privilege. If you want to charge more, our answer would be to pay nothing and put up with the investigation.'

Haviland shook his head gravely. 'My colleagues and I understood you to say so,' he said. 'But we think that is due to failure to appreciate the real position. Again I am most anxious to avoid saying anything which might seem unpleasant, but do take it from me, gentlemen, that you couldn't stand a police investigation.'

'But don't you think that's our business and not yours?' Tasker asked suavely.

'No. It's ours because you don't know what information

we are prepared to give the police, and we do. Therefore we are the best judges of the situation.'

Tasker smiled. 'If you want to impress us, I'm afraid you'll have to tell us what that information is likely to be.'

'Well,' Haviland answered, 'if you insist, I have no alternative but to do so, but you must realise that I could not supply details, as that might be giving away our privileged position. You see, I'm being perfectly straight with you.'

'It's the only way to reach a conclusion satisfactory to both sides.'

If the thing hadn't been so deadly serious, Brand would have laughed at the dignity of Tasker's bluff. Once again he wondered whether Haviland was bluffing also, or whether there really was something to fear in the situation. Well, if the man were speaking the truth, they would soon know.

'There are two things to which I might call your attention,' Haviland went on. 'The first is that the safes from which our £415 and the formula for our secret process were extracted were opened by keys—as of course you know. When I say our process was extracted, I don't mean removed: I am aware that it was not taken away, but merely read and returned. Well, neither safe was opened by the Chayle keys: therefore keys were specially cut for the purpose. You follow?'

'Your reasoning sounds conclusive.'

'The police agree with it at all events. Now these keys were not cut by Clay; he hadn't the knowledge or skill. They were cut by someone who obtained possession of either my or Mairs's bunch.'

Tasker nodded.

'I have surely only to mention a certain journey I had the pleasure of taking with my friend—I hope I may say, my friend—Mr King. A journey in the tea car of the 4.50 from Waterloo to Portsmouth on the 27th of last July. I stupidly fell asleep in the train that afternoon. There was some little matter of a shortage of sugar. Twice I passed my sugar bowl to my travelling companion: once before I helped myself and once after. When I add that I afterwards found on my bunch of keys a tiny scrap of wax, you will see that I could scarcely avoid jumping to a certain conclusion.'

'That is indeed interesting, but I don't see that it affects the present argument.'

'No? That's because, as I have said, I have had to keep back a little fact. A very little fact, but quite conclusive. That fact is known by the three of us alone, but there is no reason why it should not be divulged to the police. If such became necessary I would say that a possible significance of it had just struck me, and did they think there was anything in it? They might be trusted, I think, to do the rest. That's the first of the two matters.'

'Very interesting indeed,' Tasker said again.

'I think so too,' Haviland answered, 'but to my mind this second item is a good deal more interesting still. We know who bought the car. I'm not going to tell you *how* we know, for the reason already given. But we can give absolute proof, if necessary. And you don't need me to point out that whatever could be argued about bowls of sugar, only one explanation exists about the buying of cars.'

'Yes,' said Tasker dispassionately, 'I think of the two, that is the more interesting piece of information. A pity though that you have to keep back everything that makes it convincing.'

'Mr King may not think so,' Haviland returned.

'However, it's now a matter for your good selves. I have given you a hint of the line our information would take. I only undertook to give a hint, and I explained why I could not give you more. The next move, gentlemen, is up to you.'

'But, Haviland, suppose your theories were correct, which I deny, do you mean that you would be willing to become accessories after the fact?'

'Certainly not. I've explained how we should avoid that. The same method would be adopted in each case—that we had the information, but didn't realise what it involved.'

'Do you think that would be believed?'

Haviland shrugged. 'It wouldn't matter. It couldn't be disproved.'

'Then morally at least, you would be willing to compound a murder?'

Haviland made a disclaiming gesture. 'We have no responsibility for what happened. Nor are we the guardians of public morality nor yet the forces of the Crown. No, Tasker, we are, I hope, about to be friends and partners. We don't wish trouble to our friends.'

From this position neither argument nor blandishments could move him, and Tasker finally said he would like to retire with his colleagues to talk the matter over. While they were away, there was the whisky and the cigars and he hoped his visitors would make themselves at home.

'Let's go to your office, Brand,' said Tasker in serious tones, 'I may want you to get out some figures. I'm afraid,' he went on when the door was shut, 'they've got us. I've rather come round to Brand's view that we should agree to their terms. What do you say now, King?'

King shrugged. 'I'm a bit shaken myself,' he admitted.

211

'If Haviland is prepared to swear it was I who passed him the sugar, it might be awkward enough. I've got an alibi for the night of Clay's death, but not for that train journey.'

'I think we should settle,' Brand declared earnestly. These views he found very disquieting.

'I don't think we should settle straight off,' Tasker returned. 'I suggest still trying for better terms. But if they won't give way I think we must.'

After a little more discussion this was agreed to, and Tasker went on. 'Now look here, I want some figures to argue from. First I want a statement of our costs for the new process, our estimated output with the new plant, and our estimated profits. I want these to show,' and Tasker became technical. 'I think, Brand,' he resumed, 'we could best get them out together, so that's why I suggested we should come in here.' He turned to King. 'While Brand and I are doing this, King, I wish you'd make me out a short statement of how you reached the process. I don't mean the story of your journey to Chayle'—he smiled slightly—'but a rough note of the experiments which you say put you on the right track. It has occurred to me that it might make a good bluff. Can you do that quickly?'

'In ten minutes. I've got all the experiments written up, and I've only to type out a covering note, showing how they're connected.'

'Good,' said Tasker, 'then get at it.'

King went into his office next door and began clicking away on his typewriter. Tasker, as always, knew just what he wanted and kept Brand busy getting out figure after figure from the books. These he wrote down as Brand gave them to him.

'I may not use this,' he said in respect of more than one, 'but I want to have it in case of need.'

King also seemed to know what he wanted. The noise of his typewriter was continuous, except on one or two occasions when Brand heard him opening and closing his safe. Then, as usual, came unmelodiously some bars of Schubert. Brand, whose nerves were on edge, swore. 'I wish to heaven that blessed march had never been written,' he grumbled. 'If I've heard it once, I've heard it six million times!'

As if King had heard the protest, the 'Marche Militaire' came to an untimely end and his speaking voice was heard instead.

'You don't want dates, I suppose, Tasker?'

Tasker paused. 'No, don't trouble,' he called back; 'just the experiments.'

'Right-ho!' shouted King, and the typing began again. Presently the clicking stopped and King came in.

'Do you think this is complete enough?' he asked Tasker, holding out two typewritten sheets. 'It's a sort of synopsis of the job, correlating the experiments. These old sheets I've attached contain the details of the individual experiments.'

Tasker looked at the work and agreed that it was what he wanted. He had not however got all he required from Brand, and King looked over their shoulders till the financial statement was complete.

'These are tip-top,' Tasker said at last. 'With these figures and King's experiments, we should be able to do something.'

Thus girded for the fray, the three men returned to the scene of the battle.

16

Tragedy Comes Again to Chayle

In this final round they found Haviland unexpectedly obdurate. Tasker put up a well reasoned case. He said he admitted that their aims and objects were identical, to get as much money out of the process as they could on the one hand, and on the other to avoid unpleasantness. Then he went on to figures, pointing out that while figures were not so important as principles, they had to deal with them. He stuck to it that the process used at Joymount had been worked out by King, produced the record of the experiments, and explained that they had been at the expense of carrying these out and of providing the necessary new plant. For this they were entitled to an adequate return. At the same time they recognised that Chayle could do them a service for which they agreed that it was right that they should pay. They thought that the twenty-five per cent that they had suggested was ample for this, but they didn't want to quarrel with their new friends, and they were willing, if it would settle the question, to propose an even division of fifty-fifty.

However, with the utmost suavity Haviland declined anything less than seventy-five per cent. In vain Tasker argued. Seventy-five per cent, the others thought, was a liberal offer. It was not for them to dictate Joymount policy, but they sincerely trusted their new friends would see their way to come to terms.

In the end Tasker agreed. It was obvious that with the views of all concerned there was nothing else that he could do. When Tasker gave way, he gave way with a good grace. King looked disappointed and sulky, but Brand was delighted.

'I'm sorry,' Tasker said when the great decision had been made, 'that I didn't get these notes typed in duplicate. I'll tell you what we'll do. Let's initial these sheets, then I'll prepare two copies on decent paper, initial them both, and send them over to you with these notes. You can check them over with the original, initial them, and return one copy. Then we can get our lawyers to work on the final document.'

From Haviland's manner, Brand thought he would have preferred making the copy then and there, but he apparently decided that, having stood out for so much, he would give way on non-essentials.

'There's just one point unsettled,' Haviland added. 'Rumours about this affair are bound to leak out. Our visits to one another are known and will be talked of. Now you know as well as I, that to make a mystery of anything is to ask for publicity. I suggest therefore that we say at once that we are considering a working agreement between the two firms with the object of reducing our costs. By that we'll kill rumour and suspicion. Of course we mustn't mention the royalty or anything that would suggest the process.'

This seemed an excellent idea to Brand, but before Tasker could reply, Haviland went on.

215

'It happens that the first five clauses are contained on the first page of our draft agreement. Let so much be generally public. The sixth and seventh clauses on your second sheet to be secret. In fact I would go so far as to suggest that we have two agreements. One drawn up by our lawyers—your Sheet No. 1. The second, a secret agreement drawn up by ourselves. How does that appeal to you?'

With this all were fully agreed, and both sheets were initialled by Tasker and Haviland for their respective companies.

'Now,' Tasker continued, 'that business for the evening is over, let us turn to something more agreeable. Let us drink to our future success. In the hope that we might come to terms I brought over a bottle or two of celebration vintage from my house. Open it, like a good fellow, Brand.'

Brand opened the champagne and they drank to their new association. For half an hour or more they chatted in the most amicable manner, and then Haviland said they must be going.

'We'll see you to your launch,' said Tasker, determined to maintain to the bitter end the high level upon which the affair had been conducted. The six men accordingly made their way down from the office, through the works yard, and out on to the wharf.

The loading of the coaster was still in progress, and though it was nearly full moon, the wharf was brightly lighted by lamps. Decauville trucks full of cement were running from the yard, and the bags were being lifted by the vessel's winches and swung aboard. It was a fine night, but cold. The tide was nearly full and a strong south-westerly breeze was blowing, which had put up a choppy sea. The tiny waves were jabbling among the piles beneath the wharf and the launch, moored to the steps, was fretting uneasily at her painter. Brand knew that out in Southampton Water, and particularly where the Solent opened out beyond Calshot, there would be quite a sea from the long fetch.

'You'll have it a bit dirty going home,' he said to Samson, with whom he was walking.

'Do no harm,' Samson returned. 'She's as dry as a bone in a head sea. She's mine, you know, so I couldn't listen to anything against her. I engined her and I'm very proud of her.'

Brand said he ought to be, and with unctuous farewells the Chayle party set off.

The three Joymount men stood for a moment in silence, watching the launch as it passed under the stern of the coaster and headed out for Southampton Water. Brand was sure that they had done the right thing. Under the circumstances it was the nearest approach to security they could have achieved. All the same it was with a sigh that he saw the launch disappear.

'Well,' said Tasker shortly as they turned away, 'that's that.'

It seemed to sum up everything that was to be said on the subject. Neither of the others replied.

Though the situation admittedly left a good deal to be desired, Brand felt happier that night than he had since the first visit of Haviland and Mairs. The weight of anxiety which he had been carrying had largely lifted and the future seemed rosier. With luck, he thought, the worst of their troubles were over. He began to look forward to a period of moderate prosperity and freedom from the fears which for a time had pressed so heavily on his mind.

It happens, however, that such a state of complacency is not infrequently the prelude to disaster. Unhappily it was so on this occasion.

Next morning a dreadful blow fell. It seemed bad enough when Brand heard of it, and yet its full horror did not dawn on him at first. It was only when he thought over it and discussed it with the other two that he realised what it might involve.

He had gone to the works that morning at his usual time, and as usual had begun the day by going through his letters. It happened that one letter referred to a certain matter of special urgency, which at the time was engaging the attention of himself and Tasker. Desiring to consult Tasker upon it, Brand immediately left his office and made his way to Tasker's. Tasker was also engaged with his mail, but he looked up as Brand entered.

'It's that Hudson case,' said Brand, sitting in the visitors' armchair. 'Here's a letter from Hudson himself.'

Tasker stretched out his hand for the paper, but he had not more than taken it when his telephone rang. He picked up the receiver.

'Yes, yes,' he said impatiently; 'speaking.' There was a pause and as Brand watched he saw the other's expression change. Impatience rapidly became surprise, then incredulity, and finally horror.

'My heavens!' Tasker said in an awestruck voice. 'That's terrible news, Superintendent. I can scarcely believe it. Both *dead*, you say?'

Brand was again on his feet. 'What is it, Tasker?' he exclaimed urgently.

Tasker shook his head to demand silence, then as if he couldn't keep the information to himself, he said in that same horror-stricken voice: 'Haviland and Mairs are drowned!'

Brand stared helplessly at Tasker.

Haviland and Mairs! *Drowned!* Impossible! Brand pictured them as he had seen them on the previous evening: full of life and health and energy: planning for the future as if they had unlimited years before them. And now . . . Dead!

They must have capsized on the way home. And Samson had been so cocksure of his launch! Brand recalled his remark to him about the weather. And Samson had boasted of how dry the boat was in a sea! Well, it looked as if he had been wrong.

But Tasker was speaking again. 'Yes,' he went on into the instrument, 'that's correct. They were here, all three of them, till about half past ten. They left then to return to Chayle in their launch . . . Oh yes, everything was perfectly normal so far as I could see . . . Yes, we saw them start . . . *Absolutely* sober, and as I say, perfectly normal in every way.' There was a longer pause and then: 'Certainly, Superintendent, we shall all be here. If you send a man, he can see us at any time.'

Tasker slowly replaced the receiver and stared at Brand with horrified eyes. He did not speak, and Brand questioned him eagerly.

'What is it, Tasker? Tell me. Did they capsize on their way back?'

Tasker shook his head. He seemed not only filled with horror, but also wholly mystified. For a moment more he remained silent, and then at last he spoke.

'No,' he said slowly, 'they didn't capsize. The launch was blown up!'

Brand stared in speechless amazement.

'Just off Cowes,' went on Tasker, 'on their way home. Samson was picked up uninjured. The others went down with the launch.'

Brand swore in a shaky voice. 'Went down with the launch!' He stood staring at Tasker, then went on. 'You say blown up? *Blown up?* How under heaven could the launch have been blown up?'

'That's what the Superintendent wants to know. Apparently Samson can't explain it.'

'The petrol's got spilled somehow,' Brand went on. 'She was a petrol launch. Samson engined her himself.'

Tasker nodded without speaking.

'It was very choppy last night,' went on Brand. 'They would have caught it badly when they were past Calshot. Something has got adrift and broken the feed pipe.'

'It looks like it. A ghastly business!' Tasker shivered.

'I must tell King,' Brand said and hurried to the laboratory.

King was quite overwhelmed by the news. He seemed as much horrified as Tasker and a great deal more mystified.

'You say the launch sank?' he repeated. 'But why should she sink? The petrol would burn it, but it wouldn't sink it.' He paused, then added: 'But I suppose it would eventually. It would burn away the sides till the water came in.'

'If a fire broke out they wouldn't be able to steer, and she'd get broadside on and quickly fill—if she didn't go over altogether.'

'That's so,' King admitted. 'Yes, it must have been that, I imagine. Does Tasker know?'

'It was he told me. The police rang up to enquire. Come and see him.'

For some time the three men discussed possible causes, without however advancing any more likely theory than that put up by Brand. Then they spoke of the dead partners. But the special circumstances made it inevitable that they should soon turn to the effect the tragedy might have upon themselves.

'I don't see,' said King, 'that it'll make any difference to us. The agreement we initialled last night will be carried out by and with Samson. If all three had perished things would have been different. But as it is I take it the agreement stands.'

Tasker shook his head. 'It's not so simple as that, I'm afraid. This will bring up the entire question of our negotiations. The police will want to know what those three were doing here, and we must settle what we're going to say.'

The others saw the urgency of this. Brand, whose fears were at once aroused by the probability of a police investigation on unpleasantly intimate matters, was for telling the complete truth. But Tasker vetoed this at once.

'We can't under any circumstances admit to the royalty,' he said decidedly. 'How can you suggest such a thing, Brand? Just think what it would mean. We tell the police we have agreed to pay a royalty. They at once ask why? Then we have to tell of the process. They say to themselves, "Oh, so these people at Joymount have the Chayle process. They're the people we've been looking for since the Clay affair took place." They begin to investigate—and we're done. Why, they have only to bring an expert through both works to see that the processes are identical. And remember, you two. After the verdict at that inquest the question of an accident to Clay couldn't arise. So it works round to this, that if we give away about the royalty your necks are in danger.'

'What about your own, Tasker?' asked King. 'What about accessory after the fact, which you made so much of to Haviland?'

'As I've told you before, I know nothing of the fate of Clay. I've got your written statement that you discovered the process yourself, and I know of my own knowledge that you were experimenting on it for six weeks. If I were asked to explain why I agreed to pay the royalty I would say that I thought Chayle was entitled to it, as we had used their work. It was from their stuff that we got the new ingredients required. All we did was to discover a way of incorporating them.'

In spite of his dismay at all this, Brand could not withhold his admiration at Tasker's adroitness.

'*But*,' went on Tasker before he could speak, 'if the existence of the process became known, I'd probably lose my profits and certainly have a hell of a time of worry. I'm therefore as anxious as you to keep it dark. Now do you both agree that we must keep the royalty secret?'

There was nothing else for it, Brand saw only too well. And King speedily expressed the same opinion.

'I suggest then,' Tasker went on, 'that we do what Haviland himself suggested: admit to the first sheet of our draft agreement, but not to the second. Our object in making the agreement was, as he said, to reduce our costs, and if we're asked how the agreement could accomplish this, we might say that we hoped, besides speeding up deliveries and so on, that our stores could be ordered jointly, thus getting reductions for quantity. You get the idea?'

The others nodded.

'Of course,' Tasker went on, 'the situation is complicated for us by the fact that we don't know what Samson will say. But as it's equally in his interest to keep the process a secret, he'll probably say the same.'

'What about ringing him up?' Brand suggested.

'Of course,' King approved. 'That's the thing to do.'

Tasker was not enthusiastic. 'I thought of that,' he said doubtfully, 'but I wasn't sure of its wisdom. In any case he's probably made his statement to the police by now.'

'What if he has?' King objected. 'Wouldn't it be better to know, if only that we may tell the same story.'

Tasker nodded. 'Yes, there's that in it,' he admitted and picked up his telephone.

'Oh,' he went on into the instrument, 'he's just come in, has he? I wonder if he would be too busy to speak to me? Mr Tasker of the Joymount Works.' There was a pause and then: 'Oh, Samson, I'm glad to hear you're able to be at business. We've just heard the news and I rang up at once. I just can't say how horrified and distressed we all are. It seems perfectly incredible. Can you tell any particulars?'

Again there was a pause and again Tasker went on. 'It sounds entirely beyond belief. You've no theory then? . . . Amazing! . . . Well, look here, Samson, I don't want to introduce business at such a time, but I presume we may follow poor Haviland's advice and make our five-clause agreement public? . . . Yes, I think so too. Well, you must be busy; I'll not keep you. But do, Samson, accept our heartiest congratulations on your own escape, and our condolences for those two poor fellows.'

Tasker replaced the receiver. 'He says the five-clause agreement was what he mentioned to the police, so that's all right. But the whole affair seems quite beyond comprehension. He says it was a regular explosion and that he can't account for it at all.'

King shrugged. 'It doesn't seem so extraordinary to me. If the petrol got adrift, as we've supposed, it would get spread all over the bottom of the boat by the rolling. Then if it got alight it would all go off together.'

'Samson sounds very much upset. I don't expect he's been able to think very clearly as yet.'

'No wonder!' Brand exclaimed. 'I don't know how he can face the office.'

Brand himself was also a good deal upset. Apart from the horror of the tragedy it meant a police enquiry at Joymount—about Chayle—and the very idea of such a thing gave him cold shivers.

'I can't see why you should have hesitated to phone,' King said to Tasker. 'Why did you think it mightn't be wise?'

Tasker moved uneasily. He looked very grave. 'Well,' he said at length, 'it amazes me that neither of you chaps should see what was in my mind. Directly I understood there was some mystery about the affair, I thought of something. Has it not occurred to either of you that if the thing can't be explained, the police may suspect'— instinctively he lowered his voice—'foul play?'

Brand started. Such an idea hadn't entered his mind. King, too, seemed taken aback.

'Oh, get away, Tasker,' King retorted. 'You're not serious? Who could have done such a thing?'

'That's just it,' Tasker answered grimly. 'We could.'

'Nonsense! How could we?'

'I don't mean that we really could, of course. I mean, the police might think so.'

Brand was appalled. Such a suspicion would lead to the most searching investigation. If it did, they could scarcely hope to keep the royalty a secret. And if the royalty became known to the police, they had already agreed that he and

King were as good as hanged! Oh, no, it was not possible! He couldn't admit such a thing for a moment.

Neither, apparently, could King, who seemed equally moved. 'But, look here, Tasker,' he was saying; 'you're talking nonsense. Suppose it was foul play, which as I see it, there's not the slightest reason to imagine. But suppose it was. We couldn't be guilty. I presume you'll admit that if it was malicious, someone must have put the explosives on board? Well, none of us were near the blessed launch. We can prove that easily enough.'

'I know we can prove it,' Tasker returned, 'and I know it'll establish our innocence. It's not a charge of murder that I'm afraid of. It's the mere possibility of a serious police investigation—here. I don't see how that could be made without the whole business of the process coming out.'

King did not agree. Even supposing such a ridiculous idea were entertained, proof of its falsity would be available so immediately that further investigation would not be undertaken. He could not understand Tasker's attitude. It was not like him to be an alarmist.

Brand was faintly comforted by these arguments, but he still remained horribly upset by the idea of what might be coming. It was with misgiving that he braced himself to meet the amount of enquiry which was certain.

All three men were surprised to hear nothing further from the police that day. It was not till the following morning that the affair was followed up. Then Brand got another shock. It was not the local Superintendent who called, but no less a person than the Scotland Yard officer who had acted in the Clay case.

However, the enquiry, when it came, was mild and reassuring. Chief-Inspector French was civil and obviously

accepted their statements. All three were sure that the idea
of foul play had either not occurred to him, or had been
dismissed from his mind. He laid no stress on the nature
of the proposed agreement with Chayle, clearly taking it
for granted that it was quite ordinary. He was thorough
enough in getting an account of the visit and details of the
start, but he touched on no other subject. On departure he
thanked them for their help, saying that one or more would
be called to give evidence at the inquest, the date of which
was not yet settled.

Brand was greatly relieved when he and his sergeant had
gone, for though their visit had turned out so much less
trying than he had expected, it still had been an ordeal. It
was evident that, in spite of the confident way in which
they had talked, both Tasker and King had found it so too.

This feeling of confidence continued to grow as the days
passed and no further communications were received from
the police. They had not been called to the inquest, which,
they saw by the papers, had been opened and adjourned.
Doubtless, however, they would be called later.

Once again what had been a bad period in Brand's life
seemed to be drawing to an end. The adjourned inquest
once over, he need have no further fears. Once again the
men of Joymount began to settle down and to enjoy their
profits.

PART IV

Elucidation

17

French Returns to the Assault

The rapid progress he had made at the commencement of the case of Clay and the burnt car had made Chief-Inspector French superstitiously fearful lest this good luck should not continue. He had noticed that when things went well at first, some serious snag not unusually developed later on. If the converse had proved true he would not have so much minded, but unhappily a bad beginning did not necessarily mean a satisfactory finish. Sometimes he became despondent and thought that the balances of Chance were unequally weighted against him.

In this instance, his fears did really seem to have been justified. The case had had a brilliant opening. In the first few hours he had proved that Clay had been murdered and that the car accident had been a fake. Almost immediately after that he had developed an excellent theory of the guilt of two of the members of the Joymount staff, a theory which had seemed to cover all the circumstances.

But at this point his progress had ceased. His theory remained a theory. He did not abandon it; it seemed to him as good as ever. But try as he would, he could get nothing which proved its truth.

One of his fundamental ideas was that the process had been stolen by some person or persons connected with the manufacture of rapid-hardening cement. But here again he could learn nothing. If such a theft had taken place, he might expect to find some other firm putting out cement at a cheaper rate than the rest. But none appeared to be doing so. He had discussed the point with Haviland and Mairs, and they had agreed with him. They had indeed expressed the view that if any firm were found selling below the general level, it would be proof of guilt.

They had gone on to make an important offer, which French had accepted. They had, they said, an elaborate machinery for watching the market, which would immediately bring any such development to their notice. They promised to have this machinery operated with the greatest vigilance, and they undertook immediately to advise French if they learned of any firm offering cuts in prices. For the moment, therefore, he was satisfied to leave this matter in the Chayle hands, their interests and his own being so obviously identical.

He did not, however, rely for a long time on Chayle's detective organisation. As soon as he had completed the more immediate enquiries and was free to look further afield, he arranged through the Yard for an exhaustive watch to be kept, not only on rapid-hardening cement prices in the open market, but also on the possibility of secret rebates. So far as he could learn, however, the Chayle men were correct in saying that no such cuts had been made.

He had then turned his serious attention to Joymount.

He had not exactly suspected the Joymount men, but he had considered them in connection with the affair, principally because of the geographical position of their works. Besides being near Chayle, they had a launch by which the body could have been transported from the Island to the mainland. But in the absence of reason to suppose they had obtained the process, French saw that his other suspicions did not amount to anything at all. The men of any other firm were equally likely to be guilty.

All the same, he had made a number of unobtrusive enquiries at Joymount, mostly from workmen. Especially he had questioned the night watchman, and the skippers and crews of two small steamers which had been moored at the Joymount wharf on the night of Clay's presumed murder. From them he had obtained information which seemed to prove he was working on the wrong lines.

From the night watchman he had learned that some technical investigation had been in progress for a month prior to the tragedy, involving a certain amount of night work. Further that during the night of the tragedy itself both King and Brand had been in the building. They had arrived about ten o'clock and had left about three in the morning. They had been in the chemical laboratory, and it would have been impossible for them to have left between these hours, unknown to the watchman. Obviously, if this testimony were correct, they could not have gone to Chayle.

French did not really suspect the other two men of the four on the Joymount photograph, any one of whom Fisher of the Southampton garage had said might have bought the car. These were Campbell, a fitter, and Armour, a fireman. All the same, French had made it his business to find out where both of them had been on the night in question. Both, he had ample proof, were at home.

French had then considered the question of a boat or launch. He had inspected the Joymount boathouse, in which all the craft used by those connected with the works were kept. He had seen that it would be difficult—though not impossible—to take out a boat unnoticed by a person on the wharf. Discreet enquiries had found the two steamers which had been at Joymount on the night in question, and none of those on board had seen or heard any such boat. He learned, moreover, that on that Sunday night there had been a thick fog, and because of it all the longshoremen and coastguards he spoke to were doubtful as to the possibility of navigation.

These researches seemed to French provisionally to eliminate the Joymount staff. He was not greatly impressed by the evidence that Brand and King could not have left the works during the night, but the difficulty of crossing to and from Chayle in the fog seemed pretty considerable. If Joymount had been putting out a cheap cement, he would have assumed that in some way these difficulties had been overcome, but as they were not, his suspicions seemed rather gratuitous.

The affair had dragged on in this way for some time, and then French had returned to Town and reported to Sir Mortimer Ellison. The Assistant-Commissioner had listened and then shrugged. As a result of that shrug French had let the case stand and had taken up other work. It was understood, however, that if price fluctuations occurred in the cement market, he would immediately resume the investigation. It was admittedly a most unsatisfactory result, but no one concerned could see any way to improve it.

Then one night some three months later, the case was again brought to his notice, and in a most dramatic way.

It was getting on towards four in the morning when his telephone rang. Practice had taught him to waken instantly at such a summons, and by the time he had learned that the call was from the Yard, he was his usual quiet, efficient self. A message from the police station at Cowes had just come in. Would French take it and they would put it through?

It was his friend Superintendent Hanbury, and he had startling news. Haviland and Mairs of the Chayle Works had been drowned on the previous evening by an explosion on their motor launch, and Samson had been picked up just as he was about to sink. At first sight there were certain suspicious features in the case, and he had communicated with his Chief Constable. From him he had received instructions to get in touch with French, and ask him to go down as soon as possible. The Chief Constable was himself communicating with the heads of the Yard.

As a result of this communication, French found on reaching headquarters that orders had come for him to go down at once. Sergeant Carter had also been sent for and was ready to accompany him.

The first train for the Isle of Wight left Waterloo at 5.40 a.m., and by hurrying, French was able to make his preparations and catch it. He rang up to advise Hanbury, and the Superintendent replied that breakfast would be ready on their arrival, and that over the meal he would tell what had happened.

The journey was uneventful. The two men reached Southampton just before eight, walked down to the harbour and caught the 8.15 boat for Cowes, where they arrived in an hour. A few minutes later they saw the welcome sight of coffee and ham and eggs, and Hanbury began his story.

Beyond the main fact, however, that an accident had taken place, he had not much to tell. It appeared that about 11.45 on the previous evening an explosion had been observed about a mile north-west of the Egypt Point Light. It happened that a resident living above the Esplanade was taking a last breather at his hall door before turning in, when he saw a flame suddenly rise from the sea, flicker for a moment, and then vanish, while four or five seconds later came a dull boom. Believing something must be seriously wrong, this gentleman had rung up the police. Information was at once conveyed to the harbour, and within a comparatively short time four launches had put out. Three of these had searched the area in question without finding anything, but the fourth obtained some information.

A small coasting steamer was lying in the area, apparently at anchor, and when Mr Locke, the owner and navigator of the fourth launch, came nearer, he saw that she had lowered a boat. He accordingly drew alongside to make enquiries. From the skipper he learned that she was the S.S. *Benbolt*, on a voyage from Cardiff to Gosport with coal. When about a mile off the Egypt Point Light he, the skipper, noticed a small vessel coming towards them. He expected her to pass about a hundred yards to port. As she came abeam he saw she was a small petrol launch. She was tumbling about a good deal in the choppy sea. He paid her no particular attention, but he happened to be actually looking at her when a tremendous explosion occurred on board. Its centre was in the stern, and so far as he could see, the whole stern was blown to bits. In a moment the flame went out, leaving the area black as jet.

He at once reversed his engines and got his boat out. The boat, he estimated, reached the scene of the disaster within five minutes of the crash. It cruised around and almost at once came on a man clinging to a lifebuoy. He took him aboard, transferred him to the steamer, and went back to search for more survivors. He had been searching ever since, but without further result. The launch must have sunk, carrying down with her the remainder of those on board, if any.

Meanwhile a stiff glass of grog and dry clothes had enabled the survivor to give some account of himself. His name, he said, was Noel Samson, and he was chemical engineer to Messrs Haviland & Mairs, of Chayle. He, Haviland and Mairs, had been over at the Joymount Company's works on the Hamble, and were returning to Chayle. The launch was his, and he had been steering. When they had come off Cowes, he noticed that their grappling had broken adrift owing to the rough sea, and was knocking about in the bows. He had accordingly handed over the wheel to his principal, Mr Haviland, and had himself gone forward into the bows to make the grappling fast. He was stooping down in the bows to lift it back into its chocks when there had come an appalling explosion in the stern. Immediately he had found himself struggling in the water. How he got there, or what became of the launch, he did not know. He struggled against the high sea for some moments, and though he was a swimmer, he felt himself being overcome. He was sure he would have been drowned, had not he happened to touch something which, when he had grasped it, he found to be a lifebuoy. This had supported him till a boat had come and he had been lifted out of the water.

Locke had taken Samson aboard his launch and run him back to Cowes, where the coastguards and police had asked for a statement. Samson had appeared completely mystified by the occurrence. He supposed the petrol must have in some way got alight, but this did not seem to meet the case for three reasons. First, there was no reason why it should have either leaked or gone on fire. He had had the launch for some years, and till then everything had functioned perfectly. On many occasions he had been out in worse weather, so he did not believe the motion could have had anything to do with it. The second reason was more puzzling still. The explosion had not seemed to Samson like burning petrol. When petrol gets alight the fire is undoubtedly rapid, but still there is a definite process of bursting into flame. In this explosion there was none. It had been instantaneous. It had gone with a crack, as if some high-power explosive like dynamite had been used. Thirdly, and most convincing of all, it seemed evident that the stern must have been blown off the launch, so rapidly had it sunk. This would not have obtained if the affair had been due to petrol.

Against this view, however, Samson stated most positively that no explosive of any kind had been on board.

Hanbury had thought this statement very unsatisfactory and his uneasiness had been increased by the fact that here were three of the men who had figured in the Clay affair. He had therefore rung up his Chief Constable, and after a telephonic discussion the latter had determined to recall French, if he were available.

'Have you communicated with the Joymount people?' French asked when Hanbury's recital came to an end.

'Yes, first thing this morning. I rang up Tasker, their

managing director. He confirmed Samson's statement. Haviland, Mairs and Samson were over with them at Joymount last night from shortly before nine till about half past ten. They were discussing some business which Tasker wanted kept secret, but which he had no objection to explaining in confidence. The two firms were considering a working agreement, and it was to talk about this that they had met at that late hour. The three men left at the hour stated. They had all seemed perfectly normal—perfectly sober and all that sort of thing, and the launch had appeared to be in perfectly good order.'

'It doesn't look too well,' said French after a pause.

'That's what the Chief Constable and I thought,' Hanbury returned. 'We decided at all events that it should be looked into. And we thought that in case there might be come connection with that previous affair, you were the man to do it.'

'At first sight it would look as if there must be some connection,' French went on. 'It would be something of a coincidence if there were two separate tragedies in the same firm within three months of each other.' He paused in thought, then went on. 'There's another interesting thing in it, Super, and that is that they were coming from Joymount. We've been looking for another firm of rapid-hardening cement manufacturers who were connected with the Clay affair, and as you know, had Joymount in our minds. Yes, I agree: the thing should certainly be looked into.'

During the progress of the Super's story French had obtained the necessary details, such as addresses, all of which had been noted by Carter. Breakfast by this time having been finished, French stood up.

'Well,' he said pleasantly, 'that's a good start you've given us, Super,' though whether he was referring to the story or the meal he didn't say. 'I'll begin by going round all these people you've mentioned. Can you run me out to Chayle or shall I hire a car in the town?'

'I'll run you out,' Hanbury returned, and was proceeding with another remark when a constable entered the restaurant and whispered to him.

'Is that so? Right. I'll go back directly,' he answered. Then he turned to French. 'They've found one of the bodies, it seems. The coastguards were out searching and they're just bringing it in. I suppose you'll wait and see it?'

French agreed, and the three men walked back to the police station. Hanbury rang up the police doctor, and when the remains were brought in they proceeded at once to make an examination.

The body was Mairs's, and it was evident that death had occurred from drowning. He was uninjured save for the feet, one of which was almost blown off and the other cut and lacerated. This showed the force of the explosion, and also that it must have been centred in the bottom of the boat.

While the doctor was examining the remains, French busied himself with the clothes. He went through the pockets carefully, but without finding anything which threw light on the tragedy. There were a number of papers and these, though sodden, were still legible. But there was nothing helpful in any of them.

French thereupon borrowed Hanbury's car and he and Carter were driven out to Chayle. French had rung up Samson's private house, but the engineer had replied that he was just about to start for the works. It was therefore in his own office that French found him.

After the introductory remarks demanded by courtesy, French turned to business. Would Mr Samson please tell him all he could about the affair?

It was evident that Samson had had a severe shock, from which he had by no means recovered. His manner was nervous, his hands shook, and more than once he lost the thread of his story.

He had not really a very great deal to tell. He said that for some time they had been considering extending their business, and as Joymount was close by and therefore convenient, they had thought of taking the place over as a going concern. For various reasons this had not afterwards seemed feasible, and they had turned their attention instead towards a working agreement. They had accordingly entered into negotiations with Joymount, and on the previous evening they had come to provisional terms. He used the word provisional, because the agreement had to be submitted to the Joymount board of directors. But Tasker had had no doubt that it would be approved.

Their conference had been arranged for 8.45 on the previous evening, and they had arrived at Joymount punctually—indeed slightly ahead of time owing to a strong following wind. The Joymount representatives had met them in a friendly way, and their business had been little more than to register the agreement which both sides had already reached. Tasker had typed out some clauses which had been considered and finally initialled. That brought it to about ten o'clock. Tasker had then insisted on their dividing a bottle of champagne to celebrate their achievement, and this took about half an hour. The three Joymount men came out to their wharf to see them off, and they had parted with congratulations on both sides.

No sooner had they started than Haviland said that as they had finished the conference earlier than they had expected, he would very much like to call for a few minutes at Hamble to enquire for his sister. Haviland's sister had married a Major Ashe, and they had rung him up to say that she had had a son that day. He would look in for a moment if the others did not mind waiting. Both, of course, said they didn't, and they put in at Hamble.

The Ashes lived about half a mile from the hard, and Haviland set off to walk. Mairs and Samson remained in the launch. They smoked and chatted over their recent meeting, while Samson amused himself by rubbing up the bright parts of the motor. After a while Haviland returned to say that his sister and the child were doing well, and they started for Chayle. Samson then repeated his story of the explosion.

Though Carter had taken the statement down in shorthand, French had made occasional notes of salient points. These he now studied. Then slowly he began to ask questions.

'This whole disaster strikes one as a very extraordinary affair. Can you offer any theory as to what might have really taken place?'

'Absolutely none, Chief-Inspector. It's just about the most mysterious thing I've ever been up against.'

'You think it wasn't the petrol? It's a petrol launch, isn't it?'

'It was,' Samson returned wryly. 'No, I don't see how it could have been the petrol. There are three reasons why,' and Samson repeated the arguments he had put up to Hanbury; the excellence of the petrol installation, the rapidity of the explosion, and the fact that a petrol fire would not have immediately sunk the launch. To this was now added the fact that a petrol explosion would never have caused the injuries found on Mairs's body.

'Supposing then it was not a petrol explosion,' went on French, 'it follows that some other explosive found it's way aboard. Now, how could that have been?'

'It couldn't have been. I had none and I'm positive that neither Haviland nor Mairs would have brought any aboard without mentioning it. In fact, if either had done so, I should have seen it.'

'Quite so.' French nodded, then sat forward and spoke more gravely. 'Now *if* this was not a petrol explosion, and *if* neither you nor Mr Haviland nor Mr Mairs took any explosive aboard, it follows that someone else must have done so. See where that leads us?'

Samson saw it only too clearly. From his manner French judged that he had seen it from the start.

'Now I'd like to ask you two more questions. First leave out of account how such explosive could have been put on board and fixed up to go off at the right moment, and confine your attention to another point. Tell me who, in your opinion, might have wished such an accident to happen. Wait,' he held up his hand as Samson would have spoken, 'I want you to understand that answering this question does not mean that you are accusing anyone. If you imagine that any person or group of persons might have been glad to have you and your friends out of the way, your saying so will merely indicate to me a possible line of research.'

Samson smiled a trifle grimly. 'If I thought anyone had tried to murder me, I should only want to get him hanged. But I don't suspect anyone. And in any case, I don't see how anyone could have tampered with the launch.'

'That is my second question,' French went on. 'Why do you think the launch couldn't have been tampered with? Weren't all three of you away from it during your meeting?'

'Yes, but there were a lot of people about the wharf. You know it, do you?'

'Yes, I've been there.'

'Well, we came in at the steps at the end of the wharf, close to the boathouse. Both the berths at the wharf were occupied by steamers, in fact, we had to go round the stern of one of them, which was projecting past the end of the wharf. Now that boat was loading: some hurry job in Plymouth, Tasker told us. She was loading when we went in and she was loading all the time we were there, and she was loading when we went away. No one could have tampered with the launch without being seen by the men.'

'And did none of the men see anyone?'

'I don't know that. I mean that under those conditions no one would have risked monkeying with the launch.'

'There's something in that,' French admitted, though with a mental reservation.

'Now there's nothing significant in this question,' he went on, 'I ask it as a matter of routine. Were the three Joymount men whom you went to meet, actually in your presence during the whole time you were out of your launch?'

Samson smiled. 'That cat, I'm afraid, won't jump, Chief-Inspector,' he declared. 'They were not in our presence all the time, but there's nothing in it all the same. On our arrival King was waiting for us on the wharf. We went with him straight from the launch to their offices. Tasker and Brand were there. None of them therefore could have

242

tampered with the launch *before* our meeting. And after our meeting they came down with us and saw us off. It's true all three went out of the room in the middle of the negotiations to discuss one or two points in private. But they were within hearing all the time.'

'All three?'

'Yes. They went just across the passage and we could hear the murmur of Tasker's and Brand's voices, though we couldn't hear what they were saying. We also heard King's voice at intervals. He was typing some figures for Tasker, I think, for we heard his machine going, and at intervals he broke into song, as his habit is.'

'So that whoever may be guilty, it wasn't one of those three?'

'It certainly was not.'

Again French sat thinking silently. His first idea had been that some of the Joymount people had after all murdered Clay and stolen the secret process, and that Chayle had somehow got wise to it and was holding it over them to obtain some business advantage: black-mailing them really. If this were so, to fake an accident which would destroy all three of the men who had this fatal knowledge would be a likely enough move. But now he began to wonder if he hadn't been too ready to jump to conclusions. There were undoubted difficulties in the theory.

French was an immense believer in reconstructing his cases from the point of view of time. Now, while the affair was fresh in Samson's memory, he obtained as accurate a timetable of their movements on the previous evening as the engineer could compile. This he noted in Bradshaw form as follows:

243

8.00 leave Chayle wharf.
8.40 arrive Joymount wharf.
8.50 begin conference.
10.00 finish conference and begin celebration.
10.30 leave Joymount wharf.
10.35 arrive Hamble.
11.20 depart Hamble.
11.45 explosion.

'Tell me,' he said, 'did you know before you left Joymount that you were going to Hamble?'

'No,' said Samson, 'none of us knew that. I believe Haviland only thought of it himself after we started. It was not till we had headed downstream that he suddenly suggested it, and I had to alter our course.'

'Could Haviland have mentioned it to any of the Joymount people?'

'As a matter of fact, he didn't. I was with him all the time and I should have heard him if he had.'

French asked a number of further questions, but without learning anything more, and presently, with thanks to Samson for his help, he and Carter took their leave.

18

French Gets Help from Routine

The interview with Samson had given French a number of lines of enquiry, and as they drove back to Cowes he arranged them in his mind in the order in which they could be most conveniently dealt with. The result was that he spent some minutes first with Hanbury, and on the telephone to Goodwilly in Southampton and Crawford in Eastleigh, arranging a programme of joint work. Then he further commandeered the superintendent's car to convey himself and Carter to Ryde, where they arrived in time to catch the 2.55 boat to Portsmouth. From there they took the ferry to Gosport and after a short search among the shipping, they found the small collier *Benbolt*. By four o'clock they were on board and asking for the master.

French did not expect to learn much from his call, but he took it first on his programme for two reasons. First, he knew where the *Benbolt* was at the moment, but if he waited till she had discharged her cargo and left Gosport, it might be long enough before he found her again. Secondly, via Ryde, Portsmouth and Gosport was as good a way as any to Joymount, where he really wanted to go.

As he had foreseen, Captain Jones had little to add to his statement to Locke. He repeated it in detail, agreeing with Samson that petrol would never have produced so sharp a detonation.

French had hoped to begin his investigations at Joymount that day, but it was now too late. There was one enquiry he could make, however, and he began by looking up some place to stay near Joymount. He decided on Swanwick, to which they took the first train.

At the hotel he rang up Major Ashe, saying he wished to call that evening with reference to the death of his brother-in-law, and after dinner he hired a car and set off with Carter. By nine o'clock the two men reached Brantings, Major Ashe's house near Hamble.

Here they speedily confirmed a part of Samson's story. Haviland had called on the previous evening to enquire about his sister. His visit had been unexpected, and he had explained that it was due to a sudden idea which had occurred to him after leaving Joymount. Owing to the late hour the times of his arrival and departure had been noted. He had reached Brantings at 10.45 and left at 11.10.

French took the opportunity of being in the neighbourhood to walk from the house to the hard at Hamble, and found that it took about eight minutes. This pretty well confirmed Samson's estimates that they had arrived at Hamble at 10.35 and left at 11.20.

Swanwick was convenient for Joymount, and next morning the two men got the car again and drove down to the works. They asked for Tasker and were immediately shown into his office.

French was considerably impressed with Tasker's quiet efficiency. The managing director received his visitors with courtesy, but without effusion, and asked what he could do for them.

'I understand, sir,' French explained after the usual introductions had passed, 'that it was from here that the party were going when the accident happened, and I want you to tell me everything you can about their visit in the hope of clearing up some of the mystery which surrounds their fate.'

Tasker was very willing to tell all he knew, though he did not think anything he could say would be of much use to the Chief-Inspector. He had been terribly shocked when he had heard what had taken place. The affair was a complete mystery to him and he could form no opinion of what had happened. As to a statement, he thought that it would be better if the Chief-Inspector would ask questions, which he would answer as completely as he could.

French began with the object of the visit, and Tasker told of the first coming of Haviland and Mairs, and their suggestion that the two firms should in future work in co-operation instead of in competition. He recounted the various negotiations which had taken place, and said that the meeting on the fatal Tuesday evening had been to put in writing the conclusions which had by then been reached. This had been done, and he produced and handed over the first sheet of the agreement, bearing as it did his own and Haviland's initials and the date.

French read the document carefully, noted that the works were being treated on a basis of absolute equality, and returned the paper. He then went on to enquire as to the details of the interview. Tasker was perfectly open, but could tell him nothing which added to his knowledge. So far as he, Tasker, could see, everything was perfectly normal about both men and launch. He was however obviously surprised to learn that the trio had not gone straight back to Chayle. The launch, he said, had headed downstream, and he had not seen it turn across towards Hamble.

French then enquired if any of the three visitors had been out of Tasker's sight for any time during the visit. Tasker replied, 'only for ten or fifteen minutes,' and went on to say that he and his friends had left the conference for about that time, in order to get out certain figures which he thought he might require in the discussion. Both Brand and King had helped him with these, Brand on the financial side, and King on the technical.

French next asked if the three Joymount men were together during the time they were out of the conference room. To this Tasker replied that they were—practically. He and Brand had been in Brand's room working together and King had been in his next door, typing some required data.

All this confirmed Samson's statement. French had never, as a matter of fact, suspected Tasker of crime—only Brand and King. When therefore he had got all the information he could from Tasker, he went on with somewhat greater eagerness to interrogate Brand.

Brand however corroborated Tasker on every point. French was not surprised at this. Either their statements were true, in which case they would naturally be the same, or they were false, in which case they would have carefully arranged what was to be said. But French's interest was aroused by Brand's manner. He seemed nervous, even apprehensive, and was obviously relieved when his interrogation was over. It almost looked as if he knew something material. On the other hand French felt satisfied that he was innocent of the launch explosion, his horror and bewilderment at the disaster being obviously genuine.

King, whom French next interrogated, also told the same story, and when he considered the corroboration of Samson, French felt that he must accept the statements. This corroboration of Samson's was very convincing, as had the Chayle engineer suspected the Joymount men's guilt, he would have been the first to declare it.

Another of Samson's statements was that, whenever the explosive might have been put aboard the launch, it could not have been done while at Joymount. To test this conclusion was the next item on French's list.

He went down to the wharf with the three men and got them to point out to him where the launch was moored, and also to explain just what work had been in progress during the time of the visit. Then he began to note and consider.

The wharf was of simple construction. The river bank had been sloped down uniformly and pitched with stones to preserve it from wave action. On this sloped bank was erected the wharf proper, which was composed of reinforced concrete piles, carrying a reinforced concrete deck. About halfway up the longer piles and visible only at low water, were horizontal walings, tying the various piles together, both longways and crossways.

The structure was about a hundred feet long, and at the right hand end were the boat steps. These followed the slope of the pitching, but were raised about two feet above it, so that the bow or stern of a boat could come to the steps at any state of the tide. On the other side of the steps to the wharf the small basin had been dredged, on to which the works boathouse opened.

On the Tuesday night, so Tasker explained, the Chayle launch had been moored to the steps. Though the tide was fairly high, the water was still seven or eight feet below the top of the wharf, and it would have been quite impossible for anyone to have got into her otherwise than from the steps. Two small steamers were at the wharf. That nearest the steps, the *Lucy Jane*, was taking a cargo of cement to Plymouth, and as it was to fill an urgent order, work had been carried on till midnight. Under the circumstances no one could possibly have gone down the steps to the launch unseen by the workmen.

Of these workmen, Tasker explained, two were concerned with the general direction of operations and with tallying on behalf of the company and the carriers respectively. There was at the winch on the steamer a driver, and there were six men wheeling forward and loading the bags of cement, though these latter were alternatively on the wharf and in the works yard. The wharf moreover was well lighted.

As French pictured the scene, he became convinced that Samson was correct in saying that no one could have reached the launch unnoticed by these men. The launch itself would have been out of sight, being screened by the end of the wharf. But the approach to the steps would have been in their full view.

French next had the Joymount men who had been present sent out to him. The tallyman was absolutely positive that no one had passed. So were the six wheelers, and as there had never been less than three of them on the wharf at any one time, French felt he must accept their statements.

His belief in their reliability was strengthened by the fact that they had noticed the presence of all those who were known to have used the wharf.

French left Joymount with the unhappy consciousness that what had seemed a promising line of investigation looked like petering out. As he and Carter drove back to Swanwick he felt that he must try elsewhere for his solution. Arrived at the hotel he sat down, lit a pipe, and gave himself up to thought.

From the moment he had heard the details of the explosion, the idea of a time bomb had been subconsciously in his mind. He imagined that someone wishing the destruction of the Chayle principals, had hidden a time bomb in the launch. This idea still seemed to him more probable than any other, but he now began to reverse his original opinion that the bomb had been placed at Joymount. He wondered if it could have been set before the launch left Chayle.

This led him back to the beginning of the Clay case, for he could not but think the two crimes were connected. Had he been wrong from the beginning in his views on the Clay case? Was it connected, not with any theft of the process, but with something relating to Chayle alone? It was almost beginning to look like it.

French saw that this question, whether or not the presumed time bomb could have been placed during the launch's stay at Joymount, must be settled definitely. For all the time it would take, it would be well to have the testimony of the crew of the *Lucy Jane*. He therefore telephoned to the police at Plymouth, asking them to find out if the *Lucy Jane* would be there on the following day.

The reply was waiting for him at Southampton. It said

that the *Lucy Jane* had discharged her cargo and was leaving for Weymouth that afternoon, in ballast.

French was pleased. Weymouth was a good deal nearer than Plymouth. He found there was a train about four which got to Weymouth about 6.30. When it left, he and Carter were on board.

The *Lucy Jane* had not arrived by ten that night, but next morning when they went down to the harbour, she was there. French went aboard at once.

He made exhaustive enquiries. The man who was working the steam winch admitted that someone might have passed on the wharf unseen by him—though actually he had not seen anyone, but the tallyman was quite positive that no one had. So also was another man who had been engaged in carrying out some repairs to the port light casing.

French left Weymouth entirely convinced that the evidence was unassailable. No person had tampered with the launch while it lay at Joymount.

In the train back to Southampton he continued puzzling over his problem. He was beginning to accept the time-bomb-put-in-at-Chayle theory. Nothing else indeed seemed possible.

Then suddenly a devastating idea occurred to him. A time bomb could not have been used at all!

He had already noted the fact that if such a bomb had been employed, it must have been by someone who knew the Chayle plans accurately. Samson's launch ran at about ten knots, and as the distance from Joymount to Chayle was about nine standard miles, the time taken for the journey averaged about three-quarters of an hour. The explosion had therefore to be timed within that three-quarters. Now the time of the stay at Joymount could probably have been estimated fairly accurately. In fact, French thought, had Tasker and company been guilty, they could have arranged the start at any time to suit themselves. But the Chayle party did not return at the time Tasker and company had expected. They delayed at Hamble for no less than forty minutes. If then a time bomb had been set, it would have gone off at Hamble.

The innocence of the Joymount men seemed indeed definitely established by the fact that the explosion had not taken place until some thirty minutes after the launch had left Hamble. If it had occurred immediately after the departure, it might have been possible to argue some inaccuracy in the setting. But as it was, the explosion did not take place till half an hour after the launch had been expected to arrive at Chayle.

The more French examined this idea, the more conclusive it became. The argument was unanswerable. But then—if a time bomb had not been used, he didn't know what could have happened.

The problem was exasperating. When they reached Southampton he was still puzzling over it. But, on leaving the train, he banished it from his mind. This was the time for action, not theory. Until he had got his facts he needn't worry over much about fitting them together.

The inquest on Mairs's body was to be opened that afternoon in Cowes, but as Hanbury had arranged with the coroner that the proceedings would be adjourned after taking evidence of identification, French did not think he was called on to attend. He therefore looked up the list of enquiries he had made, and decided he would devote the remainder of the day to pushing forward one important line of investigation—the effort to find out where the explosive might have been obtained.

This matter was one of those in which he had asked the co-operation of the local men and he was anxious to know just what had been done about it. He began therefore by calling on Superintendent Goodwilly at the Southampton headquarters.

'The explosive?' said Goodwilly, when after some general discussion French had put his question. 'Well, we've made a start on it, but we've got nothing so far. We've been to all the likely shops and dealers in the area and checked up their sales for some weeks past, but without getting anything. We've got out a list of all the contractors who use explosives, including all quarry owners, but there hasn't been time to go round them yet. I'm also going to question everyone who has a licence for firearms. Then, of course, there are the military and naval authorities, though I'm not dealing with them. The Portsmouth men are seeing them, but I don't know if they've done so yet.'

'You've not been idle, Super,' French complimented. 'Let's ring up and see how the others are doing.'

Calls to the superintendents and officers of forces in the surrounding country showed that a vast deal of work was being done on the matter, but so far entirely without result. It looked as if tracing the explosive wasn't going to be easy.

In arranging what was to be undertaken locally, French had reserved for himself the investigation of what he had then supposed were the two most likely sources of supply— the chalk quarries belonging to Joymount and Chayle respectively. There would, he thought, just be time to visit the Joymount quarry that afternoon, and he decided to get on with it at once.

When at the works on the previous day he had taken the precaution of obtaining a note from Tasker to the quarry foreman, and he and Carter now set off, Goodwilly supplying them with a car.

The quarry was some distance from the works, the quarried chalk being taken there by motor lorry. It represented the usual blemish on the smooth green side of the Downs, an irregular amphitheatre of whitish rock, cut into shelves and ledges and precipices, and strewn over with heaps of broken stones and boulders. From a small shed near the entrance came the coughing of an oil engine, compressing air for the drills. Distributed over the face were men, though what they were doing was not obvious from a casual inspection. Beside the shed containing the engine was another with the word 'Office' painted on the door. French pushed this door open and looked in. A man was writing at a rough desk.

'Good morning,' said French. 'Are you the foreman?'

The man somewhat doubtfully admitted it.

'Then,' French went on, 'I want a bit of help from you. I am an officer from Scotland Yard,' and he went through his little formula, continuing: 'I've seen Mr Tasker about the same matter, and he asked me to give you this,' and he handed over the note.

The foreman was obviously thrilled. He got off his stool and pushed it under the desk. Having by this means nearly doubled the floor area, he asked French to come in. French did so, as did also as much of Carter as there was room for.

'It's about this case of the launch being blown up,' French

went on. 'We don't know whether it was petrol or an explosive that did the damage, so we're trying to find out if any explosives are missing from anywhere in the neighbourhood. We have of course no reason to suspect that any were taken from here. Every quarry foreman is being asked the same questions I'm going to ask you now.'

Taking silence for consent, French then requested the man to explain how their explosives were dealt with.

The foreman was intelligent and gave his information clearly. Summarised, it was as follows:

The explosive used was gelignite, as it tended to shatter the rock, and so reduced the proportion of big stones which had afterwards to be broken up for the crushers. He requisitioned it by the dozen boxes, and when it came it was stored in the explosives shed, a small specially constructed building quarter of a mile away. A cartridge was a cylindrical shaped block of pure gelignite, the most commonly used size being about three inches long by about three-quarters of an inch in diameter. They used bigger cartridges for the deeper holes. Gelignite was a yellowish compound, stiff like cheese, and each cartridge was wrapped in waterproof paper.

Gelignite could not be exploded by mere heat, and would burn like a stick if put into a fire. It had to be detonated with a small explosive detonator, or it *might* go off from a sudden sharp blow or a spark. No steel tools were used in working with it, for fear that by striking a flint, a spark might be produced. For exploding it in the holes, detonators were used, little things about an inch and a half long by a quarter of an inch in diameter, something like long thin revolver cartridges. These were set off either by a fuse or an electric spark. If the Chief-Inspector cared to come across to the hut, he could see the things for himself.

French walked over, asking questions on the way. No, the detonators must not be wet, or they would not explode. If they were in water, detonation by a fuse would be impossible, but electrical detonation could be used. The detonators were sold with the necessary wires fixed and waterproofed. Detonators were used by unwrapping the paper from one end of the cartridge, making a hole in the gelignite with a wooden awl, pushing in the detonator with the wires attached, and replacing the paper wrapping. So arranged, the gelignite would explode on the passage of a low tension current.

Before starting for the shed, the foreman had called over one of the workmen, who, he explained, was in charge of the explosives. This man accompanied the party. French now saw that he only had a key to the store. He commented on this.

'Yes,' the foreman answered. 'We're very careful about the key. There are only two in existence, one that this man has, and one that's locked up in the safe in the office. No one here can get any explosives except what this man gives out, and he's responsible for the stock and never leaves the door unlocked.'

This was an important point and French went into it thoroughly. After taking evidence from a number of workmen, he became satisfied on the following points:

1. No one but the charge hand or someone who had access to the office safes could have opened the store.
2. The charge hand had not lent his key to anyone, and no one could have got it unknown to him.

3. The charge hand never left the store while it was unlocked.

4. No one but the charge hand was allowed to enter, or had entered, the store.

5. The charge hand passed out the required explosives, and no one could have removed any unknown to him.

6. The charge hand was obviously a reliable man, and French was convinced that he was telling the truth so far as he knew it.

The remaining point on which French made enquiries was however by no means so clear. He asked the charge hand whether if the door had been opened with another key, and if one cartridge and one detonator had been removed, he would have noticed the loss?

At first the man said he would, but on further consideration he was not so sure. The cartridges and detonators were not counted, and the removal of one of each—particularly of the detonators, which were small—might escape notice.

French left the quarry feeling convinced of three things. Firstly if such a theft had been made, it could only have been done by someone who had access to the spare key in the office safe. Secondly, that almost certainly Tasker, Brand, and King had access to the key and could have robbed the store at night; and lastly, that if they, or any one of them, had done so, the chances of proving it were practically nil.

Not very well pleased with his afternoon's work, French decided that he would complete this part of the investigation by next morning visiting the Chayle quarries.

Here history repeated itself. The Chayle explosives were dealt with in practically the same way as those of Joymount, and here again it would unquestionably have been possible for anyone who had access to the Chayle safes to obtain the spare key of the store and remove the explosive.

In the case of Chayle, however, a further point had to be taken into account. Someone had obtained a mould of the Chayle safe keys. Admittedly, since then Haviland had had the locks changed, but if it had been possible to copy the old keys, might it not have been equally possible in the case of the new? This consideration widened almost indefinitely the range of French's enquiry, and he felt rather sick about it.

In a slightly despondent frame of mind he called at the police station in Cowes for a consultation with Hanbury before returning to Southampton.

19

French Gets Help from a Theory

When French reached Southampton his despondency had grown rather than diminished. Hanbury's report had been completely negative. Not only had the Superintendent failed to learn any new facts, but he had no ideas as to where new facts might be sought. And French found himself in very much the same predicament.

The trouble was not the lack of definite problems to be solved. It was rather that he could not see how the solution of any one of these problems was to be reached. There was the question of whether the process had been stolen, and if so, whether the launch affair was connected with the theft. There was the problem of whether the Clay murder was connected with either or both. And with regard to the launch crime there were the three essential conundrums: Where and how had the explosive been put on board, how had it been made to go off at the right moment, and who was the agent responsible? French chafed as he thought of the amount that was still to be learned. If he could solve even one of these problems it would be an ease to his mind and might well lead to a further advance.

He concentrated on the question of whether the two crimes were connected, and if so, whether both arose out of the theft of the process, or from some other incident or incidents which might have happened at Chayle, and of which he as yet knew nothing. All the evening he thrashed the matter out in his mind and when he went to bed he took it with him.

He couldn't sleep that night. The problem had taken such a hold on him that he couldn't rest till he had reached a solution. He *must* reach a solution, as otherwise he would find himself at a loose end next day. Should he assume the crimes had nothing to do with the process and concentrate on Chayle? Should he go there in the morning and begin general enquiries into the lives of Haviland, Mairs and Samson, in the hope of coming on some fact which would throw light on the situation? If not, what was he to do?

Then he had a revulsion of feeling. Here was a valuable secret, and it seemed incredible that these two crimes should not have been in some way connected with it.

Once again his mind swung back to its former view. There was no evidence of any kind whatever connecting either crime with the process. There was no evidence that the process had been stolen. There was no evidence that the safe which contained it had been opened. The formula was in its accustomed place on the morning after the Clay affair, and there was no sign that either it or any of the other papers in the safe had been disarranged. Most important of all, no other firm was putting out cement at a reduced price. No, it didn't seem as if the process was the real source of the trouble.

For hours French tossed on his bed, worried and exasperated, racking his brains to try to find a solution. But none came to him. At last he turned his attention to the other set of questions: how exactly had the explosion been brought out? But here again he was baffled. In vain he turned and twisted the facts in his mind. There was no light anywhere.

Suddenly, just as he was feeling that at all costs he must get a little sleep, a fresh idea flashed across his mind. For a moment he didn't realise its true implication, then a gradually quickening excitement took possession of him.

Yes, here was something he had overlooked! Here was something vital! Here at last was a way by which the explosion could have been caused. The more French thought of it, the more convinced he became that it was *the* way. Yes, he was sure he was right! He had solved the greater part of his problem. Thankfully he switched off his light, rolled over, and fell asleep.

He was more thankful still as he went downstairs some four hours later. Not infrequently it had happened that conclusions reached during the comparatively fevered watches of the night, looked anything but promising when viewed in the more sober light of day. But this time his new theory had stood the test of examination by the critical judgment of morning. By the time he had dressed he had gone over all his conclusions in his mind, and was satisfied that in this puzzling case he had at last reached the essential truth.

His new theory of the crime was simple and obvious, and he was now only puzzled to know why he hadn't reached it sooner. Once again, he thought, he had gone wrong through failure to follow the facts. He had allowed himself to be led astray by preconceived ideas. He had believed that certain things were likely or unlikely as the case might be, and unconsciously he had allowed his judgment to be warped by these probabilities. Well, it was another lesson to him to build on facts and facts only, leaving probabilities to their proper function of suggesting lines of investigation.

As he ate a practically solitary breakfast—he only talked to Carter when he had nothing else to think of—he reviewed his argument.

First of all, the nature of the explosion proved the disaster to the launch to have been intentional; in other words, it had been deliberately brought about with an object. What was that object?

He had jumped to the conclusion that the object was the destruction of Haviland, Mairs and Samson. It was really this which had led him to connect the affair with the process; to suppose that Joymount had stolen the process; that Chayle had got wise to the theft; and that Joymount wished to blot out what might become exceedingly inconvenient knowledge.

But might not this fundamental assumption be false? Was this not the point at which he, French, had jumped to a wholly unwarrantable conclusion? How did he know the object of the crime had been to destroy Haviland, Mairs and Samson?

He didn't know it. It was a guess. And it was recognition of the fact that it was a guess that had put him, during the night, on the right lines. He had realised that this assumption of the motive for the affair had simply clouded the issue and prevented him from seeing the truth.

Sweeping away this false assumption had enabled him

to answer the second series of questions relative to the placing and exploding the charge.

Suppose the crime, instead of being a partial failure, had been a complete success. Suppose that Haviland and Mairs had been killed, but not Samson; why? Because Samson had killed the others!

This idea, French saw at once, cleared away all his difficulties. Samson, and Samson only, could have arranged the whole affair.

Samson had unlimited facilities for secret access to the launch. It was his property, and he could without comment go out in it or work at it in the boathouse at any time that he chose. He could easily have hidden a bomb in the stern, with a string attached, which could have been led forward to the bows. A pull on the string at the correct moment would have caused the explosion.

But was such a thing likely? French thought so: for several reasons.

First, there was the overwhelming reason that, so far as he could see, it was the only way in which the thing could have been done. This in itself was proof, but there were a number of other supporting facts.

If Samson were not guilty, it was certainly a strange coincidence that the small anchor, or grappling, should break loose, and Samson should go forward to make it fast, at just the moment that the explosion should occur, and moreover that the launch should at that moment be close to another vessel.

French pictured what might have happened. Before leaving Chayle, Samson sets his bomb and lays his cord, arranging them so that neither will be seen. When he considers the time propitious he spins his yarn about the grappling, goes forward, stoops down so as to be protected by the motor casing, and pulls his cord. The bomb goes off and a hole is blown in the bottom of the boat, which sinks. Samson has taken the precaution to have a lifebuoy at hand, to which he clings till he is picked up. He undoubtedly runs some risk of drowning, but for this very reason he is sure he will not be suspected of murder.

To French all this seemed entirely satisfactory. It brought him, however, direct to the question of motive. Had Samson a motive for wishing the deaths of the other two men?

On this point French knew nothing, but he remembered noticing a curious feature of Samson's manner. The man had always seemed sullen and as if nursing a grievance, particularly against Haviland. Here was a likely line for investigation, which he must undertake at once.

Among the routine details given him by Hanbury were the names of Haviland's and Mairs's solicitors. French thought that a visit to both was indicated.

Both lived at Cowes, and Carter rang them up and arranged interviews for that morning. French and he took the next boat, duly presented themselves at Messrs Dacre & Johns, and asked if they could see Mr Dacre.

French soon realised that it was not going to be easy to get his information, and he was therefore careful not to demand it, but to ask for the solicitor's help as a favour.

'I want you to keep it to yourself, Mr Dacre,' he said confidentially, 'but I should tell you that there is a suspicion amounting almost to a certainty that this affair was not an accident, but that murder was committed.' Mr Dacre made a sharp exclamation, but French went on. 'If so, you, as the representative of the late Mr Haviland, will doubtless be as anxious as I am to get the murderer brought to justice. It is with this in view that I should like to ask you a question or two. I very much hope, sir, that you can see your way to give me this help, which both of us know you are not bound to do.'

Dacre was sincerely shocked at the news. It appeared that he was a personal friend of Haviland's as well as his man of business, and he had evidently had no idea that the affair could have been anything but an accident.

'I should be glad to help you,' he said when he had duly expressed his feelings. 'But you know, Chief-Inspector, that in these cases it is usually wise to say nothing. However, let me hear what you want, and I'll do what I can for you.'

French wanted a general statement of Haviland's position, chiefly from the financial point of view. He wanted to see his will. He wanted to know whether he had enemies, and if so, the reason for their enmity. In fact, he wanted any information which might indicate a motive for the crime.

Mr Dacre appreciated the position, but exhibited the caution of the legal mind. Finally he said he found himself unable to produce the will, but that otherwise, broadly speaking, he would answer his visitor's questions.

But when he had done so, French found that he was little the wiser. Haviland had been comfortably off, if not rich, though of course, Dacre pointed out, such terms were relative. He was married and all his money, with the exception of a few trifling bequests, went to his family. His only son was going to be a doctor, and there was no one who could replace him at the works. As to enemies, Mr Dacre knew of none, nor could he give any information which would account for such a crime.

Mr Lewisham, Mairs's solicitor, upon whom French and his satellite next called, was not such a stickler for etiquette. Under the circumstances he made no difficulty about answering French's questions. Mairs, it appeared, had been unmarried and had had no near relatives. He had left his property, which was not large, in roughly equal thirds to Haviland, Samson and a distant cousin, a captain in the merchant service. Lewisham scouted the idea that his client's death could have been due to foul play, saying he was a good sort, liked by everyone. He certainly knew of no enemies, and he didn't believe there had been any.

From all this it seemed to French that not only would Samson come in for a small amount of money on the death of Haviland and Mairs, but he would become practical chief of the business. It was not a company, and by paying Haviland's executors their share of the profits, Samson would apparently be able to do as he liked. For this he might well have risked a good deal.

While interviewing solicitors, French thought he might as well see Messrs Dagge & Trimble also, the solicitors for the Chayle firm. The office was close by, and he and Carter turned in and presently were received by Mr Trimble.

Trimble, however, was giving nothing away. He pointed out that he was now solicitor for Mr Samson, and as such must await Mr Samson's instructions before discussing business.

'Well,' said French, 'in saying that you've really answered my principal question. I wanted to know who I have to deal with in connection with Chayle. Is Mr Samson in sole charge, or are there other partners in the background who must be considered?'

Trimble thought over this and evidently considered it

innocuous. 'You have to deal with Mr Samson,' he answered. 'There's no one else at present. Presumably the Haviland interest will put in a representative later, but for the moment Mr Samson is the works.'

Here, then, was an undoubted motive. At the same time, it did not satisfy French. Firstly, it seemed scarcely adequate, and secondly, it did not account for that undoubted air of grievance which Samson had always borne. French wondered could he get anything out of the man himself.

'Nothing like trying,' he thought, and getting a car, was driven with Carter out to the works.

Samson saw them at once and French lost no time in getting to business.

First with impressive seriousness he pledged Samson to silence. Then he told him that his suspicion had been practically confirmed that the launch affair represented an attempt on the lives of its three occupants. Further progress however was made difficult by the fact that Haviland and Mairs had both seemed such extraordinarily good fellows, straight and generous and openhanded, making friends everywhere and without a serious enemy in the world. Samson became less enthusiastic at this, and as French continued to lay on the soft soap, he could restrain his feelings no longer and fell into the trap.

'They weren't such saints as all that,' he said at last. 'They were like you and me and the next man—just ordinary.'

French thought the time was not ripe and continued his adulation. Samson reacted better than he could have hoped.

'Ah nonsense, man,' he protested at last. 'They could do the dirty like anyone else. Who have you been talking to?'

Here was something definite at last. French seized on it

like a bulldog. What did Mr Samson mean by that? He must have known of some instance or he wouldn't have spoken in such a way.

Samson became suddenly wary and would have withdrawn. But it was no use. French stuck to it, and at last forced the engineer into the dilemma of either replying or taking the responsibility of keeping back apparently vital evidence. At last the whole thing came out.

Samson had been deeply and bitterly resentful against both the dead men, but specially against Haviland. He had been treated badly, he considered, about the process. He had worked at it almost day and night, for over four years. Practically all his spare time had been put into it, as well admittedly as a good deal of the firm's, though not, he swore, to the neglect of his ordinary work. When he had completed his invention he had informed the others. On the excuse of considering the plant which would be required to work the process, they had learnt the details, and Haviland had then turned round (the phrase was Samson's) and told him that the work had been done in their time and the experiments carried out with their materials and apparatus, and the resulting invention was not his, Samson's, but the firm's. Samson had seen with bitterness that he was in the other's hands. He had no money to develop his process apart from Chayle, while if he had approached another firm, Haviland might have prosecuted him for selling Chayle property.

Haviland however had not acted so badly in the end. When the process became a going concern, Samson was made a partner, the process being taken as representing his share of the capital. But Samson had felt that this concession had only been made to keep him at Chayle, and his sense of grievance had remained keen.

French saw that here was all the motive he required to build up his case. On the one hand there was hatred and a rankling sense of injustice against the two dead men, and on the other a material financial gain as well as an increase of freedom and prestige if they were out of the way. Yes, the motive was now entirely adequate.

And the other great essential of a police officer's case against a suspect was equally met. As well as motive there was opportunity. Samson could have obtained the necessary gelignite and detonator from the Chayle quarry, he could have placed it in the launch, and at the proper moment he could have exploded it, while taking the necessary precautious for his own safety.

As to proof, the third desideratum in such cases, French was not on such sure ground. There was the negative proof that he believed there was no other way in which the crime could have been carried out. Negative proof however was always unsatisfactory, and incidentally went no distance with a jury. But where to get positive proof French did not see.

One other consideration occurred to him, which, though not in the nature of proof, was entirely consistent with the theory of Samson's guilt. Might not Samson have deliberately chosen the run from Joymount to Chayle in the hope of throwing on to Joymount any suspicion which might be aroused? He would be aware that the police would learn of the negotiations in progress with Joymount, and that they already knew of the existence of the process. Would it be too much to suppose that he would have foreseen the very theory being reached, which French had been working on? French thought he would be bound to foresee it. And if so, the launch disaster would undoubtedly suggest that Joymount had taken this way to rid themselves of their enemies.

This suggestion, added to the apparent fact that Samson himself had had the narrowest escape from drowning, would tend very efficiently to transfer any suspicion from Samson to Joymount.

All the same French was still not satisfied. He wanted positive proof, something that would directly connect Samson with the crime. How was he to get it? He did not see.

Now ensued some days of the hateful worrying type which every investigator knows so well, when any real progress seems quite impossible. French was convinced that there must be some further fact, which if he could only get hold of it, would give him the proof he wanted. But if there were, it remained elusively hidden. French felt badly up against it, and grew short in the temper and a trying companion for the unhappy Carter.

This was not to say that during those wearing days either of them were idle. On the contrary, they worked hard from morning to night. But it was always in following up clues or making enquiries which led to nothing. French saw an immense dossier of facts piling up, but they were all negative facts: they proved that this and that and the other would not support his theories, but not that his theories were right or wrong.

During this period he was also much afflicted by the well-meant efforts of his fellow men. In this case, as in most others, large numbers of people thought they could help him to solve his problem, and wrote him letters and called to see him with mysterious information which, they said, would lead him straight to his goal. This phase of the public mind is usually best seen when the description of a wanted individual has been published. In such cases the individual in question is invariably possessed of the marvellous power of reduplication. He is seen in scores of places simultaneously, details of each appearance being sedulously furnished to the police. The worst of it is that no single one of these communications can be dismissed without investigation, since, however unlikely, it may contain something of value. Many a *cul-de-sac* of enquiry did French and his helpers explore as a result of the misplaced zeal of the public.

For about a week this state of stalemate went on, and then an idea occurred to French which he hoped would end the deadlock and start him once more on the road he wished to travel.

In the evening he had had a fire put on in his bedroom, and he retired there after dinner with the intention of once again going over the case from the beginning, in the rather faint hope that some hint might become disclosed which up to then had eluded him.

With the utmost concentration he worked through his notes, and he had almost given up in despair, when he came for the nth time to his theory of what had happened in the boat prior to the explosion. He had postulated a cord, running from the bows aft, the pulling of which had exploded the charge. Now it occurred to him that an electric circuit, which would ignite the detonator directly, might have been easier to arrange.

Though at first sight this seemed a quite trivial point, as a matter of fact it proved one of the most important he had yet considered. Indeed he afterwards admitted it formed the start of the line of enquiry which led him eventually to his goal.

His first idea was not so much that the electric circuit would be easier to arrange, but that the cord would be more difficult. Indeed as he thought over it he saw that he had rather taken things for granted. It would, of course, be possible to arrange some apparatus for the cord to work: it might, for example, pull the trigger of a pistol, or it might release a weight or a spring which would explode the detonator. But all such would have more or less serious objections.

In the first place the apparatus would have to be designed and made, and the making of it might be seen and awkward questions might be asked. Next any such apparatus would occupy a certain space—perhaps the pistol the least of any—and as it had to be so hidden that the victims should not see it, size was a matter of importance. Third, at best the apparatus would be experimental and untried, which would be extremely undesirable. In fact French now felt sure a cord would only have been employed if no better method were available.

The electric circuit however supplied an ideal means. Here nothing would have to be designed, as detonators fitted with the necessary wires were to be had by the hundred in the Chayle explosive store. Moreover the space occupied was negligible. It was true that one or more dry batteries would have to be used, but these need not be placed in the stern where hiding space was limited, but could be put anywhere that was convenient. About this plan moreover there was nothing experimental. For decades electric discharge had been in everyday use.

French followed up his idea. Suppose electric discharge

had been used, how exactly would the apparatus have been arranged?

The actual explosive cartridge with the detonator buried in it would be placed in the stern, as was proved by the report of the captain of the *Benbolt* and the injuries to Mairs's feet. The switch must have been in the bows for Samson to press. Wires must therefore have been run from bow to stern. The battery would probably have been hidden somewhere in the bows out of sight of the victims.

French recalled Samson's description of the launch. It had been a fifteen-foot ship's boat, and was entirely open, save for a couple of feet in the bows, which Samson had decked over as a protection against bad weather. It was broad of beam and an excellent seaboat. Samson had bought it, and had then put in the motor. This he had placed amidships, building over it a removable cover. The screw shaft he had laid along the bottom, covering it with a set of false bottom boards. One of these boards was movable to give access to the bearings. The petrol was stored in a tank in the bows.

French tried to picture just how the connecting wires might have been led, and as he did so, one point seemed to stand out. They would have been made fast to nails or other fixed objects. They would not have been left loose, lest the plunging of the boat should have shaken them out within sight of Haviland or Mairs. Possibly they had been laid beneath the moveable board alongside the screw shaft, or perhaps looped up under the stern side seats.

Now if they had been made fast, they would still be in position. The ends next the explosive would of course have been blown off, but the intermediate section and the switch in the bows should remain in place.

French wondered if an examination could be made of the launch.

If the switch and wires were found, it would constitute absolute proof of Samson's guilt.

Next morning before leaving the breakfast table French put his conclusions to Carter. By this he not only obtained the sergeant's opinion, but—which he considered much more important—he still further cleared up his own mind on the various points at issue. Satisfied after their discussion that his ideas were sound, he rang up Hanbury and asked him to arrange an early conference with his Chief Constable.

20

French Gets Help from the Sea

French had already met Major Considine at conferences on the case and he had been much impressed by his ability and by the up-to-date way in which he looked at things. Sir Mortimer Ellison had said that Colonel Tressider was what was called in certain circles a downy bird, and that if he said anything wanted looking into, he, French, might take it from him, Sir Mortimer, that it did. French had come to think the same could be said of Major Considine.

By a lucky chance it happened that the Major was expected at the police station in Cowes that morning, and by eleven o'clock he and Hanbury were seated at one side of a table in the latter's office, with French and Carter opposite.

'Well, Chief-Inspector,' Major Considine began, 'I was glad to hear you wanted a conference. A prelude to action, eh?'

French shrugged. 'I'm afraid, sir, not the kind of action you are hoping for. I'm not in a position to suggest an arrest.'

'But it means progress of some kind?'

'Yes, but the last kind you will want to hear of. I want, sir, a good deal of money to be spent.'

The Chief Constable shook his head. 'That's a bad hearing certainly. However, in this world we must pay for our pleasures. Let's hear the worst.'

'It arises out of a theory I've formed, sir, and which I'd like to put up to you before we go any further. I was considering just how the charge on that launch could have been exploded at exactly the right moment,' and French went on to describe his idea of Samson's guilt, the use of an electric circuit, and his belief that the switch and wires must have remained in position, ending up by pointing out the completeness of the proof against Samson their discovery would be.

Considine and Hanbury were obviously impressed.

'And what exactly do you propose?' the Major went on.

'What of course I would like,' French returned, 'would be to have the launch lifted. However as I presume that's out of the question, I was going to ask you for a diver.'

Considine moved uneasily. 'Cost a hell of a lot of money, I'm afraid. What would it cost us, Hanbury?'

'Not such a great deal, I fancy, sir,' the Super answered. 'I happen to know that the Eureka Salvage people over in Southampton are very slack at present. I'm sure they'd be glad to do the thing cheap. Shall I ring 'em up and ask?'

'I suppose you'd better.'

Some telephoning took place and then Hanbury reported. 'The manager says he couldn't give a figure because he doesn't know how long the job would take. He says they might spend quite a time finding the boat. But he's slack and he'd do it for practically cost price. You see, sir,' he went on confidentially, 'he has to pay his men retaining wages, and it would save him money to get them working.'

'Well, we can't run into it blindly. He could give us a figure per day, I suppose?'

Further telephoning produced a maximum figure per day which Major Considine thought the police finances could bear, and it was decided to go ahead with the work.

'When can he start?' asked the Major.

'Tomorrow morning, if we give him the order at once.'

'Very well; get it out and I'll sign it and you can post it immediately.'

After still more telephoning it was arranged that the salvage company's boat would leave Southampton at six next morning. The salvage manager thought it might save time if he sent a man over to Cowes to try to locate the area of search. This man would cross that afternoon by the 2.20 boat, and the manager asked that someone would meet him.

''Pon my soul, I think I'll go with you tomorrow,' Major Considine declared. 'Let's see. I have an appointment in Ryde tomorrow at eleven. I'll come on to Cowes and if you're still there I'll go aboard and see how you're getting on.'

French said with unction that he would be very pleased if the Chief Constable could find it convenient to be present, and the conference terminated.

'Now, Carter,' French said as they left the station, 'for something that'll interest you. What about a spot of lunch?'

Carter said the chief was full of brainy ideas that day, and they turned into a convenient restaurant.

On the arrival of the *Medina* they made the acquaintance of Mr Tim O'Brien, a burly gentleman in a peaked cap and dungarees, with shrewd eyes and a tongue which betrayed his native land. 'Is it the Chief-Inspector ye are?' he said to French, and thereafter appeared to consider him an old friend.

'Yes,' he went on apropos of nothing in particular, 'there was one time a job—' and he began an involved reminiscence which French had to interrupt with pertinacity before he could make headway with the business in hand.

They called at police headquarters to pick up Hanbury. 'Mr O'Brien here,' French explained, 'has come over to help us to get the area defined over which we'll search tomorrow. He says that in this job the time will go in locating the launch, and that the diving won't amount to much.'

Hanbury nodded to the salvage man. 'Have you any notion how we should set about it?' he asked.

'We were discussing that on the way up,' French answered. 'It seems there's a chance of getting something. We have that gentleman who saw the explosion and we have Locke and the three other men who went out in launches, and we have the skipper of the *Benbolt*, and lastly we have Samson. Mr O'Brien thinks that if we got them all to give us positions and took the mean, we couldn't be very far wrong.'

Hanbury nodded again. 'We'll go up and see Dr Sadler,' he said shortly, and led the way along the shore towards the west.

'Dr Sadler's the man who saw the flash,' French explained to O'Brien as they walked. 'A retired doctor of science, I think you said, Super?'

'Yes. An astronomer, I believe. He's not been here long: under a year.'

'Barring he was a shipmaster itself,' said O'Brien, 'an astronomer's just the boy we want. He'll be acquainted with taking bearings and he'll have noted where the thing happened.'

The Irishman proved a true prophet. Dr Sadler, though apparently slightly taken aback by the size of his deputation, quickly grasped what was required of him.

'Oh yes,' he said at once, 'I can help you there. But in one dimension only, I'm afraid. I can give you the bearing of the flash fairly accurately, but its distance only very approximately.'

'Sure, doctor, that's the best of good news,' broke in O'Brien. 'It was the bearing we'd hoped to get from you, though we scarcely expected it. But we never thought you could tell us the distance, and for the life of me I don't see how you'd know it.'

Sadler smiled rather wanly. 'Only by an estimate of the time between the flash and the boom,' he explained. 'Naturally very approximate, but still a rough guide.'

'Faith now, but that's clever. I'll warrant you didn't think of that, Chief-Inspector?'

'I didn't,' French admitted. 'We're going to be a good deal in your debt, Dr Sadler.'

'Not at all,' the scientist returned. 'I'm rather fond of looking at the lights at night, when it's clear enough to distinguish them, as it was that night. I suppose it's because it's the next best thing to looking at the stars, which I've been doing all my life. But of course you're not interested in that. Well, as I was saying, I was looking at the lights. I had just identified the Calshot Point Light when the flare went up. It was about ten degrees west of Calshot.'

O'Brien was enthusiastic. 'We couldn't have asked for

better than that,' he declared warmly. 'It would be about a point, doctor?'

'About that. There are really about eleven degrees in a point, but a point is as near as I could go.'

'A point west of Calshot,' the salvage man repeated. 'And where would you say that would be, doctor? See the west end of that long grey shed? What about that?'

'Just about that, I should say. If the boat sank at once, I've no doubt you'll find her close to that line.'

'Aye, be jabbers, we've to think about that too. If she didn't sink at once, goodness only knows where she mayn't have got to.'

'She must have sunk pretty quickly,' French pointed out, 'because of where Samson was picked up.'

'True for you, Chief-Inspector.' O'Brien gazed through a pair of binoculars in the indicated direction. 'Bad cess to it,' he went on, 'I can't pick up another bearing. You see,' he turned to French, 'if you can get two bearings on a line to the one side of where you're searching, the skipper can see where he is for himself. But if you can only get one bearing someone has to stay ashore and signal port or starboard to the ship. I expect I'll be for that.'

'If you want to signal you can do so from my front garden,' said Dr Sadler. 'It's fairly private.'

O'Brien was obliged. This would suit him exactly. He would be up about seven if the morning were clear. 'And now, doctor,' he went on, 'you were saying about the distance the flash was away. We'd thank you to tell us about that.'

'I estimated between four and five seconds passed between the flash and the boom,' Sadler answered. 'If so, at eleven hundred feet per second that means about a mile or less from the house—say three-quarters of a mile from the shore.'

'That agrees pretty well with what Captain Jones of the *Benbolt* said, and also with Samson's statement,' French pointed out. 'Both said they were about a mile from the shore.'

'Good enough,' O'Brien declared. 'We'll not get it much nearer than that.'

'Better see Locke all the same,' Hanbury suggested. 'We can get hold of him quite easily.'

'Yes,' French approved. 'The more, the merrier.'

Having thanked Dr Sadler for his information, they returned into the town in search of Locke. They ran him to earth in his club, and he at once confirmed the other evidence. 'A mile,' he declared, 'would be the outside figure. I should say three-quarters would be nearer it.'

In the street once more, French took Hanbury aside. 'There's one thing we mustn't overlook,' he pointed out. 'Suppose for argument's sake Samson is guilty. Suppose he sees the diving going on and tumbles to what we're doing. Suppose that the wire and switch are there. Well, he'll know at once that he's for it. You see?'

Hanbury nodded significantly. 'That's true, Chief-Inspector. You think he might slip his cable?'

'I think we'd be wise to keep him under observation till this affair is over.'

'I'll arrange it,' Hanbury declared, and the men separated.

It was not yet light when next morning the optimistically-named steamship *Eureka* left Southampton with, in addition to its crew and much strange apparatus, two passengers, Chief-Inspector French and Sergeant Carter. As is somewhat unusual for passengers without maritime connections, they occupied positions of honour on the bridge, the guests of the skipper.

Captain Soutar was as taciturn as his satellite O'Brien was talkative. He explained briefly that the morning was fine, that the bridge was the only place there was room to move on that damned hooker, and that they would be at the scene of operations in about an hour, and then relapsed into a moody silence.

In darkness they sailed down the famous waterway and it was not till they were near their objective that the south-eastern sky began to brighten and the low lines of the various coasts came dimly into view.

The crew however had not been idle during the run. Apparatus was being brought on deck and overhauled. Winches, of which there seemed to be a vast number in every part of the ship, were clanking slowly and unsteadily, getting heated up and cleared of condensed water. The diver, a hercules named Kendrick, was screwing and unscrewing the valve of his helmet, which lay on a packing-case beside him, as if dissatisfied with the way it was working. French went down and began to chat with him, taking the opportunity of explaining exactly what he wanted him to look for. 'And by the way,' he went on, 'it's all very confidential. So I want you to keep what you see to yourself.'

The giant nodded. 'I've got you,' he agreed, and went on to talk of the job. 'Where you're going to lose the time,' he said, with a deplorable absence of originality, 'is searching for the blinking boat. With a small thing like that we may pass right over her and the grabs may miss her. And in these waters we may get a dozen hulls before we strike the right one.'

'You're not encouraging,' French smiled.

'On the other hand we may come on her first shot. You never know your luck. But once we find her, your job won't take long.'

French watched the proceedings with interest. First the ship was taken to within half a mile of the shore and manœuvred on to the line with her bows pointing towards Calshot. It was still too dark to see the burly O'Brien and the flags that he would afterwards use, but red and green lights seen in the correct direction were taken to be his contribution to the proceedings. Strange objects were then lowered over the stern and checked carefully for depth and the ship moved slowly forward, steering to right or left according to the colour of O'Brien's light. For something over half a mile they crawled on, and then, turning, came back to where they had started from.

'O'Brien moves a few feet to the side each time,' Captain Soutar explained, 'so that we may sweep all the ground once and none of it twice, but where the tide runs strongly like here, it's chancy work.' He shook his head lugubriously.

French was soon to learn its monotony. Backwards and forwards they swept, slowly and painfully and quite without result. O'Brien had early come into view and exchanged his lights for flags. Time was passing and French was beginning to get peckish, when a cry went up from the men who were operating the drags.

It appeared that they had hooked an obstruction, and for a few moments all was ordered confusion. The engines were stopped and anchors were dropped in three directions, to hold the *Eureka* stationary over the object. It was all done with immense skill, but it took time.

Captain Soutar was, however, no sooner satisfied as to their position than Kendrick was ready to go down. At the first call of an obstruction he had begun to put on his gear. French had never seen diving and was immensely interested. First the giant put on numerous socks and sweaters and a beret, and then drew on the strong rubbered canvas dress. French was surprised to find that the sleeves ended at the wrists, the hands being ungloved. Rubber bands round the wrists made a watertight joint, so he was assured, but it seemed to him that the wrists must be badly constricted. However, Kendrick didn't seem to mind. French noticed, however, that he looked very sharply to see that the bands were properly in position.

For a few minutes the man sat in the dress, entirely clothed up to the brass ring which went round his neck. Then he gave a wave of his great hand and his assistant lifted on the heavy brass helmet, screwing it fast. Two other men were now working the pump, which was supplying air to the imprisoned diver. Huge boots with enormously thick leaden soles were quickly strapped on, and Kendrick was ready to go down.

Giant and all as he was, he could scarcely move under the weight of his trappings. They would, however, be balanced by the buoyancy of the air in the dress once he was under water, so it was explained to French. He was assisted to a ladder which had been lowered over the side, and he began to descend. First the great boots disappeared beneath the water, then his body and the powerful electric light he was carrying, and at last his round polished helmet, its glass window winking like the eye of some brazen cyclops. In a moment nothing was to be seen of him except the rubber air supply tube, leading down like a water-snake heading for the depths, the twitching rope which he held in his hand, and the fizz of the bubbles of surplus air, released from the automatic valve in the helmet.

He was a surprisingly long time going down. He had to take his time, so it was explained to French, because of the increasing pressure, too sudden an alteration of which might be dangerous. 'In deep work,' said the skipper, 'the going down and coming up takes most of the time. But here it's shallow enough to do it without much delay.'

'What would happen to him if he was too quick?' French asked.

'Nothing very much here,' Soutar answered. 'But if a man came up suddenly from a great depth his eardrums would go and his blood would boil. An increase of pressure's all right if it's the same inside and out. But high internal pressure and low external will kill you. We have airtight chambers on board and if a man comes up too quickly we rush him into the chamber and blow up the pressure till it's equal to what he was under below. That puts him right again.'

'And then what happens, because he's surely just as much cut off in the chamber as below water?'

'We let the pressure down slowly so that he has, so to speak, time to leak off inside. Then he's all right.'

There was a telephone in Kendrick's helmet and one of the assistants was wearing earphones. This man now came forward.

'He says we've hooked a small steamer, sir,' he explained. 'There's no sign of the boat anywhere round and he's coming up.'

'We need scarcely hope to get it first shot,' the skipper said to French. 'It's a pity it's so deep, else a plane might have seen it on the bottom. But it'ld be too small for a plane to pick out at that depth. Better go down, gentlemen, and have something to eat. I'll join you when we get under way again.'

As soon as Kendrick had come aboard the anchors were raised and the sweeping began again. French and Carter did full justice to the rough but excellent meal which was provided, and then with pipes drawing comfortingly, they watched from the bridge the slow back and forward traverse of the ship. Time began to drag. French realised that what he had been told about the difficulty of finding the boat was only too true.

About two o'clock a motor boat came out of Cowes harbour and headed for them. It brought Major Considine and he came on board and showed a good deal of interest in their progress. Once again he shook his head on hearing Captain Soutar's gloomy prognostications as to the time the search might take, but before he could give expression to any opinion there was a shout from the stern. Another sunken object had been hooked.

As if for Major Considine's benefit, the previous operations were repeated. Anchors were dropped and Kendrick put on his dress and went down. Again there was a considerable delay, and the others waited anxiously for news. But again they were disappointed. There was a wreck all right, but it was the very ancient remains of a sailing ship, a brig.

As if it was all part of the day's work—as indeed it was—Soutar got his anchors up again and restarted the sweeping. Major Considine soon found he had had enough of it and departed in his launch, leaving the others carrying steadily on.

Presently daylight began to wane and O'Brien once more had recourse to his coloured lights. And then, just as it was getting on to quitting time another object was fouled.

'We'll get Kendrick to have a look at it,' Soutar decided, much to French's relief. 'If it's what we want we might get back tonight.'

The tedious preparations were once more made and Kendrick went down. He had with him the powerful electric light, which at first glowed mysteriously in the water, disappearing gradually as the man got deeper. There was less delay than previously and then the telephone sounded.

'He's on to it this time, sir,' reported the assistant. 'There's a big hole blown in the stern.'

'Fine!' said French warmly. 'That's really good.'

The skipper thought it was a better bit of luck than they deserved. 'We might have looked for that for a fortnight,' he said. 'So small, you know.' Then to the assistant. 'Is he going to make his examination now?'

Kendrick, it appeared, was already engaged on it. 'That's all right,' Soutar grunted. 'We'll get home after all.' Then again to the assistant. 'Tell him when he's done to have a talk with the Chief-Inspector before he comes up.'

Twenty minutes passed slowly and then there was a call from below.

'He wants an inch-and-quarter spanner sent down,' the assistant explained.

'Inch-and-quarter spanner to Kendrick,' Soutar directed.

A man hurried off and returned in a moment with the tool. It was quickly tied to a cord with a slack loop round the diver's life-line, and after telephoning down, was dropped overboard.

'He's got it,' said the assistant in a moment.

There was a considerable further delay, and then the telephone sounded again.

'He says he doesn't need to speak to the Chief-Inspector,' the assistant explained. 'He can explain better when he comes up.'

Soutar nodded, and in due course the illumination appeared once again in the water, and the diver came aboard.

'It's the boat all right,' he said when his helmet was lifted off. 'There's a big hole in the stern. I'll just get this blessed dress off and then I'll be able to talk easier.'

'Come to my cabin when you're ready,' said Soutar, moving back to the bridge with French. 'Now,' he went on, 'you can have this place to yourself to discuss your business. I have things to do below. Make yourself at home.'

French thanked him and sat down with Carter. Presently the diver made his appearance and took his place opposite them. French handed over his cigarette-case.

'Well,' began Kendrick, 'there was something there all right, but it wasn't what you expected, Chief-Inspector.' He gave a slightly sardonic smile. 'Not by a long way,' he added, with apparent satisfaction.

'Tell me,' said French.

'I'll tell you, sir. I found the boat at once: the ladder was nearly on her. There's no one knows his job like the skipper, I will say. Well, I worked round to the bows and made sure of the name to start with. She was your boat all right.'

'Pretty lucky that, from all you people have told me,' French commented.

'We might have got her in a week and we mightn't have got her in a fortnight, and here we've got her the first day.

I'll say you're lucky. But we aren't.' He grinned. 'We might have made a pot out of you.'

'I expect you'll do that in any case.'

'Not as much as we'd have liked. Well, then I had a look at the stern, where you said the explosion had been. And it had. There was a hole three feet each way in her bottom, just in the stern sheets. The propeller shaft even was bent a bit, so it must have been a tidy shot.'

'Could you tell where the explosion had been placed?'

'Yes, easy enough. The bottom planking was blown downwards, and the false bottom boards above the shaft were blown upwards, so the charge must have been between the two.'

'We thought that would be the likely place. It wouldn't have been seen there.'

'Not unless someone lifted the loose board to get at the bearings.'

'Which was very unlikely at that time in the evening.'

Kendrick nodded. 'I daresay that's so. However, that's nothing to do with me. Then I had a look up in the bows for the switch or press that you were expecting. There wasn't one.'

'There wasn't one?' A feeling not far removed from dismay took possession of French.

'No, nothing like it.'

'And no wires?'

'Not in the bows. There was nothing.'

French thought ruefully of his theory about Samson. If this were true, as of course it must be, it looked as if that theory was a wash out.

'Do you think the switch and wires could have been washed away?' he went on.

'Sure they weren't.'

'Why so sure?'

'I'll tell you. Because I found the real cause.'

'For goodness' sake, diver, go ahead with your story. What did you find?'

For answer Kendrick took a small object out of his pocket and set it gingerly on the table. 'I found that,' he said, then relapsed into silence.

French stared in bewilderment. It was a strange enough looking little piece of apparatus. First there was a small piece of iron about three inches long, one end of which was flattened into a narrow plate with a hole in the middle. The other end was shaped into a spindle of about half an inch diameter, and on this spindle worked an arm, also about three inches long. The arm stood out at right angles to the spindle, and could be rotated about it. A wire spring, however, tended to prevent this rotation and to press the arm in one direction. It was like part of a turnstile, in which the upright post in the centre corresponded to the spindle, and one of the four rotating members represented the arm.

But it was not so much on the spindle and arm that French's attention was concentrated, as on what the arm held. Clamped to its free end was a push bicycle cyclometer. The toothed operating wheel at the end of the cyclometer had been removed, and its place was taken by a round wheel, its rim covered with rubber. The wheel was about an inch and a quarter in diameter; that is, it stood out beyond the barrel of the cyclometer. From the opposite end of the cyclometer came two insulated electric wires about two feet long and with broken ends.

'What in the name of goodness is that?' French said. 'And where did you find it?'

'Aye, that's the question to ask,' replied Kendrick, who was evidently going to make the most of his story. 'It's where I found it that matters, for that shows what it was put there for. It was on the propeller shaft. That hole that you see in the bracket plate was slipped on to the holding down bolt of one of the shaft bearings and the nut put back on top of it. That held it in position, you understand. The wheel of the cyclometer was pressed against the shaft by this spring, and when the shaft revolved it revolved too. So the turning of the propeller shaft operated the cyclometer. From the cyclometer these wires led towards the hole in the bottom of the boat. So you see it now, sir?'

For a moment French did not quite follow, and then the horrible plan stood completely revealed. 'You mean that the running of the boat would work the cyclometer until—'

'That's it,' Kendrick interrupted, determined not to be forestalled with his climax. 'There's an electric contact on the cyclometer and when the reading gets to a certain figure the contact's made and the current passes. I found the affair fixed to the shaft at the thrust bearing beside the motor, and close by was a low tension battery for the spark to work the detonator. So there's the whole thing, clear as day.'

French swore weakly. So his theory was wrong and Samson was innocent! The thing, after all, had been set beforehand by the murderer to go off at a prearranged moment. Not indeed after a certain time had passed, but after the launch had travelled a certain distance! The call at Hamble would therefore have made no difference. So that was the explanation! Why hadn't he thought of it before?

'Did you bring up the battery?' he asked presently, and the question sounded to him as an anticlimax.

'Yes, I have it outside. Now is that all you want from below? Because if it is we can get away.'

French thought it was everything. 'You'll have to give evidence, you know,' he added.

'It won't be the first time,' Kendrick returned as he went in search of the Captain to tell him the job was done.

'Hi!' French called after him suddenly. 'Did you find that grappling out of place?'

'Yes, sir, I did. I intended to mention that. It was lying out of its chocks, and the paint was scraped where it had been slapping about.'

French thought this was final. Samson's tale was true, and he was innocent of the murders. With a sigh French signified that the interview was over.

21

French Gets Help from his Wits

As they pushed their way up the dark stretch of Southampton Water towards the growing cluster of lights at its head, French's thoughts remained busy with his case. At first sight the proof of Samson's innocence seemed clear, and the obtaining of such proof an important and welcome step forward. But second thoughts showed him that this admitted progress by no means cleared the affair up. In fact it left it more puzzling than ever. If Samson were innocent, who was guilty? This fundamental problem remained as much a problem as ever.

He returned again to the old question: Where could the apparatus have been placed in the launch?

Certainly not at Joymount: there had been no opportunity. And in the nature of the case, not during that halt at Hamble. It looked therefore as if it must have been done at Chayle. This need not now be ruled out. The use of the cyclometer would have made it possible.

But this assumption stopped short at the crucial point. It didn't indicate who was guilty.

French wondered if one of the Joymount men could have visited Chayle secretly. Here at all events was a line of investigation to be explored. Could the launch have been got at by an outsider? If so, how and when? Could the Joymount men account satisfactorily for their movements during such periods? He must go into this matter at once.

Then it occurred to him that he had been wrong in concluding that this discovery of the cyclometer eliminated Samson. Might Samson not still be guilty, and foreseeing the possibilities, either that the launch might not sink at all, or that if it did, a diver might be called in, might he not have planted the cyclometer as a blind? The cyclometer need not have been used to explode the charge. Samson could have done it by means of a second circuit, the wires of which he could have pushed out over the side before operating the switch. By this means they would have gone down clear of the launch. Yes, Samson was by no means eliminated.

But the fixing of the cyclometer and charge was not limited to the Joymount men and Samson. *Anyone* could have done it. French, now grown despondent, seemed as far away from a solution as at the beginning of the case. One thing at all events was clear: a very much more complete investigation would be needed of the personalities and conditions at Chayle.

There was of course one new clue, the cyclometer. If the purchase could be traced, it might prove invaluable. But if it had been bought at, for instance, some small shop in the East End of London—where probably such an alert criminal as he was dealing with would have obtained it—the chances of tracing it were not rosy.

On reaching Southampton, French rang up Major

Considine and Hanbury to tell them the news. Then next morning he called on Goodwilly and got him to put him in touch with an expert who would examine and report on the cyclometer. This man took the ingenious little apparatus to pieces and showed how the contact had been soldered to the 'hundreds' wheel, so that on the latter moving to the figure 1—indicating one hundred miles—contact had been made. Otherwise the expert had nothing to report, except that the change from the toothed driving wheel to the rubber edged disc had been made by a skilful workman.

While discussing the affair with the expert a new idea flashed into French's mind. He believed he saw a test which might be applied to Samson, and which, if the engineer were guilty, might surprise him into some involuntary movement or gesture. Such a reaction would not, of course, be legal evidence, but French thought it might help him to make up his own mind on the man's innocence or guilt.

Once again therefore he and Carter set off down Southampton Water, reaching in due course, first Cowes and then Chayle. Once again Samson was in his office and saw them immediately.

French began with generalities about the case, passing on to a discussion of their activities of the previous day, of which he felt sure his victim would have heard. Samson was obviously interested, and asked what the diver had found. French described the damage to the launch, but avoided all mention of the cyclometer. Then during a somewhat halting and aimless discussion he slipped in the significant remark.

'You'll be interested to know that we're just about on

to the criminal, Mr Samson,' he said in confidential tones and with a slightly lowered voice. 'Don't repeat it, but we believe we've traced the cyclometer.'

Unobtrusively but keenly French watched the engineer. If Samson had placed the apparatus, French didn't believe he could avoid *some* indication of emotion. But save for a slight look of mystification, the man's manner gave nothing away.

'Cyclometer?' he repeated. 'What do you mean?'

'We found a cyclometer on board which we're now engaged in tracing. What could it have been doing there, Mr Samson?'

Samson said he was hanged if he could tell, which occurred to French as an unpleasantly apt statement of the case. 'Where did you find it?' Samson went on.

'In the bottom of the boat. I thought you might know something about it.'

'Not a thing. Never saw it. Never heard of it. Was it just lying there?'

French made a non-committal reply. He could not be absolutely sure, but his strong impression was that Samson knew nothing about the affair. And if not, who under heaven did?

He and Carter had stood up to leave when a further point suddenly occurred to French. He thought rapidly. Yes, there might be a clue in the affair which up to now he had missed.

'By the way, Mr Samson,' he said, 'I've been entering up some details of your launch in our records. Can you add to them for me? What was her speed?'

'About ten knots in normal weather.'

'And her motor revolutions per minute?'

Samson seemed surprised. 'What's that for, Chief-Inspector?' he asked. 'I don't see how that comes in.'

French shrugged. 'You may thank your stars you're not connected with the C.I.D.,' he said confidentially. 'You wouldn't credit the amount of red tape that's insisted on. Your launch was concerned in this affair, so all details, relevant and irrelevant, have to be entered up. I've got her length and beam and draught and general construction. I want her revs. still, and details of her engine—type, horse-power, and so on—even down to the diameter of her propeller shaft.'

Samson looked as if his respect for Scotland Yard had dropped many points. However after shrugging with the air of a man who has granted his questioner a fool's pardon, he gave the information. French made a point of noting the replies, but he had really only wanted the answers to two questions, the motor's revs. and the diameter of the shaft.

For French's idea was very simple.

The chances, he thought, were in favour of a new cyclometer having been used. Few men in the position which the murderer probably occupied would own a bicycle from which an old one could be obtained. Even if he did, he would be unlikely to take it off, lest it should be missed. Still less likely would he be to steal a cyclometer from someone else's machine.

But if a new cyclometer had been used, it would be registering 0 miles when it was fixed on board. The explosion took place when it was registering 100. Therefore between the time it was put on and the disaster, the mileage indicated had increased from 0 to 100 miles. Obviously this didn't mean that the launch had travelled 100 miles;

the drive from the propeller shaft was quite different to that from the wheel of a bicycle. French now wondered could he calculate the actual distance the launch would travel while the cyclometer registered 100 miles? If so, it would give him where the apparatus was fixed.

He thought that, with the information he had just obtained, he could do so, at least approximately.

He began on reaching Cowes by visiting a cycle shop and asking to see some cyclometers. From this he learned that the original toothed driving wheel had five teeth. He learned also that cycle wheels averaged 26 or 28 inches in diameter. Then he went on to the police station and put through a couple of telephone calls. One was to the makers of the motor and propeller which Samson had used in the launch, asking them for the average revs. during normal full speed—as a check on Samson. The second was another check, to ask Diver Kendrick if he had measured the diameter of the propeller shaft.

Then taking Samson's figures, he began to work.

The first question was to find how many times the cyclometer driving wheel revolved while registering one mile. This was not difficult. The 26 inches diameter of a bicycle wheel meant about 7 feet circumference. Each rotation of the bicycle wheel—each 7 feet—moved the cyclometer driving wheel one tooth. Therefore five teeth—one complete revolution of the cyclometer driving wheel—was made every 35 feet. Dividing this 35 feet into 5,280, the number of feet in a mile, gave 150, the number of times the cyclometer driving wheel revolved while registering one mile.

The cyclometer however had registered 100 miles. Therefore its driving wheel had revolved 15,000 times.

Now the cyclometer driving wheel was of the same diameter as Samson had given for the propeller shaft. Therefore since the apparatus had been placed on board the propeller had revolved 15,000 times also.

Samson had said that the motor—which was coupled direct to the propeller shaft—revolved 450 times per minute. Therefore dividing 450 into 15,000 would give the number of minutes during which the motor had been working. French quickly made the division. The answer was 30!

The motor had then been running for thirty minutes between the time the apparatus was fixed in the boat and the explosion. French gasped as he saw what this meant.

He turned up his notes to check his memory. Yes, he was correct. From the hour the launch left Joymount until the explosion, the time of actual running was estimated to be 30 minutes! This estimate was obviously approximate, and his calculation was also necessarily approximate. But with this proviso what closer and more utterly convincing conclusion could have been reached? Here was the most absolute proof that the apparatus had been put into the launch at Hamble or Joymount! Hamble was out of the question: therefore it was at Joymount.

Of course there was still the chance that Samson's figures were wrong. But with such a result French didn't believe this for a moment. In any case, the enquiries he had made would check them up. No, he might take it that somehow the Joymount people were guilty.

And he was justified. Before he left the police station answers came in from both the motor firm and Kendrick. In each case Samson's figures were confirmed.

French's mind was in a maze of doubt as they crossed

again to Southampton. He had gone into the question of the guilt of the Joymount men on the ground, and he had been completely satisfied as to their innocence. Now it looked as if he had been wrong!

But where had he been wrong? How could the thing have been done? He could not see. He felt almost as if he was going mad. It could not have been done! And yet, seemingly it had!

His success had stimulated his brain. As they drew in to the pier at Southampton still another idea struck him. Contributory evidence was within his reach. That loading of the coaster! Was there anything to be noted about that?

He wondered. The cement trade was not an urgent trade. Cement was not a perishable commodity, and a few hours' delay in the time of its delivery would not usually be important. Of course this did not always follow. Some job might be held up for want of supplies. But normally a day one way or the other in the time of delivery wouldn't matter.

Did it not look, French thought, as if the essential of the affair was to have a number of men on the wharf that night? In other words, was there a real urgency for the sailing of the ship, or was it necessary to prove that no one went on board the launch?

French thought the point was sufficiently important to justify a run down to Plymouth. Accordingly he and Carter spent the afternoon travelling west. They arrived too late to do anything that night, but next morning found them at the harbour office.

There French's card procured them immediate attention. The coaster, *Lucy Jane*, Captain Foggatt, had put into Plymouth on the 21st of November, with a cargo of cement

301

from the Joymount Company of Hamble. French wanted
to know the consignees. Would they be good enough to
look the matter up for him?

The harbour authorities had no objection, and in a few
minutes the two police officers were on their way to the
depot of Messrs Rawle & Tomkinson, Builders' Supplies
Merchants, near Friary Station.

There they saw Mr Rawle. French explained that his
enquiries were delicate and secret, and he begged that Mr
Rawle would kindly keep them strictly to himself?
Mr Rawle said he would do anything to oblige. French
was obliged. He was interested in the coasting steamer
Lucy Jane, and was getting a record of her movements
over a certain period. The matter had of course no connection with Messrs Rawle & Tomkinson—it was with the
ship only that he was concerned. He understood she had
brought Messrs Rawle & Tomkinson a cargo of cement
about the 21st of November? Was this so, and if so, could
Mr Rawle tell him the exact date she had arrived and
whether the cargo had been promptly discharged?

Rawle couldn't say offhand, but he would find out. He
rang and gave the necessary instructions. Presently he
received certain details. The *Lucy Jane* had discharged 190
tons of cement on the 22nd November. There had been
nothing remarkable about the speed of the discharge. It
was in fact quite normal.

French asked a number of other questions, dilated on the
haste with which the trip seemed to have been carried out,
and suggested that perhaps the cement was overdue, and
was wanted urgently. Mr Rawle however said that that was
not so. The cement was received well inside the contract
date, and there had been no urgency about it whatever.

This, French thought, was extraordinarily suggestive, but not yet entirely conclusive. Though there was no urgency about the cargo, the ship herself might have been wanted elsewhere. He stepped into the post office and rang up the Weymouth police. He was still engaged upon that business of the *Lucy Jane*. He would be obliged if they would let him know when the coaster had left Weymouth, for where, and with what cargo.

The reply was waiting for him at Southampton. The ship had lain at Weymouth for two days, and then had taken aboard a lot of empty cement bags and had left for the Joymount Works!

Then there definitely had been no need to load cement on that Tuesday night! Why then had it been done? French could imagine only the one object: to have men and lights on the wharf during the visit of the Chayle contingent, so as to prove that no one could have tampered with the launch. And this late loading could only have been arranged by the Joymount men!

French thought that this fresh evidence removed the last shred of doubt as to Joymount guilt. There had been, as he put it to himself, some hanky-panky on the wharf that night. He had already tried to discover what it was, and failed. Never mind, there was one good rule to observe in cases of failure. Try again! He knew that he was now on the right lines, and that was half the battle.

The immediate question then was, How had the explosive and the apparatus for discharging it been put on board the launch unseen by the workers on the wharf? Because it now seemed certain that this had been done.

It was a question he had put to himself on many previous occasions, but never heretofore had he been able to imagine the answer. But now suddenly and unexpectedly a possible method flashed into his mind. It was a perfectly simple and perfectly obvious method, and he could have kicked himself for not having seen it sooner.

He wondered whether merely seeing it were enough? Was there any possibility of failure in it which would make a test desirable? Over this point he puzzled for some time, then he decided a test would be more satisfactory from every point of view.

He remembered that when visiting Major Ashe he had noticed that boats were to be hired at Hamble. Leaving Carter to his own devices, French went down to Hamble and after considerable trouble—it was not the season—he succeeded in hiring a light skiff for a day or two. He put down a deposit for it and rowed off alone.

He could see the Joymount wharf across the little estuary. By an unexpected piece of luck it was deserted. It was the only time he had seen it without a steamer. He rowed over to make a closer examination.

It was late afternoon when he hired the boat, and it was dark when he completed his survey and set off on his journey back to Southampton. Immediately on arrival he called to see Superintendent Goodwilly.

'I want to try a small experiment, Super,' he explained. 'You remember we discussed the possibility of an explosive being put aboard the Chayle launch while it was lying at the Joymount wharf. We decided it couldn't be done. I'm now not so sure and I want to see if I can do it.'

Goodwilly was interested and asked what French wanted him to do.

'Give me a boat and three men and some lights,' French answered. 'We'll go down to the place, reproduce as far as we can the conditions of that night, and then I'll try to go aboard the launch unseen.'

'A boat, three men and lights? I can do that. When would you like to have them?'

'I'd like to be there about four tomorrow morning.'

This was evidently not what Goodwilly had expected. However, he made no difficulty about it, and the matter was arranged.

'As a matter of fact I'm interested,' Goodwilly went on, 'and if you've room I shouldn't mind going out with you myself.'

'Cheers!' cried French. 'I shall be glad of your help.'

About three o'clock the next morning a small petrol launch left Southampton with French, Goodwilly, Carter and three constables. It was a fine morning, but cold and very dark. There was no wind and Southampton Water was calm as a duckpond. Only twice did the launch roll: when a great liner and a six-thousand-ton tramp passed them on their respective ways up to and down from the harbour. The navigation lamps shone clear and bright, but save at Southampton itself, there were few lights ashore.

Almost complete silence reigned among the men as the launch chugged busily seawards. Except for French and the Super, all would have much preferred to be in bed. But to French this experiment meant a good deal. If it were to succeed it would mean that he had solved his problem. It would not mean the end of his case, because to see how a thing might have been done is very different from proving that it was done. But if he knew he was on the right track it would prevent him from dissipating his energy on blind alleys and allow him to concentrate on that one point of obtaining his proof.

When they turned into the Hamble French had the motor stopped and oars shipped. 'If we don't make a noise,' he said, 'we *may* escape notice—which would be very much to the good. Our lights will probably be seen, but that we can't help. Let's take what precautions we can.'

Silently they drew in towards the wharf. French's luck had held, there were still no vessels alongside. Presently they floated up to the steps at the end of the wharf and made fast.

'Now everyone, out with the lights,' French directed, and he assembled everyone on the wharf.

It took only a few moments to set the stage. The lamps which were lighted on the wharf on the night of the tragedy were duplicated by those brought in the launch, and Carter and the three policemen were placed where the workers had stood, and were instructed as to the kind of lookout they were required to keep.

'That's how it was that evening,' French explained to the Super. 'I argued that no one could cross the wharf and go down those steps unseen by some one of the men.'

'I'd swear it,' Goodwilly answered. 'No one could have, and no one did.'

'Very well,' said French, 'lend me something of yours: something personal that I couldn't copy.'

'My pouch?'

'The very thing.' It had silver mountings and bore the Super's initials.

'Now,' French went on, 'I want to make some preparations. Will you wait for me and then we'll try the experiment.'

Goodwilly nodded and French moved away towards the gate into the yard and vanished behind some sheds. Goodwilly glanced at his watch and then settled down to wait. He thought that in spite of their lights they might well remain unobserved. The only windows in the works which overlooked the wharf were those of the offices, and they would now be deserted, it being unlikely that the watchman would leave the ground floor. If anyone were awake at Hamble and looked out of his window, he would see the light, but unless such a person happened to be connected with the management, it would convey little to him. French had been right to keep their movements silent.

Presently French appeared from behind the huts and approached.

'How long have I been, Super?' he asked as he came up.

'Twelve minutes,' Goodwilly answered. 'Are you ready now to get going?'

French answered the question with another.

'Did anyone pass since on the wharf?'

'No one.'

'Better ask your men.'

'My dear French, I was here myself. There was no one.'

'Ask them all the same,' French persisted.

The men, appealed to, declared that the Superintendent was correct. No one had passed.

'That's all right,' said French with satisfaction. 'That works.'

Goodwilly looked at him. 'What do you mean?' he asked.

'Only,' said French, 'that your pouch is now on the cylinder cover of the engine.'

Goodwilly looked at him keenly. 'You're a caution,' he declared, and then laughed. 'How did you do it?'

'I deserve to be kicked from here to Southampton,' French declared. 'The thing's so absolutely simple that I should have thought of it at once, but I just missed it. Come along to the other end of the wharf and I'll show you.'

They walked off behind the sheds as French had done a few minutes earlier. French edged along the works wall till they had passed the end of the wharf—the opposite end to that of the boathouse and steps. Then stooping, he crept down the pitched slope towards the edge of the water.

'You see, it's possible to get down to the sea without being noticed from the wharf,' he pointed out.

Once below the level of the wharf deck, they were secure from observation, no matter what lights might be burning there. French led the way along the sloping pitching to the end of the wharf. There he put out his hand, and catching a rope which lay along the slope and was tied to something above, he pulled it. The boat which he had hired in the afternoon appeared. With the aid of a small torch both men got aboard.

Having cast off the rope, French pushed the boat in under the wharf. There it floated in a sort of cavern between the rows of tall gaunt concrete piles, and beneath a roof which was the deck of the wharf. Quickly and silently they passed down the strange alleyway, till the bow bumped lightly on the steps. True it was the back of the stairway that they had reached, but a moment sufficed to make fast the painter and enabled French to step across the handrail. Another step would have brought him to the police launch, which was so close to the wharf as to be hidden from the watchers above.

'Our Joymount friends keep a couple of skiffs in there,' French said, pointing to the boathouse. 'It would have been easy to transfer one beforehand to the other end of the wharf. That all right, Super?'

Goodwilly was enthusiastic. French's reconstruction was unquestionably the solution of this part of the problem.

'When you led me below,' he said, 'I thought we were going to walk along the walings—I suppose the thing has walings. I never thought of the boat.'

'I thought of the walings early on,' French answered. 'But they wouldn't have worked. You could only walk along the walings at low water. But the explosion didn't occur at low water. No one could have got along them in four or five feet of water, at least not without getting wet and dripping water into the launch. And no one did get wet that night and there could have been no water dripped into the launch or one of those three would have noticed it.'

'That's really very good, French; I congratulate you. But, surely, there's a difficulty still—two difficulties, in fact? First, though this shows a possibility, it doesn't prove anything; and second, I understood that none of the Joymount people left the office during the Chayle visit.'

French nodded. 'You're right, both times. I know very well we're not through, but we're getting along.'

Goodwilly was enthusiastic about their progress as the party turned homewards. A constable was left with the boat to row it over to Hamble and collect French's deposit, and the others chugged back to Southampton.

22

French Gets Help from a Victim

After breakfast that morning, French retired to his room and set himself systematically to attack the next stage of his problem. If Joymount were guilty, as now seemed certain, why had they committed these horrible crimes? What was their motive?

It was easy enough to suggest one. He had thought of a very adequate motive right at the beginning of the case. He had seen that if Joymount had stolen the process, and if Chayle had discovered the theft, Chayle might use their knowledge to levy blackmail. Particularly strong would be their hold if in addition they could prove that the Joymount men had murdered Clay.

French saw that the kernel of the situation was whether or not Joymount had stolen the process. He *must* know this. If they had, it would be practical proof of their guilt of the murders; if not, he, French, was still completely at sea.

How could he find out?

He attacked the question from every point of view that

he could think of. Of course, he had been over the ground already some dozens of times, entirely without result. Still his entire case now depended on his reaching a conclusion. He *must* do it.

Presently he began to consider what exactly the process consisted of. Broadly speaking, an improved method of making cement. He turned this over in his mind like a cow chewing the cud. He had never been able to get actual details of the process, the tacit assumption always being that it was too technical to discuss with a layman. But Haviland had said that it involved putting in some additional chemicals which acted as a flux and reduced the amount of heating required. French now wondered what happened to those chemicals. Must they not remain in the finished product? He did not see how they could be taken out.

But if they remained in the finished product, it should be possible for an analyst to find them. Was there not here a way by which he might reach a conclusion?

French felt himself in such an extremity that he couldn't afford to ignore any possibility. Accordingly he put through a call to Professor Greenaway, a London chemist consulted by the Yard in cases of difficulty. Explaining about the process, he asked if the Professor thought the new product might be distinguishable chemically from other cements?

Greenaway replied with reason that he had never heard of the cement and therefore didn't know whether it could or not, but that if the Chief-Inspector would send him a sample, he would soon find out.

Wondering if at last he was on to his solution, French went out and bought two bags of cement, one of Chayle manufacture and one of Joymount. He had them specially packed in boxes and took them to Town as passengers' luggage. Then getting them into a taxi, he drove to the Professor's house.

He found Greenaway ready enough to help. He was, he said, interested in cements, and if there was a new one on the market he wanted to know all about it. 'You leave your packages round with the caretaker at my lab,' he directed, 'and I'll have the affair put in hand first thing in the morning.'

'You'll ring up the Yard, sir, when you've anything to report?'

'I'll ring up the Yard.'

It was not till the following evening that a message came through. Would French call round at the laboratory as soon as possible?

French, it can be imagined, did not lose much time.

'Well, Chief-Inspector,' said Greenaway. 'So far as I can see, you've got a bull's-eye. These two samples you sent me are identical, and what's more, they're different from all other brands of cement I've ever come across. And though I say it myself, I don't believe there is any cement on the market that I don't know about.'

French felt slightly overwhelmed. 'By Jove, sir! That makes a bit of difference to me. Does it mean that the two samples were made in the same way?'

'I should say, absolutely. They're identical with one another chemically, you understand, and different chemically from other brands. Physically they seem indistinguishable from others, and of course there hasn't yet been time to test for efficiency. But you may take it both your samples were made by the same process.'

French hesitated. 'I wonder, sir, if you would be

prepared to give evidence to that effect, should it become necessary?'

'That the samples are identical, yes; that they were made by the same process, no. I have no doubt of it, but, of course, I can't prove it.'

This was good, but not good enough. Again French sat in thought. 'You would know, sir, if you went through both works, Chayle and Joymount, whether their process was the same?'

'Probably. With the information I've got from the analysis I should know what to look for, and I think I should find it.'

'Then, sir, if it should become necessary, would you be prepared to make the inspections?'

'Certainly. You didn't find out for yourself if new machinery had been installed?'

'I'm afraid not, sir,' French admitted. 'There was no suggestion from anyone at Chayle of new machinery. They all spoke as if it was a different way of using their existing plant.'

'Well, I should be delighted to make an inspection. I assure you I'm immensely interested in the whole business.'

French could scarcely contain himself with satisfaction. Here was a discovery of the very first importance. It was true it did not in itself prove motive, but it was the foundation upon which such proof must and, he was sure, could be built. This was the biggest step forward he had taken since he went to Southampton!

Presently he saw that it established another very suggestive fact. It proved that the Joymount representatives had not been straight in their statements. They had not said anything which could suggest knowledge of the process, and under the circumstances this was keeping back material evidence. French was also now fairly satisfied that the agreement with Chayle must have been connected with the process. If so, it was surely very different from what had been shown him. Probably he had been put off with a part of it only.

But just here French saw a difficulty. Samson! Samson had supported these false stories. He must have known Joymount had stolen the process, and he had said nothing about it. Samson surely had everything to gain by the unmasking of the Joymount rogues. If they were defrauding Chayle they were defrauding him. Why had he lied also—against himself?

As he sat in the train on his return journey to Southampton, French pondered over this point. He could not, however, solve it satisfactorily, and he passed on to another.

This was the exasperating old friend of the placing of the cyclometer and charge on the launch. It now seemed evident that this had been done by the Joymount men at their own wharf, and he thought he knew how, but there remained that devastating question of when? None of them had had any opportunity. French metaphorically set his teeth as for the hundredth time he settled down to wrestle with the difficulty.

In the first place it seemed clear that the thing could only have been done by Tasker, Brand or King. Those three were in control. They had negotiated the agreement, and probably only those three knew the details of the process. Those three had probably determined on murder—they were the only ones who had a motive. If so, it was unlikely in the last degree that they would have trusted anyone else with their dreadful secret.

Assume, then, that one of these three principals were guilty, when could he have carried out the job?

Not when the launch arrived at Joymount. The visitors were met on the wharf by King, and conveyed by him straight to the office, where Brand and Tasker were awaiting them. There certainly would not have been time to tamper with the launch.

Equally certain was it that it could not have been interfered with just before the Chayle men's departure. The six men had remained in company right from the time of leaving the office until the Chayle party had set off for home.

It must, therefore, have been done at some intermediate period. There was one such possible and only one.

During the proceedings the three Joymount men had left their visitors on the plea of discussing the proposals in private. This was the explanation given to the Chayle men of the withdrawal, and it was convincing enough, but was the further reason given by the Joymount men to French so satisfying? Tasker had explained that he had wanted some further figures to be got out, to assist him in his bargaining. French found this harder to believe. Surely, under the circumstances, Tasker would have had all the figures he wanted before the meeting began?

The point was a small one, and yet to French it threw a certain suspicion on that withdrawal.

According to the statements of all concerned, what exactly had happened? On the suggestion of Tasker, the three men had gone to Brand's office, the reason given being that as Brand was the accountant, he could more easily get at the required figures. Tasker and Brand had then worked together getting these figures out.

In the meantime King, in response to a request by Tasker, had gone into his own office, which was next door, and had there got out a further statement, the exact details of which had not been mentioned. This was a typed statement. King had declared that he had not left the office during the period. This declaration was confirmed by Tasker, Brand and Samson. All three said they had heard King's typewriter practically continuously, and also at intervals King's voice upraised in song. Also about the middle of the period, King had called out a question to Tasker about the work he was doing. Tasker had shouted an answer and the typing had been resumed. Samson, moreover, had heard question and answer.

It was obvious, that if these statements were true, no one had left the offices. But if no one had left the offices, the Joymount trio could not have put the explosive on board the launch. Therefore by hypothesis, some, at all events, of the statements were false, and perhaps all.

French switched his mind over from the statements to the personalities of those making them. During his long experience he had become extraordinarily skilful in the reading of character and he knew, practically always, whether his informants were speaking the truth or lying. Now of these four men, Tasker, Brand, King and Samson, there was only one of whose word he would place any reliance at all, and that was Brand. It was not so much, indeed, that he believed in Brand's truthfulness, as that he considered Brand incapable of deceiving him. Brand was a man of comparatively weak character. He was timorous, and whatever his morals, French was sure he had not the stamina for serious crime.

Now French had been a good deal interested in Brand's

manner. Brand had given all the indications of a bad conscience. At French's examination, which had been of the mildest type, he had been hard put to it to overcome his terror. French was positive that he knew something incriminating and was afraid it would come out. On the other hand everything he had said about the happenings on this particular evening had borne the unmistakable ring of truth. French indeed had come to the conclusion that Brand was as puzzled about the launch explosion as he was himself.

The other three men were of sterner stuff, and French was sure they could lie without giving themselves away as Brand would do.

Was there any way, therefore, in which Brand could have been tricked by the others during that momentous ten minutes?

French thought he might expand the problem slightly. Considering the probabilities only, it seemed to him that if Brand were tricked, Samson must have been so also. It wasn't exactly likely that Samson would have been party to an attempt to murder himself.

For five minutes French smoked fiercely as he concentrated on the problem. Then he gave a little laugh and a shrug. The problem was no problem at all! If King and Tasker had employed a very old trick, King could have left the office and placed the charge. A gramophone!

What would have been easier, when King withdrew into his own office, than to set a gramophone going? It would supply all the noises of typing and movement required, besides calling out that question to Tasker. On returning to the office after visiting the launch, the gramophone could easily have been stopped and put away, its sounds

317

being replaced by those of King's real movements. The thing had been done before many times, both in books and in real life.

By this scheme both Brand and Samson could have been tricked, but—and this interested French even more—it involved the co-operation of Tasker. Tasker would have had to fix up the interlude in accordance with a prearranged programme if the gramophone were to be used, and he would have had to prevent any undesired voyages of discovery by Brand. Also King's question and the reply would have had to be rehearsed beforehand. French saw with satisfaction that if he could prove the use of a gramophone, it would give him a case against Tasker as well as King.

For another half hour French considered ways and means of learning whether a gramophone had or had not been used. Then thinking he saw his way, he left the hotel and, with Carter, went to the principal gramophone shop in the town.

He saw the manager and explained his business. He wanted to know how people could make gramophone records for themselves. Was there any apparatus sold for the purpose, and where was it to be had?

The manager was not encouraging as to the possibilities. Apparatus for the purpose had been designed and put on the market, but it had not proved very satisfactory, and most people who wanted a good record went to one of the gramophone companies and had it made by their professional staff. Practically all the gramophone companies made such records, and these were kept absolutely private.

In answer to a further question, the manager did not

believe a record could be made by a private individual which would sound really lifelike. There would almost certainly be defects which would stamp it a record.

If this information were correct, French thought it unlikely that King would have attempted to make his own record. The discovery of his trick would have been too serious. On the other hand, he would consider himself safe in employing a company, as he would not believe the question of a gramophone would arise. It would therefore be worth finding out whether any gramophone company had made such a record.

French accordingly sent a note to the Yard, giving a résumé of what the record must have contained, a note of the dates between which it must have been ordered, and a copy of his photograph of King. He asked that a letter should be sent to each of the gramophone companies, asking for information on the subject.

The next day was Sunday, and French took what he considered was a well earned holiday in the bosom of his family. On Monday morning he called at the Yard before returning to Southampton, and it happened that while he was in the building a reply to his circular came in.

It was from the Etna Gramophone Company of Reading. They rang up to say that they thought they had made the records referred to in the Yard's letter of Saturday. French could scarcely believe in his good luck. Slightly awestruck, he and Carter hurried to Paddington and took the first train to Reading.

The manager of the Etna Company was, he declared, only too anxious to oblige the officers, but they must recognise that his company gave a guarantee of privacy when making records for outside individuals. This he could not break unless he was shown that it was his duty to do so.

French took the confidential man-to-man line. 'We have reason to suspect,' he said, 'that that record was used to make an alibi, while the man it featured was engaged in committing a particularly brutal murder. You cannot, sir, shield such a man,' and he went on to give his assurance that if it turned out that the record had been used innocently, nothing that was said would be made public.

This had the desired effect, and the manager at once gave his information.

On the 14th of November he had had, he said, a telephone call from a man giving his name as Clement Allworthy, asking if the Etna Company made special records for private individuals, and if so, at what charges. The information was given him, and he said he wanted a record made, and that he would call and have it done. An appointment was thereupon fixed up for the following day.

At the time arranged he turned up, repeating the name Clement Allworthy, and adding the address: 'Cloony', Babbacombe Road, Torquay. He said he had a bet with some friends which arose out of a discussion on spiritualism. He had bet his friends that with the help of modern science he could reproduce everything that had been done at a certain *séance* at which they had all been present. One of the items included the medium's typing a message which was written on a sheet of paper in another room, and which he had not seen. This feat Allworthy proposed to reproduce with the help of a gramophone. He wanted to create the illusion that he was typing continuously, while actually he hurried to the other room, read the message, hurried back, and then typed it. The record was to be largely of typing, but it was also to have some humming and speaking which would prove his identity. It turned out that one record would not last the required time—fifteen minutes—so three were made, 'Allworthy' explaining that he had an automatic change gramophone. The records turned out to be very good, and the man paid for them and took them away. Both the manager and the operative who had attended to 'Allworthy' were positive that he was the original of the photograph which had been sent from the Yard.

'We keep the master record of every recording,' the manager concluded, 'and if you like I can let you hear these three.'

Nothing could have suited French better. He agreed eagerly and he could have shouted with delight when he heard King's voice humming and calling out his question to Tasker.

His satisfaction grew deeper as in the train back to Town he thought over what he had learnt. Here was proof of his theories as to the deaths of Haviland and Mairs. It would be utterly impossible for King to explain the purchase of the records otherwise than by admitting his guilt. And as he, French, had already seen, they proved not only King's guilt, but Tasker's also. But they didn't prove the guilt of either Brand or Samson. Both these men might easily have been, indeed almost certainly had been, deceived.

French wondered had he enough evidence for an arrest. At first he thought he had, then he realised that there was a good deal of the case of which he was still ignorant. He decided to try to get some further information before showing his hand.

Then, just as the train ran in beneath the Paddington

roof, he thought he saw his way. Could he force a confession from Brand?

Brand was obviously a man of weak character, fearful and timorous, but French imagined he was also in his way conscientious. From his observation he felt sure that the man had a secret on his mind which was worrying him intensely. That he was the dupe of the other two French now believed.

French wondered could he make him tell what he knew. Police pressure would, he felt, be powerfully backed up by the man's own internal urge, and he might not have the strength to resist both.

On reaching Southampton French explained his idea to Goodwilly, and then rang up Brand. He was sorry to trouble Mr Brand, but would he be in Southampton in the early future? He didn't think so? Well, would it be too much to ask him to come in? They had got some information which somewhat puzzled them, and they wanted his help to clear it up.

Brand said that if it was necessary he would go in specially. French thanked him, and a meeting at the police station at Southampton was fixed up for late that afternoon.

In due course Brand turned up, looking rather anxious. French had arranged the stage for the act, and Brand was shown into a dismal waiting-room. He was left there for twenty minutes, in the belief that the delay would increase his apprehension.

At last he was shown into Goodwilly's office. There he found Goodwilly, French, and Carter, all of whom looked preternaturally solemn. They greeted him briefly and without apologising for having kept him waiting.

'We want a little information from you, Mr Brand,' began

French, 'but before you make a statement it is my duty to warn that what you say will be taken down and may be given in evidence. You understand also, that you are not bound to answer my questions unless you wish to, and that you may, if you desire, have a solicitor present.'

This, delivered in a grave and almost menacing tone, had its desired effect. Brand paled and looked alarmed.

'What does that mean, Chief-Inspector?' he asked nervously. 'It doesn't mean that you're going to—to—arrest me?'

'I haven't said anything about arrest,' French returned. 'You may be able to satisfy the Superintendent and myself, in which case no harm is done. But, subject to the official warning which it was my duty to give you, we should like to get some explanations of certain matters from you.'

French had wanted to make the man uneasy and he had certainly succeeded. That he had some evil secret on his conscience, French was more than ever convinced.

'I'll tell you anything I can,' Brand declared, a trifle unsteadily. 'What do you want to know?'

'We want to know,' said French sternly, 'if you would care to make a statement as to your part in the murder of Messrs Haviland and Mairs?'

Brand's face changed. A look of absolute horror appeared in his eyes. He stared, apparently rendered motionless by distress aad fear. The three police officers watched him without speaking.

'Murder!' he gasped. 'You don't say they were murdered?' He swore brokenly.

It was not put on, the surprise. At least so French thought. And yet it was not altogether surprise either. Brand looked as if a blow had fallen which he had already feared. The silence began to run into minutes. Drops of sweat appeared on the man's forehead. He made no attempt to wipe them away. At last he went on, in a voice which had suddenly grown husky.

'I didn't know it was murder,' he declared shakily. 'I swear I didn't! I swear it!'

'Well,' said French, 'we want your statement—subject to my warning. If it's your statement that you know nothing about it, that will be taken down and we'll ask you to sign it. But I may as well say that we shall not be satisfied unless we get a lot more information than that. We should want a detailed account of your actions throughout the whole business, from the original theft of the Chayle process right up to the present time.'

From Brand's start and look of absolute consternation, French saw that he had got home. It was the original affair, the theft of the secret, and possibly the murder of Clay, in which the man had been involved. French felt sure he knew nothing about the later crime.

'As you know,' French went on, 'the theft of the process is a serious matter, because of the murder of Clay. And all that faking of the car accident is also very serious. We don't want to force your confidence, Mr Brand, but I suggest you would be well advised to tell what you know. Now we don't want to take you at a disadvantage. Would you like some time to think it over?'

The man looked so driven and worried that French felt sorry for him, though he did not allow this to appear in his face. Brand made several attempts to speak, without success. Then at last he murmured that he had nothing to say.

French slapped his notebook shut. 'Think it over,

Mr Brand. Don't make a stupid mistake which may do you more harm than good. Think it over.' He turned to Carter. 'Show Mr Brand to a room where he can think this matter over.'

Carter rose, and tapping the witness on the shoulder, motioned him to follow. Without another word both men disappeared from the room, Brand walking as if in a dream.

'He's mixed up in the theft, but innocent of the launch affair. What do you think, Super?' said French, when the door closed.

'That's my idea, too,' Goodwilly answered. 'How long shall we keep him, French, if he won't speak?'

'He'll speak all right. There's nothing he wants so much, and he'll not be able to resist his own desire. He'll see he's done for about the theft, but he'll think that doesn't matter compared with a possible charge of murder. Send him some dinner and we'll have him in again about nine o'clock.'

When Brand was brought in about nine, he attempted to bluster. He wanted to be released at once. If not, he wanted to know was he arrested, and in this case he would like to see the warrant.

'You're not arrested, Mr Brand,' French answered coolly. 'You're what is technically known as "detained". We should like to avoid arresting you, but we can't let you go until this matter is cleared up. You must see that for yourself.'

'If I make a statement will you let me go?'

'I can't promise that, sir. If you can satisfy the Superintendent and myself that you are not guilty of these crimes, yes. If not, no.'

'Well, my hotel people must be told I'm here.'

'Yes, sir, that's reasonable. We'll send any message you wish. You needn't say you're here unless you like.'

At his prisoner's request French telephoned that Mr Brand was staying over in Southampton until further notice.

Brand would not, however, make any statement. French expected him to demand the presence of a solicitor, but he didn't do this either. After a short interview he was led away and locked up for the night.

Next day it was the same. French saw him in the not uncomfortable room in which he had slept, and once again suggested that he might care to make a statement. But Brand shook his head.

'Well,' said French, 'there's a bell, and if you want to see the Super or myself, all you've got to do is to ring it.'

All that day matters remained in the same condition. Brand still wouldn't speak. French was getting very worried about the case. He had gone just about as far as he could. It would not be possible to hold the man longer than another night. Though the 'reasonable time' during which a suspect could be detained often went up to as much as a week, that was usually while his statements were being tested. French could not use detention as a sort of mental third degree.

However next morning his doubts were dissolved, and his opinion justified. Brand evidently could not face another day. He sent word that he wished to make a statement.

'I think you're wise, Mr Brand,' French assured him when they were once again seated in Goodwilly's room. 'The truth seldom does anyone any harm.'

'Not if they've not broken the law, Chief-Inspector,' Brand returned. 'As a matter of fact I have come within measurable distance of breaking it, though not really with evil intentions. I'm going to tell you about it, because I'm absolutely innocent of murder or serious crime, and I want you to believe that.'

'We'll give your statement the most careful consideration. It will be taken down and you can read it over before signing it, so as to make sure it is correct. Now, sir, will you go ahead.'

Brand began at the beginning. He told his hearers about the financial condition of the Joymount Works and the fear that they would have to close down, involving loss of employment for all those connected with it. Then he described their finding that Chayle was underselling them and getting their trade, followed by King's investigation and the discovery that Chayle were putting out a new cement. He recounted King's efforts to deduce the process, his failure, the temptation to visit the Chayle Works and learn the secret by observation, as usual stressing the fact that they did not wish to injure Chayle, but only to save themselves from ruin. He told his story in a convincing way, and French hadn't the slightest doubt that he was listening to the truth.

He remained convinced of Brand's truthfulness even when the latter reached the point at which Clay was killed. Whether it was murder or manslaughter in the eyes of the law, French believed that the deed had not been intentional. And though French knew that the young men should instantly have reported the occurrence to the police, he could well understand the reasons which prompted them to hide it.

Brand gave the whole history of the disposal of the body, so far as he knew it. He did not try to put more responsibility on King than he took on himself, though stating that the idea was King's. He convinced his hearers that he had loathed and feared the whole operation, but that he had joined in it for the simple reason that he did not think his statement would be believed, and to get rid of the body as they had done, was better than being charged with murder.

Except to ask an occasional question, French did not interrupt the narrative. It was all coming out just as he had expected it would. Indeed he was somewhat surprised to find how close to the truth had been his surmises.

Brand then went on to tell about Chayle's discovery of the theft of the secret, and their resultant proposals, which, he pointed out, amounted to practical blackmail. He told in detail of the negotiations between the two firms, leading up to the agreement which was initialled on the night of the explosion. He admitted that after the launch disaster both the Joymount men and Samson had kept back the fact that a second sheet had been included in the agreement, explaining the reason.

To the very end French believed the statement. Brand had weakly allowed himself to be made a party to theft, but French did not think he was guilty of murder. He spoke aside to Goodwilly.

'According to your own statement, Mr Brand,' he said, when at last Goodwilly had nodded agreement, 'you're guilty of complicity in a theft. Whether you'll be charged with that or not I can't say at present, and we shall have to detain you till the question is settled.' He hesitated, then his good nature got the better of his caution, and he added: 'While I can't bind myself, I may say, for your comfort, that it is not at present our intention to charge you with murder.'

His mind somewhat relieved, Brand was taken back to his room.

23

French Gets Help from the Enemy

With the details of Brand's confession added to the proofs he already had in his possession, French felt that the arrest of King and Tasker could no longer be delayed. He put the point to Goodwilly.

'Certainly, Chief-Inspector,' the Super agreed, 'I don't see what else we can do. I think we should go out there tonight and bring them in.'

'And what about Brand?'

Goodwilly shrugged. 'I don't know what to say about him,' he admitted. 'I rather incline to the view that if we get those other two for the launch murder, we might drop the Clay case. As to the theft, if Chayle won't prosecute, as I'm sure they won't, I question if the charge would be proceeded with.'

'That's my idea also,' French returned. 'I think we'll have to hold him till the Public Prosecutor is consulted, but I expect the charge will be dropped in the end.'

This was certainly to be a red-letter day in the case. While Goodwilly was obtaining warrants for the arrest of

Tasker and King, another of the lines of research French had initiated, produced unexpected but highly gratifying results.

The Superintendent at Portsmouth rang up to say that he had traced the sale of the cyclometer. One of his men, in going round the cycle shops in a comparatively poor quarter of the town, had found a salesman who remembered selling one of the kind described. He remembered the transaction, because the purchaser had seemed somewhat more well-to-do than most of his customers. The man had explained that he had promised a cyclometer to his little son, who had recently been given a new bicycle. The customer was a middle aged man, very well dressed, with a clean shaven and slightly foxy face, and the salesman would recognise him if he saw him again. The constable had reported to headquarters, and having obtained a copy of the Joymount group, he had returned to the shop and asked the salesman if it contained his customer. Without hesitation the man had picked out Tasker, saying he would swear to him anywhere.

This seemed to French the best news that he had yet received. To have obtained proof that King had bought the cyclometer would have been good; but to find that Tasker had done so was many times better. That King was guilty French could already prove, but he had not been convinced that the gramophone episode was sufficient evidence against Tasker. This new discovery just supplied the deficiency.

Admittedly there was still no proof that the cyclometer sold to Tasker was the one found in the launch. But if it were shown that Tasker's son was grown up and did not possess a bicycle, as French believed could be done, Tasker would be hard put to it to explain the purchase.

That night, separately and without knowledge of one another's predicament, Tasker and King were arrested and brought to Southampton. After being charged, they were cautioned and asked if they wished to make a statement. Tasker said that except for formally stating his innocence, he had nothing to say until he had had an opportunity of consulting his solicitor. King however raged at the officers and swore he could prove his innocence and would there and then answer any questions they liked to put. But French said that, as it was late, they would postpone the discussion until the following morning and King, protesting volubly, was removed to the cells.

It was not, however, because it was late that French declined to hear King. Frequently after an evening arrest interrogations lasted through the whole night. French wanted to be prepared: he wanted first to search the man's rooms and examine his papers. He much regretted the need for this, as he feared that King's desire to talk would have cooled after a few hours' detention, but of the two evils it seemed the lesser.

Next day French and Carter made a detailed search of both King's and Tasker's rooms, with the result that a good many papers and documents were transferred to Southampton. These French set himself to go through. Till late in the evening he studied his catch without result, then at last, as he was rather despairingly looking over the firm's order book, a sudden idea occurred to him and he remained motionless, lost in thought.

There were a number of items for machinery. He wondered what they were. If they were for the ordinary work of the firm, he was no further on. But if they were for new plant to work the process, he rather thought he had got King. Slowly a smile of somewhat unhappy

331

satisfaction twisted his features. He wanted to get his man, but he hated the final stages of the process.

Presently he got up and went across the passage to Goodwilly's room. The Superintendent was, as it happened, working late on another case.

'What about having King in now, Super?' French suggested. 'I've been through his papers, and if he wants to make a statement we ought to hear it.'

Goodwilly agreed and the simple scene was set. French, Goodwilly and Carter sat down at one side of a table in the Super's room, while a chair was set for King at the other. Then the prisoner was brought in.

'Last night, Mr King,' French began, 'you said you wished to make a statement on this matter, and that you could answer any questions that you were asked. Last night you were not unnaturally somewhat upset, and tonight you may have thought over things and be of a different mind. We should like to know whether you still wish to make the statement and be questioned?'

'Yes,' King answered truculently, 'I can clear myself and I don't see why I shouldn't be let.'

French nodded gravely. 'It is my duty to warn you once again that what you say will be taken down and may be given in evidence. Also that you needn't speak unless you like. Is it still your wish to do so?'

'Of course it is,' King retorted. 'I don't want to stay here longer than I need, and I take it that if I explain everything you can't hold me.'

'If you give a satisfactory explanation of the facts and convince the Super and myself that you are innocent, we won't want to hold you, but you must remember that you may do the opposite.'

King laughed scornfully 'Not I, Chief-Inspector. Go ahead.'

'Very well, sir; we'll hear your statement. I don't wish to influence you, but I suggest you give us an account of this whole affair, from your point of view, from the beginning up till the present time. By the beginning, I mean when it was first discovered that the Joymount profits were going down.'

This businesslike speech seemed somewhat to sober King. He thought for some moments, then began to speak.

His story, at least in the earlier stages, was identical with that of Brand's. He told of the losses of Joymount and of his instructions to investigate the position. He explained how he had tested the Chayle cement and found that it was a new product, which must therefore have been produced by a new process. He stated that the board had instructed him to try to discover the process, ending up by declaring that he had done so.

'You did so?' said French. 'How did you manage that, Mr King?'

'By hard work,' King returned. 'I made experiment after experiment till I got it.'

'Chemical experiments?'

'Yes. First I analysed the Chayle stuff and found its composition. That was easy. It contained some unusual ingredients. Then I devised methods to put the same ingredients into our cement. That was difficult, but I managed it at last.'

'Now,' said French, 'that's the first point on which you'll have to convince us. It has been suggested, you know, that you went to the Chayle Works and copied the process from a document in a safe in Mr Haviland's office.'

333

King put on an expression of injured innocence. 'That's an absolute fabrication,' he said indignantly. 'Nothing of the kind! The whole thing was worked out in the Joymount lab.'

'Well, but can you prove that?' French went on. 'How are we to know that you really did carry out such experiments?'

'I have a record of them in my safe at Joymount.'

French pointed to a side table. 'We brought up some of your papers today. Just look if it is among them?'

King ran quickly through the pile and abstracted some sheets clipped together. 'This is it,' he declared, handing the bundle over.

French took the papers and made a show of examining them. Then he shrugged. 'Unfortunately,' he pointed out, 'I'm not a chemist. How can you prove that you carried out these experiments and that they produced the result that you say?'

King shrugged in his turn. 'You'll have to get a chemist,' he said sullenly. 'I can't be made to suffer for your ignorance.'

'Quite reasonable, Mr King,' French admitted smoothly. 'Perhaps however we can get some confirmation in another way. These experiments required certain chemicals?'

'Of course they required chemicals.'

'Then how did you get the chemicals?'

'How? Why, in the ordinary way in which I got anything I wanted. I ordered them.'

French picked up the Joymount order book. 'Then,' he said with an air of triumph, 'if you ordered them, you should be able to turn up the orders.'

'Of course I can turn them up,' King answered scornfully. 'Show me the book.'

French looked considerably crestfallen as he handed it over. King ran through the pages and pointed to block after block. 'There you are,' he declared.

'That good enough for you?'

It was not quite good enough for French. He insisted on going into the experiments one by one, and getting King to point out the actual order issued to supply the chemicals used in each experiment. When he made him write down and sign this information, it really did look as if he were getting the proof he had asked for.

This detailed work took a good deal of time. However, it was finished at last, and then French asked his victim to continue his statement.

King, believing that he had scored on the question of the experiments, was more truculent and self-assured than ever. He went on to tell that he had reported his success to his board and that they had instructed him to go ahead with the making of the new cement.

'Did that require any alterations in your plant?' French asked.

This opened a further line of enquiry and here again French was very thorough. He got King to produce his drawings and then to show him the orders he had issued for the parts of the various machines.

Up till now French had been a little doubtful as to whether his idea would work out as he had hoped. But now with this further statement from King, he saw that he had the unhappy man in his hands. Unwittingly King had committed himself beyond hope of recovery.

French paused for a moment to choose his words, then went on slowly. 'Now, Mr King, your statement is this: you were instructed to try to find the process: you did so by means of certain chemical experiments which you have described: you then reported to your board: they instructed you to have the necessary machinery made: you did so. Now is that correct? Is that what you want to stick to?'

King signified that that was his statement, that it was the truth, and that the Chief-Inspector could take it or leave it as he liked.

'Very well,' went on French even more slowly, and watching the other keenly. 'Now look at the significance of these dates. On Sunday night, the 29th of July, the Chayle Works are burgled, and the watchman comes by his death. On the following Wednesday, the 1st of August, the board meeting takes place at which you report that you have discovered the process. You spend—'

King shuffled uneasily on his chair. 'That's not fair, Chief-Inspector,' he burst out. 'I can't help the coincidence of the dates.'

French held up his hand. 'Let me finish,' he said. 'After the board meeting you spend ten days in making your designs for the machinery—you said it took you ten days. Then you order the machinery. The order blocks support your statement and these dates. That correct?'

Now puzzled and uneasy, King admitted that it was.

'Very good,' went on French. 'Now I suppose you carried out the experiments which led you to discover the process before the board meeting on the 1st of August?'

For the first time King hesitated. A look of doubt, changing immediately to fear, appeared in his eyes. But he bluffed on. 'Of course,' he answered. 'The experiments were carried out during the month previous to that meeting.'

French looked at him for some seconds without speaking. Then he shook his head.

'Then how, Mr King,' he asked, 'do you account for the

orders for the chemicals used in those experiments not having been issued until *after* those for the machinery?'

It was a knock-out blow. King began to mumble something about a mistake in the dates. But he didn't complete his sentence. He had proved the dates too completely. His voice died out. French went on.

'The dates are pretty clear, you know. You obtained the process from the safe in Haviland's room at Chayle on the night that Clay died. *Then* you designed your plant and ordered your machines. As soon as that was off your mind you thought you must be able to prove that you learned the secret by experiment, and you ordered the necessary chemicals. Do you wish to say anything more on that point?'

King still sat staring. He did not try to answer. French shrugged slightly.

'I'm afraid, King,' he said not unkindly, 'the game's up. The man who made the gramophone record will swear to you. And we know all about the fixing of the cyclometer. Tell me now, is there anything more you wish to say?'

King moved with an effort. 'Only,' he said unsteadily, 'that Clay's death was an accident.'

'Yes,' said French. 'I'm prepared to take your word for that. But you should have reported the affair instead of faking that car business.'

King was utterly broken down. 'I was afraid I shouldn't be believed.' Once more he paused. 'I'd like to say, Chief-Inspector, that Brand was not in this thing. He was in it, but quite innocently. He didn't realise what I was doing.'

French nodded. 'I had come to that conclusion already, Mr King, but I'm glad to hear you say it. Your statement will be reported to the proper quarter.'

* * *

From further enquiries and the examination of the documents of all concerned, the remaining details of the case were built up. In his speech at the opening of the trial, counsel for the prosecution outlined the affair as it was then understood by the police.

The first point was the fall in the Joymount profits and the resultant commission to King to investigate the cause. King was a *protégé* of Tasker's, and Tasker had given him this job because he rightly believed him to be by far the most able man on the staff. King had justified his trust. Enquiry had told him of Chayle's rebates, analysis of their new cement, and deduction of their secret process.

To his report Tasker, who knew his King, had replied that the secret must be discovered if possible by fair means, but if not, by foul. Very early in the game King saw that he was unlikely to succeed by the first method, and Tasker then suggested a nocturnal visit to Chayle. If King could learn what he wanted by inspection, so much the better, but learned the secret must be, and methods of obtaining the Chayle keys and robbing the safes were discussed. It was Tasker who suggested the drugging of Haviland in the train which King afterwards carried out.

One of the chief obstacles in the way of the conspirators was the alertness and the conscientiousness of Brand. In his work Brand took nothing for granted. He looked so carefully into every phase of the business that neither Tasker nor King believed they could carry their plan through without arousing his suspicions. And once his suspicions were aroused, Brand would unquestionably report to the directors.

To meet this difficulty, Tasker proposed a wily scheme. Brand was himself to be involved. He was to be led into a mild breach of the law, so that if and when he discovered the truth, his tongue would be tied. He would not, of course, be trusted with anything serious, but if he did learn the real facts, he would be unable to use his knowledge.

Matters then took their prearranged course. Radcliff and Endicott were engaged, and Brand's voluntary aid was accepted, to carry out useless experiments as a blind to cover the real activities. On their alleged failure Brand was inveigled into assisting King to have a look into the Chayle works. He did not know King's real object.

Then occurred the Clay disaster—wholly unintentional and unforeseen. That night, on getting the body to Joymount, King had rung up Tasker, and the two men had met and spent the night in working out the trick with the car. Here again Brand was to be involved, so as to close his mouth effectually about the whole affair.

As time passed and the police made no move, Tasker and King began to breathe more freely. Gradually they came to believe their future assured, a future of wealth, independence and security.

Then came the knock-out blow of the visit of Haviland and Mairs, and at once these rosy dreams were dispelled. Instead of the wealth they had been counting on, there would be for them existence on a pittance; instead of security there would be the haunting fear that they might at any time be betrayed to prison or even death; and instead of independence there would be servitude under the orders of their Chayle masters.

They didn't know that Haviland was bluffing when he dictated his terms; that he suspected what had happened, but couldn't prove it. But even if they had, it would probably have made little difference. The disappointment was too overwhelming. Neither Tasker nor King could look forward to spending the remainder of their lives under such conditions. Better, they thought, to make a fight for it, even at the risk of losing, than to settle down to a poverty and a dread which might last their whole lives. The knowledge which was destroying their happiness was confined to Haviland, Mairs and Samson. If these three men were eliminated, the Joymount men's rosy dreams would become a reality . . .

From that time the idea of destroying the three Chayle representatives seldom left the minds of Tasker and King, though for a while they did not see how the murders could be carried out with safety to themselves.

Then Tasker thought of the launch explosion. Both men believed that the launch and all aboard it would simply disappear, and that no suspicion of foul play would arise. If, however, they did fall under suspicion, they were satisfied that they could overwhelmingly prove their innocence.

Tasker had, of course, deliberately typed only one copy of the agreement, so that should any of the Chayle bodies be recovered, the incriminating clauses six and seven should not be found on them. Similarly he had spaced the typescript to end the first five clauses on sheet one, so that this single sheet could afterwards be shown to the police as the whole agreement which had been negotiated. Had Haviland not played into his hands by proposing separate agreements to cover each sheet, he would himself have made the suggestion.

On this occasion when deliberate murder was contemplated, King declined to shoulder all the responsibility, and joint action was therefore decided on. Tasker was to obtain a gelignite cartridge and detonator from the company's

340

quarry, and also to buy the cyclometer and battery, while King, who had secretly visited the Chayle boathouse to make sure it would fit, was to plant his apparatus in Samson's launch. In this Brand was again to be used. Unknown to himself, he was to be furnished with evidence of his colleagues' innocence, so that his statements to the police should be made in good faith, and therefore be convincing.

To Tasker and King the escape of Samson came as an appalling catastrophe. They saw at once that Samson would be bound to suspect them, but they hoped against hope that he would be unable to back his suspicion up with evidence. Samson, indeed, admitted later that he had suspected them at first, but their guilt had seemed so impossible that he had afterwards dismissed the idea from his mind.

Having thus outlined the case he hoped to make, counsel for the prosecution proceeded to call his witnesses. The evidence against each prisoner was slightly different. Against King the following facts were proved:

The note of the Chayle process found in his safe was exactly similar to that in the Chayle office. In several cases different phrases could have been used to describe certain details, but in all these the wording was identical. In one instance, in fact, there was an error in the Chayle document, where the obviously intended phrase 'solution should be mixed' was written 'solution should mixed', and this error was repeated in King's note. It was clear, therefore, that one document was a copy of the other.

That King had stolen the process was also proved by the dates already mentioned, which showed that he had ordered the machines immediately after the death of Clay, and before he had made the experiments by which he stated he discovered the secret.

Brand's evidence, and King's own admission to the police, proved that King had been the principal figure in the burnt car fake.

But King was not being tried for stealing the process and faking the car accident. He was tried for murdering Haviland and Mairs, and for that only. The evidence against him was overwhelming.

In the first place the motive was established beyond question. An account of the blackmailing of Joymount was given by Brand and admitted by Samson. Both these witnesses swore to the suppressed second sheet of the draft agreement, which, indeed, was found in Tasker's safe.

Next, the discovery of the electric circuit operated by the cyclometer proved that the explosion had been deliberately prearranged. Further, French's deduction from the cyclometer reading was accepted as showing the apparatus must have been placed in the launch at Joymount.

The *possibility* that King had placed it was established by French, who swore that he had tried the experiment of leaving King's office window by means of a rope ladder, going to the west end of the wharf, there getting into a boat and floating down beneath the wharf to the steps, getting on to the steps, waiting three minutes and returning to the office, and that he had been able to do all this in eleven minutes. As the time King was supposed to be alone in his office was estimated at from twelve to fifteen minutes, this would have allowed him ample time.

Lastly, that King had *actually* placed it was proved from the early statements of King himself, Tasker, Brand and Samson. All four stated that certain definite sounds had come from King's office during the time that he had retired there during the last conference between the two firms. The Etna Gramophone Company's representative swore that he had made records reproducing those very sounds, and that King was the man for whom he had made them. On the suggestion of the prosecution he produced a gramophone and copies of the records, and they were played in court. The defence were unable to offer any suggestion as to what these records could have been for, other than to allow King to leave his office secretly.

The proof against Tasker consisted of four main items. First there was the consideration that without his general help King could not have carried out the crime. Second, there was proof of motive, same as in the case of King. Third, the gramophone fraud could not have been put through without Tasker's active co-operation, particularly in the answer to the gramophone question, which must have been rehearsed. Last, there was the purchase of the cyclometer, for which the defence could give no satisfactory explanation.

After brilliant speeches on both sides, and a long and impartial summing up, the jury found both men guilty of wilful murder. Appeals failed, and the dreadful sentence that murder brings was carried out.

Before their deaths both men admitted their guilt, their story being substantially as suggested by French and outlined in the opening speech of prosecuting counsel. Brand was specifically cleared by both, at least so far as guilty intention was concerned.

In the end no case was preferred against Brand, Samson absolutely declining to prosecute. Samson, indeed, asked Brand to join him in partnership, but Brand had had enough of the locality, and departed for South America, where he was afterwards understood to have made good in a new life.

As for French, his holiday from the monotony of work in London, coupled with a brief word of congratulation from the Assistant Commissioner, was his reward for the successful issue of a particularly long and tedious case.